Governess Gone Rogue

By Laura Lee Guhrke

LAURA LEE GUHRKE

Governess Gone Rogue

AVONBOOKS

An Imprint of HarperCollinsPublishers

GOVERNESS GONE ROGUE. Copyright © 2019 by Laura Lee Borio. All rights reserved. Printed in the United States of America. No part of this book may be used or reproduced in any manner whatsoever without written permission except in the case of brief quotations embodied in critical articles and reviews. For information, address HarperCollins Publishers, 195 Broadway, New York, NY 10007.

First Avon Books mass market printing: February 2019

First Avon Books hardcover printing: January 2019

Print Edition ISBN: 978-0-06-289068-9
Digital Edition ISBN: 978-0-06-285370-7

Avon, Avon & logo, and Avon Books & logo are registered trademarks of Harper-Collins Publishers in the United States of America and other countries.

HarperCollins is a registered trademark of HarperCollins Publishers in the United States of America and other countries.

FIRST EDITION

19 20 21 22 23   LSC   10 9 8 7 6 5 4 3 2 1

For fellow writers Sophie Jordan and Jennifer Ryan, because this book would not exist without you. Many, many thanks. Thanks also to Jacoby Smith for the help with Latin. It is much appreciated.

Governess Gone Rogue

Chapter 1

London, 1893

Ａnd she's off."

Ten-year-old Owen St. Clair moved to stand alongside his brother, propped his elbows on the windowsill, and rested his chin in his hands as he watched their now-former nanny, a stern, black-clad widow named Mrs. Hornsby, step into the hansom cab at the curb below. "We're to blame, you know."

"Stuff." Colin, older than his brother by exactly eighteen minutes, shook his head, a decisive move that sent the unruly strands of his carrot-red hair into further disarray. "It's not our fault the Hornsby doesn't like frogs."

"Well, we did put it in her hatbox." Owen sighed as the cab containing Mrs. Hornsby turned at the corner and vanished from view. "Three nannies in six months. I think that's torn it, Colin. Papa said one more nanny and he'd send us to Harrow."

At the ghastly prospect of being sent off to school, the twins turned, sliding down to sit on the floor of the library, their backs to the wall beneath the window as they contemplated what could well be their immediate future.

"We can't let Papa send us away," Colin said at last. "He'd be lost without us. And what would happen to Oscar?"

Both boys looked up at the gray tabby cat that was sitting on the arm of a nearby chair, a cat they'd rescued from a tree in the park one and a half years earlier. Oscar was twitching his tail and blinking his green eyes sleepily, seeming unaware of the dire future that lay ahead for his two human friends.

"He'll be lonely," Owen said. "Papa's away all the time, and the servants think he's a nuisance because he doesn't chase mice. They don't like him. They might forget to feed him. They might give him away."

"We've got to do something to stop it."

"Maybe we could take him with us? It's probably against the rules to have a cat at Harrow, but—"

"I'm not talking about Oscar." Colin turned to his brother. "I'm talking about us and being sent away. Oscar has nothing to worry about if we can convince Papa to let us stay here."

There was silence for a moment as both boys considered the problem.

"Maybe," Owen said at last, "we could find our new nanny ourselves before Papa knows what's happened. Someone we like. Someone fun. If we do that, it's a fate . . . fate—what's the word?"

"*Fait-accompli*," Colin supplied in carefully enunciated, very British French.

"That's it." Owen's nod was decisive. "And if we've already found someone, Papa can't be too angry about Nanny Hornsby leaving, can he?"

"Maybe not, but the thing is . . ." Colin paused, his freckled face scrunching up with distaste, as if he'd just eaten a persimmon. "We don't really want another nanny, do we?"

"No, but what other choice have we got?"

"Maybe we should find what we really want."

"You mean . . ." Owen stared at his brother, his expression one of both excitement and doubt. "You don't mean a new mum?"

"Why not? We've been talking about it for ages."

"I know, but—"

"Another nanny would be tiresome. School would be worse."

"That's true, but—"

"Papa's sure to marry again sometime," Colin interrupted. "What if he picks someone who doesn't like us?"

"We'd be off to Harrow like a shot. But still—"

"If we find Papa someone who likes us, she could convince him to let us give school a miss altogether."

"Possibly," Owen said, his voice making it clear he wasn't optimistic about such a plan's chances of success. "But Papa won't ever marry again. He's said so thousands of times."

"We'll have to find him a girl who's smashing enough to make him change his mind. Someone pretty, of course."

"Someone nice. Someone who won't put pomade in our hair and lecture us when our trousers get torn."

Colin nodded. "She'll have to be brainy, too, like Mama was. And fond of cats."

Oscar meowed, as if giving his endorsement of this plan.

"There's just one problem," Owen pointed out. "How do we find her?"

"That is the sticky wicket."

Both boys fell silent again, thinking hard.

"We could put an ad in Auntie Clara's paper," Owen said after a moment. "Men are always advertising for wives in the papers."

"Gentlemen don't, and Papa's a gentleman. Wait—I know!" Colin jumped to his feet and crossed the library to the writing desk. As his brother watched, he opened the center drawer, retrieved a sheet of notepaper, and closed the drawer again.

"What are you doing?" Owen asked curiously, standing up and moving toward the desk as his brother reached for the pen that was reposing in a silver holder on the inkstand. "Who are you writing to?"

"Who does everyone write to when they want to solve a problem?" Colin countered as he inked the nib of the pen. "I'm writing to Lady Truelove."

THOSE WHO WANTED to be polite would have deemed Amanda Leighton a woman of the world. Those not so inclined to civility would have called her something else, something much less romantic.

Either way, facts were facts, and though by the age of twenty-eight Amanda had lived in two different countries, earned a university education, found a profession, taken a lover, and lost her reputation, she had not gained the one experience society deemed worthwhile for those of her sex. Amanda had never managed to acquire a husband.

But then, she'd never really been in search of one. Her mother had died when she was a young girl, and she'd been raised by her father, a university professor who had scorned the traditional, marriage-minded, downright silly scope of a girl's learning, and who had personally given Amanda a first-class education worthy of any boy. More important, he'd taught her to take charge of her own destiny, not by the use of feminine wiles, but by the employment of her intelligence.

She'd become a teacher, and for the seven years since then, she'd earned her living with her brain. Sadly, not every employer understood that the rest of Amanda's body wasn't for hire.

When Mr. Oswald Bartlett put his hand on her in a way no employer ever ought to do, Amanda had demonstrated her scientific knowledge of male anatomy with the use of one well-placed knee. She had also, unfortunately, lost her job.

Not that being governess to Mr. Bartlett's four daughters had been a particularly exciting post. How exciting could it be to teach four girls how to speak French, waltz, and curtsy, especially when neither they nor their parent ever envisioned for them anything more? Still, her position with the widower had provided her with a roof over her head, two meals a day, and a minuscule, but steady wage.

Now she was unemployed, and thanks to the knee, she was facing the search for a new post with no letter of character.

Amanda leaned back in her chair, looked up from her now-cold tea, and realized that the waitress who had served her in such friendly fashion half an hour ago was now eyeing her with impatience. The goodwill she'd purchased at Mrs. Mott's Tea Emporium with one cuppa and one Bath bun was clearly gone, but Amanda continued to linger. It was far too early to give up for the day and return to her tiny flat, but where could she go?

She'd spent the past month presenting herself at every employment agency in London, to no avail. Though all had been impressed by her university education, none had sent her to interview for any governess posts. Her baccalaureate from Girton College seemed breathtakingly impressive until each agency made the inevitable inquiries and learned what had happened to her after departing that lauded institution. Once they discovered she was the same Amanda Leighton who had once taught at Willowbank Academy, whose reputation had been tainted by scandal, their eagerness to find her employment went straight out the window, and who could blame them?

Willowbank was England's most prestigious academic school for young ladies, but when one of its teachers took the son of the school's most generous and influential patron as her lover, well, that was a scandal for the ages, especially when no wedding followed in its wake. Her days as a schoolteacher had come to an end, for who wanted to put their daughters in the care of a woman tainted by scandal? Only Mr. Bartlett had been so inclined, and his reasons for hiring her were now, in hindsight, dismally clear.

These days, she was down to tutoring a few people in her neighborhood, but that wasn't enough to pay rent and buy food, and if her present state of unemployment continued much longer, her meager savings would be gone. Sadly, her prospects for respectable employment were dim, and growing dimmer by the day.

All her father's efforts, four years of university education, Tripos honors, two published papers, and seven years of teaching at one of England's most lauded schools, all obliterated by one stupid mistake, and though she was glad her father hadn't lived long enough to see it, she knew it shamed his memory. She also knew that mistake was one she ought never to have made. Aware, educated, with plenty of common sense and worldly wisdom, and yet, she'd fallen in love with a man because he'd said her eyes were like sunlight caught in the embrace of a dark forest. She'd never dreamed any man, even an aristocrat, could be so poetic. Or that she could be such a fool.

Amanda swallowed the last of her tea and glanced out the window again. Having pawned her watch a few days ago, she didn't know the time, but it looked as if it was late enough that the evening papers were out, and she decided to see if any governess positions had been posted.

Reading the papers without paying for them was tricky, but Amanda couldn't afford to pay for them. The twelve pence in her handbag and the fifteen shillings hidden away under her mattress were all she had left.

If she didn't find a post soon, she'd have to sell Papa's books and her mother's cameos. That would keep her in funds through autumn, but what would happen to her when winter came?

Fear shivered through Amanda, bringing her to her feet. Shoving dire thoughts of the future out of her mind, she put on her cloak, then took up the Bath bun that would be her evening meal, wrapped it in her handkerchief, and tucked it into her pocket. She paid her bill and left Mrs. Mott's to find a newspaper seller, but she'd barely gone a block before the sign painted on a plate-glass window caught her eye, and she paused.

Deverill Newspapers Limited, the gilt lettering read. Publishers of the *London Daily Standard* and the *Weekly Gazette*.

Perhaps she was going about her employment search the wrong way, she thought, staring at the sign. What if, instead of looking through the posts being advertised, she placed her own advertisement, noting her credentials and offering her services as a governess? Mentioning Girton would gain her some inquiries, perhaps even some interviews, and if she could gloss over her past sufficiently, she might gain a post.

Action appealed to her far more than passively waiting for a job to come along, but another look through the window caused her to doubt the soundness of her idea, at least as far as this particular newspaper was concerned, for it seemed to be either going out of business or moving to a new location. Packing crates were stacked against the far wall and most of the furnishings had been removed.

Nonetheless, there was at least one person still on the premises, she noted, spying a tall man with blond hair who was rummaging through one of the crates that lay on top of the room's only desk. He might be able to assist her.

She opened the door, and the man looked up, revealing a startlingly handsome countenance, but Amanda felt no jump in the pace of her pulse. Her affair with Lord Halsbury and the resulting disgrace had cured her of any romantic notions about men, handsome or otherwise, and besides, she had other priorities.

"Yes, miss?" He circled the desk and came toward her. "May I help you?"

"I'm not certain. I wanted to see about placing an advertisement, but—" She broke off and glanced around. "Is this newspaper out of print?"

"No, no," he assured her, "though I suppose it appears that way at present. We are moving to larger premises today."

"We?" Amanda echoed, noting his finely tailored suit as he halted before her. "You don't look like a clerk or journalist."

That made him laugh. "I imagine not," he agreed, and offered a bow. "I am Viscount Galbraith."

Amanda's surprise deepened, and perceiving it, he laughed again, gesturing to the sign on the window behind her. "My wife, Clara, was a Deverill before she married me. She and her sister, the Duchess of Torquil, own this publishing company."

"A business owned by women?" Amanda murmured, impressed. "That's unusual."

"They have a staff, of course, but everyone's at the new premises just now, trying to get things settled before my wife and I leave for the Continent on our honeymoon. I'm only here because I've lost my pocket watch, and my wife seemed to think she'd tossed it into one of these crates, so I've come in search."

"Then I mustn't keep you, my lord." She gave a curtsy and moved to leave, but his voice stopped her.

"If you wish to place an advertisement, you can write it down, and I'd be happy to deliver it to a member of the staff."

"I shouldn't wish to give any trouble."

"It's no trouble. I'll be going back to Fleet Street once I find my watch, and I can easily take your advertisement with me. I might even be able to supply you with writing materials." He returned to the desk, rummaged through the crates, and pulled out a rumpled sheet of paper and a stubby lead pencil.

"Here we are," he said, returning to her. "Not the best stationery, I fear, but it should serve the purpose."

"Thank you," she murmured, taking the offered paper and pencil from his outstretched hands. "You're very kind. What is . . . the . . . ahem—" She broke off, her face heating, for she knew it was the height of vulgarity to discuss money matters of any sort with a peer, but she could see no other choice. "What is the rate for an advertisement?"

"The rate?" He gave her a blank stare for a moment, then he laughed, making it clear she hadn't given offense. "Good Lord, I've no idea," he confessed. "What do you think would be fair?"

"I don't suppose free would be very fair, would it?" she quipped, but pride caused her to regret the half-joking words at once. "I wasn't trying to cage," she added at once. "I'm happy to pay the proper rate, of course."

His keen blue eyes swept over her, surely noting the frayed hems of her cloak and skirt, but whatever he might be thinking, he didn't express his thoughts aloud. "What if we say one halfpenny per word?" he asked. "With a three-day run?"

Even in her straitened circumstances, she could afford that, if she kept it short. Relieved, she gave a nod of agreement, and Lord Galbraith gestured to the long worktable beside the door, pulling out a swivel chair from underneath so that she could sit down.

"Now, if you will pardon me," he said, pushing in the chair for her, "I must continue the hunt for my watch."

He returned to the desk across the room, but he'd barely resumed rummaging through the crate before the door opened and another man came in, a man every bit as good-looking as the viscount, but as different from him as chalk from cheese.

Lord Galbraith had the countenance of a man who enjoyed life, a man of amiable temperament with an easy smile, a man whose fair coloring and flawless features seemed almost angelic.

There was nothing angelic, however, about the man who halted in the doorway. If this man had ever been an angel, he'd fallen a long time ago, and fallen hard.

Beneath the brim of a gray felt derby, his eyes were a clear, almost colorless green, the green of bottle glass—cool, translucent, and curiously devoid of any discernible emotion, softened into humanity only by the brown lashes that surrounded them, lashes that were long and thick and sinfully opulent.

There was nothing soft about the rest of his face, however. Its lean planes seemed to have been chiseled out of marble, as exquisitely sculpted and expressionless as any statue. There was a curious lethargy to his stance and an unmistakable weariness to the set of his wide shoulders, and to Amanda, it seemed a weariness of spirit rather than body. Though he was probably only a few years older than she, there were distinct lines etched into the edges of his mouth and the corners of his eyes, and though she couldn't tell if those lines were borne of dissipation or suffering, they nonetheless told of a man who had seen it all and done it all and who wasn't much interested in doing any of it again.

Those cool green eyes of his looked in her direction, then away at once, a glance devoid of any masculine interest. Most women would be insulted, she supposed with a hint of humor, but after Kenneth Halsbury and Mr. Bartlett, Amanda could only deem such indifference a relief.

"Ah, Jamie," Lord Galbraith greeted the man in the doorway. "You received my note, I take it?"

"I did, and when I called at the new offices, Clara told me you'd come here, insisting I must speak with you at once. I'm dying to know what could be so urgent, so I came straightaway." Despite this declaration, his drawling, well-bred voice displayed no curiosity.

"It's about the boys."

Something flickered in that weary, stone-hard countenance, a hint of life. He started toward the other man, his body moving with a sudden, disciplined energy that contrasted sharply with his former ennui.

"What about the boys?" he asked, his voice carrying a new urgency. "I'm almost afraid to ask," he added as he halted across the desk, "but what do you know that I don't?"

"They wrote a letter to the paper. I got it this morning."

"My sons are writing to newspapers?" The man called Jamie relaxed, giving a laugh. "Is that all?"

"All?" Galbraith echoed. "You don't even know what they were writing about."

"Does it matter?" Jamie's wide shoulders gave a dismissive shrug. "It's one of their pranks, obviously. One of their more harmless ones, thank God."

"You may not retain that opinion once you know what it's about. And I don't think it was a prank."

"My sons are seldom serious about anything, Rex. They adore practical jokes. Why do you think they chew up and spit out their nannies with such exhausting frequency?"

"They wrote to Lady Truelove, asking for her advice on how to find a new mother."

"What?" He stiffened, and even in profile, Amanda could see the amusement vanish from his face, replaced by dismay. "But they know I'll never marry again. We've discussed it."

"They seem to harbor hope your mind can be changed on the subject." Galbraith reached into the breast pocket of his jacket and pulled out a folded sheet of paper. "Read for yourself."

"How can you be sure this is from my sons?" Jamie asked as he took the letter and unfolded it. "Did they sign it?"

"Only with the moniker Motherless in Mayfair," Galbraith answered. "But they included a return address so that Lady Truelove could reply, and unless you've moved out of the duke's town house in the last day or two, or someone else's motherless children have moved in, this letter was definitely written by your boys."

"Of all the ridiculous, harebrained schemes they've hatched—" He broke off with a sigh, bent his head, and read the letter, then looked up again. "That tears it," he said, tossing down the sheet in obvious exasperation. "I've had enough. I'm sending them to school."

"Isn't that a bit drastic? Writing to an advice columnist isn't the most egregious thing they've ever done."

"If by that you mean it's not as bad as the time they set off firecrackers in the drawing room and caught the curtains on fire," their father said dryly, "or when they put itching powder in my valet's linen, I suppose I must concede the point."

Amanda pressed her lips together to stifle a laugh. An enterprising pair of young men, she thought. Though also a bit naughty, it seemed.

"Still," their father went on, "I suppose it's a good thing they chose Lady Truelove as their confidante. Had they written to some other newspaper's advice columnist, you wouldn't have seen it and it would have been published." He doffed his hat, tossed it on the desk, and raked a hand through his tobacco-brown hair. "I shudder to think what society's reaction to that would have been. Motherless in Mayfair, twin boys who need a mum because they're tired of all the nannies . . . everyone would know at once it's my sons."

"The boys do have something of a reputation with nannies."

"A letter like that printed in the paper doesn't bear thinking about. I'm the target of enough debutantes as it is."

"A fate worse than death," intoned Galbraith.

Jamie paid little heed to his friend's amused rejoinder. "Few bothered with me when I was only the second son. As a mere MP with a modest income, I impressed no one, but now—" He broke off with a humorless laugh. "It's amazing how much more appealing I am now that I'm next in line to be the Marquess of Rolleston. Poor Geoff hadn't been gone a month before young ladies were commenting on my lonely widower's life. The last thing I need is their pretenses of concern for my poor motherless boys, who are so desperate for maternal affection that they're writing to newspapers."

"No harm was done. Surely you're not serious about sending them to school because of this?"

"Why shouldn't I send them?" Jamie countered, a defensive note in his voice. "God knows, they've done enough to deserve it. And the timing's ideal now that their latest nanny's gone."

"Another nanny already? What happened this time?"

"The same thing that always happens. They made the poor woman's life a torment, and she decided she'd had enough."

Amanda raised an eyebrow. Heavens, what did these boys do to their nannies? Given the firecrackers and the itching powder, she supposed anything was possible, but she had no opportunity to speculate on the topic, for Galbraith spoke again.

"The autumn term at Harrow has already begun."

"They could still be admitted, if Torquil puts in a word."

"Given that our brother-in-law is a duke, I'm sure you're right, but sending the boys in the middle of term would be terribly hard on them. Why not just engage another nanny?"

"After seeing a dozen nannies come and go during the past three years, I am forced to concede that no woman I could hire is capable of managing my sons."

Amanda's amusement deepened, and she wondered what this man would do if she piped up, declared his contention totally wrong, and demanded the chance to prove it as the boys' next nanny. A tempting idea, but after a moment of consideration, she discarded it.

Though she was in desperate need of a job, it sounded as if this man's misbehaving sons would soon be off to school, and no nanny would be required. And, as she had so recently discovered, working in a widower's house put a woman in a very vulnerable position. Amanda slid a glance over the powerful frame of the man by the desk, concluded that he wouldn't be as easy to incapacitate as the stout, middle-aged Mr. Bartlett, and decided she wasn't quite desperate enough to put herself at risk of a man's unwelcome advances again.

She forced her attention to her own task, and the voices of the two men faded as she stared at the blank sheet of paper before her. "Post wanted," she scribbled. "Girton-educated woman seeks position as governess. Sober and respectable."

She paused over the last word, biting her lip. Respectable? Such a lie, that, but what else could she say?

As she grasped for an additional word or two that would put her in the best light to potential employers, the viscount spoke, his insistent tone breaking into Amanda's thoughts.

"Be honest, Jamie. Is school really the best solution? Or is it simply the most expedient?"

"Careful, Rex," Jamie answered, and though his voice was light, there was unmistakable warning beneath the words.

Galbraith, however, did not take heed. "I realize being in the Commons takes most of your time. And it's understandable that you want to keep occupied. Losing Patricia must have been a devastating blow, but it was devastating for the boys, too."

"Do you think I don't know that?" Jamie countered, his voice suddenly fierce. "Damn it, Rex, I know you adore giving out advice to all and sundry these days—"

Galbraith suddenly coughed, interrupting his friend's irritation, and it was a moment before Jamie continued, and when he did, it wasn't to chide his friend for offering advice. "At this point, I see no reason not to send them to school. They're old enough to go."

"Barely. And are you sure they're ready for Harrow?"

Jamie gave a short, unamused laugh. "Better to ask if Harrow is ready for them. I shall be lucky if they last a term without being expelled."

"You miss my point. Are they ready from an academic standpoint?"

Those words struck a chord, Amanda could tell, for Jamie muttered an oath and looked away.

"It would be difficult," he admitted after a moment. "Nannies have managed to teach them the rudimentary subjects, of course—spelling, arithmetic, penmanship, a bit of French . . ." He paused, grimacing. "It's not much, I know."

"Not enough to prepare them for Harrow and Cambridge, certainly."

"One can't really expect much more from a nanny. And no woman can prepare a boy for Harrow and Cambridge anyway."

Amanda barely managed to suppress a derisive snort. Heavens, if she'd believed such claptrap, she'd never have applied to Girton, much less graduated with honors. And Girton, she longed to inform his lordship, was a *Cambridge* school.

Before Amanda could give in to the impulse to say any of that, however, Jamie spoke again.

"What they need, I suppose," he said slowly, "is a tutor."

With those words, Amanda's indignation vanished, and her chest tightened with longing. If only she could be a tutor.

Unlike governesses, tutors were men, and therefore, they were allowed—even expected—to teach subjects of substance, like mathematics, science, and history, not just French and how to waltz and curtsy.

But there was no point in wishing for such a post, so Amanda forced her attention back to her task. She read over her advertisement, added the address of her lodgings and a request that any interested parties write to her there, then she put down her pencil, satisfied. All that remained now was to pay for the ad, but when she looked across the room, the two men were still deep in their own conversation.

"Yes, but Jamie, it's clear they wrote to Lady Truelove because they *want* a mother. Need one, too, if their behavior is anything to go by."

"They had a mother, one mother. And she died. Any stepmother would never be anything but a second-rate substitute. They don't need that."

"But what about you? Do you ever stop to consider that a wife might be what *you* need?"

"That's rich, coming from you, last season's most notorious bachelor."

"But I'm this season's most happily married man."

Jamie made a dismissive sound between his teeth. "You've been married a week. I hardly think it counts."

"But it does, Jamie, because I know how lucky I am. My friend," he added, his voice turning unmistakably grave, "Patricia's been gone over three years, and you've been living like a monk ever since she died. And now that you're in the Commons, you're also working like a dog. Wouldn't coming home to a wife be an agreeable thing after your long, hard days at Westminster? And it would be good for the boys, too."

"Enough." Jamie's voice had not risen, but nonetheless, the word was like the crack of a whip in the nearly empty room. "I am not remarrying. Ever. I neither want nor need a wife, and the boys will have to accept that."

Galbraith merely grinned in the wake of this unequivocal declaration. "You're so out of temper these days. You may not need a wife, my friend, but you clearly need a woman. Badly."

"Unless said woman is willing to offer herself up for an hour or so at some pleasure palace, I'm not a bit interested."

With those words, Amanda's cheeks began to burn, making her appreciate that though she might be a woman of the world, with both her innocence and her reputation lost to history, she was still capable of being embarrassed.

She gave a prim little cough, and the two men glanced in her direction. They looked away at once, but it was clear from their fleeting expressions of surprise that they'd completely forgotten she was in the room.

There was a moment of awkward silence, and then Jamie reached for his hat. "The only thing I need is a tutor who can prepare my sons for Harrow. I'd best get on with finding one."

"I'm sure Merrick's Employment Agency can provide you with some applicants. And I'll ask Clara's staff to place an ad for the post in our papers, to watch for tutor positions wanted, and to inform you at once if they see anything pertinent. Would Tuesday suit for conducting interviews?"

"Yes, though how the servants will manage the boys in the interim, I can't imagine. Now that the rest of the family has decamped to the country, my valet, a footman, and the assistant cook are the only ones in the house. By the time Tuesday arrives, the twins will have run them all ragged, poor devils."

"You could watch the boys yourself, for a change. Parliament's in recess now."

"Which doesn't mean I've any free time." Jamie picked up the letter his sons had written and shoved it into his breast pocket. "I'm off tomorrow for Windermere's Friday-to-Monday. We've got to hammer out the details of my education bill. Colonel Forrester is insisting we make changes or we won't have his support. And then, I have to spend a few weeks in York—"

"You're always off somewhere when Parliament's not in session. That's half the reason those boys of yours are always in trouble."

"I've had enough lectures from you, Rex, so do something useful before you and Clara go off on honeymoon, and help me find a tutor, will you?"

With that, Jamie donned his hat, gave a nod of farewell to his friend, and turned to depart.

Amanda quickly lowered her gaze to her advertisement, pretending vast interest in reading it as he walked past her toward the exit. *I could apply for that post*, she thought in vexation as the door closed behind him, *if only I were a man.*

Women, alas, could not be tutors, not to boys. It wasn't done. And social conventions aside, she wasn't willing to subject herself to the risk of unwelcome advances from a widower, even a grieving one who seemed uninterested in making any. And the widower in question didn't believe a mere woman could manage his sons, so he'd never hire her anyway.

Galbraith's steps sounded on the floorboards, approaching her, and Amanda came out of her reverie with a start.

"My apologies for ignoring you, miss," he said, halting beside her chair as she stood up.

"No need to apologize, my lord." Amanda handed him her ad and the borrowed pencil, then reached for her handbag. "One ha'penny per word, I believe you said? For three days?"

When he nodded, she opened her bag and extracted the nine pence required for her advertisement. "Will it be possible to insert this in the next three issues of the *London Daily Standard*?" she asked, placing the coins in his palm.

"Of course." He glanced at the sheet of paper in his hand, then back at her. "Given your university education, I'd already have a post for you if you were a man," he said, smiling as he looked up. "How unfortunate that a woman can't be a tutor."

"Yes," she agreed with feeling, and turned away. "Very unfortunate."

It WAS NEARLY dark by the time Amanda reached her lodgings in Bloomsbury. Her street was well lit, her building respectable, and her landlady very kind, but if she didn't find employment soon, she'd be forced to cheaper accommodations, which would mean a darker street and a seedier neighborhood.

Trying not to think about that, she entered the lodging house and paused beside the parlor doorway to bid her landlady, Mrs. Finch, good evening, then she mounted the five flights of stairs to her garret flat. A bit of the remaining daylight came through the flat's only window, providing enough illumination for her to find the lamp and matches. But as light flooded her tiny room, the sight of the sparse furnishings and worn carpets made her feel even more dispirited than before.

Years of study and hard work to obtain her baccalaureate, she thought as she removed her hat and cloak, and what had she done with it? Tossed it aside for the ardor of a poetic aristocrat who had demonstrated in the end that his poetry was more worthy than his character.

Papa would be so ashamed of her.

Pain squeezed her chest, and Amanda shoved aside thoughts of her father, for knowing she'd thrown away all he'd done for her hurt too much
to contemplate. She hung her hat and cloak on the pegs in the wall by
the door and removed her jacket, realizing as she did so that the middle
button was loose.

Deciding to mend it at once, she crossed to the washstand, pushed
aside the creamware pitcher and basin, and laid the jacket on the washstand's green marble surface. She bent down and retrieved her sewing
basket from the floor beneath, but as she straightened, her attention was
caught by her reflection, and she stilled. Studying the countenance that
stared back at her, she wondered in bafflement what it was about her that
had inspired the illicit passions of both a dashing, poetic gentlemen and a
respectable, middle-aged banker when she'd never sought the attentions
of either.

Well, if she was some sort of temptress, it surely couldn't be because
of her hair, she decided, making a wry face. Her mass of rebellious black
tendrils had been tamed into temporary submission this morning by
hairpins and combs, but given the humid weather, the pile of curls atop
her head now had a texture that to her critical eyes made her look like an
unkempt poodle.

Amanda sighed and moved on, studying her face.

It wasn't a homely countenance, by any means, but there seemed nothing particularly lust inspiring about it. Blunt lashes, a straight nose, a
pointed chin, and a square jaw—nothing out of the common way, in
other words. Certainly nothing that seemed remotely wanton. Beneath
black brows that were too straight for delicacy, a pair of hazel green
eyes stared back at her, and though they did have gold flecks in them,
she couldn't see that they were reminiscent of sunlight embraced by a
dark forest. She certainly didn't see the face of a seductress whose best
romantic offer had included a house in a discreet neighborhood, money,
and jewels, but no wedding ring.

She set aside her sewing basket and glanced down, though she knew
her figure wouldn't provide any solution to the mystery. For one thing,
she was taller than many men, including both her former lover and her

former employer. Her waist—what there was of it anyway—stubbornly refused to mold into the coveted wasp shape, no matter how tightly she laced her corset. And her clothes could hardly inspire masculine attention, for they were plain, severe, and almost prudishly modest. Black skirt, high-necked white blouse, ruffled jabot, cameo pin—all the usual trappings of an ordinary middle-class woman.

Trappings.

Struck by the word, Amanda stared at her reflection. Her hair, her skirt, her corset, her cameo pin—these were just trappings, and yet, the very fact that she was wearing them made her vulnerable to hazards men seldom faced. Had she been a man, she would not have lost a job or been ruined by a love affair. She would not have been imposed upon by an employer. Men were expected to have physical desires, permitted to have lovers. Women, she'd learned the hard way, were not.

The trappings of her wardrobe denoted in a glance not only her gender, but also her place in the world, one that could not be altered in any significant way by her own actions and initiative. Her affair with Lord Halsbury had been a stupid mistake, but even had she not made it, her choices in life would still have been far more limited than any man's. However intelligent she was, or how educated, or how hardworking, she could not change the fact that she was female, nor that the world thought females inferior.

How unfortunate that a woman can't be a tutor.

Viscount Galbraith's words echoed through her mind as she stared at herself in the mirror. Only a man could teach truly challenging subjects. Only a man, she thought, lifting one hand to touch her hair, was safe from a male employer's advances.

Only a man . . .

Suddenly, Amanda was yanking out hairpins and combs, her hands shaking as she sent corkscrews of midnight black tumbling around her shoulders. When all her hair was down, she cast the pins and combs aside, and as they scattered across the marble surface of the washstand, she had the strange, exhilarating sensation that she was casting off chains.

She returned her attention to the mirror, set her jaw, and reached into the sewing basket. But then her hand stilled, and her courage faltered.

It's impossible hair, she shouted silently to her reflection, trying to bolster her resolve. *I've never liked it.*

She was ruined, she reminded herself. Ruined, shamed, and nearly destitute. This was no time for silly feminine sentiments about her hair.

Amanda took a deep breath and grabbed the scissors.

Chapter 2

Everyone in society knew that James St. Clair, born the second son of the Marquess of Rolleston, had always been the bad seed of his family, nothing but trouble from the day of his birth. As a boy, he'd been told time and again by his father that he'd never amount to anything, and he'd spent his entire youth proving the old man right. Before the age of twenty, he'd managed to get himself sent down—and due to his father's influence, reinstated—by both Harrow and Cambridge, expelled by both White's and Boodle's, and disinherited by his parent at least half a dozen times. After university, he'd put his education to what he deemed its best use by brawling and drinking his way through every London pub from South Kensington to Spitalfields and becoming proficient at every form of cards and dice the gaming hells could offer.

But when he was twenty-one, and despite his father's predictions about his future, Jamie somehow managed to achieve one great success. He won the hand of Lady Patricia Cavanaugh, the sister of the Duke of Torquil, who'd been the prize catch of the season the year she debuted, and in marrying her, Jamie at last redeemed himself in the marquess's eyes.

The irony, of course, was that he'd never given a damn about earning his father's good opinion because his father was a prize bastard. Truth be told, if he had ever considered Rolleston's wishes when choosing his bride, he'd have married a cancan dancer in a music hall and really done the old man in. Falling in love with the sister of a duke had been completely unintentional, but for Pat's sake, he'd set himself on the straight and narrow path. And when she had presented him with twin sons of his own, Jamie had vowed to be a very different parent from the cruel, vicious man who had sired him.

A decade later, however, his beloved Pat was three years in her grave, and without her, Jamie felt as soulless and empty as he had before she'd entered his life. And despite his vow to be a better father than his own, Jamie's sons were proving to be every bit as wild and ungovernable as he'd been at their age. In fact, as Jamie surveyed the latest carnage done to the nursery, he feared they might even be worse.

"Where in blazes did they get red paint?" he asked, turning to Samuel, who was standing nearby with a rag and a tin of turpentine. "After that business with Nanny Hornsby and the frog, they were supposed to be confined to the nursery for a full week, and to my knowledge there's no paint in the nursery."

"I'm so very sorry, sir," the footman burst out. "I was with them, of course, but then the bell rang, and Mrs. Richmond had gone to the butcher's, so I had to go down. It was Lady Tattinger at the door, inquiring after the Duchess. I told her their Graces had already left for the country, but you know how the baroness rattles on and on, and I couldn't get away—"

"Yes, yes," Jamie cut in and waved a hand to the red streaks all over the white plaster walls. "But the paint, Samuel? Where did they get the paint?"

"I gave it to them, I'm afraid. They wanted to play clock golf when their nursery confinement was over," he rushed on before Jamie could reply. "But when I fetched the set from the attic, I saw that the paint was coming off the numbers, and I suggested we spend the afternoon repainting them. It's something for them to *do*, you see, sir, and they're best if they have things to do. But we'd barely begun when the bell rang, and I went down . . . I was only gone a few minutes . . . I never thought . . . I never dreamed . . ." He paused again, lifting his chin and squaring his shoulders, looking suddenly younger than his twenty-five years. "Shall I pack my things and go, sir?"

"You think I intend to dismiss you?" Jamie shook his head, appalled by the very idea. "God, no. With those boys of mine, I need all the help I can muster. No, Samuel, your job is safe, you may be sure."

The footman didn't seem quite as relieved by that news as he perhaps ought to have been. "Thank you, sir."

"As for this mess, cease your attempts to clean it up. We shall have the boys do it. Fitting punishment, I say."

"Begging your pardon, sir, but I'm not sure putting turpentine in their hands is the best idea. After the firecrackers . . ."

His voice trailed away, and Jamie's mind immediately began envisioning a second Great Fire of London. "I see your point," he said hastily. "Find a painter and arrange to have the job properly done."

"Yes, sir. Thank you, sir."

"Where are the boys now?" He glanced toward the doorway that led to the nursery bedrooms. "In their room?"

"Oh no, sir, I couldn't have them up here." Samuel waved his rag in the air. "Not with the fumes."

"Quite," Jamie agreed, leaning back as the acrid scent of turpentine hit his nostrils. "They must be with Mr. Hoskins?"

"No, sir. You see, Mr. Hoskins is . . . um . . . that is, he . . ."

The footman paused, and Jamie noted the servant's apologetic expression with growing dismay. "Good God, Samuel, you're not telling me my valet's gone off as well?"

The footman's silence gave him his answer.

"What did they do to him this time?" Jamie demanded. "Itching powder again? Or an emetic in his tea, perhaps?"

"My lord, I don't believe it was anything the boys did. Not any one thing in particular, I mean. Mr. Hoskins did leave a note, I understand, before he departed, and he might have explained his reasons there."

"Explanations don't matter, I suppose. We both know the true reason he's gone." Samuel, he noted, did not attempt to dispute this contention. "The boys are with Mrs. Richmond, then?"

"Yes, my lord. I asked her to serve their high tea down in the kitchens. Eating up here would be terribly unappetizing."

Jamie glanced at the gruesome red streaks on the walls and was glad

Torquil wasn't here to see the latest damage to the ducal residence. "It would be no more than they deserve."

"Perhaps, but it wouldn't be healthy, sir."

Given the turpentine fumes in the air, Jamie couldn't help but agree. "They shan't be able to sleep up here tonight, I suppose. You'd best make a room ready elsewhere."

"Yes, sir. What do you mean to do—about the boys, I mean?"

"I suppose I must do something," he muttered, looking forward to the prospect with the same degree of joy he usually reserved for visits to the dentist. "What, I'm sure I don't know, for no form of punishment ever seems effective." He paused, sacrificing pride and forcing a smile. "You know my sons as well as anyone, Samuel. I'd welcome your suggestions."

The footman lifted his hands and let them fall in a helpless gesture that spoke more eloquently than any words.

Not surprised, Jamie gave a sigh. "I'll leave you to it, then."

He departed the nursery and went to the kitchens, where he found the twins wolfing down veal ham pie, Scotch eggs, and fat rascals with their usual hungry enthusiasm—displaying, he was chagrined to note, not a whit of concern over their earlier ruination of the nursery room walls or the fact that they'd managed to cause the departure of two servants within less than twenty-four hours.

He stepped into the kitchen with a decided stomp of his boots, and at the sound, his sons looked up from their evening meal. One glance at his face, and forks clattered to plates, and their happy abandon vanished.

"Good evening, gentlemen," he said with his most severe frown, folding his arms. "I understand you've had quite a busy day, writing letters to newspapers—"

"How do you know about the newspaper, Papa?" Colin interrupted.

"Don't interrupt," he ordered, in no mood to be sidetracked. "I know about that letter because I find out everything you do, gentlemen. I know about the frogs you put in Mrs. Hornsby's hatbox that led her to quit. I know about the damage you did to the nursery room walls. And I know that your antics have now lost me my valet."

They hung their heads, but as much as he wanted to believe this display of regret was genuine, Jamie had been down this road far too many times to fool himself with that sort of wishful thinking. Unfolding his arms, he started across the room toward the table where they sat.

Giving a nod to Mrs. Richmond, who was standing by the stove nearby, he pulled out an empty chair across from his sons. Still with no idea of what he was going to say or do, he sat down, but as he studied their bent heads, all he could think of was how closely their bright, carroty hair resembled Pat's, and how much better a parent she'd always been than he.

"Do the two of you know what you've done?" he asked at last, and the inanity of the question made him wince. "Do you know," he went on, trying again, "how much trouble you're in?"

They both nodded, but they did not look up nor reply, and Jamie was once again at a loss.

He had to impose some sort of punishment. He thought back to his own boyhood and all the times he'd been called to his father's study, of all the times he'd stood, bent over, staring at the floor with gritted teeth, the only sound in the room the snap of a willow switch against his bare ass. Physical punishment was the only kind he'd known as a boy, and he refused to consider visiting that sort of cruelty upon his sons, but what else was there? What could he do that he hadn't already tried?

Inadequacy swamped Jamie suddenly, inadequacy and despair.

I can't do this, Pat, he thought. *I can't do this without you.*

But even as that thought went through his head, he knew he did not have a choice. "Why?" he asked, trying to gain time with the question so that his mind could come up with some alternative to his father's willow switch and his own failed methods of discipline. "What were you thinking? Why would you deface the walls of the nursery in such a way?"

"We didn't mean to deface anything," Owen mumbled, staring at his plate. "We just wanted to paint the walls."

"But why?"

"It's red paint, Papa," Colin said as if that were explanation enough, but when Jamie, baffled, didn't reply, Colin looked up, his blue eyes glistening. "Red was Mama's favorite color."

A memory flashed through Jamie's mind before he could push it away, a memory of watching Pat dress for a ball. Half a dozen years ago it must have been, and nothing special about the event to mark it in his memory, and yet he could still recall every detail of the moment—Pat's stunning red gown, her copper-and-ginger curls glinting in the lamp-light, her adorable freckled face as she'd looked over her shoulder, and her merry laughter at the maid's dour comment that redheads weren't supposed to wear red.

Really, Parker, don't you know by now I never do what I'm supposed to?

Pain twisted in Jamie's heart like a knife, and he jerked to his feet, feeling a sudden, desperate need to get away. "Well, don't do anything like that again," he muttered, and turned away before either of the twins could discern what he felt. They'd suffered enough already; they didn't need to see his pain.

He walked to the stove where Mrs. Richmond was dishing toad-in-the-hole onto plates, and he worked to regain a sense of equilibrium. "My valet has left my service, Samuel tells me. Did he leave a letter of resignation?"

"He did, my lord." She set down her spoon, pulled the letter from her apron pocket, and handed it to him.

He glanced through it, and though the twins were not the stated reason the valet had given for departing his employ, Jamie suspected Hoskins's desire about wanting a post with Continental travel was nothing but an excuse.

"As you know, Mrs. Richmond," he said, folding the letter and putting it in his breast pocket, "I'm leaving tomorrow for Lord Windermere's house party in Kent. With Nanny Hornsby gone, I hope you will be willing to assist Samuel with the boys in my absence?"

"Of course, my lord," she answered, but only a fool would believe she sounded the least bit willing.

For Jamie, however, any affirmative answer was enough. "Thank you," he said, and turned to depart, but her voice stopped him before he reached the doorway.

"My lord?"

He paused, looking over his shoulder. "Yes?"

"When . . ." The stout little woman gave a cough. "When might we expect a new nanny to arrive, if I may ask?"

Jamie cast a glance over his shoulder and found both his sons watching him.

"I'm not hiring another nanny," he said, returning his attention to the cook as shouts of happy relief rose up behind him.

Mrs. Richmond, however, did not share the boys' elated opinion of this news. "No nanny?" she murmured, going a bit pale.

"I've decided a tutor is what's called for. A stern fellow," he added, noting with some satisfaction that his sons' shouts of joy had faded into apprehensive silence. "A strict disciplinarian, to whom I shall give a very free hand. He'll make those sons of mine toe the line, Mrs. Richmond, you may be sure. Applicants are coming to be interviewed for the post on Tuesday, and someone will be hired by the end of the day."

"Tuesday?" The cook swallowed hard. "It'll take as long as that?"

"Only because I have to be away. It's only four days."

"A long four days, my lord."

"We shall have to muddle through as best we can."

He turned away, but as he departed, he did not miss Mrs. Richmond's reply, uttered in a low voice behind his back.

"Easy for you to say. You won't be here. You're never here."

Most men would dismiss a servant for such impertinence, but Jamie couldn't afford that luxury. He needed all the help he could get. Besides, he'd never thought it right to punish people for telling the truth.

FOR JAMIE, THE next few days proved quite productive. In the relaxing atmosphere of the country, with a bit of excellent trout fishing and grouse hunting to soften his stance, Colonel Forrester had agreed to support Jamie's education bill when the Commons reconvened.

Colonel Forrester was not the only one who had enjoyed Windermere's hospitality. For Jamie, it was a welcome respite from his usual grinding workload, but he had no illusions that Samuel and Mrs. Richmond were enjoying a similarly pleasant interlude, and upon his return Monday afternoon, he was relieved to discover that neither of his two remaining servants had decided to depart the household during his absence.

Nonetheless, Jamie did not want to push his luck. Immediately upon his return, he began paying calls at various London employment agencies. He spent all of Tuesday interviewing applicants, determined to engage a tutor before the end of the day, but by late afternoon, he feared his goal might have been a bit unrealistic.

Despite the newspaper advertisement inserted by Galbraith on his behalf and the efforts of the agencies, only twelve men came to be interviewed, underscoring the fact that his sons had something of a reputation. Worse, after interviewing nearly all of them, Jamie had not found one he'd even consider hiring.

Some were so timid that sending them up to the nursery would be like sending lambs to the slaughter. Others were too elderly and frail to keep up with his energetic young sons, others were painfully inept, and still others were far too much like his own father for his liking. One, in fact, described teaching methods so vicious that it gave Jamie chills to think he'd ever been in charge of anyone's children.

And then, of course, there were the ones so dull they put a body to sleep.

"Lord Kenyon?"

Jamie gave a start at the sound of his name and opened his eyes to find the portly man opposite giving him a quizzical stare across the desk. "Yes, quite so, Mr. Partridge," he agreed hastily, though he had no idea what he was agreeing with. "I'm sure you're right."

"Repetition is the key to learning Latin, my lord, as you surely are aware. *Adduco, adducere, adduxi*—"

"Of course," he interrupted, vivid memories of instruction in loathsome Latin coming back to torment him anew. "And your approach to mathematics?"

"My approach is the same, my lord, regardless of subject. Memorization is the key to all learning. Drilling is what boys need. Drilling," he repeated, pounding the fist of one hand emphatically into the palm of the other as he spoke. "The wearing of their minds into grooves of correct thought through constant repetition is what will prepare them for Harrow."

Having attended that lauded institution himself, Jamie had no doubt the other man was right, and yet, such teaching methods left him curiously dissatisfied. "That is the conventional wisdom, I know," he said, and paused. Partridge was the best candidate he'd interviewed today, and yet, he couldn't seem to utter the offer of employment. The man's education was first-rate, his letters of character laudatory, and Jamie's own situation desperate. What was making him hesitate?

"Regimentation and memorization are all very well," he said after a moment. "But don't you have the desire to imbue your pupils with something more?"

"More, my lord?" Mr. Partridge blinked, clearly taken aback. "But what more is there?"

What, indeed. Jamie didn't even know himself the answer to that question. Considering it, he rose and turned toward the window. Blinking a little against the bright afternoon sun outside, he shaded his eyes with one hand and looked down to where Colin and Owen were playing in the park across the street. They were attempting to fly kites and having little success, for the breeze today was not a strong one.

Samuel was seated near them on the grass, watching, but doing little to assist their efforts. Jamie couldn't blame him. The poor fellow was probably exhausted.

He returned his attention to his sons, observing Colin as the boy started across the grass at a run, his box kite bouncing along the ground behind him. The toy managed to take flight, rising about twenty feet before it came hurtling back down, straight for a park bench, impelling the young man seated there to toss aside his sandwich and dive out of the way.

The kite hit the bench right where the young man had been sitting. Hands on hips, he shoved back his brown derby hat, and stared at the mess of broken wood, torn silk, and kite wool for a moment, then he turned toward Colin and said something.

For a moment, Jamie feared the man might be angry, but that didn't seem to be the case. He was pointing at the kite and gesticulating with his arms, true enough, but it didn't appear that he was scolding the boy. He seemed, instead, to be explaining something.

Whatever he was saying, it must be interesting indeed, for Colin was actually listening. Owen, too, for he had stopped attempting to launch his own kite and was crossing the grass to join his brother.

Jamie, equally intrigued, continued to watch as the young man removed his tweed jacket and his hat and tossed them onto the bench. He raked a hand through his unruly crop of dark hair, turned to Samuel, and nodded to the crate nearby as he began rolling up his shirtsleeves.

He must have asked a question, for the footman gave a nod in return, and the stranger bent down to rummage in the crate. A moment later, he straightened, a diamond-shaped kite of blue silk in one hand and its attached skein of kite wool in the other. Giving a quick glance behind him, the young man dropped the kite to the ground, then he began moving backward across the grass at a rapid clip. Suddenly, as if by magic, the kite caught the slight breeze and jerked upward off the ground. The man continued to walk backward, letting out kite wool as he went, allowing the kite to climb into the sky.

Seeming satisfied that it was high enough, the young man circled back around to where the boys were standing. There, he relinquished control of the kite to Colin and knelt on the grass beside him to help guide the toy and keep it from tangling in the tall elm trees nearby.

"Lord Kenyon?"

Mr. Partridge's voice penetrated his consciousness, and Jamie turned from the window, reminded of the task at hand and the decision he had to make. But when he looked at Mr. Partridge across the desk, he knew that at least as far as this candidate was concerned, his decision was already made. Pat had been passionate about knowledge, education, and learning. She would not have wanted her boys to be drilled as if they were in a regiment of the army. He would keep looking.

"I believe you have answered all my questions, Mr. Partridge," he said, gathering up the other man's excellent letters of character and holding them out across the desk. "Thank you for your time."

The other man took the dismissal with good grace. "My lord," he said, accepting his letters and offering a bow. "I bid you good day."

Jamie started around the desk. "I will show you out."

"No, please," Mr. Partridge said, causing Jamie to halt his steps. "Don't trouble yourself, my lord. I am sure you are short of staff, with everyone in your family off to the country. I can find my own way down." With another bow, he departed.

Jamie bent over his desk, inked a pen, and scribbled a few notes next to Mr. Partridge's name. Experience had taught him to take down his impressions of every person he interviewed to watch the boys, for there had been many over the years, and he couldn't possibly remember them all. He also knew that because no one he'd ever hired stayed long, he might have to give those applicants he'd interviewed and rejected a second look at some point in the future.

Setting aside the pen at last, he straightened and glanced at the clock, then at the list of appointments, noting in some dismay that he had only one remaining candidate to interview. Holding out little hope, he yanked the bellpull on the wall, indicating he was ready for Mrs. Richmond to bring the last applicant up to the study.

While he waited, Jamie turned again to the window, but he found that the young man in the park was gone. Colin was still flying the kite, however, and with what was probably more luck than skill, he was managing to keep it out of the trees. Owen had pulled out another kite, one of a delta shape, and was running backward with it across the grass just as the stranger had demonstrated.

"Mr. Adam Seton, my lord."

Mrs. Richmond's announcement tore Jamie's attention from his son. He turned, and at once, blinked in surprise, for the black-haired man coming across the room toward him hat in hand was the same young man from across the street.

That is, Jamie amended at once, if he was a man. Upon closer inspection, he seemed more like a boy to Jamie's eyes—slender and beardless and in need of a haircut, tugging at his high collar as adolescent boys were so inclined to do. Unlike most boys, however, his face was free of spots, his skin pale as milk but for a faint pink tint in his cheeks from the chill outside.

He couldn't be more than half a dozen years older than the boys he aspired to teach, but when Jamie looked into the younger man's eyes, he found cause to wonder.

They were strange eyes, dark umber green with lights of tawny amber, and they seemed far older than the rest of him. There was knowledge in those eyes, and experience, and a curious intensity of passion more suitable to a poet or political revolutionary than a tutor. Adolescent girls no doubt found the fellow madly attractive, and Jamie knew if he had any daughters, this interview would already be over.

It might soon be over anyway, he thought, glancing down over an atrocious suit of brown tweed that was frayed, disheveled, and far too big. Jamie suspected his own sons might be to blame for its creased elbows and grass-stained knees, but nonetheless, Seton's unkempt appearance underscored his age and lack of sophistication. Only very young men displayed such a cavalier disregard for their clothes.

All in all, Mr. Seton did not seem capable of being the stern taskmaster London's wildest pair of hellions required, but Jamie supposed it could do no harm to conduct an interview.

He glanced past the other man to the servant by the door. "Thank you, Mrs. Richmond. You may go."

As the cook departed, closing the door behind her, Jamie returned his attention to the youth opposite. "How old are you, Mr. Seton?"

There was an infinitesimal pause. "Nineteen."

Jamie folded his arms, raised an eyebrow, and waited.

"Seventeen," the young man amended with a sigh.

Jamie gave a laugh, his first impression confirmed. "You can't seriously think I'd consider you as a tutor for my children. You're far too young."

"I may be young, but I'm a very good teacher."

"Indeed? And where have you taught?"

Those eyes slid away, and the silence answered his question.

"I see." Jamie unfolded his arms. "And why were you talking with my boys?"

The young man frowned, looking puzzled. "How did you—" He broke off and glanced past Jamie to the window, then back again, comprehension easing away the bewilderment. "I was in the park, yes."

"And you were talking with my sons."

"I was." The young man's wide mouth tipped at one corner in a wry curve. "That is, if your sons have red hair, freckles, a passion for kites, and a loathing for nannies."

"My sons talked to you about nannies?"

"No, we talked only of kites. But their anathema for nannies is widely known."

Jamie stirred, not appreciating the reminder. "Do you always converse in parks with children to whom you have not been introduced?" he demanded.

"Do you always watch your sons play from a window across the street?"

He inhaled sharply, feeling that shot like an arrow through his chest. "Take care, Mr. Seton," he said. "Cheek won't gain you the post. Answer my question, if you please."

"I like children. Is talking to them such a crime?"

"A crime, no, but I can't help being curious as to your intent."

That puzzled the young man. "My intent?"

"Were you attempting to gain an advantage over other applicants by playing with my sons? Perhaps hoping they would bring their influence to bear on my decision whom to hire?" Even as he spoke, he knew he was being unfair, but the impertinent question about the window had flicked him on the raw—probably because it was so damnably perceptive.

He wasn't the only one flicked on the raw, it seemed. Seton's chin lifted a fraction, displaying a hint of rebellion that harkened to the passion Jamie had sensed earlier. "First of all, I don't curry favor with anyone, my lord. It is not, let me assure you, in my nature to do so. Second, I happened to be in the park, waiting for my allotted time to be interviewed. I was having my lunch and minding my own business when your son's kite came crashing down and nearly landed on my head. I decided that before he injured anyone, he ought to be taught how to fly a kite properly."

"On a day like this, no one can fly a kite properly."

"I did."

That point, Jamie was rather chagrined to note, could not be argued. "I can't think how. There's scarcely any breeze today."

"A strong breeze isn't necessary, not if one has the proper kite. A box kite's no good on a day like this. It's too heavy, which is why your son failed to successfully launch it. You need a diamond or delta-shaped kite when there's so little wind. As I explained to your sons, it's a matter of physics."

Jamie was a bit taken aback. "You were explaining physics to my sons? With a kite?"

The young man looked back at him steadily. "Can you think of a better way to explain a fundamental principle of physics to a pair of children?"

"No." Jamie gave a short laugh, appreciating that he'd just lost an argument to a seventeen-year-old. "I can't, actually."

He paused, considering, then went on, "Aside from your ability to fly a kite and explain to a child how it's done, what makes you presume to believe you are qualified to teach my sons? They need to be groomed for Harrow. How can someone your age be capable of doing that? What preparatory school did you attend?"

"I did not go to preparatory school, my lord. Nor any sort of school, actually." Mr. Seton swallowed, tugging at his collar again, as if the admission had been a difficult one to make. "I was educated at home, by my father. I was . . . ahem . . . too sickly for school."

Given the twins' exuberance, that was not a compelling reason to hire the fellow, and yet, Jamie was strangely reluctant to dismiss him. "So, your father was an educated man. What schools did he attend? Harrow? Eton?"

"St. Andrews, in Cambridge. Massachusetts," he added when Jamie frowned at the unfamiliar name.

"Your father was American?"

"Yes. After St. Andrews, he attended Harvard, receiving his baccalaureate. He then became a tutor there, and in time, a professor."

"And where is he now? Still in America?"

"He's dead."

"My condolences." Jamie paused, for he didn't want to be cruel in the wake of such a pronouncement, but facts were facts. "If you never went to school, I can only assume you've no one to vouch for your capabilities as a student, and you're clearly too young to have much practical experience as a teacher. Have you any references to offer?" he asked, even as he wondered why he was bothering to put the question.

To his surprise, Mr. Seton nodded. "I do, yes," he answered, and bent as if to reach for something on the floor beside him—an odd thing to do, to Jamie's mind—but then, he stopped, straightened, and reached into the breast pocket of his jacket instead. "I have two."

He pulled the folded sheets from his pocket and held them across the desk.

Jamie took them and glanced over the first one. "And who is this Mrs. Finch?" he asked, looking up when Seton didn't answer. "Is she a woman of prominence?"

"I'm afraid not." The young man's lips twisted into a wry, sideways smile. "She's my landlady."

"I beg your pardon?"

"At my lodging house. It's a respectable place," he added as Jamie gave a disbelieving laugh. "I'm teaching her the piano, and—"

"How useful for boys going to Harrow," he cut in, tossing the letter aside.

"I am also giving her lessons in French and German."

"That's a bit more impressive than piano, I suppose," he muttered, unfolding the second letter and glancing at its contents. "And Mr. Hugh Mackenzie? Who is he?"

"He's the pubkeeper at the end of my street." The young man's cheeks went red as Jamie laughed again. "I'm teaching him maths."

"You're teaching mathematics to a pubkeeper? What on earth for?"

"Perhaps because he wants to learn?" One of his straight black brows lifted, taking on a sardonic curve. "Or is it your opinion that only those of the peerage have a thirst for knowledge?"

"In considering whom to hire, I will take your impertinent character into consideration, Mr. Seton."

The younger man bit his lip, suitably chastened, but if Jamie had expected an apology, he was fated for disappointment. "At first," Seton said after a moment, "Mr. Mackenzie merely wanted to know how he could discern if tradesmen were cheating him, so I offered to teach him how to keep proper account books. Double-entry bookkeeping requires a solid knowledge of basic arithmetic. And the ability to use an abacus is quite helpful, too."

"You know how to use an abacus?"

"I do, yes. So does Mr. Mackenzie, now."

Despite himself, Jamie was rather impressed. "Still," he said, "a pubkeeper isn't much of a reference, and my sons hardly need the education one would give a clerk."

"We've moved on to algebra and geometry now, if that makes you feel better."

Jamie frowned, but this time, he ignored the cheek. "Tell me," he said instead, "are a landlady and a pubkeeper the only references you have?"

Seton stirred, looking uncomfortable, giving the answer to that question even before he spoke. "Well, I am only seventeen, after all," he muttered.

"Just so. And my sons are the grandsons of a marquess and the nephews of a duke. They require a tutor of far greater experience than you possess."

"If you can find one willing to teach them. Your sons are quite the hell-raisers, if the scandal sheets are to be believed."

Jamie did not appreciate the reminder. With an abrupt move, he gathered the letters and held them out. "Thank you, Mr. Seton, I'm afraid you won't do, but I appreciate your time."

The young man hesitated, seeming inclined to say more, but thankfully, he checked the impulse. "I reside in Red Lion Street, Bloomsbury. Number twelve," he said, taking his character letters from Jamie's outstretched hand. "You can write to me there, my lord, if you change your mind."

"I shan't change my mind. Why should I?"

The youth hesitated a moment longer, then turned away. "Oh, I don't know," he said vaguely as he walked to the door and opened it. "After all," he added, looking at Jamie over one shoulder, "servants can only tolerate so much itching powder in their underwear and so many firecrackers in the drawing room before they've had enough." With that parting shot, and a decidedly provoking grin, Seton vanished out the door, leaving Jamie frowning at the doorway and wondering how in hell the scandal sheets had learned about the itching powder.

Chapter 3

*T*hree shillings for the clothes, Amanda thought in aggravation as she walked up Park Lane toward New Oxford Street to catch the omnibus home. Money squandered in a useless endeavor. And it was all her own fault, for she'd been unforgivably cheeky.

Do you always watch your sons play from a window across the street?

As she recalled the impudent words that had come flying out of her mouth, Amanda grimaced. Employers, she feared, did not take kindly to criticisms of that sort.

But damn it all, he'd made her angry with his accusation that she'd been sucking up to his sons in the park in order to obtain the post. And his dismissive tone when he'd spoken of Mrs. Finch and Mr. Mackenzie had added fuel to her fire. *Toplofty snob*, she thought with a derisive snort. Who was he to talk as if the recommendations of ordinary, middle-class people were somehow unworthy of consideration?

Amanda sighed and stopped walking, then turned to lean back against the wall of the building beside her. Who was he? He was a man with a smashing job to offer, and she was an idiot for letting her temper get the better of her.

Now, she was worse off than before. To obtain those letters of character for Adam Seton, she'd sacrificed her only current source of income by offering future lessons free of charge in exchange. Though she'd muffed her interview, her obligation to Mrs. Finch and Mr. Mackenzie remained.

In addition to the money she'd sacrificed, there was also her wasted time—four days of practicing a deeper voice and a manly walk and trying to grow accustomed to the strange, rather salacious sensation of wearing trousers. And though casting aside a corset had seemed so liberating on the first day, after four days without one, her back ached. And if all that wasn't enough to put her thoroughly out of sorts, she'd cut off all her hair.

Amanda straightened away from the wall and doffed her hat to rake a hand through what little remained of her once plentiful mane, and as the cropped strands slid through her fingers, she felt an absurd desire to cry.

She'd abandoned every shred of her femininity and for what? So that her temper and her tongue could cost her a job. On the other hand, did she really want to work for a man like him? An image of Lord Kenyon's pale eyes, so icy and remote, flashed through her mind, and his voice, so well-bred and dismissive, echoed back to her.

My sons are the grandsons of a marquess and the nephews of a duke.

"Oh, well, the nephews of a duke," she muttered, her desire to weep giving way to renewed irritation. "My word and la-di-da."

Their lineage was all very well, but those boys were also absolute hellions. Even their father had admitted as much, and the newspaper accounts she'd read over the weekend had only reinforced the truth of his assessment. The notorious antics of Lord Kenyon's sons, she'd discovered, were widely known to the gossip columnists, who had devoted a great deal of space in the Saturday editions to gleeful speculations about what the twins might have done to drive not only their latest nanny but also their father's valet out of the household.

Her encounter in the park with the boys had given Amanda an impression that differed somewhat from the general understanding, but then, she was aided by years of experience. She'd been around enough children to know that very few were lost causes. The twins, she felt, could be helped to straighten out, but that task would prove almost impossible if something wasn't done before they reached adolescence.

Either way, they weren't her concern, since she hadn't gotten the job. With that reminder, Amanda shoved aside any inclinations to anger or self-pity and chose to look on the bright side. Selling the locks of her hair would recoup some of the money she'd spent. More important, her disguise had worked. She'd prepared for the possibility that Lord Kenyon would see through her straightaway, and the fact that he hadn't done so showed she could apply for other tutoring positions. Not at the agencies, of course, for she'd visited those multiple times already, and she didn't want to risk that someone would recognize her. But she could look through the newspaper advertisements for tutoring posts. Unlike governesses, good tutors were a rare and sought-after commodity. A job offer could still come her way, as long as no one looked too closely into her father's academic credentials.

Amanda settled the brown derby back onto her head and resumed walking, her determination renewed. When she reached New Oxford Street, an omnibus was just pulling up to the corner, but she did not join the queue waiting to board. Instead, she turned in the opposite direction, toward the entrance to the park and the Marble Arch, where dozens of newspaper sellers plied their trade.

She stopped in front of the first one she came to. "How many of the evening dailies do you have for sale?" she asked the elderly man on the other side of the stacks.

"Let me see . . ." He looked down, rubbing the tips of his gnarled fingers over his thick gray mustache as he began counting. "Nine . . . ten . . ." He looked up. "Twelve, altogether."

Amanda hesitated, doing some quick arithmetic, reminding herself that she'd already spent more than she ought. If this mad idea to find work as a male tutor didn't succeed, she'd be destitute long before the new year.

The man stirred, looking past her shoulder, and when she glanced back, Amanda realized a queue was forming behind her.

"Which ones ye be wanting, sir?"

That question snapped her attention back to the newspaper seller in front of her, and she had the sudden desire to laugh.

Sir.

Hell, if that wasn't an encouraging sign from the heavens, she'd eat her brown felt derby. And stone broke in January or stone broke in September, did it really matter much either way?

Amanda took a deep breath and reached into the breast pocket of her jacket. "I'll take them all."

MR. PARTRIDGE LASTED less than three days. Hired Tuesday night, he was gone by Friday morning, and though his stated reason for leaving was the sudden illness of a relative, Jamie felt certain a pair of angelic-faced, red-haired devils had more to do with his departure than the influenza visited upon some distant cousin.

Jamie looked up from the man's resignation letter to the grim faces of Samuel and Mrs. Richmond. "It seems we shall have to begin again."

"Perhaps . . ." Mrs. Richmond gave a cough. "Perhaps he could be persuaded to come back when his cousin is better. It might only be a few days."

"Or it might be weeks," Samuel pointed out. "If there's a sick cousin at all."

Either way, Jamie knew waiting weeks for the man's unlikely return was not a viable option. And even if it were, what could be done with the twins in the meantime? He was supposed to be departing this evening for a three-week tour of Yorkshire.

Sending the boys to Ravenwood would have been ideal, for there was far more to occupy their mischief-making minds at Torquil's estate than there was here in London. But the duke had flatly refused to consider the idea of having his nephews down to Hampshire without at least a nanny to accompany them, a refusal for which Jamie could not blame him. And for his own part, he was far too busy for a jaunt to Hampshire. He'd won his seat in the Commons by the slimmest of margins, and he needed to spend his time before the next Parliamentary session on work, not play. He couldn't postpone his trip north, for he had visited his constituents in Yorkshire only once since his by-election a year ago, and he certainly did not have the time to go off with the boys for punting and tennis at Ravenwood. Hell, he hadn't yet managed to carve out the time to find himself a new valet, much less go on another exhaustive hunt for someone to watch the boys.

"Samuel is right, Mrs. Richmond," he said, putting aside Mr. Partridge's letter. "Someone must be found immediately."

"You'll hear no argument from me, my lord," the cook replied. "Perhaps another visit to the agencies?"

But Jamie knew that wasn't likely to accomplish much. The morning following his interviews, he'd called upon the agencies again, but they'd been able to offer no additional candidates for his consideration and left with little choice, he'd hired the pedantic Mr. Partridge.

"I will pay another call at the agencies before I leave," he promised without much hope. "My train for Yorkshire doesn't depart until five o'clock."

"You're still going north then?" Mrs. Richmond glanced at Samuel, then back at Jamie, her dismay obvious. "You don't think it might be best to postpone the trip, given the circumstances?"

Jamie shook his head. "I've postponed one visit to my home district because of the twins. I can't afford to do so again. I have a duty to my constituents, Mrs. Richmond."

"Your constituents?" The cook's frustration was obvious, but before Jamie was obligated to reprimand her and receive what was likely to be her resignation in response, Samuel tactfully intervened.

"What about taking the boys with you to York?" he suggested. "Your father's servants could take charge of them for a bit, couldn't they?"

Just the idea of having his sons anywhere near his own father without being there himself left Jamie cold. "That's not possible."

"What about the other applicants you interviewed on Tuesday?" Mrs. Richmond asked. "Was there not at least one acceptable candidate besides Mr. Partridge?"

At once, a pale face with intense hazel eyes came into Jamie's mind.

I may be young, but I'm a very good teacher.

"No," he answered. "Not even one."

The faces of the two servants made it clear they thought he was being far too punctilious. "Perhaps the agencies have some new candidates," he said and stood up. "Have my driver fetch the carriage, Samuel, and bring my luggage down, would you?"

A few hours later, however, it was clear that Jamie's hope of finding a tutor before his departure north would go unfulfilled. Tutors qualified to prepare boys for public school were not only rare, he was told, but were also in great demand. Such men could, it was pointed out to him with tiresome frequency, pick and choose their pupils, and though Jamie was never told straight out that no qualified tutor would want to take on his sons, the inference was clear, and by late afternoon, he was forced to admit defeat.

Out of time, he telephoned the house at Upper Brook Street and informed Mrs. Richmond that he had been unsuccessful, and that she and Samuel would be required to supervise the twins until he returned from Yorkshire. He softened the blow with a raise in their wages and a pledge to shorten his trip from three weeks to two, but as his carriage took him to Victoria Station, Jamie feared it would not even be one before he received a telegram from Torquil informing him that both servants had resigned, the twins had been fetched to Ravenwood, and that he would be expected to come to Hampshire and retrieve them immediately.

He stared out the window as his carriage made its way along the Holborn Road, his mind working to find some way of circumventing that possibility.

He could ring Merrick's and have them send along another nanny, of course, but he still felt quite strongly that hiring a tutor was the best solution. And what competent nanny would agree to a post that was only temporary?

He could begin perusing the Situations Wanted advertisements in the papers, though he doubted worthy applicants would need to insert such advertisements. He could write to various acquaintances, inquire if they knew of any possible candidates for the post. He could also write to Harrow for recommendations. Eton, too—but only if things got truly desperate. All that took time, however, and he needed someone now, not weeks in the future.

His carriage came to an abrupt stop. Lost in his own contemplations, Jamie paid little heed at first, but as the minutes ticked by and the vehicle did not move, he opened the window and stuck his head out.

All he could see ahead was a solid line of hansom cabs, broughams, omnibuses, and dog carts, each vehicle as motionless as his own. He wasn't worried, for his train didn't depart for forty minutes yet, so Jamie drew back inside the carriage and closed the window. But as he relaxed again in his seat, the street sign painted on the corner caught his attention, and he paused.

Red Lion Street.

The name was familiar, though he wasn't sure quite why, for this was Bloomsbury, a section of London he seldom had cause to visit. Here, artists, émigrés, and bohemians existed alongside respectable, solidly middle-class families, and none of these mingled much with gentlemen of his station. He doubted he'd ever set foot in Red Lion Street in his entire life, so why should the name strike such a familiar chord?

As if in answer to that question, the words of Adam Seton came back to him.

I reside in Red Lion Street, Bloomsbury.

The carriage jerked into motion again, rolling past the corner, but Mr. Seton's voice continued to echo through Jamie's mind.

Number twelve. Write to me there if you change your mind.

He wasn't changing his mind. Leave his boys to be managed by a boy of seventeen, one so unqualified it was laughable?

Mathematics and geometry . . . French and German . . . can you think of a better way to explain physics to a pair of children?

With an oath, Jamie reached up and pounded on the ceiling for his driver to stop the carriage. Moments later, he found himself walking beside a row of terrace houses, where the front stoops were indifferently whitewashed and chalk drawings of children's hop-score games littered the sidewalk.

Number twelve was a tall, narrow structure of soot-dusted red brick and dark blue shutters, with window boxes of purple asters and curtains of white Nottingham lace. Stepping around a group of girls playing jump-the-rope, Jamie ascended the front steps and tapped the knocker, wondering if he was following the dictates of fate, or if desperation was making him soft in the head.

The door was opened by a thin, henna-haired woman of about fifty. "I've no rooms to let just now," she began, then stopped, her eyes widening in surprise as her gaze traveled slowly down over Jamie's well-cut clothes.

"I should like to see Mr. Seton," he said, holding out his card. "If he is receiving this afternoon?"

"Mr. Seton?" The landlady looked up, frowning as if the name were not familiar. "Mr. Seton, you say?"

"Mr. Adam Seton. I was given to understand he lives here?"

She blinked several times, but just as Jamie began to think the whole thing a great joke, perhaps concocted by Rex at his expense, her brow cleared. "Oh, Mr. *Seton!*"

"He does live here, then?"

"Why, yes, of course." She laughed, touching one hand to her forehead as she took his card with the other. "He's not in at present, Mr.—"

She broke off to glance at the card, then back at him. "Your . . . ahem . . . your lordship," she amended. "I am sorry, but as I said, Mr. Seton is out."

Jamie pulled out his watch, considering. Ten minutes to Victoria, five to secure a porter, five more to find his seat. He could afford to spare a few minutes. "I may wait, I trust?"

"Oh, my lord, I don't know when Mr. Seton will be back. He could be hours yet."

"I realize that."

With a little laugh and a shrug, the landlady stepped back to allow him in, then led him through a doorway to the right of the foyer into an overcrowded parlor of maroon velvet draperies, mahogany furniture, and Benares brasses. An upright piano stood in one corner, and a pair of scraggy-looking potted ferns struggled for survival in the dim light of the room's only window.

"Do sit down, please, my lord."

Jamie did so, settling onto one end of a faded crimson velvet settee. Removing his hat, he gestured to the instrument in the corner as she took a seat on the settee opposite him. "Mr. Seton is teaching you piano, I understand. And French and German?"

"Why . . . umm . . . yes." Her voice had a strange inflection. It might have been amusement, though he couldn't imagine what she'd find amusing about his question. "Yes, yes, he is. Would you care for tea?"

He shook his head. "Thank you, but I should not wish to impose upon your hospitality, madam. Tell me, is Mr. Seton a good teacher, do you think?"

The amusement vanished, and she wriggled a little in her chair, rather as a child might do when caught misbehaving, making Jamie wonder if Mr. Seton's assurance of his abilities had been nothing but empty boasting.

Mrs. Finch's reply, however, when it came, was quite unequivocal. "He is very good. Patient, kind. Never a sharp word."

"And is he a man of good character? Respectable and honest?"

"Oh yes. Always pays on time, quiet, sober."

"Does he do well with children? Do you know?"

"Oh yes, my lord. The children are always coming 'round asking Mr.—ahem—Mr. Seton for help with their lessons, and that's a good sign, isn't it?"

He had no chance to ask another question, for the sound of the front door opening intervened.

"Ah," Mrs. Finch said, turning to look over her shoulder to the open doorway. "That'll be Mr. Seton now, I expect."

Sure enough, the object of their conversation appeared, but he moved past the doorway without a sideways glance, making the floorboards creak as he headed for the stairs.

"Mr. Seton?" Mrs. Finch called after him. "You have a visitor."

The creaking stopped. After a few seconds, it resumed, and a moment later, the younger man appeared in the doorway, his eyes widening at the sight of Jamie. "Lord Kenyon? What are you doing here?"

Mrs. Finch spoke before he could reply. "Isn't it obvious, dear boy? He's come to see you." She glanced back and forth between them, then stood up. "I'll leave you to it, then," she said, chuckling as she left the room, though Jamie couldn't see what she found so amusing. He had no time to consider the question, however, for Seton spoke again, returning his attention to the matter at hand.

"Why are you here, my lord?"

Rather wondering that himself, Jamie rose, studying the boy in front of him. Seton's credentials were laughably lowbrow, his experience almost nonexistent, and the scope of his academic knowledge open to question. His suit—the same ill-fitting one he'd worn the other day—was no longer grass stained, but it was every bit as worn as Jamie remembered. In addition, the knot of his tie was hopelessly crooked, and his cuff, peeking out from his jacket sleeve, was stained with ink. On the other hand, his ease with the twins the other day had been unmistakable. Other children seemed to get on well with him, if Mrs. Finch could be believed. And Colin and Owen couldn't very well torment and hound out of the house the same fellow who'd shown them how to properly fly a kite, could they? He might last awhile—at least until Jamie returned from Yorkshire and could find someone more qualified.

"Lord Kenyon?"

"I'm here because there's a question I forgot to ask you the other day. Tell me, Mr. Seton—" Jamie broke off and took a deep breath, hoping he wasn't making a dreadful mistake. "How's your Latin?"

Chapter 4

Only a self-deluded fool would think Lord Kenyon wanted to hire her. He looked as if he'd rather hire the devil, but there was no other reason for him to be here, asking about her Latin, and Amanda was so relieved for a second chance that she couldn't help a grin. "Changed your mind, did you?"

"Wipe that smirk off your face, Mr. Seton, or I shall change it again."

She obeyed at once, reminding herself that cheek had nearly done her in during their first interview. "*Mea Latina est magna*," she said, answering his question, careful to maintain the deep, masculine tones she'd been practicing. "*Et vobis?*"

"It's good enough to know you're telling the truth," he muttered. "At least about Latin."

Wisely, she didn't reply, and he went on, "Your wages will be four pounds per month, with room, board, three meals each day, and tea. You will have one day out each week, as well as one half day for Sunday service. You do attend church, I trust?"

No, synagogue, she wanted to say, but she checked the impulse just in time. "I do, my lord," she answered with solemnity. "Religiously, in fact."

He frowned, but if he had any suspicion her reply was somewhat tongue-in-cheek, he didn't express it. "Good," he said instead. "Pack your things at once, go to the house in Upper Brook Street, and present yourself to Mrs. Richmond."

She blinked, laughing a little. "What, this minute?"

"That is what 'at once' usually means, Mr. Seton. Mrs. Richmond, or Samuel, the footman, will show you the nursery and your room, see you settled, and introduce you to your charges. When I leave here, I will telephone them to expect you." He pulled a notecase out of his breast pocket, retrieved three one-pound notes, and held them out to her. "Here."

"What's this?" she asked without taking the money. "Surely you don't pay wages in advance?"

"Of course not. This is for a new suit of clothes."

Amanda glanced down, dismayed, wondering what she'd got wrong about a gentleman's wardrobe. "Is there a problem with my clothes?"

"Not if your intent is to look like a decaying cabbage. Otherwise, yes. I expect those in my employ to be properly dressed, Mr. Seton," he went on, seeming not to care that he'd just compared his new employee to a rotting vegetable. "Particularly those who will be exerting influence over my children. On your first day out, you will present yourself to my tailors, Joshua and Firth, in Regent Street, inform them that you are there at my request, and have yourself fitted for a new suit of clothes. And since I have no time to assure them before I leave town that I am standing the expense, you will have to pay for the suit in ready money. Three pounds should be adequate."

Amanda knew there could be no visit to his tailors, but she took the notes without argument. "You're going away?"

"Yes, this afternoon. I shall be in Yorkshire for the next two weeks."

She frowned, puzzled. "But you hardly know me. And you are willing to put your children completely in my care while you are miles away?"

"Are you in the habit of questioning everything your employer says or does?" he countered, a clear warning that she was again flirting with insubordination. But, really, what sort of man abandoned his children to the unsupervised care of someone he barely knew?

As if reading her mind, he said, "You are being hired on a conditional basis, Mr. Seton. While I am away, Mrs. Richmond and Samuel will be keeping close watch on you. When I return, I shall observe and assess the quality of your instruction myself, then decide whether or not to make your position permanent."

The fact that he was going away was probably a blessing for her. It would give her time to settle into not only her new post but also her new identity. "Fair enough."

"There is one other thing I must make clear, Mr. Seton. My sons, as you know, are full of high spirits—"

"That's one way of calling a goose a swan," she cut in, laughing a little, but at the forbidding look he gave her in return, Amanda smothered her humor.

"As I said," he went on, "my sons are high-spirited. However, I will tolerate no form of physical punishment, so if the willow switch or belt is your idea of discipline—"

"It most certainly is not!" she interrupted again, too appalled to be polite. "Any teacher that resorts to such methods is not only vicious, but also incompetent."

Something about his countenance changed—it didn't soften, exactly, but its harsh lines relaxed a fraction, and she realized her words had been a relief to him.

"I am gratified to hear that," he said. "For your sake, I hope you mean it. I also hope that you are as respectable and honest as your landlady's assurances deem you."

He was watching her keenly as he spoke, and apprehension prickled along her spine. It took all the fortitude she possessed not to squirm under his unrelenting stare. He looked every inch the haughty aristocrat, the sort who in another age would have had no qualms about ordering a dishonest servant pitched over the castle rampart and into the moat. She wasn't usually the sort to be intimidated by anyone, but then, she also wasn't accustomed to living a lie.

"If Mrs. Richmond has any concerns about the quality of your teaching or your treatment of the boys, or any difficulties with you whatsoever, she has the authority to sack you on the spot," he went on, still watching her closely.

Amanda worked to keep any hint of apprehension from showing on her face. "I understand. And I accept your terms," she added, even though he hadn't asked for her acceptance.

He studied her a moment longer, then gave a nod. "Good. Now I must go, or I shall miss my train."

Without waiting for an answer, he bowed, donned his hat, and stepped around her, heading for the door.

Amanda turned, watching his broad back as he walked away. "And if I have any concerns or difficulties?" she called after him. "What then?"

"An unlikely possibility," he countered over his shoulder without pausing. "Since you're such a good teacher."

With that incisive rejoinder, he departed, leaving her staring at the empty doorway, dazed and astonished by what had just happened.

"I'm a tutor," she murmured, trying to make it seem real. "I'm a tutor. I didn't muff it. I got the job."

Relief flooded through her—relief, elation, and incredulity so profound that she burst out laughing. "Well, now, Papa," she added, glancing overhead as if talking to her parent in the heavens, "what do you think of that?"

An hour later, however, as she faced the dubious stare of Mrs. Richmond, even Amanda's ebullient mood faltered a bit.

"Saints preserve us, I never thought he'd hire *you*," Mrs. Richmond muttered, planting flour-dusted hands on ample hips and eyeing Amanda with unmistakable dismay.

The emphasis on the pronoun showed that she not only remembered taking Amanda up for her interview three days earlier, but also that she hadn't been much impressed, and her present demeanor proved she wasn't changing her opinion just because Amanda had been hired. "How will you keep those boys in line? Why, you're little more than a child yourself."

Amanda opened her mouth, but she had no chance to allay the housekeeper's concerns.

"Now, Mrs. Richmond, what's the use of that sort of talk?" another voice put in, and Amanda looked to her right, where a big, blond, very handsome young man in striped livery stood by the stairs at the end of the servants' corridor, the same young man who'd been watching over the boys during their outing in the park. "You'll be scaring him off before he's even begun. I'm Samuel, by the way," he added to Amanda with a friendly smile as he came toward her. "First footman."

"Only footman, he means," Mrs. Richmond corrected. "All the other servants have gone to the country. You'd best come in," she went on, moving back in the corridor to allow Amanda inside.

"I remember you," the footman said as she stepped through the trades-man's entrance, suitcase in hand, and into the corridor. "From the park. You flew kites with the boys."

"Yes." Amanda set down her suitcase, then turned and retrieved the case of books the driver of her taxi had placed by the door. "That was me."

"What's this?" asked Mrs. Richmond as she moved around Amanda and closed the door. "You met the boys in the park?"

"Mr. Seton showed them how to launch their kites when there wasn't any wind," Samuel explained. "Rather smashing, I thought. The boys loved it."

"He exaggerates my abilities," Amanda told the cook, smiling. "There was a bit of wind."

"Speaking of wind, Samuel," the housekeeper put in, "best stop using yours to no purpose, and take Mr. Seton upstairs to the boys."

"That's why I'm down here," the footman replied. "I heard the trades-man's bell go and thought I'd save you the trouble of taking him upstairs. She's making apple tarts for tomorrow," he added to Amanda with a wink as he came forward to take the crate of books from her arms. "We wouldn't want anything to get in the way of that."

"And what makes you think there'll be any for you?" the cook countered, urging both of them toward the staircase. "Go on with you. Those boys shouldn't be left alone too long, or heaven only knows what mischief they'll be getting up to."

"They are a handful, no denying it." Samuel's voice was carelessly offhand, but Amanda did not miss the warning look he gave the housekeeper or the forced smile on his face when he returned his attention to her. "But they're good lads, for all that. And now that they have a tutor to take charge of them and lessons to occupy their minds, they'll settle down nicely, I'm sure."

Her crate in his hands, he turned to start down the corridor, giving Amanda a nod to follow, but as she bent to retrieve her suitcase, she caught the cook's muttered reply.

"Settle down?" the woman said under her breath as she walked in the opposite direction. "Roast this poor boy alive, and eat him, more likely."

Samuel evidently heard the cook's remark as well, for he gave Amanda a rather weak smile over one shoulder as he led her up the servants' staircase. "Don't mind Mrs. Richmond. She's a bit of a pessimist, is all."

"Well, she has some justification for that point of view, I suppose," Amanda said with determined good cheer. "Given the number of nannies that have come and gone in the past."

Samuel paused at the top of the stairs, bringing Amanda to a halt several steps below him and turning to look at her over one shoulder. "Lord Kenyon told you that?"

"No. I read about it in the papers. And as you already know, I met the boys for myself the other day. I think I have a pretty good idea of what I'm facing."

His brows rose as if he felt she didn't have a clue, but he didn't say so. Instead, he pressed one shoulder to the green baize door, shoved it open, and led Amanda through it into what was clearly the family living quarters.

Her feet sank into thick, luxurious carpets as she followed the footman across a wide landing, up another flight of stairs and down a long corridor, but though they passed several exquisitely carved rosewood and mahogany tables, she couldn't help noticing that there was nothing on any of them—no vases, no lamps, no bric-a-brac of any sort. She found that odd, for though she'd had little association with the aristocracy, she'd had enough contact with that segment of society to know they adored showing off their priceless family heirlooms. Such barren surroundings seemed quite strange, even to her untrained eyes.

As Samuel led her through the door to the nursery, however, the explanation for the lack of decor in this part of the house became painfully obvious. The twins were running in circles around the nursery's large front room, one chasing the other around a large table. A gray tabby, clearly desiring to stay as far above the fray as possible, was perched atop the bookcase, watching the scene below with that air of lofty superiority cats always managed so well.

"Here we are," Samuel said, shouting to be heard above the din as he set Amanda's crate of books on the floor, but if he hoped his announcement would give the boys pause, he was mistaken.

Amanda watched their antics for a moment, waiting, but when they didn't even glance in her direction, she wasn't surprised.

"It's the rain, you see," the footman said, his voice filled with apology. "Other than a few brief outings in the kitchen garden, they've been cooped up indoors for the past three days. When the weather turns fine again, you can take them across to the park, and then, I'm sure they'll be . . . they'll be . . . better."

"I'm sure," she said, not believing it for a second.

Walking around the boys, who had still made no acknowledgment of her arrival, she paused by one of a pair of windows and was glad to note there was no ivy or trees that the boys could use to climb down. She didn't much care for the bars on them, but then, most nurseries had them.

At the far side of the large room, a chalkboard hung on the wall. In front of it stood a desk, facing two smaller ones, the latter a pair of school desks with hinged tops and attached chairs. They were, she noted, bolted to the floor. A wise decision, she decided, glancing again at the boys, who were still running in circles and wailing like escapees from Bedlam.

"Which way are the bedrooms?" she asked the footman, raising her voice to be heard above the din even as she strove to keep its timbre deep and convincingly manly.

Samuel gestured to a closed door on the right-hand wall. "You're just through there. The boys share the room beyond yours."

Amanda received news of this arrangement in some dismay. "I won't have my own room?"

"When we had a nanny, she had her own room, of course. A woman needs that sort of privacy. But now that we have a male tutor, Lord Kenyon felt it would be better if . . . if . . ."

His voice trailed off, but it wasn't hard for Amanda to guess the reason for the new arrangement. "They have to go through me if they wish to sneak out in the middle of the night? Sneaked out before, have they?"

Samuel gave her a look of apology that confirmed her theory. It was a sensible precaution, and a male tutor didn't need a separate, private bed-room, but these arrangements made things deuced difficult for her. With adjoining rooms, the boys could walk in on her at any time. Still, perhaps once she had them in line and there was no fear of them sneaking out while she was asleep, she could request a room that was truly separate. Until then, she'd just have to be careful to always change her clothes in the bathroom or with the doors locked.

She turned toward the door Samuel had indicated, vaguely noting as she turned the handle that the boys behind her had gone suddenly silent and still. But it was only as she pushed the door wide and stepped over the threshold that she realized the reason for their silence, as a shower of ice-cold, rank-smelling liquid drenched her from above.

Amanda gasped in shock as loud guffaws of boyish laughter erupted behind her. Grimacing at the odious smell, she rubbed a hand over her wet cheek, well aware that the entire left side of her body was soaked through. When she glanced down, she saw that her white shirt cuff was now stained a mucky, brownish-green.

"Mr. Seton, are you all right?"

Samuel's voice overrode the boisterous amusement of the twins and succeeded in breaking Amanda's momentary shock. "Of course," she said briskly, her voice loud enough to carry to the laughing boys. "It's only water, after all." She took a sniff and grimaced, appreciating that whatever concoction they had drenched her with contained not only water, but also a generous quantity of fresh horse manure from the mews. But how had they managed it?

She glanced up, noting a galvanized pail overhead, suspended by a rope from a hook those two scamps had somehow managed to screw into the ceiling. The pail had been cleverly positioned so that it would tip its contents with the opening of the door, and despite being the victim of their joke, Amanda couldn't help admiring their ingenuity. But then, she'd known from the beginning that they were too clever by half.

She looked at Samuel, who was watching her with sympathy, and she forced a laugh. "They thought a bit of dirty water would put me off?" She gave a snort of disdain. "Hardly."

Hoping she'd made it clear she was not so easily intimidated, Amanda stepped over the puddle on the floor into her bedroom. Rattling her suitcase a little to shake off the droplets of brackish water, she set the suitcase down in a dry spot. "Samuel, I suggest you fetch some towels."

"At once, Mr. Seton. There's a bathroom and water closet at the end of the corridor here, and I can clean this up while you change."

"No, thank you," she countered, turning around and returning to the nursery. "I appreciate the offer," she added with a brief smile, "but it's not necessary. Just fetch the towels and a bucket of hot, soapy water, if you would."

He departed, and Amanda turned her attention to the laughing boys, trying to ignore the powerful stench on her clothes.

"Well, gentlemen, that was quite a greeting," she said with determined good cheer. "And I really must thank you, for you've done me an enormous favor."

The laughter stopped abruptly, and Amanda took advantage of the silence. "With this little trick of yours, you've demonstrated one of the areas where your education has been deficient," she told them. "I'm much obliged to you."

"What do you mean?" one of the twins demanded, frowning at her.

Opening her eyes wide, she pretended to be astonished by the question. "Well, you only got me wet on one side." Gesturing to the contraption above the door and hoping she wasn't playing with fire, she went on, "You positioned your pail in the wrong place. Had I been playing this trick on you, I'd have been able to give you a thorough soaking all over, because unlike you, I possess a fundamental knowledge of engineering."

She gave them a beatific smile. "I am more grateful than I can say, and I will be adding lessons in engineering to your curriculum, of that you may be sure."

Two pairs of keen blue eyes in two identical freckled faces glared up at her for a long moment. She studied them carefully in return, for though she already knew their names, their matching gray suits and bowl haircuts made it almost impossible to discern which one was Colin and which was Owen.

"I know who you are," the boy on the left said abruptly, breaking the silence. "You're the man from the park."

"I am."

She'd hoped her rapport with them the other day would make things easier, but now, as she studied their resentful faces, she appreciated that the opposite was closer to the truth. They felt betrayed, she realized; before, she might have been considered a friend, but now, she was a traitorous enemy, something for which even her excellent kite-flying skills could not atone. Ah, well. Their resentment couldn't be helped, and there would be plenty of time for them to discover how nice she really was and how much fun lessons with her could be. For now, the only thing that needed to be understood was that she was in charge, and if the hostility in their eyes was anything to go by, fixing that fact in their brains would not be an easy task.

Out of the corner of her eye, she caught movement and turned toward the doorway as Samuel entered the nursery with a pail of steaming, soapy water and an armful of towels.

"Put them there, Samuel, if you please," she directed, pointed to the large round table in the center of the room. "When is their high tea?"

"Six o'clock."

She nodded and moved around the twins as the footman followed her instructions. "Is it brought up here, or do the boys come down?"

"I usually bring it up."

She glanced at the clock on the mantel. "Excellent," she said, and began ushering the footman toward the door. "Then we will see you again in about half an hour."

The footman gave her a dubious look. "Are you sure I can't stay and help you settle in?"

"How kind of you, but it's not necessary. I do have one question." She paused by the door, gesturing to the knob. "I see that this door has a lock. Does it also have a key?"

"It does, sir. Two, in fact." The footman leaned back in the doorway, reached overhead, and retrieved a skeleton key from the top edge of the casing. "This is the spare. Mrs. Richmond has the other. I'll retrieve hers to have one made for you. In the meantime, you can use this one."

He held the key out to her, and she took it. "Thank you, Samuel," she said, putting the key in her trouser pocket. "You may go."

The footman hesitated a moment as if reluctant to leave her on her own, but then, he gave a nod and departed.

She turned around to find the twins watching her, and she was pleased to see a hint of apprehension in their faces. Good—apprehension was a much more encouraging sign than bored indifference would have been.

"You can't lock us in," the boy on the left told her before she had any chance to speak. "What if there's a fire?"

Her intent in obtaining a key was to keep them out of the nursery whenever she wasn't watching them herself, for she had no intention of being showered with any more manure-laced water or subjected to any other tricks they might have in store. But she couldn't see any harm in allowing them to think she was capable of keeping them prisoner, if necessary. "A fire is most unlikely," she countered. "Unless you intend to start one?"

"Of course not," the other boy said with dignity. "We're not arsonists."

"Quite so," she said gravely. "But you do like firecrackers, I hear."

"That was an accident."

"Don't tell him any more, Owen!" his brother cut in. "We don't have to explain anything to him."

The name caused Amanda to glance over both boys again. Eventually, of course, she'd be able to see the subtle differences between them, but for now, she needed something, anything, that would distinguish them in her mind, and after several seconds of study, she found it in the dark red scab of a healing cut on Owen's left hand.

"Colin is right," she said at last. "Everyone is entitled to keep some secrets. Still, given this apparent distrust on your part, I'd be quite justified in possessing some of the same, wouldn't you agree? For the time being, however, I am choosing to trust you, and I should advise you not to betray that trust. Now," she went on, grabbing two towels from the table before coming to stand directly in front of them, "since our meal isn't until six o'clock, we have plenty of time for your first lesson, and I'm glad, because it's a very important lesson, one you'll find useful in every aspect of your lives."

"What subject?" Owen asked, earning himself a sideways kick from his brother.

"Consequences." Smiling brightly, she held out the towels.

Neither of them moved, but it was Colin who spoke first. "You can't really expect us to mop the floor?" he said with derision. "Cleaning is for servants. We are gentlemen."

"Gentlemen? Oh my word and la-di-da." Her smile didn't falter, and her hands holding the offered towels remained outstretched. "Perhaps it's my plebian upbringing, but I don't care two straws if you're gentlemen. In my schoolroom, the ones who make the mess clean it up."

"That would be you, then, wouldn't it?" Colin countered at once. "You spilled the pail."

Amanda laughed. "A clever argument, but futile. This mess was caused by you and your brother, and you two will clean it up."

Colin's gaze locked with hers, and though his eyes and coloring were completely different from his father, she could see a certain familial similarity in the narrowing of his eyes and the set of his jaw. "We don't have to do what you say."

"Yes, you do," she answered at once. "Because if you don't, you'll be shipped off to Harrow faster than you can spit."

"And you'll be out of a job."

"I can easily get another job," she lied, still smiling, "but you'll still be stuck at Harrow."

Neither Colin nor his brother appeared to have a comeback for that, and with simultaneous heavy sighs, they snatched the towels from her outstretched fingers, and set to work, cleaning up the mess without too much complaint. In this newfound, albeit tenuous, spirit of cooperation, Amanda assisted them by retrieving their soiled towels, but she had barely disposed of them through the laundry chute that some enterprising soul had had built in one corner of the room when Samuel returned with the boys' evening meal.

As the boys consumed Cornish pasties, oatcakes, potted beef, and bread-and-butter pudding, Amanda did not join them. Instead, she accepted Samuel's offer to watch over them while she had a bathe and changed her soiled clothes.

The bathroom was enormous, for like most baths in wealthy households, it had once been a bedroom. There was a separate water closet, a long washstand laid with white marble and topped with two porcelain basins and matching pitchers, and a cupboard filled with soft, snowy white towels, jars of castile soap, and giant, misshapen sea sponges. Even more delightful, the claw-foot tub was connected to a set of water pipes coming up through the floor, with taps for both hot and cold water. She was amazed by such luxury, though she supposed in a duke's household such things were commonplace, and she lingered in the bath longer than she probably ought to have done. But at last, clean, freshly dressed, and glad now that she'd had the foresight to purchase more than one second-hand suit, she returned to the nursery, where she found that full-scale war seemed to have broken out in her absence. Thankfully, however, it was the sort of war that didn't hurt anyone.

With Samuel's help, the boys were placing toy soldiers on the floor in military formations, blue on one side and red on the other, preparing for what seemed to be a pitched battle of epic proportions. The cat, still atop the bookcase, didn't seem interested in the warfare going on below, for he was asleep, one gray paw over his eyes.

Samuel was the first to spy her standing in the doorway. "Ah, Mr. Seton," he greeted. "The boys are reenacting Waterloo."

"Yes, I see." She entered the room, stepping carefully around a platoon of French troops, and walked to the table, but if she'd hoped for a bit of supper, she was disappointed, for the only food that remained was one half-eaten pasty.

"I'm afraid they ate your share before I could stop them," Samuel said apologetically, rising to his feet. "They had ravenous appetites this evening."

Amanda glanced at the twins. She couldn't see Owen's face, for he was bent over his troops, but she could see Colin's, and the tiny hint of a smirk that curved the elder twin's mouth made her suspect their appetites had been less of a consideration than the notion of scoring off her, but she didn't express that theory aloud. "Yes, so it seems," she said pleasantly, smiling back at the boy.

Colin jerked his chin and looked away, returning his attention to his soldiers.

"I'd best be getting back to my duties," Samuel said, his words evoking a torrent of protest from the two boys, which he ignored as he edged his way around the toy soldiers and started for the door. "I'll have Mrs. Richmond make a fresh tray of supper for you, Mr. Seton," he offered, pausing by the door. "Just ring when you want it, and I'll bring it up."

"Oh no, please don't bother," she said at once, not wanting to take further advantage of a fellow servant's goodwill, knowing she might well need his help often in the days ahead. "You have your own work to do. I'll come down and fetch it myself once the boys are asleep. When is their bedtime?"

"Didn't Lord Kenyon tell you?"

She made a face. "He didn't tell me anything, to be honest. He was in rather a rush to catch his train."

"I see. Well, they usually have a bathe at half past seven, and bedtime is at eight. That is," he added ruefully, "if you can get them bathed and into their pajamas in half an hour."

"Is that such a difficult business, then?"

"Sometimes," the footman admitted and turned toward the bookcase. "I shall see you in the morning," he added as he plucked the cat off the top, earning himself a slew of hissing protest from the animal. "I bring breakfast up at half past eight."

Arms outstretched, holding the squirming, angry animal away from his body, Samuel left the nursery, kicking the door shut behind him as he departed.

"Do you want to play, Mr. Seton?" Owen's voice asked behind her, and Amanda turned around just in time to see Colin give his brother an exasperated scowl.

"What?" Owen countered, not the least bit intimidated by his twin's displeasure that she'd been invited to join. If Amanda had any illusions, however, that Owen's invitation was borne of a genuine desire for her company, those illusions were dispelled by his next words. "I don't want to be Bonaparte, and if Mr. Seton plays, I can be von Blücher instead."

Colin rolled his eyes, but gave in. "Oh, all right, he can play, too," he muttered, moving on his knees to a position behind the red-uniformed soldiers. "You need to be over there," he told Amanda, pointing to a place across the room.

She moved to the indicated spot, but as she glanced over the neat rows of her blue-painted French army, she felt a bit out of her depth. Toy soldiers was a game she'd never played, not as a child, nor as a teacher. Still, in her role as a male tutor, she supposed she'd have to display at least a pretense of competence at boys' games. And how hard could this one be, really? She knew all about the Battle of Waterloo.

Her knowledge of military history, however, proved wholly unnecessary, for she'd barely knelt behind her troops before Colin and Owen were both coming at her in a full-frontal assault, sweeping their soldiers at her in a growing pile and taking hers down with them, and though they punctuated their efforts with an impressive barrage of sounds meant to be cannon fire and shot, their efforts paid little heed to historical accuracy.

Unless she wanted to be mowed down along with her troops, Amanda was forced to give way, and she retreated, moving backward on her knees until she hit the opened toy cupboard behind her and she could retreat no farther and all her troops had been knocked over. With at least a dozen of Wellington's troops still standing, the boys claimed victory for their British and Prussian forces with a triumphant yell.

"Let's do the battle of Carthage next," Owen suggested, but with a glance at the mantel clock, Amanda was forced to negate that plan.

"Not tonight," she said, standing up. "It's half past seven, so it's time for a bathe. Then bed."

Ignoring their groans and protests, she retrieved pajamas from the armoire in their bedroom, shoved one pair into each boy's arms, and pointed to the door.

"March, soldiers," she ordered, following them as they walked out of the nursery and down the corridor to the bath, noting in amusement how they dragged their feet as if they were facing a firing squad rather than a bath.

Once the tub had been filled halfway with warm water, Amanda left them to it with a reminder to also brush their teeth, and she returned to the nursery.

Her suitcase was still lying on the floor of her room, still open from when she'd retrieved her change of clothes earlier. She pulled out a fresh shirt and a set of underclothes for the morning and placed them on the dressing table, then put away the few remaining items of her masculine wardrobe. Closing her suitcase, she placed it on top of the armoire, then went to give the nursery a full inspection.

She unpacked her crate of supplies, and as she put her books on the shelf, she was pleased to see plenty of excellent titles already there. In the toy cupboard was a vast quantity of toys, puzzles and games—plenty of things, it would seem, to occupy a pair of ten-year-old boys. Their need to make mischief clearly had a deeper cause than a mere lack of distractions, and it didn't take much reflection to know where to put the blame.

At once, an image of Lord Kenyon's hard, lean face came into her mind, but Amanda shoved the image away. Neglectful parents created a sad gap in a child's life, but they were as much a part of her job as French lessons and arithmetic, and a particularly common tale for children of the upper classes. The only thing she could do was attempt to fill the gap as best she could. It might take some doing in this case, particularly where Colin was concerned, for it was clear that boy was the primary instigator of the twins' mischief making.

A sound caught her attention and she looked toward the door as the object of her thoughts entered the room, followed by his brother. Their wet hair and the way their pajamas stuck to their skin confirmed that they had indeed taken their bath.

"Did you brush your teeth?" she asked.

"Yes, sir," they said in unison, a surprisingly passive response. When she ushered them to bed, they complied without complaint. As she tucked them in, she couldn't help wondering if behind this display of docility and cooperation, their minds were conjuring more trouble, and after nearly an hour with not one peep coming from the other bedroom, Amanda, fearing the worst, decided to check on them.

To her happy surprise, she found them fast asleep. She paused between their beds, studying one face and then the other, and even she could hardly believe these two sleeping boys were the same holy terrors who'd driven off twelve nannies in three years and arranged for a shower of manure tea to pour down on her head. Right now, they looked deceptively angelic.

She watched them several moments longer, but they did not move, and their breathing was deep and even. Satisfied, she withdrew into her own room, closed the door softly behind her, then went downstairs to fetch herself a tray of supper, retracing the route Samuel had led her earlier in the day.

She found the kitchens at the far end of the servants' corridor. Samuel was nowhere in sight, but Mrs. Richmond was seated at a long central worktable, reading a newspaper and drinking a cup of tea, with the boys' cat curled at her feet. She looked up as Amanda came in.

"Good evening, Mr. Seton," she said, smiling. "Boys asleep?"

"They are, yes."

"That's a relief, I'll wager. Come down for your supper, have you?"

Standing up even as she asked the question, she crossed to the stove, where she took up a thick pad and removed an iron skillet from the lower oven. "I heard about the trick the boys played on you earlier," she said as she placed the skillet on top of the stove and reached for a spoon from one of the hooks on the wall. "Terribly naughty of them to do something like that," she went on as she placed oatcakes on a plate and spooned potted beef over them. "And on your first day, too. Samuel and I felt ever so badly for you. We ought to have checked the rooms beforehand."

"Please don't blame yourself," Amanda replied. "It's just a bit of dirty water, and no harm done."

"Well, you're taking their first prank in stride, I must say."

Was it her imagination, Amanda wondered, or did the cook sound a little surprised? Unbidden, Lord Kenyon's initial opinion of her echoed through her mind.

You can't seriously think I'd consider you as a tutor for my children. You're far too young.

Amanda smiled to herself, wondering what his opinion would be if he knew she was actually more than a decade older than she'd claimed, and female to boot.

He'd sack you in a heartbeat, girl, Amanda reminded herself sternly, and set aside any humorous imaginings on the subject.

"I've cleaned your suit," the cook told her as she poured a cup of tea from the teapot by the stove. "I'll take it up in a bit, where it can dry in your room. Sugar and milk in your tea?"

"No, thank you. I drink it plain."

Teacup in one hand, the cook added two Cornish pasties to the plate with the other, then turned to bring her meal to the table, but Amanda spoke, stopping her. "Could I just take it on a tray?" she requested. "I don't want to leave the boys alone too long."

"That's probably wise," Mrs. Richmond said as she placed Amanda's meal on the requested tray. "One never knows what those two will take it into their heads to do on their own."

"They're asleep just now," Amanda said, taking the tray, "but I have no doubt they're dreaming of fresh deviltry for me at this very moment."

"I wish I could disagree," the rotund little woman said with a sigh, "but I'm afraid you're right. Still, it's good you know what you're facing. And they're fine boys, Mr. Seton, honestly—not a hint of true malevolence or wickedness in either of them. They are a bit wild, no denying it, but if you can stick it, they'll settle down, I'm sure. Give them a chance. Don't let them scare you off."

Amanda smiled. "I'm not easily intimidated, I assure you."

With that, she returned upstairs. After verifying the boys were still sound asleep, Amanda ate her meal in the nursery, and after Mrs. Richmond had brought up her cleaned suit, she took it into her room and prepared for bed.

She hung the pieces of her suit on the pegs in the wall beside the armoire, then set the lamp on the table closest to her bed, putting the matchbox beside it at the ready. She took the precaution of locking the door into the boys' room before she changed into her pajamas, then she unlocked it again and extinguished the light. Moving carefully in the dark, she walked to the bed, pulled back the sheets, and slid between them.

Her first day posing as a man, she thought, smiling as she settled more comfortably into the mattress, and she'd gotten through it with no one the wiser. And her unexpected shower notwithstanding, the boys had been surprisingly cooperative so far. Perhaps this was going to be an easier post than she had feared.

That thought had barely gone through her head when Amanda felt a strange tickling sensation along her ankle, and her smile vanished as she came to the awful realization that something was in the bed with her, something small and slimy and very much alive.

With an involuntary shriek, Amanda tore back the sheets and leaped out of bed.

Through the closed door into the boys' room came a stifled but unmistakable slew of giggles, but she paid little heed as she hopped up and down on one foot, frantically shaking the other to remove whatever blasted creature was clinging to her ankle, as she reached for the matches. She lit the lamp, raised it high, and took a long, sweeping glance over the floor, but there was no sign of the insect that had invaded her sheets. It was only when she turned toward the bed that Amanda realized precisely what had been crawling up her leg.

"Ugh," she muttered, her lip curling in disgust. "Slugs."

About two dozen of the repugnant little creatures were wriggling and squirming their way across the bed. Others, less fortunate than their fellows, had been squished by her body weight, and their flattened gray corpses were smeared over the sheet. She twisted, lifting one arm to glance at her backside, a glance that confirmed her flannel pajamas were in a condition similar to that of her sheets.

"Oh," she breathed, outraged. "Those little devils."

More giggles sounded from the other room, and Amanda stiffened. She turned toward the door and saw that it had been opened a crack. Two faces, one above the other, could be seen through the opening, but after a second, the door closed again amid another bout, louder this time, of boyish laughter.

As the latch clicked, Amanda's outrage dissolved, giving way to a very different emotion, one that many of her former pupils would have recognized in the narrowing of her eyes and the lift of her chin.

"Oh, the game's on, now, gentlemen," she vowed, returning her attention to the bed, setting her jaw grimly as she stared at the still-squirming slugs. "The game is *on*. And by God, I'm going to win it."

Chapter 5

As a young man, Jamie had been a rebel, prone to all manner of wild impulses, but he'd come to believe himself transformed by the passage of years. He'd come to think that love, marriage, and fatherhood had changed him into a man of maturity and good sense, but as the evening train carried him north to Yorkshire, he began to wonder if the cavalier, reckless ways of his youth were indeed truly behind him.

This sudden predisposition to question his own character was due, of course, to his hiring of Adam Seton. It had seemed his best—his only— option at the time, but now, five hours later when the deed was done and he was over two hundred miles away, he found himself plagued by doubts.

Seton was only seventeen, and though he had seemed mature for his age, one couldn't be sure that was really so. When Jamie thought of himself at seventeen, he knew he'd been anything but mature.

Even worse, Jamie didn't really know anything about the fellow, except that his father was American, a fact that was hardly reassuring. Seton's letters of character had been laughably insignificant, his manner decidedly impertinent, and the quality of his teaching open to question. Granted, his landlady seemed satisfied with his tutoring abilities, but was that assessment worth a damn?

Perhaps his doubts came from the fact that he'd never hired anyone to watch his boys who hadn't been thoroughly vetted by an employment agency. In addition, he'd always conducted much more thorough interviews than the one he'd given Seton, and as Jamie stared past his reflection in the window to the inky blackness beyond, all sorts of heretofore unimagined consequences of his hasty decision this evening began running through his head.

He tried to tell himself he was getting worked up over nothing, but the farther the train carried him from London, the greater his worry became, and by the time his train reached York, hiring Seton seemed less like the only possible option and more like the rash impulse of a desperate man.

Or, worse, a selfish one.

Jamie moved in his seat, guilt stirring inside him. Hiring someone to watch over one's children wasn't something to be done on the spur of the moment. It ought to be a carefully considered decision, but in the rush to get on with his own plans, he hadn't bothered with any of that.

Is school really the best solution? Or is it simply the most expedient?

Rex's question of a week ago came echoing back, taunting him because he knew it was a valid one. Upon losing Nanny Hornsby, his first thought had been to reach for the easiest, quickest answer to his problem, and while it was true that he hadn't actually sent the boys away to school, the course he'd chosen instead had also been one primarily of expedience. If anything happened . . .

Sudden, unreasoning fear clenched his guts.

He closed his eyes. He was being fanciful, even absurd. In addition to Seton, there were two servants in the house. When he'd telephoned Mrs. Richmond from Victoria Station, he'd instructed that she and Samuel keep a close eye not only on the boys, but also the new tutor. Still, Jamie couldn't help wondering now how conscientious in their duty the servants would be.

He'd already taken advantage of every scrap of goodwill they possessed, pressing them into service as substitute nannies every time the need had arisen. Rather than keep close watch over Seton and the boys, wouldn't these two long-suffering servants be more inclined to enjoy a respite from that responsibility and stay well away from the nursery as much as they could?

The train slowed, coming into York Railway Station, and Jamie opened his eyes again, relieved by the distraction. Telling himself to stop imagining things, he donned his hat and coat and pulled his dispatch case from the rack overhead. When the train stopped, he exited the carriage, stepped down onto the crowded platform, and secured a porter.

"I'm transferring to Knaresborough," he explained. "Which platform?"

"Platform five, sir," the porter answered, jerking one thumb over his shoulder to the building behind them. "Straight across the station and to the right. Train departs in forty minutes." He paused, glancing over Jamie with a practiced eye. "First-class carriages are at the front."

Jamie nodded. "What about my trunk? I've no valet with me."

"If you bought a through ticket, your trunk should be transferred automatically. But," he added as Jamie pulled his luggage ticket and half a crown from his pocket and held them out, "I would be happy to supervise its transfer personally, sir," he said, taking both from Jamie's hand.

"Excellent. Thank you."

The porter pocketed the tip, noted the luggage number, then handed the ticket back, touched his cap, and turned to carry out his promise while Jamie entered the station. After crossing the crowded main foyer, he turned to the right and made his way toward Platform 5, pausing along the way for a cup of tea and a hot cross bun in the station's refreshment room.

The train was already in by the time he arrived at Platform 5. He boarded one of the first-class carriages and shoved his dispatch case into the overhead rack, but he'd barely settled into his seat before a newspaper kiosk caught his eye through the window. Perhaps he ought to get a paper? It would be a welcome distraction from the absurd and groundless fears whispering to his imagination.

He glanced at the kiosk again, but when he read the headline of the newspaper on display, he knew reading it would prove no distraction at all. Quite the opposite, in fact.

SECOND CHILD GOES MISSING IN WEST END. NO RANSOM DEMANDED. SCOTLAND YARD BAFFLED.

With a curse, Jamie jumped to his feet and reached for his dispatch case.

HE MANAGED TO exit the train before it pulled out, but it was too late to retrieve his trunk. Adjourning to the ticket office, he requested that his trunk be shipped from the station at Knaresborough to his London residence, then he paid over the required fee and asked about return trains to London. Informed that the earliest one departed at eight o'clock the following morning, Jamie bought a return ticket and adjourned to the Royal Station Hotel, where he secured a room and telegraphed Lord Weston and Lord Malvers, his most influential supporters in his district, that a family emergency had arisen at home and that any speeches, gladhanding, and political meetings would have to be rescheduled. He also sent word to Rolleston, informing his father that their first joint tour of the estates would also have to wait.

Rolleston would be livid, of course, and Malvers, a cantankerous old devil, wouldn't like it either, but their opinions on the subject were not what caused Jamie to spend an anxious, sleepless night. His brain insisted upon envisioning his sons in all manner of ghastly circumstances, each more awful than the last, making sleep impossible.

The following day, he arrived back at Upper Brook Street in the early afternoon, tired, disheveled, and worried sick, and when he entered the nursery, the sight that met his eyes only seemed to confirm all his worst fears, for Mr. Seton was tied to Colin's desk with a gag in his mouth. The twins were nowhere in sight.

Heart in his throat, Jamie crossed the nursery. "For God's sake, what's happened?" he demanded, sliding the gag forward and pulling it from between Seton's teeth. "Have the boys been kidnapped?"

"Kidnapped?" Seton echoed, his voice hoarse from the gag. "Are you joking?" He gave a laugh. "God help any kidnapper that ever got hold of those two."

That point, Jamie was forced to admit, had some validity. "But where are they?"

"Oh, I'm sure they're somewhere about the house," Seton replied in obvious chagrin. "Crowing about how clever they've been, no doubt, and having a jolly good laugh at my expense."

Jamie shut his eyes for a moment, filled with profound relief. "The twins tied you up?"

"Well, I certainly didn't do it to myself," Seton muttered, sounding so testy that Jamie almost smiled. He caught it back, however, reminding himself sternly that his sons' tying up their tutor was not something to laugh about.

Seton certainly didn't seem to find it amusing. Gold sparks glittered unmistakably in those dark, hazel-green eyes, and a frown had drawn his severe black brows together, marring the almost feminine smoothness of his forehead.

It wouldn't do for Seton to quit in a huff, especially since it was becoming clear to Jamie that his worries had been overblown. "I will discipline the boys for this, I promise you."

"No, please don't interfere." Seton shook his head, signs of temper abating. "I would prefer you leave this to me, my lord. They have to be made to understand that I am quite willing to discipline them when necessary, and that I don't need to go running to you for help in order to do it."

Jamie could have pointed out that his help was just what Seton did need at this particular moment, but he refrained. "How did this come about?" he asked instead, circling the desk and kneeling down to begin freeing the other man from his bonds. "How could you allow them to do this to you?"

"They wanted to play Cowboys and Indians. They promised faithfully that they would do their lessons for the rest of the day without complaint, if we played the game first." Seton paused to give Jamie a rueful look over his shoulder. "And if I'd play the part of the cowboy."

Jamie gave him a pitying look in return. "And you agreed to that?"

"To gain their undivided attention for the entire day without a battle, one game seemed a small price to pay. And I thought it would provide the opportunity for a history and geography lesson about the American West."

"Except that you agreed to be the cowboy. Don't you know in that game, the cowboy is always the one captured and tied up?"

"Of course I know that." Seton scowled. "I'm not a complete dolt."

The current circumstances left that declaration open to question, but again, Jamie decided it was best to employ tact and continued his task without replying.

"I thought it wouldn't matter, you see," Seton went on, sounding a bit defensive in the wake of Jamie's silence. "As long as they tied me to Colin's desk, rather than Owen's, I was sure I'd have a clear means of escape."

Jamie paused to study the two desks before him, but he couldn't see what form of escape Colin's desk might provide that Owen's did not. The oak seats, hinged oak tops, and wrought iron frames appeared identical. Both seemed quite sturdy and were securely bolted to the floor. "Sorry, but I don't follow."

"Colin's desk is beside the bellpull. If they did a flit after tying me up, I'd just catch the pull between my teeth and give it a tug, which would summon Mrs. Richmond or Samuel, who could then untie me."

"Ah." Enlightened, Jamie glanced up at the wall beside Colin's desk, and he almost laughed out loud as he saw why the tutor's plan had gone astray. The silk rope of the bellpull was considerably shorter than it ought to have been, well out of reach of Seton's teeth, and when Jamie glanced around, the stepladder against the wall and the scissors and tasseled length of rope on the floor nearby told the rest of the tale.

"Your plan," he managed, grinning behind the tutor's back, "doesn't seem to have worked so well."

"Don't I know it." Seton stirred in his seat, straining against his bonds. "Just untie me, my lord, if you please, so I can find those scamps and return the favor."

"I admire your tenacity, Seton," Jamie answered as he complied. "Most of your predecessors would be thinking to hand in their notice just about now."

"Over this?" Seton made a sound of derision. "This isn't as bad as—"

"As bad as what?" Jamie asked, looking up again, feeling a hint of alarm. "What else have the twins done to you?"

"It's not important. Just get these damned ropes off."

"I'm trying, but the knots are tight." Pausing again, he leaned back, retrieved the scissors, and began working the blades back and forth to cut through the thick strands of rope, careful to avoid cutting the other man in the process. "If I'd known they would take it into their heads to start tying people up," he muttered as he worked, "I'd never have taught them to make sailor's knots on the boat."

"You have a boat?"

"Torquil does. The Cavanaughs are a sailing family."

"How lucky for me," Seton replied tartly. "What are you doing here anyway?" he added, ignoring Jamie's answering chuckle. "I thought you were to be gone a fortnight."

"That was my intention, but I couldn't rid myself of the nagging fear that I'd put my children at risk by leaving them in the care of a complete stranger with somewhat dubious references. So, I changed my plans and came home."

"My references are not dubious! You met my landlady yourself. And—" He broke off, twisting his head to stare at Jamie over one shoulder, shaking back the unruly curls that had fallen over his forehead. "Wait. What do you mean, you feared you'd put the boys at risk? You thought they might be in danger?" Clearly nonplussed by that idea, he blinked. "From me?"

It did seem terribly melodramatic now. "Let's just say I began to wonder if I'd been a bit precipitate in my decision to hire you. I'm quite relieved to find my fears of danger unfounded. At least as far as the twins are concerned. I must confess," he added, "in all the ghastly scenarios I envisioned on the train coming back, I never imagined you as the one in jeopardy."

Seton looked away with a sniff. "I deserve your ridicule, I daresay, for allowing them to trick me this way. But it won't happen again, that I can promise you."

That was a vow Jamie had heard from many nannies over the years, but he didn't say so. Instead, he concentrated on his task, and after a few more saws with the scissors, he succeeded in freeing Seton from his bonds.

The tutor gave a sigh of relief, slid out from behind the small desk, and turned to face Jamie, rubbing his wrists to restore circulation to his hands. "Thank you. Now, I'd best find those sons of yours. My lesson on American history might have been scrapped, but I also had a jolly good science lesson planned for this afternoon, one it took Samuel some trouble to help me arrange, and I've no intention of letting our efforts there go to waste."

"That's all very well, but I don't see that you'll be able to teach them anything if they are able to gain the upper hand with you as easily as they've done today. I won't be here to step in and rescue you every time they play a trick, you know."

Seton's pointed chin went up a notch. "There will be no need for you to do so, my lord," he said with dignity. "I've given them the benefit of the doubt once, and they abused it. I shan't give them another. No, it shall be noses to the grindstone for the foreseeable future." He turned and started for the door. "I'll have them so occupied with their lessons, they'll have no chance to play any more tricks on me."

Given past experience, Jamie wasn't particularly sanguine about Seton's chances of success there, but he decided to give the other man the benefit of the doubt. At least for now.

IF AMANDA HAD learned nothing else about children during her seven years of teaching them, she'd learned one thing. A child's ears were often a teacher's best weapon.

"A promise is a promise," she said, keeping a firm grip on Colin's ear with one hand and Owen's with the other as she propelled them up the stone stairs of the cistern room where she'd found them hiding with a stack of penny dreadfuls and a bag of sweets. "I've played Cowboys and Indians. Now it's time for the two of you to fulfill your part of our bargain."

"How did you get away?" Colin demanded as she led them into the house and started up the servants' staircase. "We tied those knots tight."

"Not tight enough, obviously."

"Ow, ow," Colin wailed as she turned on the landing, pulling the boys with her. "You're hurting me."

"Me, too," Owen wailed, taking the cue from his brother. "Me, too."

Amanda, well aware of just how much force to apply in situations like this, was unimpressed. "Rot," she pronounced, shoving the green baize door open with her foot. Ignoring their protesting squeals, she led the two boys through the door, across the gallery, and down the corridor.

When she reached the nursery, Lord Kenyon was gone, much to her relief. Letting the boys trick her had been galling enough, but the fact that their father had witnessed just what a mug two ten-year-olds had made of her was downright humiliating, and not, she feared, a good testament to her abilities as a tutor.

Amanda shoved each boy—none too gently—into his seat, adding, "Don't move, either of you, or by heaven, I'll have you on your knees scrubbing floors like a pair of scullery maids for the rest of the day."

"You already made us scullery maids," Colin muttered, glaring at her and rubbing his ear. "You made us clean Mrs. Richmond's big copper pots this morning first thing."

"That was for the slugs. For tying me up, you'll be polishing silver this evening after high tea."

A chorus of protest greeted that announcement.

"You can't do that!"

"After high tea, it's supposed to be playtime!"

Amanda was unimpressed. "As I told you yesterday, actions have consequences. If you want any playtime in the future, I suggest you stop trying my patience with silly jokes." She circled her desk to stand behind it, glad to see that in her absence, Samuel had brought up the supplies she'd asked him to gather for her. After unfastening her cuff links and rolling up her shirtsleeves, she cleared off her desk and set to work.

Ignoring the two boys, she placed a heavy, oilskin tarp over the desk to protect its rosewood surface and put a shallow wooden tray on top, then she retrieved a glass beaker from the crate, stuck a bit of modeling clay to the bottom, and affixed it to the center of the tray.

As she worked, she could sense the two boys watching her with resentful eyes, but she continued to pay them no mind. Whistling a tune, she took out a jar of flour and another of water and mixed the contents of both in a bowl to make a smooth paste of flour glue. Once she was satisfied with the consistency of the mixture, she set the bowl aside, pulled a handful of newspapers from the pile on the tray, and began crumpling the sheets into hard balls. These she glued around the beaker, cramming them tightly together as she built them into the cone shape so necessary to her experiment.

It was only when she had completed the next step of cutting her remaining sheets of newspaper into strips that curiosity—Owen's, at least—

overcame resentment. "What are you doing?" he asked as she dunked a strip of newspaper into the glue mixture.

"I'm making a volcano."

Colin's sound of disdain interrupted before she could say more. "Out of papier-mâché?" he said. "How boring."

"Oh, very boring," she agreed cheerfully. Bending down, she placed her sticky strip of paper along the base of her makeshift mountain, then looked up to meet Colin's still hostile gaze over the top. "Until it erupts."

That surprised him, she could tell, though he tried not to show it. Donning an air of disinterest that didn't fool her for a second, he looked away. Lifting the hinged top of his desk, he extracted his slate and some colored chalks, then he closed his desk again and began to draw.

Owen, however, continued to watch Amanda, and after several minutes of silence, his curiosity won out again. "Can you really make it erupt?" he asked.

"Owen!" his brother hissed, glaring at him. "Stop fraternizing with the enemy!"

Amanda almost smiled at that terribly grown-up turn of phrase, but she managed to suppress it just in time. She didn't want them to think she was laughing at them, for that might endanger what she hoped would be the start of a truce. Pressing her lips together to hide her smile, she reached for another strip of paper and said nothing.

"I'm not fraternizing," Owen protested, craning his neck to watch Amanda as she circled to the side of her desk and continued to build her volcano. "I'd just like to know if it's really going to erupt, that's all."

"It can't!" Colin said decisively.

"Can't it?" Amanda countered without pausing in her task. "We'll see."

"But how?" Owen asked. When she didn't answer, he stood up and came across to her desk for a closer look, ignoring his brother's protests. "It's just a big lump of papier-mâché."

"At the moment, that's true," she agreed. "But by the time I'm finished, it will look very much like Mauna Loa. Do you know where that is?"

He hesitated, then shook his head.

"It's in a place called the Sandwich Islands."

"Captain Cook went there," the boy said unexpectedly.

"He did." She paused to smooth out an uncooperative strip of paper, then went on, "We'll paint this, of course, and we'll add some black rocks, and perhaps some trees—not many, though, because it's hard for trees to grow around a volcano."

"Because of the lava," Owen said, nodding in understanding. "When it cools, it turns into rock, doesn't it? Can you really make it erupt? The volcano, I mean."

She laughed. "I can. Would you like to help me?"

"Why should we help you?" Colin cut in before his brother could answer.

"No reason at all since you've decided I'm the enemy. But I'm curious about something . . ." Amanda paused, straightening, and looked at Colin over Owen's head. "Would you mind telling me why? What have I done to earn your animosity?"

The boy looked away without answering, but Amanda persisted in a nonchalant sort of way as she resumed her task. "You don't want to go to school—at least, that's what I've heard. But if I weren't here, you'd probably be halfway to Harrow by now. So how am I the enemy?"

Owen turned, looking over his shoulder at his brother as if expecting Colin to offer an explanation, but Colin didn't speak. Instead, he picked up his chalk and resumed doodling on his slate.

"No explanations to the enemy, is that it?" she said, resuming her task with a shrug. "Very well, if that's how you want to play it. But I'm not going anywhere, so if you persist in not speaking to me, you'll find your lessons terribly dull. Still, it's your choice, I suppose."

"You're not the enemy, exactly," Owen began, but he was cut off at once by his brother.

"Why should we have to explain things to you?"

Colin's voice was hard, so hard, in fact, that Amanda was startled. She looked up, watching the boy as he shoved aside his slate, tossed down his chalk, and glared back at her. "You're a tutor, aren't you? And tutors are supposed to be clever, aren't they? You ought to know why we don't want you here. Unless . . ." He paused, his deep blue eyes narrowing to slits. "You're not really very clever, after all."

Amanda already had a pretty fair idea of what lay behind the boys' petty rebellions, but she could see no point in voicing her theories out loud, not to the twins anyway. "Guessing would be quite improper," she said without pausing in her work. "You've made it clear you don't want to explain, and if I were to continue to press you, it would be an invasion of your privacy."

An expression of what might have been disappointment—or perhaps chagrin—at her lack of curiosity flickered across Colin's face, but it was gone in an instant, and he looked away.

"Besides," she went on, resuming her work, "I have a great deal yet to do if I'm to make this volcano erupt before dinner. Would you care to help me, Owen?" she asked, turning her attention to the boy beside her.

He hesitated, staring at the strip of newspaper she held out to him, then he nodded and pulled it from her outstretched fingertips. Ignoring his brother's obvious disapproval, he brushed glue over the paper, then pressed it against the side of Amanda's creation and reached for another.

For several minutes, they worked together in silence. Colin made no move to help them, nor did he speak, but whenever she glanced in his direction, Amanda found him watching them, and she found that a hopeful sign, even though every time their eyes met, he looked away.

"There now," she said at last, standing back to survey the papier-mâché mountain she and Owen had created. "That looks about right, I think. We'll take it to the kitchen."

She wiped her hands on a damp rag, then handed the rag to Owen so that he could do the same. She then pulled her suit jacket off the peg by the door, slipped it on, and retrieved the tray containing her creation. "Mrs. Richmond can put this in a warm oven while we're out so that the glue will dry."

"We're going out?" Owen asked, falling in step beside her as she started for the door. "Where?"

"The park."

"The park?" Owen's freckled face lit up. "Good-oh! Are we going to fly kites?"

"Not today. We must find rocks and trees to put around our volcano. Best put on coats and hats, boys," she added, including Colin in this suggestion even though he had made no move to follow. "There's a sharp wind today."

Owen paused by the door to grab his mackintosh from its peg. "C'mon, Colin," he urged as he slid his arms into his coat and reached for his cap. "Why are you just sitting there?"

"I don't want to go."

Amanda paused, too, turning to look at the boy over her shoulder. Since it meant a postponement of lessons, she'd hoped he would be as eager as his brother for an outing in the park, but Colin turned his face away from them, his chin high, his profile stiff and proud.

"Don't be stupid," Owen chided, jamming his cap down on his head. "If I have to go, you have to go, too."

"No, I don't!" Colin looked at Amanda, his round, freckled face twisted, confirming her suspicion that under the wild and rebellious hellion who'd put slugs in her bed and cut the rope off the bellpull, there was a hurt and neglected little boy, and Amanda's own frustration rose up, frustration toward the parent who'd brought about this sad state of affairs.

"I don't have to do anything just because he says I do," Colin went on, jabbing a finger in Amanda's direction. "I'd rather stay here."

"But there won't be anyone to watch you," Owen pointed out.

"Samuel can watch me."

"Samuel has his own duties," Amanda put in before Owen could reply. "But you don't have to come with us if you don't want to," she went on before Colin could argue with her. "You can come down to the kitchens instead."

At once, he slid out from behind his desk. "I'll do that," he told her, a declaration meant to sound as if he'd chosen this course himself, as if it had been his own idea. "It's lunchtime, and I'd rather have sandwiches and tea than go to the park and look for stupid rocks."

Amanda opened her eyes wide. "Oh, but you surely don't think you'll be having anything to eat, do you?"

"Why not? It's nearly one o'clock."

"And because the trick you played on me delayed our lessons today, I'm afraid lunch is now delayed, too."

"That's not fair."

"Life's not fair. Best get used to it. And if you keep arguing with me," she added as he opened his mouth again, "you'll put us so far behind schedule, we'll have to give lunch a miss altogether."

"Colin, shut up," Owen pleaded. "I don't want to miss lunch."

Colin ignored that. "But what am I supposed to do while you two are gone?"

"Well, you could make a start on polishing that silver," she suggested brightly. "Or you could bring paper, pen, and ink, and start on today's assignment."

His frown was wary. "What assignment?"

"Our excursion is part of today's science lesson. If you don't feel up to participating, that's all right, but I shan't allow you to be idle. While your brother and I are studying rocks in the park, you will compose an essay about them. By the time we return," she added, her brisk voice overriding the child's groan of dismay, "I expect you to be ready with a full explanation to give your brother of the differences between sedimentary, metamorphic, and igneous rocks."

"But I don't know anything about rocks." His blue eyes narrowed accusingly. "You've failed to teach us about them."

"Oh, you needn't worry. There's a book on the subject up here. *Rocks of the World and Where to Find Them*, I think it's called. Third shelf," she added as if to be helpful, nodding to the bookshelves behind him. "Right side, near the end."

He scowled at her.

She smiled at him.

The clash of wills lasted a full ten seconds, but at last, Colin capitulated and tossed down his chalk.

"Change your mind?" she asked, donning an ingenuous air as he came to join them by the door and began to put on his coat.

"Obviously." He rolled his eyes. "You don't think I'm going to sit in the kitchens, all by myself, polishing silver or writing about rocks, do you? Dull as ashes, that."

"I couldn't agree more," she said gravely and turned away. "Come along, gentlemen," she called over her shoulder as she started down the corridor with her papier-mâché volcano. "I know Colin doesn't want to miss lunch, and neither do I, especially since I asked Mrs. Richmond to make jam roly-poly for us."

Shouts of surprised approval from behind her greeted this news, and Amanda couldn't help grinning. An endorsement of jam roly-poly at lunch wasn't much of a victory, she supposed, and it was certainly no guarantee of future success, but since it was the first speck of approval she'd received from these two since her arrival, she'd take it. She'd take it gladly.

Chapter 6

*G*iven that he'd planned to be away two weeks, Jamie had nothing of crucial importance to do in London, but that didn't mean he could afford to be idle. After freeing Seton and giving strict instructions to Mrs. Richmond and Samuel to keep a more watchful eye on the boys and their tutor this afternoon than they had this morning, he lunched at his club, and upon his return, ensconced himself in his study.

For the next several hours, he caught up on his correspondence, including handwritten notes of apology to those with whom he had intended to meet during his tour of Yorkshire. After putting all his letters in the tray by the front door for Samuel to post that evening, he decided to check on Seton and the boys to see how they were getting on. When he went to the nursery, however, he found it empty.

He journeyed below stairs, but though he found Mrs. Richmond and Samuel in the kitchens, neither Mr. Seton nor his charges seemed to be anywhere about.

"They went for an outing," Samuel said in answer to his query on the subject. "They were going across to the park," he added, shoving a scoop of coal into the scuttle by the stove.

"No, no," Mrs. Richmond corrected, looking up from the pastry she was rolling out. "They returned ages ago. They had lunch, then polished some of the silver, and then they—"

"Silver?" Jamie and Samuel interrupted in surprised unison.

"Punishment," the cook said, nodding her head with a grim sort of relish that reminded Jamie of just how close to the breaking point his sons had pushed the staff. "Worked them like kitchen maids for over an hour, Mr. Seton did."

"Ah." Samuel gave a nod of understanding and dumped another scoop of coal into the scuttle. "Because of the slop water yesterday, I imagine."

"Slop water?" Jamie asked, his surprise giving way to dismay. "What slop water?"

"Just a little joke, sir," Samuel hastened to explain. "No harm done."

Past experience made Jamie rather inclined to doubt that reassurance, but before he could pursue the matter further, Mrs. Richmond said, "Seton already punished them for the slop water. They had to scrub some of my big copper pots for that, and they did it first thing this morning. No, polishing the silver is because of the other thing."

"Ah," Samuel said again with another knowing nod. "The slugs."

"Slugs?" Jamie knew what that meant even as he spoke. "In Seton's bed, I suppose? Or in the drawer with his linen? Hell's bells," he added in exasperation, "it's only been twenty-four hours. How could they possibly inflict so much torment on the poor fellow in such a short space of time? Never mind," he added at once. "It was a stupid question."

"Now, my lord, don't be worrying," Mrs. Richmond said in a placating tone that increased his worry rather than eased it. "Just having a bit of fun, they were. You know how they are."

He did know, all too well, and it was becoming quite clear that he needed to sit down with Seton and obtain a full report of exactly what had been going on in his absence. "And where are the boys now?" he asked Mrs. Richmond.

"Kitchen garden," she said promptly, waving a floury hand in that direction, and Jamie turned to start down the corridor for the back door. "Setting off a volcano."

Jamie stopped and took a step back to stare at her through the doorway, not certain he'd heard that right. "I beg your pardon?"

"That's what they said, my lord. They built a volcano and they're going to make it erupt, they said."

"And you let them?" he asked, his dismay deepening as various scenarios of disaster ran through his mind. "Good God, Mrs. Richmond, didn't the firecrackers demonstrate that the twins can't be trusted with anything that explodes?"

"Erupts, sir," she corrected. "They're making it erupt."

"Yes, yes, all right," he conceded impatiently. "Either way, I can't believe you raised no objection to this—" He paused as another thought struck him. "But where is Seton? Why the devil isn't he putting a stop to this?"

"Put a stop to it? Oh no, my lord. He's helping them make it. It's a— now, what did Mr. Seton call it, Samuel?"

"A scientific experiment," the footman replied as he took up the now-empty coal bucket and rose to his feet.

"That's it," the cook said and resumed rolling dough. "Although it didn't look very impressive to me. Just a big, gray lump when I saw it."

Scientific experiment or no, an erupting volcano seemed as fraught with hazard as firecrackers. Given what he'd been hearing about slop water and slugs and having seen for himself just how hapless Seton had proved to be at a simple game of Cowboys and Indians, Jamie decided he'd better investigate this scientific experiment for himself.

When he reached the kitchen garden, however, he found to his relief that nothing was on fire and nothing was erupting—at least, not yet. Seton and the boys were kneeling on a tarp laid in one of the garden's now-fallow vegetable beds, with their science experiment between them. The volcano seemed to have been painted, for it was no longer the big gray lump Mrs. Richmond had described. Now it was brownish-black in color, with red streaks down the sides, representing—he could only assume—streaks of lava. The volcano reposed on a tray, black pebbles piled all around it, along with a few small twigs and bits of lichen to represent trees and grass.

"But how are you going to make it erupt?" Colin was asking as Jamie approached unnoticed, observing them over the garden's low brick wall.

"I'm not going to do it," Seton said, rising up on his knees, a jar in each hand. "You are."

This news was met with exclamations of excitement, and Jamie, concerned but not sure he wanted to interrupt, paused by the garden gate.

Leaning down, he folded his arms on top of the brick wall and continued to watch, prepared to jump in if disaster occurred.

"Now, Colin," Seton said, "you will take that pitcher of hot water there and pour all of it into the volcano. Owen, once he's done that, you will add three drops of the soap, six drops of the red dye, and three drops of the yellow, please."

When Seton instructed the twins to add a quantity of bicarbonate to their experiment, vague memories of Jamie's own childhood lessons in chemistry came back to him, and when the boys were told to add vinegar to the mixture, he understood what was coming.

The "eruption" was immediate, and so was the reaction of the twins. Jamie grinned as the boys scrambled back from their creation with squeals of delighted astonishment as bright orange foam poured from the top of the volcano and spilled down the sides. It did look rather like molten lava, and though the tutors at Harrow would never have chosen such an unorthodox method for demonstrating a chemical reaction, Seton's volcano certainly made a much more exciting show than any ordinary glass beaker would have provided.

Pat, Jamie thought, would have loved it.

Science had been her passion, and she'd adored mucking about with chemicals and doing various experiments. She ought to be here now, vibrant and alive and making volcanoes with her boys, not lying in the cold, damp earth of a churchyard grave.

Suddenly, he felt the emptiness—that big, dark space that had been inside him ever since he could remember, a void filled for all too brief a time by the warmth and laughter of a freckle-faced girl.

His eyes stung. Blinking, he looked away, hating that he knew how it felt to have a heart in his chest instead of a gaping hole. He wished he'd never known. Then perhaps having that heart ripped out of him three years ago wouldn't have hurt so much.

"Papa!"

Colin's voice rang out, and then both boys were coming toward him at a run, and Jamie ducked his head, savagely dabbing a thumb and forefinger at his eyes so they would not see as he moved toward the garden gate. By the time the boys reached him, his eyes were dry, his face—he hoped—impassive.

He caught both boys up at once, lifting one under each arm as if hefting sacks of potatoes, making them laugh as he carried them through the gate and across the garden to where Seton was standing by their science project.

"We thought you were gone to Yorkshire," Colin cried, still laughing as he set them on their feet again.

"I was, but I changed my mind." He nodded a greeting to the tutor, then glanced at the volcano, which was still oozing a bit of orange foam from the top. "Conducting science experiments, I gather?"

"We made a volcano erupt, Papa," Owen told him.

"Yes, so I saw. Pretty amazing, what?"

"It was! Mr. Seton says it's because vinegar and bicarbonate make carbon dioxide gas when you mix them together. And the soap with the gas makes the foam. We dyed it to look like lava."

"Did you come to help us, Papa?" Colin asked.

"Alas, no. I have business to conduct this afternoon—"

Groans of disappointment from both boys interrupted him, but it was Colin who spoke first. "You're just back. How can you have business? You always have business," he added accusingly before Jamie could reply.

Guilt pricked him, and he looked away. "It's tragic, I know," he said lightly. "Believe me, I'd prefer to remain here, making volcanoes erupt with you."

Before either of the boys could attempt to persuade him to that course, however, he turned to their tutor and spoke again. "Mr. Seton, might I have a word with you ere I go?"

Seton's dark hazel eyes widened a fraction, in apprehension or surprise, Jamie couldn't be certain, but the younger man nodded readily enough. "Of course, my lord," he said, brushing dirt from his knees before turning to the twins.

"Colin, Owen," he said, "I want the two of you to take everything back to the kitchen and wait for me there. I'll be along shortly. While you wait, you will begin recording in your science journals everything we did to build our volcano and make it erupt, including precise measurements of all the chemicals we used and a description of the reaction we obtained."

To Jamie's surprise, the boys moved to comply with these instructions without any protest and only a bit of a squabble over who would have the honor of carrying their creation. Once Seton had settled the matter by charging Colin, as the eldest, with responsibility for their science project, the twins folded up the tarp, gathered the various vials they had used, and adjourned to the house with their volcano in a fashion that was almost agreeable.

"Miracles never cease," Jamie murmured, watching them go.

"My lord?"

"Nothing." He turned his attention back to the tutor. "I was simply enjoying this rare moment of domestic peace and accord."

"Moment is probably right." Seton raked back the longer locks of hair that had fallen over his forehead, giving Jamie a rueful look. "We'll see how long it lasts."

"Are you saying it won't?"

"With children around, domestic peace never lasts, I'm afraid."

"I daresay you're right. I'm curious how you intend to manage them when the next skirmish breaks out."

Seton gave him a cheeky grin. "I have my methods."

He raised a brow. "Polishing silver?"

The grin faded from the tutor's youthful, gamine face. "You don't approve."

"I am hardly in a position to disapprove," Jamie countered dryly. "And though I'm not sure their efforts with the silver will pass muster with Mrs. Richmond, I realize that they must be punished for misdeeds."

"Not punished," the tutor corrected at once. "I prefer not to use that word. It implies cruelty. Suffice it to say, all actions have consequences, and that is the lesson they must learn, one they have failed to learn in the past."

"You don't hesitate to speak your mind, do you, Seton? That wasn't a criticism," he added before the other man could reply. "Merely an observation. And rather along the lines of what I wanted to speak with you about." He gestured to the path. "Shall we?"

They started toward the house, and Jamie went on, "I do appreciate your philosophy of disciplining them when they misbehave, and I recognize the need for it. But I do have concerns and questions."

"Of course."

"I would like to discuss them, as well as hear what sort of curriculum you have planned in the coming year and what goals you hope to achieve. I shall be in for dinner this evening, and I would like you to join me after you've put the boys to bed, so we can discuss these matters."

"Dinner?" The lad stopped on the path, turning to give Jamie a confounded stare. "Dinner?"

"Yes, Mr. Seton, dinner," Jamie replied, stopping as well, and he couldn't help being amused at the younger man's continued blank stare. "The final meal of the day, served at some point between tea and bedtime, usually around eight o'clock."

"It's quite kind of you, but—"

"If you manage to be here for long, Mr. Seton, you'll come to appreciate that I'm not the sort to do things out of mere kindness. As I said, I want to discuss the boys, and since I'm free this evening—which is, I assure you, a rarity—I thought dinner would be a suitable time for that discussion."

Seton shifted his weight and looked away, clearly uncomfortable. "I believe it's customary for a tutor to take his meals with his pupils," he muttered, and resumed walking.

"So it is, usually," Jamie replied, falling in step beside him, "but I think we can make an exception."

They reached the door that led from the back garden into the house before Seton could reply, and since the younger man had arrived a step ahead of him, Jamie took it for granted that he would open the door, but unexpectedly, the tutor stepped to one side and turned toward him in an oddly expectant fashion.

That took him back a little, but then Seton spoke, and Jamie's impression that the younger man had expected him to open the door faded as he realized the tutor's true purpose in stopping.

"I appreciate your interest in what I'm teaching the boys," he said, "but it's hardly necessary to devote an entire meal to a conversation about it."

"But we both must eat, Mr. Seton. And I think it is necessary, for I need to learn more about your teaching methods, and about you."

"Me?" He looked a bit alarmed by the prospect, and though Jamie was now fairly sure the other man wasn't about to take off with his sons and hold them for ransom, he found Seton's hesitation a bit worrisome.

"You will be exerting a great deal of influence over my sons during the coming two years. I would have thought you'd welcome the opportunity to reassure me as to your character."

"I do welcome it," the lad said at once. "Of course I do."

It was a fervent assurance, yet not particularly convincing. Seton sensed the fact, for he spoke again. "It's just that . . . I'm not . . . I mean . . ." He paused, squirming like a cat on hot bricks, his cheeks as pink as a girl's. "I don't go into society much," he mumbled after a moment.

How terribly young he is, Jamie thought, sympathy mingling with amusement as he noted the lad's flushed cheeks and nervous manner. His own youth seemed like a long time ago, but he could still recall how awful it was to be seventeen. "We're just two bachelors having a meal," he said gently. "It's not as if you'll be dining at Buckingham Palace, you know."

"No, my lord." His voice was faint, with perhaps a hint of panic in it, but he seemed to realize for himself how out of proportion such a reaction was to a simple invitation to dinner, for he gave a cough and spoke again, more heartily this time. "I accept your invitation, of course. Thank you, my lord."

"You needn't look as if you're bracing yourself for your execution, Mr. Seton. I shan't be calling you on the carpet for what happened this afternoon, if that's your fear. Quite the opposite, for I have now seen for myself that you were right."

"I was?" The younger man blinked, seeming too confounded by this seemingly inexplicable concession to be pleased by it. "Right about what?"

"You *are* a good teacher."

Seton stared at him for a moment as if that was the last thing he'd expected to hear. Then, suddenly, he smiled, a wide smile that lit up his entire face, softening the severe, finely cut lines of jaw and cheekbone, reminding Jamie again of how young the fellow was, and how vulnerable.

He felt a sudden, protective instinct rising in him, one he recognized at once—the need to defend and shield from harm those who might not be quite up to defending themselves. It was a feeling akin to what he often experienced if he saw one of the boys take a tumble or have a nightmare, and yet, it wasn't precisely the same.

Jamie stared, striving to define the feeling more precisely, but then, Seton's smile vanished, and the feeling slipped away, making him realize how absurd it had been. His only duty to this young man was to be a fair employer. Besides, Seton was an intelligent chap who, despite his youth, had seemingly lived in the world long enough to take care of himself. What need had he for Jamie's protection?

The younger man stirred, looking away, making Jamie realize he'd been staring, and he quickly spoke again.

"I hope that's settled then?" he asked, reaching for the knob and opening the door. "I shall see you this evening at eight. And don't worry any more about putting on your Sunday manners," he added over his shoulder as he stepped across the threshold into the servants' corridor. "I'm far more interested in turning your life inside out than I am how you hold your knife and fork."

AMANDA WATCHED LORD Kenyon's back as he walked away, his last words echoing through her head like harbingers of doom and erasing the all-too-brief moment of exaltation she'd enjoyed over his compliment to her teaching abilities.

. . . turning your life inside out . . .

Amanda closed the door, then leaned her back against the wood, a knot of apprehension forming in her stomach at the thought of having dinner with him.

She'd expected a thorough interrogatory before being hired, of course. She'd prepared for that, and though her infamous past had necessitated several crucial deceptions, she'd striven to stick to the truth as much as possible. But she hadn't thought Lord Kenyon would take much further interest in her once she'd begun her job as long as she did it well. Most fathers didn't bother much about their children and were quite happy to leave the care of them in the hands of wives, nannies, tutors, and governesses. Indeed, during the year she'd lived with the Bartlett family, Sir Oswald had never once inquired about his daughters' lessons, and only rarely about their welfare. At Willowbank, she could count on one hand the number of fathers who had visited their daughters or taken them for outings. And from what she'd observed thus far, Lord Kenyon certainly didn't seem a more attentive father than the average.

Still, he was within his rights to make inquiries of her anytime he liked, and she'd better be prepared with satisfactory answers. If he found anything about her odd or out of place, he might start digging more deeply into her life, and that would be disastrous. The life of Adam Seton, though good enough to pass muster in an interview, would hardly bear up under a more thorough investigation.

She thought she'd have some breathing room while Lord Kenyon was in Yorkshire, time and space to rehearse her new role and practice living life as a man before she was put under any serious scrutiny. The boys, after all, were only ten, and weren't likely to be aware of any subtle differences between their current tutor and the various other men of their acquaintance. Children, bless them, were much more inclined than adults to take things at face value. No, any mistakes she made wouldn't likely be perceived by the boys.

As for the two servants in the house, they were probably quite relieved to return to their own duties and leave the boys fully in a tutor's care, and they wouldn't be likely to notice much either during the brief moments when they brought meals to the nursery or she took the boys down to the kitchens for a round of disciplinary scrubbing.

Lord Kenyon, however, was a different matter. His unexpected return and invitation to dinner left her no time to practice or prepare. She imagined those clear green eyes studying her over a dining table, and her stomach tightened, the apprehension inside her deepening into dread. Those eyes, she'd wager, didn't miss much.

And she'd already made at least two mistakes in front of him. During her initial interview, she'd almost reached for her handbag before remembering that she no longer carried that useful little item. And just a few moments ago, she'd stopped by the door here and waited for him to open it, something a man, however young and gauche he might be, would never do. He'd noticed that, she knew, and his puzzled frown told her he'd thought it odd. She was reasonably sure she'd covered her gaffe well enough, but knew she couldn't afford to make another one in front of him.

That fact meant dinner would be fraught with danger. A prolonged meal required a great deal of conversation, not only the sort of an employer probing into his employee's life, but also the sort of manly conversation no woman was ever privy to. That, she appreciated, left her every bit as vulnerable to discovery as any discussions about her past, because there was no way to anticipate what might come up. What did men talk about among themselves? Port vintages? Horse racing? Football? Politics? She had no idea.

Just two bachelors sharing a meal.

Amanda's stomach gave another nervous lurch, and she caught herself up sharp with the reminder that she'd chosen this course. How had she expected it to be? Had she really thought it would be all smooth sailing once she was in the household?

The truth was that she hadn't allowed herself to think about anything at all beyond getting the job. She'd been so focused on that, she hadn't considered what it would be like to act a part every waking minute of every day. Now, as all the ramifications of her future came roaring into her mind, she appreciated just how difficult the task ahead would be. This wasn't just about one evening of dodging inconvenient questions about her fictional past. This was about her entire life.

Suddenly, potential hazards were springing up in her mind like mushrooms popping out of the ground after a rain. He wanted her to go to his tailor for a new suit. How would she get out of that? And what about games and sports? She was all right when it came to games for girls—jacks, hop-score, jump-the-rope, that sort of thing—and she could play a decent, if not brilliant, game of rounders or croquet. But boys played football, cricket, and rugby, games she'd never played in her life. Lord Kenyon would surely expect her to know these games, to play them with his sons. He had the sort of strong and fluid grace that spoke of an athlete, and if he ever watched her pretend any sort of competence at boys' sports, she'd be sunk. He'd undoubtedly played enough football and cricket at school to know a fraud when he saw one.

There were other hazards to consider. If there was ever occasion to dance, she'd have to remember to lead. And to stand whenever ladies entered a room. And pull out chairs for them, open doors, pick up hand-kerchiefs. And, of course, there were all the womanly things she'd have to avoid doing . . . oh God.

Amanda straightened away from the door in alarm as another thought struck her, a ghastly one she'd never considered until this moment. What about her menses? Mrs. Richmond would surely notice when that time came around. How could she ever hide her monthly cycle from the woman who did the laundry?

Amanda's dread deepened, threatening to dissolve into panic. She leaned back against the door again, folded her arms over her tightly bound breasts, and took several deep, steadying breaths. She hadn't come this far just to be outdone by trivialities. There were ways to cope with all these things, and she would just have to tackle each one as it came up. Otherwise, she'd be overwhelmed. For now, tonight's dinner was the only thing she needed to worry about.

She started toward the kitchen to fetch the boys and tried to look on the bright side. It was only one meal, not a daily occurrence. All she had to do was make a few manly sounding remarks about the excellent joint of beef, force down a glass or two of port, and steer the conversation away from herself and her own checkered past. How hard could that be?

Chapter 7

She was almost there. Keeping the ends of the half-formed bow of her tie clenched tightly in her fingers so the blasted thing wouldn't come undone, Amanda simultaneously tried to shove the wide loop of white silk in her right hand through the smaller loop at her throat. She then pulled the ends into the proper shape, tightening the knot as she tried to balance the proportions on both sides, then she lowered her hands and leaned back from the mirror to survey the results.

It was crooked. Again.

With an oath of exasperation, Amanda pulled at the ends to undo her latest pathetic attempt. Of all the things her father had taught her growing up, she wondered in aggravation, why hadn't tying his ties been one of them?

Taking up the ends of white silk, she started again from the beginning. "Right end shorter than left," she muttered, repeating for the sixth time what the old tailor in Petticoat Lane had told her when he'd sold her the secondhand clothes of her gentleman's wardrobe. "Cross longer end over shorter end, then bring it up through the neck loop—"

"Having a problem?"

Startled, Amanda jumped, letting go of the ends of her tie, and she turned her head to find Colin watching her from the doorway to the nursery, grinning in unmistakable amusement.

"You are supposed to be getting ready for bed," she told him severely, "not spying on me."

"I am ready for bed," he answered, gesturing to the flannel pajamas he was wearing as he crossed to her side. "And it's not spying since I have to go through your room to get to mine."

With no way to refute that very valid point, Amanda turned her attention back to her task. "Pull it tight," she went on under her breath, suiting the action to the words. "Let the longer end hang down, fold the shorter end in half . . ."

She formed the bow again and tugged the ends into place. "Well?" she asked, turning toward the boy. "What do you think?"

Colin's howl of laughter gave her the answer even before he spoke. "Awful. One side's twice as big as the other."

She returned her attention to the mirror. "It is, isn't it?" she agreed dismally. "I fear I shall never be any good at bow ties. A four-in-hand is so much easier."

"Do you want me to do it up for you?"

Surprised, she turned toward him. "Do you know how?"

"Of course. Owen and I both do. Samuel taught us."

"Not your father?"

"He's too busy to teach us things like that. Especially now."

"Why now, especially?"

"Because he's in the Commons." Colin's expression became dismal. "Once Parliament starts again, we'll hardly ever see him."

Amanda might have been relieved by that news, but the forlorn expression of the little boy beside her made that impossible, and she decided one of the things she'd have to talk with Lord Kenyon about at dinner was the lack of time he spent with his sons. "Being in Parliament is very important work," she said, thinking to comfort the child, but even as the words came out of her mouth, she realized how lame they sounded.

"More important than us," Colin muttered. "That's sure."

"I don't think that's true. The way he talks about you, he seems very fond of you and your brother. In fact . . ." She paused and took a breath, hoping she wasn't about to utter a bald-faced lie to a child. "I think he loves you both very much."

To her surprise, Colin nodded in agreement with that contention, though he didn't seem much impressed by it. "He loves us, but he doesn't want us around."

"If that were the case, he'd have sent you off to school already."

"The only reason he hasn't is because he doesn't think we're ready yet. That's why he decided to hire a tutor this time instead of another nanny. A tutor would bring us up to the mark, he said, and make us ready acad . . . acad . . ."

"Academically?" Amanda supplied.

"That's it. He said that was important because if we weren't ready, we'd fail our examinations and be sent home, and he didn't want that to happen. I overheard him telling Samuel all about it, the night before we met you in the park."

Amanda had a sneaking suspicion Colin had overheard that conversation because he'd had an ear to the keyhole, but now was not the time for a lecture on the immorality of eavesdropping. "So that's why you don't want a tutor," she said instead. "But then, why do you keep driving nannies away?"

He looked away with a sulky frown and didn't answer.

"Surely you know," Amanda persisted, "the more nannies you drive off, the more you exasperate your father and the more likely school becomes?"

Colin shrugged, staring at the floor. "At least if we're in trouble, he's paying attention." His voice was a mumble, and yet, the bitterness in it was unmistakable. "Otherwise, he can barely stand to look at us."

Amanda had already appreciated that their father was a neglectful parent, but when she tried to imagine that he might feel animosity for his sons or resent their needs, she couldn't form the picture. He'd worked himself into a profound state of worry over the idea that he might have put his sons in danger by hiring someone he knew so little about. He was an inadequate parent, perhaps, but not an indifferent one. "I don't think that's true."

"Yes, it is. We remind him of Mama, and he doesn't like it. We look like her, you see."

Amanda's heart constricted with compassion. "I'm sorry," she said, not knowing what else to say.

"Doesn't matter." Colin gave another shrug and looked up. His face gave nothing away, and yet, the very impassivity of his expression told her that he was much less indifferent than he wished to appear. "So," he said, waving a hand toward her chest, "are you ever going to tie that thing?"

Amanda looked down in dismay at her still-undone neckwear.

"I'm not sure I can," she confessed and looked at him. "Will you help me?"

"Maybe." Colin tilted his head, considering, giving her a look far too shrewd for a boy of ten. "What have you got to trade?"

"Oh, so you want something in return? That's not very gentlemanlike."

"It's not very gentlemanlike not to know how to tie a tie either."

"If you ever do go to Harrow, I shall make sure the tutors there put you on the debating team. You'll be excellent."

He grinned. "Got any sweets?"

She had some Belgian pastilles in her drawer, but she wasn't sure buying the child's assistance with chocolate was a good idea. "You already had dessert," she reminded. "Two helpings of Spotted Dick."

"That was ages ago."

"Two hours," she corrected. "You'll get much further with me if you don't exaggerate."

"Well, it seems longer. And besides, I'm hungry." He glanced at the clock on her mantel. "You've only got seven minutes to get downstairs, or you'll be late. Being late for dinner is very bad."

"Well, yes, I know that, but—"

"Papa won't like it. He hates when people are late."

Amanda, desperate, capitulated. "I've got four chocolates," she said, kneeling in front of the boy. "I will trade them for a lesson."

"Done." He picked up the ends of her tie and began manipulating the silk, explaining as he went, using similar instructions to the ones the tailor had given her, but when he'd finished, the results were clearly not satisfactory.

"Crooked," Colin said, shaking his head and undoing the bow.

"I thought you knew how to do this," she muttered, wondering if Colin had made her for a mug again.

"I do know how! But," he added, frowning in concentration, "it's harder when you do it on somebody else. There," he added, tugging the ends into place and once again leaning back to study his handiwork. "Got it this time."

She rose and turned to the mirror, and she didn't know whether to be relieved that she now had a perfectly done bow tie or chagrined that a ten-year-old had tied it with more skill than she, and with far less effort.

"Second drawer of the chiffonier," she said. "And you must share them with your brother," she added as he tore to the other end of the room and opened the requisite drawer to retrieve the chocolate.

"Share what?" Owen asked, coming into the room.

Amanda pulled her black dinner jacket off the peg inside the open armoire. "Chocolates," she explained, slipping the jacket on over her white shirt and white satin waistcoat. "Two for each of you."

Owen's face lit up at once. "Smashing!" he said, and joined his brother at the other end of the room as Amanda retrieved a linen handkerchief from the armoire and tucked it into her breast pocket, careful to leave the corner sticking out.

"Into bed, both of you," she ordered, returning her attention to the boys and jerking a thumb toward their room.

They both nodded and moved toward their own room without voicing any objections, though whether that was because she'd managed to establish some semblance of authority over them or because their mouths were full of chocolate, she couldn't be sure.

The second dressing gong boomed down below, the sound reverberating along the corridor and through the open doorway that led into the nursery, meaning she only had five minutes left, and she hastily followed both boys into their room.

"There," she said a few minutes later, smoothing Owen's counterpane over him before straightening away from the boy's bed. "I will be having Samuel come up periodically to check on you," she added over her shoulder as she started for the door, "so no mischief making while I'm gone."

With that, she took up the lamp and reentered her own room. There, she gave herself one last glance in the mirror and made a token effort to smooth her hair. But she'd barely raked back the sides with a bit of po-made before the grandfather clock on the first floor began sounding the hour and she was forced to give up on her unruly curls as a lost cause. She wiped her hands on a spare handkerchief, cast the scrap of cambric aside, and ran for the door, but the chimes had long since died away by the time she had raced down the corridor, across the landing, down the three flights of stairs, and into the drawing room.

Lord Kenyon was already there, waiting for her, faultlessly attired in black evening clothes despite his lack of a valet. "Seton," he greeted, taking a sip from the half-empty glass in his hand as Amanda skidded to a halt in front of him.

"Sorry I'm late," she panted, trying to catch her breath.

"There's no need for apologies. I already told you we're not standing on ceremony tonight since it's just the two of us. Sherry?" he asked, gesturing to the decanter and cordial glasses atop the nearby liquor cabinet.

Shaking her head in refusal, she sucked in another gasp of air. "I don't think there's time for it. I heard the clock chime the hour as I came down, so Samuel will be announcing dinner any second."

"He already did. Not to worry," he added at her sound of dismay. "I told him to delay ten minutes since you weren't down yet. Have a drink," he invited, turning to reach for the sherry decanter. "You look as if you need it."

"You're not upset?" she asked in puzzlement as he poured sherry for her.

He paused, giving her a surprised glance. "Should I be? Ten minutes is hardly long enough for Mrs. Richmond to start squawking about cold soup and overcooked meat."

"I was given to understand that you detest unpunctuality."

"Me?" He made a scoffing sound and set aside the decanter. "I don't know where you heard that," he said, held out her glass of sherry, and took another sip of his own. "I'm usually the last one down to dinner. Of course, that's mainly because I can't seem to keep a valet—"

"That scamp," Amanda interrupted as she took her glass from his outstretched hand, half laughing at how easily Colin had tricked her out of her chocolates. "That conniving little scamp."

He raised an eyebrow. "You are referring to one of my sons, I take it?"

"Colin." She shook her head, still laughing a little, wondering just how long it would be before she could discern when that child was having her on.

"He's the reason you came tearing in as if the house was on fire? Not that I'm surprised," he added as she nodded. "He loves a good joke. As you ought to know by now," he pointed out, lifting his glass.

She made a face at this reminder of what had happened earlier in the day. "He told me you hate it when people are late. I know, I know," she went on, watching him shake his head as if amazed by her gullibility. "But it seemed quite logical to suppose he was telling the truth. You're in the Commons. Surely you value punctuality. It must be quite inconvenient when Members are late for votes and things like that."

"Well, it's true that at Westminster one has to be on time for absolutely everything. It's *de rigueur*. But here at home, I'm not so punctilious, much to Torquil's dismay."

"Is the duke such a stickler, then?"

"Terribly. But just now, he's at the country house in Hampshire, with the rest of the family. When he's here, though, everyone jumps to attention."

Amanda wasn't sure she liked the sound of that. "Will he be coming to London often?"

"Well, he is in the Lords, so he'll come when there's an important vote on. But as I'm sure you know, those in the Lords don't have to be present nearly as often as those in the Commons, so I don't expect we'll see much of him. As for the rest of the family, they won't return to London until spring, when the season begins."

"And will we go there?"

"To Hampshire? We might for a few days at Christmas, but I doubt I'll have time to be away much more than that."

She breathed a sigh of relief. By Christmas, she hoped to be much more at ease in her new role.

"My lord?" Samuel's voice had them both turning toward the door. "Dinner is served."

Amanda gulped down her sherry, set her glass aside, and fell in step with his lordship as they followed Samuel out of the drawing room and down the corridor.

"You see?" Lord Kenyon said as they entered an unexpectedly small dining room with an oval table set for two. "No standing on ceremony here, Seton. We're not even in the formal dining room tonight."

She glanced around, noting soft yellow walls, dark wood furnishings, and a definite lack of grandeur. She was also profoundly grateful for the soft, mellow dimness of candlelight. "Does the family often dine here when in residence?"

"For breakfast, always. Dinner, too, if we have no guests." He pulled out a chair, and Amanda almost moved to take it, but caught herself in time and circled to the chair at his right hand instead.

Once they were both seated, Samuel served them a clear soup and poured white wine. "Will there be anything else, my lord?" he asked. "Or shall I prepare to serve the fish?"

"Nothing else, Samuel, thank you," he replied, but as the footman started for the door, Amanda gave a cough.

"Samuel?"

The footman turned at the door to look at her. "Sir?"

"If you could check on the boys a few times while we dine, I would be grateful. I don't trust them on their own."

Samuel gave her a look of understanding. "Of course, Mr. Seton."

With a bow, the footman departed, and remembering her plan to keep the conversation away from herself as much as possible, Amanda turned to Lord Kenyon and spoke before he could.

"Speaking of the boys," she said as she picked up her soup spoon, "I'm sure you want to know how close they are to being ready for Harrow."

"I wasn't planning to ship them off next week, obviously," he replied as he picked up his own spoon. "But, yes, I would like to know where they stand."

"It's early days yet for a full assessment. But," she added hastily, "I can present you with the curriculum I'd like to implement, and you can tell me what you think of it?"

"By all means."

She gave an outline of her lesson plan for the twins, and she successfully managed to keep the conversation on the boys throughout the soup course and the fillet of sole that followed it.

"You are placing a great deal of emphasis on math and the sciences," Lord Kenyon said as Samuel cleared away the fish plates and replaced the wineglasses with fresh ones. "Particularly chemistry, I assume, from what I saw this afternoon?"

"This afternoon wasn't really a lesson. My main purpose with the volcano was merely to gain their interest. Until I do that, and establish my authority, of course, any lessons will have limited value."

"With the former, I've seen how you intend to accomplish your goal. But what of the latter?"

"It's a matter of consistency more than anything. Rules and the consequences of breaking them, establishing a routine . . . these things are vital to order and discipline, which are vital to learning."

To her surprise, he sighed. "Shades of Mr. Partridge."

Amanda frowned, uncomprehending. "Sorry. Who?"

"Never mind." He shook his head. "It's just that I'd hate the boys to be bored by too much regimentation."

"What do you take me for?" She sat up straighter, pretending to be affronted. "I'll have you know, I am not a boring teacher."

"Well, no," he agreed dryly. "I'm sure they find tricking you all the time vastly entertaining."

She grimaced, thinking his words a reproof, but as Samuel came to the earl's side with a dish of beef fillets, the footman's conspiratorial wink over his head bolstered her spirits.

"I suppose," Lord Kenyon said as Samuel moved to serve Amanda, "you'll get the hang of their tricks eventually."

"My idea is to stop their tricks altogether," she replied.

He looked doubtful, but didn't say so. "I'm heartened that you aren't ready to wave the white flag just yet, Seton," he murmured.

"After one day?"

"You wouldn't be the first," Samuel muttered, earning himself a pointed look from the earl. Abashed, he withdrew and fetched the sauce for the beef.

"I must say, I was surprised by what I saw in the garden," Lord Kenyon commented. "I didn't expect you to be launching straightaway into a subject like chemistry."

"You think it beyond their abilities?"

"On the contrary, I expect they'll take to it like ducks to water. It's what they'll do with the knowledge that worries me."

Amanda smiled. "I'll be there to ensure they don't make their own itching powder or light up any firecrackers."

His answering look was wry. "You can't blame me for being concerned, considering I lost a valet due to the former, and they almost set the whole bloody house on fire due to the latter."

This was her chance. "You realize why they do things like that?" she asked. "Why they cause trouble and play pranks on the servants?"

If there was any trace of amusement in his face, it vanished. "Of course," he answered stiffly. "They want attention."

"Not just anyone's," she corrected. "Yours."

"Yes, I quite realize that," he said, his voice cool. "When I'm in town, I give them a bit of my time each day."

He clearly thought that an adequate dispensation of his father duties, but Colin's face earlier told a different tale. "It's not enough," she said. "They are two lonely little boys, and they need their father. They've already lost their mother—"

She broke off at the sight of his icy green eyes staring her down, and she knew she'd gone too far.

"You have been in my home just over twenty-four hours, Mr. Seton," he said. "By your own admission, that is too early for you to assess the twins' academic knowledge. Don't you think it's also a bit too early for you to determine their emotional needs?"

Some needs are plain enough, she wanted to retort, but as much as she wanted to offer a strong lecture about the quality of his parenting, she knew if she gave it, she'd probably get fired. Perhaps once she'd proven herself and gotten the twins under control, her opinions would have value, but until then, she had to tread carefully.

"You asked for this meal to hear my assessment of the boys," she said quietly. "Neither they, nor you, would be served by one that is less than honest. It may have been impertinent of me to speak as I just did, perhaps, but tact is not in my nature."

"So I'm discovering," he agreed, his voice dry.

At that moment, Samuel reentered the room, sparing Amanda any further reprimands, but she couldn't say that was much of an improvement, for as the footman moved around the table, placing spears of asparagus on their plates, the silence between her employer and herself seemed stifling. When the footman departed again, Amanda watched him go with a hint of envy, wishing she could escape as well.

"Still," Lord Kenyon went on, forcing her attention back to the conversation at hand, "I cannot deny the truth about my sons, however bluntly it is conveyed. Once the Commons is back in session, I will try to arrange my schedule so that I can give them more of my attention." He reached for his glass and lifted it, meeting her eyes over the rim. "Truce?"

This concession was so unexpected, it took Amanda a moment before she was able to set down her knife and fork and reach for her own glass. "Truce," she agreed.

They each took a sip of wine, but as they resumed their meal, she appreciated that one concession on his part did not mean she could let down her guard, and she opened her mouth to launch a new subject, but he spoke before she had the chance.

"Watching your experiment with the boys this afternoon gave me some insight into your methods. A bicarbonate and vinegar volcano for a chemistry lesson, a little physics along with the kite flying—all meant to gain and keep their interest. It's an unusual way of teaching."

"You prefer something more orthodox?"

"On the contrary, I'm glad that you intend to keep their lessons interesting. And besides . . ." He paused, staring down at his plate for a moment. "My wife would have approved of your lesson today," he said at last. "Education was very important to Pat, and she was especially keen on chemistry."

"That's an uncommon thing for a woman."

"Yes." With an abrupt move, he began slicing his beef. "She wanted to be a doctor, but of course, that wasn't possible."

"There are women doctors," Amanda couldn't resist pointing out.

"I doubt any of them are the sisters of dukes."

"She could have been the first."

"She wanted to be, but her father did not approve, and he refused to stand the fees. That was before we met, but I know it was a great disappointment to her, always."

"How would you have felt about that?" Amanda asked, curious. "Would you have married her had she been a doctor?"

He shrugged, set down his utensils, and leaned back with his wine. "I'd have married Pat—doctor, or debutante, or Gaiety Girl—it wouldn't have mattered to me what she was."

"Yes, but in general terms," Amanda persisted, "would you have married a doctor?"

"If not for Pat, I'd never have married at all."

Silence fell between them again, and Amanda searched for another subject. It wasn't easy. They'd rather exhausted the topic of the boys, and she found him unbearably difficult to talk to about anything else. "Making your home with your in-laws is a bit unusual, isn't it?"

"I suppose."

Desperate, she tried again. "Don't your own relations have a house in town?"

His face did not change, not a muscle moved. His countenance seemed frozen, and it was a moment before he spoke. "My father," he said slowly, "lives in Albermarle Street."

"That's quite near Westminster. Given that you're in the Commons, wouldn't living there be more convenient than here?"

"Only in some ways." Unexpectedly, he smiled, and Amanda sucked in a sharp breath, for she'd never seen a smile like that—brilliant, dazzling, and devoid of any shred of feeling.

God in heaven, she thought, *the man's a glacier.*

Swallowing hard, she tried again. "And you have no desire for your own household?"

"The duke has a large family, and I prefer that the boys have family around them."

"But not your own family?"

The smile vanished. "The Cavanaughs," he said, his voice hard, "are my family."

Samuel reentered the room at that moment, and Amanda looked away, heartily relieved by the interruption. This dinner was beginning to give her frostbite, and as the footman began to clear the plates, she had no choice but to resume the only topic she could seem to discuss with him.

"As I told you, it's early days, but perhaps I ought to give you my initial impression of where I think the boys stand at present. If you'd like to hear it?"

He seemed to relax, and Amanda had the curious feeling a danger had passed. "Of course."

Deciding the remainder of the evening would go much better if she could somehow manage to lighten the mood, she said, "For one thing, your sons have a sincere appreciation for the animal kingdom. Slugs," she added, "seem to be of particular interest to them at present."

She was rewarded with a faint, almost imperceptible smile. "Yes, I believe I heard something about that. Perhaps outings to collect insects should be on your agenda?"

"Only if I can keep the specimens under lock and key," she quipped.

His smile widened a fraction, giving her a hint of hope the glacier could be thawed. "A wise precaution. Are there any other subjects for which they seem to have an aptitude?"

"Oh, yes," she said at once. "Engineering. Specifically buckets, and how best to make them tip over."

A choked sound from by the sideboard had them both glancing at Samuel, but the footman merely pressed a fist to his mouth and gave a cough. Mumbling something about dessert and port, he departed the dining room.

Though it was clear Lord Kenyon knew about the slugs, he seemed unaware of the twins' other little prank, for he gave her a dubious look. "Dare I ask what my sons have been doing with buckets?"

"It's probably better if you don't. Suffice it to say, I'm adding lessons in engineering to their curriculum. I must say, I was quite impressed by their knowledge of military history. They seem to know a great deal about the Battle of Waterloo, for example."

"That's Samuel's influence. He's mad about history."

"And do I have Samuel to thank for their knowledge of Cowboys and Indians?"

"No. I fear I'm the one responsible for that. But in teaching them that game, I never thought—" He broke off, making a smothered sound, and then, suddenly, he began to laugh. "It never occurred to me they'd play that game quite the way they did today."

His laughter deepened, seeming to fill the room, and Amanda could only stare. She'd never heard him laugh before, and the change it wrought to his countenance was stunning. The glint of humor in his eyes warmed their pale green depths. His smile, unlike the earlier one he'd given her, was wide and genuine, softening the hard planes of his face and the carved edges of his mouth instead of freezing them in place.

Amanda watched in amazement as the hard shell of her employer shattered into pieces and revealed a man of flesh and blood, a man capable of humor and perhaps other, deeper passions, a man who seemed no longer coldly handsome, but devastatingly attractive.

The transformation was so earth-shattering that Amanda could not move or speak; she could only stare, and as she did, her body instinctively responded. Beneath her masculine evening suit, tingles danced along her spine. Under her high gentleman's collar and silk bow tie, her throat went dry. Within manly oxford shoes, her toes curled. Every nerve within her pulsed with a new, fully feminine awareness.

She'd thought she couldn't feel this sort of thing anymore. She thought desire was dead in her, killed by the heartbreak, betrayal, and shame that had followed in its wake. But now, looking at the man across from her, she realized all the gloriously feminine yearnings that had once destroyed her life were still within her, waiting to be reawakened.

Think like a man.

Amanda swallowed hard, striving to remember that vow and the role her new life required, but as she looked at Lord Kenyon across the table, her entire body awash in sensations she hadn't felt for over two years, it seemed impossible and absurd. How could she possibly think like a man when everything in her was remembering how it felt to be a woman?

Oh God, Amanda thought, sick with dismay, *what the hell am I going to do now?*

Chapter 8

Riveted by her discovery, dismayed by her body's traitorous reactions, Amanda couldn't seem to move, or think. She could only feel as arousal awakened within her for the first time in years, opening within her like a flower unfolding its petals.

She'd tried so hard to forget all this—the sweet, piercing pleasure that could come from something as simple as an attractive man's laugh or the sight of his smile. The warmth pooling in her belly and spreading to every cell and nerve ending, the exhilarating pump of her blood through her veins, the intoxicating glory of romance—how could she ever have thought to forget all this?

No, she shouted silently, her mind appalled by her body's sudden treachery. *No, no, no.*

Lord Kenyon seemed to sense the change in her, for his laughter faded away, and a slight frown of puzzlement creased his brow. "Mr. Seton? Is something wrong?"

The masculine address penetrated her dazed senses, and Amanda forced herself to say something.

"No." The word that had been pounding through her brain moments ago came out of her mouth as a strangled sound, woefully unconvincing. "No," she said again, more emphatically, remembering too late that she'd never had a great talent for concealing her emotions. With him watching her, however, she knew she'd better learn that trick, and learn it fast.

"Nothing's wrong," she lied, working to don the mask of cool indifference he seemed able to put on so effortlessly. "It's just . . . it's only . . ." She paused, trying to suppress the feelings rushing through her. "That's just the first time I've heard you laugh."

The moment the words were out of her mouth, she realized they sounded nothing like what a man would say.

Think like a man.

She took a deep breath and tried again. "You're not what I would describe as a merry sort of chap, so hearing you laugh was rather a surprise."

"Yes, well . . ." He paused, a faint smile still curving the corners of his lips. "It's not often a man sees his children's tutor trussed up like a chicken."

"You don't seem to find the fact that your sons tied me to a desk and left me there particularly distressing," she said, trying to sound severe, but she feared she merely sounded out of breath. "I begin to see just why you've been through so many nannies."

"Forgive me," he said, not seeming the least bit repentant. "But in hindsight, it seems so absurd, you tied up, the bellpull cut, the scissors on the floor. Who wouldn't laugh?"

Amanda latched onto the subject of the boys' trickery like a lifeline. "I was a mug. I can't deny it," she said, making a face at him. "I'm surprised you didn't sack me on the spot for being so gullible."

"You wouldn't be the first person my sons have taken in."

"Perhaps, but I was sure I'd be able to see through any of their tricks. Their nannies, I thought, may have fallen by the wayside left and right, but I would be different. Arrogant of me, I suppose."

"Well, you were a bit overconfident, perhaps." He paused to consider, leaning back with his wine, still smiling. "No doubt you thought that, being a man, you'd have better luck with them than their nannies had."

"Quite," she agreed at once, with perhaps too much fervor. "Absolutely."

Feeling in need of a drink, she reached for her wine, but then paused, struck by a thought. "Is that why you didn't hire me straight away? You thought I was too cocky?"

"Partly. I thought you were far too young to be so confident of your abilities. It had to be a pose. And—" He broke off, frowning a little. "I thought you far too impertinent for a lad your age. It flicked me on the raw."

She studied him thoughtfully for a moment. "You don't like it when people speak their minds, do you?"

"I'm not used to it—at least, not now that I'm in politics. No man in politics can afford to say what he really thinks about anything, or he'd never be elected. But you would be wrong to think I don't value honesty. I do value it." He paused, looking at her steadily. "Very much."

Her stomach gave a sudden, nervous lurch, and she looked away, feeling as transparent as glass. Fortunately, however, Samuel reentered the dining room, saving her from having to come up with a reply, and as the footman cleared their dinner plates and wineglasses, replacing them with dishes of syllabub and glasses of port, his presence was a welcome distraction. By the time he had set a bowl of fruit and a plate of cheese on the table and departed again, Amanda felt once more in command of herself.

"If what you say is true," she said, "then why did my cheek in our first interview offend you?"

"It didn't offend me, precisely. It's only that it reminded me of someone." He paused, his hand holding his spoon poised above the crystal dessert dish in front of him. "My wife was always exceedingly blunt in her opinions," he murmured, smiling a little, as if remembering. "Cheeky as hell, that woman."

Amanda stared, dismayed and rather chagrined. "I remind you of your wife?" she blurted out, then wanted to kick herself.

He looked up, his smile widening into a heart-stopping grin. "I'd hardly go that far," he drawled. "No offense, Seton, but my wife was much prettier than you."

Amanda ought to have been relieved by that remark, but instead, she felt a wholly feminine desire to toss her syllabub in his face. Fortunately, he lowered his gaze to his dessert, and she managed to refrain. "I'm sure," she muttered, and decided to return to the subject they'd been discussing. "So, what made you change your mind?" she asked as she picked up her dessert spoon. "Why did you hire me?"

"Pure desperation," he confessed. "Not a very good reason, I know, and I only appreciated that I might have put my sons in a harmful situation after I was halfway to York. I've never hired anyone to oversee my children whom I know so little about."

"If it's any comfort to you," she said before he could work to improve his knowledge on that score, "many parents—servants, too—have inadvertently put a child in harm's way. One moment's inattention in a shop, for example, and your child vanishes. Parents, like everyone else, are human beings, and prone to human error. Not that hiring me was an error," she hastened on as he raised a brow. "My point is that you're bound to make mistakes. The only thing to do is the best you can."

"You're right, of course, though I confess, I take little comfort in it. I don't . . ." He set aside his spoon and looked up. "I'm not a particularly good father, Seton."

"I wouldn't say that," she demurred, thinking of her conversation with Colin. "You're a neglectful father, certainly, and far too indulgent. But you could be a very good father, I think, if you took a little trouble."

"God," he muttered, laughing a little, "you really don't mince words, do you?"

"No," she admitted. "Besides, it does your boys no good for me to give you false opinions of your abilities as a parent. Far better for me to tell you the truth."

Those words were barely out of her mouth before she appreciated the blatant hypocrisy in them, and she hastily reached for her glass, gulping down half its contents, shivering a little at the port's burning sweetness.

"Really, Seton," he murmured, picking up the decanter on the table and leaning forward to refill her glass, "if that's how you drink an excellent vintage port, I shan't bother having Samuel open a second bottle."

Lovely, she thought with an inward groan. *Now he'll think I drink like a fish.* "A second bottle," she mumbled, "wouldn't be wise anyway. I'm not used to spirits."

Unexpectedly, he grinned. "Given your profession, I'm glad to hear it. Speaking of which," he added when she didn't reply, "we've gone a bit far afield. The purpose of this dinner was for me to find out more about you and your teaching. But we're almost finished with dessert, and all I've managed to learn is that I not only neglect my sons, I also spoil them."

Acutely self-conscious, she suppressed the urge to wriggle in her chair, but she refused to soften her critical assessment in order to pacify him. "Do you disagree?" she asked instead.

He looked away. "I'm hardly in a position to disagree. But, I confess, I find it hard to know what to do with them. One of life's little ironies, that."

She frowned, puzzled. "Ironies?"

Leaning forward, he plucked an apple from the bowl on the table and picked up a fruit knife. "One would think," he said meditatively as he began to peel his apple, "I'd know exactly how to handle my sons. Acorns, after all, don't fall far from the tree."

"You were wild as a boy?"

He paused and looked up. "That seems to surprise you."

"It does," she confessed. "You don't seem the least bit wild to me."

"No? How do I seem to you?" he asked, tilting his head as he looked at her. "Don't pull your punches now, Seton," he added when she hesitated. "I'm curious to know."

Had he asked that question two hours ago, her honest opinion would have been that she thought him one of the coldest men she'd ever met. Now she didn't know what to think, or what to say. "You always seem fully in command of yourself," she said at last. "Not wild at all. Self-controlled, even rigid. But then, it's hard for me to know what you're really like," she added, lest he take offense. "You've got such a poker face that most of the time, I have no idea what you're thinking or feeling."

"I see." He looked down at the apple in his hands, frowning thoughtfully. "It's a trick I learned as a boy," he said softly. "Not showing how I really felt about anything. In our household, I learned very early that was one's safest course."

"Safest?" she echoed, struck by the word, suddenly uneasy. "What do you mean?"

"It doesn't matter." He looked up, giving her a shrug and a careless smile, but she wasn't fooled, for the mask was plain to her now. "But just because I didn't let anyone see how I felt, it didn't mean I wasn't wild as hell."

"But were you as wild as your sons?"

"Worse, I'm afraid. Far, far worse."

She thought of herself this morning, tied to a desk and watching in dismay as Colin had climbed the stepladder with scissors in hand, grinned down at her—the devilish little imp—and cut the bellpull. "Oh dear," she murmured. "Your poor parents."

"My mother died when I was three—cholera. As for my father . . ." He paused again, and he was silent so long, Amanda feared he wasn't going to finish what he'd been about to say. But at last, he spoke again. "As for my father, you need not feel any compassion for him. God knows," he added with a laugh as he resumed peeling his apple, "he's never bothered to feel that emotion for anyone else."

There was no humor in his laugh. Quite the contrary, for it seemed to underscore the biting cynicism of his words. "My father, you see, believed with absolute conviction in the maxim, 'Spare the rod, spoil the child.'"

Appalled, she stared at him, the words he'd spoken to her at the lodging house echoing through her mind, words fraught with a new, more sinister significance.

I will tolerate no form of physical punishment, so if the willow switch or belt is your idea of discipline . . .

"I see," she murmured. Physical punishment was not unknown to her, of course. It was quite a common practice, and she'd known many parents and teachers who employed it, but she never had. Just the idea of it never failed to make her slightly sick.

"I, of course, responded to my father's notions of discipline by learning to pretend I didn't give a damn. And by being as ungovernable as possible, of course," he went on, his voice so matter-of-fact that he might have been discussing the weather. "The more he tried to control me, the more harshly he punished me, the more I rebelled."

This was not the time, she decided, to point out that his own method of parenting, the antithesis of his father's, came with its own set of problems and had a similar result. It was clear he already knew that.

"But you're not wild anymore," she said instead, watching him as he continued peeling the skin from the apple with his knife in a long, curly strip. "You're a responsible Member of Parliament, and you don't have a rake's reputation. So, what changed you?"

His hands went still. "I met my wife."

At that simple declaration, Amanda's heart twisted in her chest, though what emotion she felt was hard to define. It was compassion and understanding and something else—a little tinge of envy, perhaps. Lady Patricia Cavanaugh had not only captured the heart of a rake, she had also reformed him, proving that a common female fantasy could, once in a blue moon, become reality. In Amanda's case, the result of loving a rake had been ruin. "I see," she said, unable to think of anything else to say.

With an abrupt move, he set aside the knife and sat back with his peeled apple. "Why I'm rattling on this way mystifies me, for I'm not a talkative man, as a rule."

"Yes," she agreed, smiling a little. "I've appreciated that point."

"I've told you more about myself and my family than I ever tell any-one. Hell, I've even told you about my father, and that is something, I can assure you, I never do."

"Never?"

"Never." He looked up, studying her as he took a bite of apple, then he said, "You're remarkably easy to talk to, Seton."

Considering the fact that she had been striving to keep the conversation on him and his sons rather than herself, that wasn't as surprising to her as it might be to him. "Well, as you said, you don't really know me, and it's often easier to talk to someone you don't know."

"True. And it helps that you're a man."

She gave an involuntary laugh, but it was not, sadly, a masculine-sounding laugh, and she hastily covered it with a cough. Reaching for her glass, she took another swallow of port and strove for something manly to say.

"For my part," she said at last, setting down her glass, "I find women extraordinarily difficult to talk to. But," curiosity impelled her to add, "I wouldn't have thought a man like you would have that problem."

"No?" He ate another bite of apple as he considered that. "I'm curious what makes you say that."

She thought of his laughter of a short time ago, and her toes curled again in her shoes, heat unfurling in her body. "Just an impression."

"An erroneous one, I assure you. At least, nowadays. I have found that my present life is much easier if I limit my conversations with women to the bare minimum—especially when it comes to the women of my own set."

"You mean women of the ton?"

He grinned, a charming grin that sent her stomach plummeting. "Well, a man doesn't really have to worry about what he says to a woman of the demimonde."

She blushed again, making him laugh. "I take it," he added, "you've had no experience in that regard?"

Amanda looked away, her face hot, and she feared if she didn't turn this conversation, he'd be offering to take her to a brothel.

"But you," she said, feeling a bit desperate, "you're a man of the world. You grew up among the aristocracy. You've been married, and to a duke's sister no less. Why would conversing with women of your own set discomfit you?"

He made a face. "It didn't used to do."

"Ah," she murmured, remembering his conversation with Galbraith in the newspaper office. "As a second son with a small allowance and a new MP with a minuscule salary, you've been considered a poor marriage prospect, but now that you're the heir . . ."

"Just so. You grasp the point admirably. Because I was so damnably wild, my father had disinherited me, and I showed no signs of wishing to heal the breach, making it unlikely I'd ever receive more than the minimum income the estate is required to pay me. I also had no desire to marry—I was having far too much fun for that. So, the women of my set left me in peace."

"Yet, you did marry."

"Had anyone tried to force Pat on me, I'd have run for the door, but we met quite by accident. I never expected to fall in love." He paused, a faint smile curving his lips. "It hit me like a ton of bricks the first time I saw her face. And somehow, despite my wild reputation, I won her over." He gave a laugh. "I can't think how."

Amanda wouldn't have understood it either two short hours ago. She understood it now. She tore her gaze from his laughing face and took a swallow of port.

"The rum thing is . . ." he said, and paused for another bite of apple. "After I married, I became much more intriguing to other women—the married ones anyway. I've shocked you," he added as Amanda made a stifled sound.

"I'm not shocked. Well," she amended as he raised an eyebrow, "maybe I am, a little."

"I didn't reciprocate, if that's what's you're thinking," he said dryly. "As I said, I loved my wife. She was laughter and sunshine and music—everything that was good in the world. And when she died . . ."

He paused, set aside his half-eaten apple, and reached for his port. "Sorry," he said lightly, and took a drink. "Being maudlin at dinner is in terribly poor taste. My apologies."

"There is no need to apologize, my lord."

"As I told you, you're a good listener, so that's my excuse." He looked down at his glass, running his finger idly up and down the stem. "The point is, now that I'm set to become the Marquess of Rolleston, set to inherit a lucrative slew of estates and investments, I have become the thing every man dreads."

"Wealthy?" she guessed jokingly.

He gave a shout of laughter. "No, Seton." He paused, lifting his glass in a toast. "A desirable *parti*," he corrected, and took a drink.

"Even though you already have a son to inherit after you and a second son as well?"

His smile faltered a little, taking on a brittle curve. "It appears there are quite a few women who care more about money for themselves than they do about securing future titles for their sons."

"There can't be that many women so mercenary," she said, compelled to defend her own sex, momentarily forgetting that she was supposed to be a member of the opposite one. "There can't be," she amended. "I refuse to believe it."

"You're so young," he murmured.

"Or perhaps you're just terribly cynical."

"No perhaps about that," he agreed at once. "But I don't want to shatter your ideals about the fair sex before you've even had the chance to appreciate their finer qualities—of which there are many. But for my own part, I often find the company of women exhausting. You, Seton, have been more enjoyable company than any woman could possibly be."

It was meant to be a compliment, but Amanda couldn't say she found it so. In fact, it had the curious result of making her feel rather depressed.

"But," he added before she could manage an expression of thanks that didn't include a healthy dose of sarcasm, "we've talked about me long enough." He leaned forward, setting down his glass, making her fear that the interrogation was about to commence. "One of the main purposes of this dinner was for me to find out more about you, and we're nearly done and I haven't uncovered a thing. You're an oyster, Seton."

She pretended not to understand. "I thought you would prefer to discuss the boys. They're far more important than I am."

"You said yourself there's not much to report in regard to the boys, and God knows, I've bent your ear long enough about me, so we've come to you by default. Your father was American, I believe you said. What brought you to England?"

She might have known she wouldn't be able to avoid talking about herself all evening. "My mother was English. She fell gravely ill when I was twelve. She wanted to return home," she explained, glad she'd decided from the start to stick to the truth as much as possible. Telling lies, she was only just beginning to appreciate, was an exhausting business. "So, my father resigned his chair, and we came back to England. Mama only lived six months after that—it was cancer, and it overtook her very quickly. But at least she was able to see her homeland again, be reunited with a few of her relations, and be buried here, as she'd wished. Papa and I were both glad of that."

"I'm sorry about your mother. Cancer is quite painful, I understand."

His voice was offhand, but not perfunctory. Nor was it gushing with sympathy, and yet, its very lack of pathos caused Amanda's throat to constrict. "Yes," she said at last, surprised by the catch in her own voice, and how hard it was to talk about her mother's death, even after almost sixteen years. "Very painful."

"If your mother's relations are here, why are you not with them? Why are you out in the world alone at your age, earning your living?"

"Probably for the same reason you don't live with your father," she quipped, reaching for her port.

She'd meant it as a joke, but he didn't laugh. He jerked upright in his chair, his expression suddenly the hard, remorseless one she was used to, and she felt a jolt of fear, wondering if she'd somehow given herself away. But his next words obliterated that notion.

"What did they do to you?" he asked, his voice low, fierce, and vibrating with anger, and she realized that he was not angry with her, he was angry *for* her.

Amanda's chest tightened, and though she opened her mouth to answer, no words came out. She could only look at him, pleasure flooding through her, the simple pleasure of knowing he cared, however superficially, about her well-being. That a man would express such concern for her welfare was like a balm over the wounds of her past experience, and she was lost for a reply.

"Did they abuse you?" he demanded. "Beat you, hurt you—what the devil?" he added, sounding confounded as Amanda shook her head and began to smile. "God, Seton, why are you smiling, in heaven's name?"

At once, Amanda wiped the smile off her face and looked away. Reaching toward the plate between them, she picked up a crumbled bit of Stilton and ate it, not sure how much to say. Her mother's relations hadn't abused her, they simply refused to have anything to do with her now, but she could hardly tell Lord Kenyon the reasons for that.

"I only meant," she said at last, "that my mother's relations are tiresome, and I have no desire to live with them. They were by no means abusive. But thank you," she added, "for worrying on my behalf."

"Yes, well," he muttered, and it was his turn to look away, "anyone would, I daresay."

"No," she correctly softly, shaking her head. "Most people wouldn't, I'm afraid."

She regretted the words at once, afraid they smacked of self-pity, but thankfully, he didn't make a show of sympathy that would have embarrassed them both. "Either way," he said, sounding a bit nettled, "I still don't see what you were smiling about."

"Oh, that." She paused, struggling for a way to explain that wouldn't give her away.

Think like a man, she told herself, reaching for another bite of cheese to give herself time.

"It's good to know my employer's in my corner, that's all," she said after a moment, striving to sound offhand. "I like to think it means I've passed muster."

That sounded manly enough, she decided, but she made the mistake of looking at him and all her hard-won efforts to think like a man went straight out the window.

He was watching her, smiling a little, his head tilted to one side, the tawny lights in his tobacco-brown hair glinting in the candlelight, shredding any notions she had of forgetting she was a woman. "Is my approval important to you all of a sudden?"

It was. Dear God, it was. And why? Because tonight she'd begun to appreciate how handsome he was and how charming he could be. Her throat went dry at that rather galling realization, and she looked away. "Not a bit," she lied.

"Good," he said, grinning, his eyes teasing. "You're cocky enough already, and I wouldn't wish to make you more conceited."

"No fear." She grinned back at him as she picked up her glass of port. "The moment I start to think how amazing I am, those boys of yours knock me right off my trolley."

He laughed, making Amanda appreciate again just why women wanted to console the grieving widower. He thought it was solely because of his newfound position as Rolleston's heir, but she knew it was much more than that. Despite his casual parenting, it was clear that he loved his sons, and nothing appealed to women more than a man who loved his children. Oddly enough, the fact that he was rather inept at raising them had the curious effect of making him even more appealing. And now that she'd seen beneath his cool inscrutability, she knew there was humor in him, and intelligence.

Her gaze slid to his mouth. There was passion, too. The passion of a man who had loved his wife so much that he'd become a monk after her death, avoiding feminine company like the plague. No wonder the women of his set found him wildly attractive. Amanda suddenly wanted to kick herself for her own obtuseness.

"It must be hard," he murmured, breaking the silence, "to be forced to manage completely on your own at your age. Is there no one who can look out for you?"

Amanda stiffened, those words like a splash of cold water, reminding her that his attractiveness to women had nothing to do with her, and it never would. And she didn't want it to. "I look out for myself," she said stiffly and set down her glass. "I prefer it that way."

"Of course," he agreed at once. "I didn't mean to imply otherwise. Every young man wants to make his own way, and I appreciate that you're proud, Seton, but as you go on in life, you'll find that things are much easier if one has family, or at least a few friends, standing by."

She'd had both, once upon a time. Her eyes burned, and she looked away, feeling weak, stupid, and terribly fragile, all the emotions she most despised. She was not like this, she thought, frustration flaring inside her, her father's reminders to her in the wake of her mother's death coming back to her. She was not fragile. She was not weak. She didn't need to be looked after.

Thankfully, the mantel clock chimed just then, saving her from having to reply.

"Half past ten already?" she said and shoved back her chair. "Forgive me, my lord, but I really must bid you good night. I'm by way of being a . . . um . . . an early to bed man, especially nowadays. Those boys of yours run me ragged, I must confess, and I need my rest."

"Of course," he said as they both stood up. "We'll talk further when I return from York. We'll have dinner again, and you can give me a report on my sons' progress."

Her dismay at the idea of spending another evening with him was blunted somewhat by the news of his departure. "You still intend to go north then?"

"I must. I'll take the Monday train, I think."

"So soon?"

"If I don't visit my constituents now, while Parliament is still in recess, I won't have another chance until the Christmas holiday, which is a horrible time for political meetings. And now that I'm satisfied you don't intend to kidnap my sons, I see no reason to delay."

She made a face. "Given what happened this morning, it's far more likely they'll try to kidnap me and have me shipped off on a boat to Shanghai."

"I'm not sure that's the sort of thing you ought to be telling me. It's not very reassuring."

"I said they'd probably try. Not that they'd succeed. No, by the time you return, I will have those boys shipshape and Bristol fashion, I promise you. After this morning's humiliation," she added as he gave her a dubious look, "my pride demands it."

"Very well. When I return, you can tell me all about how you've managed things, and you can crow about your success to your heart's content. But," he added at once, "I will also expect to hear more about you. I shan't let you evade the subject of yourself so much the next time we talk."

She pasted on a smile. "I shall look forward to telling you all about me."

With that, she gave a bow, just as a gentleman should, and left the dining room, glad dinner was over. Granted, it hadn't been quite the interrogation she'd been dreading, but nonetheless, being in his sights all evening, acting a part, striving to say only enough and not too much, had been exhausting. And despite her vigilance, she knew she had made mistakes.

In her own room, she closed the door behind her with heartfelt relief, vowing that the next time they dined together, she would be fully accustomed to her new role. To be convincing, she had to not only talk and act like a man, but also to *think* like one.

Suddenly, the notion left her feeling a bit bleak. Damn it all, she thought, aggravated with herself, being a woman had always been more of a hindrance to her ambitions than a help. It would be far, far better to just forget altogether that she was a woman.

An image of Lord Kenyon flashed across her mind, and just the memory of his brilliant smile and the unexpected sound of his laughter were enough to bring back a faint, womanly thrill, and Amanda leaned back against the closed door of her room with a groan. Forgetting she was a woman, she realized in chagrin, was going to be harder than she'd ever imagined.

Chapter 9

Lord Kenyon left for Yorkshire on the early train Monday morning as he had planned. The boys were disappointed, of course, but though Amanda felt badly on their behalf, she couldn't help being relieved for herself. Dinner with him had underscored just how difficult it was going to be maintaining her lie under his watchful eyes. Worse, their evening together had reminded her of her own femininity, something that had no place in her new life.

She had no intention of crying off, however, not only because she had no money and no other job prospects, but also because she already loved being a tutor, and despite their talent for trouble—or perhaps even because of it—she was becoming quite fond of her charges.

In the wake of Lord Kenyon's departure, things did get a bit easier for Amanda. During the three weeks that followed, she established a set schedule for the twins, and though they balked at every opportunity, Amanda stuck to her guns. Flexibility could come later; for the present, a set routine was crucial to establishing order, and whether it was bath time, playtime, bedtime, or lessons, Amanda kept them up to snuff and made short shrift of any excuses.

She found a laundry only a block away from the house, and when her monthly came, she was able to sneak the soiled rags in and out of the house in a burlap sack she hid in folds of her mackintosh, using the pretext of dashing out with letters for the post.

She avoided the other two servants as much as possible, keeping to herself in the nursery even after the twins were in bed. Reasons were easy to find—assignments to grade, lesson plans to make, a little quiet time alone, the feeling she shouldn't leave the boys, even when they were supposed to be asleep. Mrs. Richmond and Samuel didn't seem to take offense at her desire to remain upstairs in the evenings, though Amanda suspected that was borne of relief that the twins were no longer in their care as much as it was a respect for Amanda's privacy.

Even on a set schedule, the boys remained a handful, challenging her authority at every turn, but her plan to exhaust them into submission with constant activities and outings did prove somewhat effective. Unfortunately, that strategy also had its drawbacks.

"Amanda?"

At the sound of her name, she gave a start, jerking upright in her chair. "Hmm?" she mumbled, blinking as she tried to clear her sleep-dazed senses. "What?"

Across from her, Mrs. Finch was shaking her head. "Poor child," she murmured. "You're dead on your feet. What have those aristocrats in the West End been doing to you?"

"I'm perfectly well, Mrs. Finch," she assured the woman opposite, but the huge yawn that immediately followed this assurance told a different story.

"No, you're not. You're exhausted. I can see it in your face. Three weeks you've been in this new post, and each week when I see you, you seem more tired than the week before."

"Two energetic boys rather wear one out."

"You don't need to come here on every day out, you know."

"But I do," she reminded. "I'm tutoring you, just as I promised. And," she added when her former landlady waved aside that consideration with a dismissive gesture, "I'm also tutoring Mr. Mackenzie. Would you have me go back on my word to him, too?"

"Hugh Mackenzie's quite able to take care of himself without any lessons from you, my dear. Why he felt he needed to learn mathematics escapes me."

"He wants to be sure his pub is making a profit."

She sniffed. "I've not met a Scot yet who didn't know down to the penny where his money was."

Amanda pressed a smile from her lips and refrained from pointing out that Mr. Mackenzie's Scottish heritage hadn't yet deterred the landlady from walking out with him on a fine night for ice cream or a music hall revue. "Mr. Mackenzie aside," she said instead, "even if I wanted to rest on my days out, my charges would never allow it. Those boys would be storming into my room every fifteen minutes with some new scheme or idea. And I haven't the blunt to shop or attend entertainments. No, Mrs. Finch, if I want any rest, I'm afraid you're stuck with me on Tuesday afternoons for a bit longer."

The older woman smiled, leaned over the polished Jacobean dining table where they had been doing lessons in French, and patted Amanda's hand. "Then at least let me offer you tea."

It was just on four o'clock, a bit early for tea, but Amanda didn't argue. A cuppa was her former landlady's cure for everything from colds to cholera, and since her eyes were heavy and her head a bit groggy from her lack of sleep and her all-too-brief nap of a few moments ago, a cup of Mrs. Finch's strong India tea would be just the thing. "That sounds lovely, thank you."

Mrs. Finch turned in her chair to give the bellpull in the wall a tug, and moments later, Ellen, the lodging house's parlor maid, came at a run, brushing self-consciously at her black dress and white apron. "Yes, Mrs. Finch?"

"Tea, Ellen, if you please, for Miss Leighton and myself. And bring some of those nice digestive biscuits, too."

The maid cast a dubious eye over Amanda's brown wool trousers and waistcoat before returning her attention to her employer. "Yes, ma'am," she murmured.

She departed for the kitchens, returning a few minutes later with a tray of tea things and sweet biscuits. Depositing the tray in front of her employer, she gave Amanda's clothes another puzzled glance, then left again.

"Ellen doesn't seem to know what to make of my new wardrobe," Amanda commented, laughing a little as Mrs. Finch poured tea.

"Can't say as I blame her, dear. I hardly recognize you myself. Gives me a turn, it does, every time you come to visit." She added sugar and milk to Amanda's teacup, shaking her head. "Such a waste, if you ask me."

Amanda frowned in bewilderment as her former landlady slid her teacup across the table. "What's a waste?"

"You in men's clothes. You're such a pretty girl. If you took a little trouble, you could be a beauty."

"I doubt that," Amanda said. "And this shameless flattery," she added with mock severity before the other woman could protest, "shall not impel me to go easier on you over French verbs." She held out her hand, and the other woman handed her the sheet of paper that contained the work of her latest lesson.

"I still don't know why such a disguise was necessary," Mrs. Finch said as Amanda took a gulp of tea, picked up a pencil, and began scanning the other woman's essay for errors.

Amanda paused, her fingers tightening around her pencil. "For me to obtain any post, some sort of subterfuge was always going to be necessary, I'm afraid." She forced herself to look up and meet the other woman's gaze. "Given my past."

Mrs. Finch sighed. "I supposed you're right. And I admit when you first came here, I had my doubts about letting rooms to a woman like you." She wagged a finger at Amanda in somewhat maternal fashion. "And if I'd seen you with any gentlemen followers hanging about, I'd have tossed you out straightaway, my girl."

"Yes, ma'am," Amanda agreed, well aware of the fact. Like most people, Mrs. Finch had known everything there was to know about her the moment she'd first given her name, but thankfully, the landlady had taken pity on her and decided, albeit reluctantly, to let her a room. Thinking of that, Amanda's conscience pricked her. "I know I put you in a difficult position asking for that letter," she mumbled. "I'm sorry. It's just that I couldn't see any other way."

Mrs. Finch merely seemed amused. "Don't be sorry, child. If I didn't want to do it, I'd have refused. Simple as that. Besides, I've done a few things in my time that would make my late mother turn in her grave, God rest her soul."

"Really?" Amanda was intrigued. "Like what?"

The older woman's amusement faded a fraction. "I'll not be saying, but I know as well as anyone that life is hard for a woman alone in the world. We're entitled to take a few liberties with the truth now and then, if you ask me."

So that was why she'd let Amanda a room here. Some dark secret in her own past. Amanda's curiosity deepened, but it wasn't her business, so she didn't pry. "Still," she said instead, "let me thank you again. And you needn't fear that you'll get into trouble over this. As I told you when I applied for the post, if I'm caught, I'll take all the blame. I'll tell his lordship I've been posing as a man all along and you and Mackenzie were duped by me just as he was."

Mrs. Finch made a derisive sound, waving a hand. "Oh, I'm not worried about that. I can hold my own with any man, even a lord. And don't worry about Mackenzie either. He's always happy to play a trick on a Brit. Enjoying himself hugely, I'm sure, that his lordship's been fooled into thinking a slip of a girl like you is a man." She paused for a chuckle, then sobered and shook her head, becoming earnest again. "No, that character letter isn't what I'm concerned about."

"Then what is worrying you?"

"You, my dear."

Amanda stared, astonished. "You're worried about me? But why?"

"Because I'm fond of you, you silly goose!"

"Oh." Amanda colored up, feeling a rush of warm affection. "It's very good of you, ma'am," she replied, "but honestly, you needn't worry."

"Well, someone has to," the other woman countered incisively. "Because I'm still not sure you know what you're doing. Cutting off your hair, posing as a man, of all the harebrained schemes. Those boys need someone to watch them, all well and good. You want to change your name, no harm in that, and perfectly understandable, I say. But what I don't see is why you couldn't have just applied to be a nanny."

"Because a nanny wasn't what Lord Kenyon was looking for," she reminded, and returned her attention to the paper in front of her, marking an error in the French text with her pencil. "He required a tutor."

"There are other jobs." Mrs. Finch gave a sniff and picked up her teacup. "And more fish in the sea than ever came out of it. On the other hand . . ."

She paused, and Amanda looked up again to find her former landlady grinning at her like a mischievous child. "Most of the available fish aren't nearly so good-looking."

Amanda stirred on the hard kitchen chair, remembering just how and when she'd come to that exact realization about his lordship, and the blush in her cheeks deepened, much to her aggravation. "Oh, stop," she muttered.

"I'm twice your age, and he made even my heart go pitter-pat. Why you'd want to dress like a man in front of him, I can't think."

"As I said, I didn't have a choice. And it hardly matters how I dress, since he is my employer."

"He's a widower, isn't he?" Mrs. Finch gave her a knowing smile. "I'll wager he's lonely."

Amanda thought of him, of how he'd looked, staring down at his apple, melancholy in his face.

I met my wife.

She forced the image away. "My former employer, Mr. Bartlett, tried to show me just how lonely widowers are," Amanda countered dryly. "I was—and I remain—unimpressed. And in any case, I doubt Lord Kenyon would appreciate a pretty woman even if she were right under his nose. He wants nothing to do with any of us."

"Don't you believe it! I know men and their ways. They always appreciate a pretty woman. As a nanny, you'd have at least a chance of catching his eye. As it is . . ." She paused to glance over Amanda's brown suit and shook her head with profound disappointment.

"For someone who was concerned I'd have gentlemen followers," Amanda said in some amusement, "you seem far too inclined to find me one."

"Lord Kenyon wouldn't be that sort," Mrs. Finch replied, looking a bit shocked by the notion. "He seems a most respectable gentleman."

So did Lord Halsbury, she almost replied, but she bit back that dry rejoinder. "If you think any woman, however pretty, has a chance with Lord Kenyon," she said instead, "you are sadly mistaken. And," she added before the other woman could offer any more thoughts on men and their ways, "even if you're right, it hardly matters, since in his eyes, I'm not the nanny, I'm the *male* tutor. And," she added for good measure, "I'm not the least bit attracted to him anyway."

At once, her toes curled in her shoes and heat spread throughout her body, making her appreciate that her words had been more of a wish than a declaration of fact. Acutely aware of the hot blush in her cheeks, she gave a cough and tapped the papers before her with the tip of her pencil, striving for a brisk and businesslike manner. "Now, about your essay—"

"Of course, it may not be too late to catch his eye, if—"

Amanda groaned, appreciating that the other woman was not going to be deterred from this topic, and set down her pencil. "If you have some vision in your mind for a great romance here and a happy ending for the ruined but repentant girl, do give it up, Mrs. Finch. His lordship thinks I'm a man. And since it's doubtful he has any romantic predilections of that sort," she added with a touch of humor, "a romance between us is most unlikely, don't you think?"

"Maybe. Maybe not." She gave a shrug and took a sip of tea. "He'll see through this disguise of yours eventually, my girl."

"I hope not, but for the sake of argument, suppose he does? What are you suggesting? That if I'm caught, I ought to play the helpless female and throw myself on his mercy?"

"Why not? Some men have a deep sense of chivalry."

"I fear Lord Kenyon would be far more likely to give me the sack than make me a romantic offer, even an illicit one."

"That isn't what I meant, dear," Mrs. Finch said with a touch of prim reproof. "But you did what you did in order to survive. It wouldn't go amiss to tell him that, if it becomes necessary. And to underscore the bleakness of your circumstances and the fact that you are alone in the world, helpless and poor."

Amanda had no intention of doing any such thing, but she didn't say so. "Goodness, you make my life sound like a penny dreadful," she teased.

Mrs. Finch sighed. "I can see you are not taking what I say seriously. Do you have any sort of plan for your future?"

"Of course I do. I just need enough time in Lord Kenyon's household to save a bit of money. A year, perhaps, and then—"

"A year?" Mrs. Finch interrupted with lively scorn. "You're lucky you've lasted this long. How will you ever manage a year?"

"Well, however long I last, I just need to save enough of my wages for passage back to America before I'm found out. In America, I can easily find a teaching post, even without any references. I'm sure they need teachers on the frontier, and they're probably not too picky about whom they hire."

"The American frontier?" Mrs. Finch looked appalled. "Oh, let's hope it won't come to that."

It would, she feared. Her past would always come back to haunt her as long as she stayed in England. In America, though, she had the chance for a fresh start. She just needed enough money to get there.

"I don't want to hear any talk about you going off to America," Mrs. Finch said, breaking into her thoughts. "If he tosses you out, you come straight back here. I could do with another parlor maid. You'll have to share the attic with Ellen and Betsy, of course, and domestic service isn't the sort of work that an educated young lady ought to do, but at least you'll have a roof over your head, food to eat, and a decent wage."

Amanda was too overcome by such a kind gesture to speak for several moments. "Thank you, ma'am," she said at last. "You're very good."

"Nonsense," the landlady said tartly. "You still owe me quite a few more lessons before we're square about that letter, and I've no intention of letting you out of your obligation so you can go gallivanting off to another continent."

Amanda wasn't fooled by the acerbic reply, but she let it go. She was, first and foremost, a realist, and she knew Mrs. Finch's offer was one she might need to take up. She'd learned the hard way what it meant to burn bridges.

"Yes, ma'am," she murmured respectfully, and picked up her pencil.

BY THE TIME Amanda arrived back at Upper Brook Street, night had fallen, and the door into the servants' corridor had barely shut behind her before a distinctly anxious voice was calling to her.

"Mr. Seton? Mr. Seton, is that you?"

"Yes, Mrs. Richmond," she called back, and began unbuttoning her mackintosh. "I've returned."

The cook appeared in the doorway at the other end of the corridor. "Thank heaven you're back at last!"

Noting the urgency in the cook's voice, Amanda paused, her mackintosh halfway off her shoulders. "What's happened?" she asked sharply. "Are the boys all right?"

"The boys?" Mrs. Richmond made a dismissive sound, wiping her hands on her apron as she hurried down the corridor toward Amanda. "Oh, they're all right. Aren't they always? It's the rest of us that suffer."

Relieved, Amanda slid the rest of the way out of her mackintosh and hung it on the peg closest to the door. "What's the trouble?"

"His lordship's returned." Pausing halfway along the corridor, the cook pulled the pieces of a man's black evening suit from the pegs along the wall. "He arrived less than an hour ago."

Amanda frowned, puzzled. "Wasn't he supposed to be arriving on the afternoon train tomorrow?"

"He was, but one of his friends, Baron Weston, was returning to London tonight, so they arranged to come back together. Want to discuss some issue before Parliament reconvenes on Thursday, I expect. It's put things in a tumult around here, let me tell you." She paused to draw breath, then went on, "The boys' dinner is a bit late, I'm afraid—"

"They haven't had dinner?" Amanda made a sound of dismay. "But it's after seven."

"Now, Mr. Seton, I know you're quite the army general about that schedule of yours, but the delay couldn't be helped. His lordship wanted to see the boys straightaway when he arrived, and if his lordship wants to see the boys, it's not our place to gainsay him."

"Of course not," Amanda said at once. "I realize that. And I'm glad he wants to spend time with them."

"It wasn't much time, sadly. Half an hour and a bit was all he could spare."

"Half an hour? Is that all? But he's been away three weeks." Amanda paused, bewildered and a bit disappointed. "On his first evening back, wouldn't he want to spend more time with them than that? Perhaps dine with them, or—"

"Dine with the boys? What, an earl dining in the nursery?" She laughed. "Don't be a goose! No, he's going out this evening. Lord Weston's hosting a little dinner party, I understand, so he'll be off to Grosvenor Square in a bit. I've had to unpack his trunk, draw a bath, and press an evening suit and a fresh shirt for him. I've scarce had time to draw breath."

"Of course, of course," Amanda said soothingly. "And I'm sorry I wasn't here to help. Had I known he was arriving back early, I'd have come home sooner. But why—"

"I've no time to talk now," the cook interrupted before she could ask why Samuel had not been able to assist. "I really must get on with the boys' dinner. Here," she added, thrusting the suit she carried into Amanda's arms.

Amanda took the garments automatically, but the moment her fingers touched the fine, luxurious wool, she knew this evening suit didn't belong to her. "This isn't mine."

She tried to hand the clothes back, but Mrs. Richmond didn't take them. "I know it's not yours, Mr. Seton," she said impatiently, looping a white satin bow tie around Amanda's neck. "Heavens, you are in a daze tonight, aren't you? I laundered your evening suit and put it back in your room ages ago, the morning after your dinner with his lordship, in fact. Though heaven help us, you do need a new one, and no mistake. You must have noticed it in the armoire, surely?"

"Of course," Amanda began, but she was again interrupted.

"This is one of his lordship's evening suits. It's been in his dressing closet and it needed a brush and a press so he could wear it this evening. I've done that, so you can take it up to him. You'll have to do for him, you know," she added over her shoulder as she turned and began walking away. "Samuel's out this evening."

"Out?" Amanda curled her fingers tightly around the black superfine in her hands, a sinking feeling in the pit of her stomach. "What do you mean?"

"Samuel asked if he could have the evening off, and since Lord Kenyon wasn't expected back until tomorrow, I agreed. That means you'll have to valet. He asked me to send you up the minute you returned."

"Me? Valet his lordship?" Dismayed, Amanda stared at the cook's retreating back. "But I can't!" Her voice rose a notch with those words, gaining a more feminine pitch, and she forced herself to pause, clear her throat, and take a breath.

"He's been doing for himself for the past fortnight," she said at last. "He can't do so for one more night?"

Mrs. Richmond stopped by the kitchen door and turned, her astonished face telling Amanda she was doomed. "Why should he have to do for himself?" she countered, her voice surprised and a bit irritated. "He has you, doesn't he?"

Amanda hastened to smooth things over. "Yes, of course, but I won't be any good to him at all. I've never valeted anyone, nor have I ever had a valet. I've no idea how it's done."

"Then, I hope you're a quick study." Mrs. Richmond started to reenter the kitchen, then paused again. "Well, don't stand there gawping," she said, jerking a thumb toward the ceiling. "He's already running late."

She vanished into the kitchen, and Amanda's dismay deepened into dread.

"You don't understand," she whispered, staring down the empty corridor. "I can't do this."

Even as she spoke, however, Amanda knew she had no choice. Taking another deep breath, she turned and started up the servants' staircase.

JAMIE SHOVED UP the sleeves of his dressing robe and burrowed into yet another drawer of the chiffonier in his room, exasperated that he couldn't find even one white bow tie.

Cravats, ascots, Napoleons, and various other pieces of neckwear were unceremoniously raked out of the drawer and onto the floor as he searched for the elusive slip of white satin that was *de rigueur* for any dinner party. "I really need a valet," he muttered under his breath for perhaps the hundredth time in the past month. "This is becoming ridiculous."

The tap on his door did not distract him from his purpose. "Come in," he called, shoving aside a handful of derbys and continuing to rummage through his tie drawer, barely noticing when the door did not open. But when the knock came again, he looked up, noting with some impatience the closed door's reflection in his dressing mirror. "For God's sake, come in," he shouted, and returned to his task.

The door creaked as it swung inward, and Jamie glanced up again, noting that Seton was standing in the doorway, looking paler than ever, the pieces of Jamie's evening suit clasped to his chest.

"Seton, at last!" he exclaimed. "I thought you'd never arrive in time to help me."

He resumed his search, but after a moment, he looked up again, frowning as he realized Seton had not moved from the doorway. "Well, don't just stand there, man, hugging my suit as if it's a demirep," he urged, beckoning with an impatient hand. "Lay it out on the bed, then help me dress. I'm terribly late."

"I thought you didn't care much about punctuality," the younger man replied as he came in, closed the door behind him, and proceeded to comply with his instructions.

"I do when it's a dinner party," Jamie assured, returning to his own task. "It's the height of bad manners to be late for that, and at Weston's, it would be disastrous. He's got a French chef, temperamental as an opera singer. I'm already a last-minute addition to the party, and if I hold up the show, the fellow's likely to resign in a fit of pique and Weston will be cross as hell with me. I need his support for the education bill and he's dancing around it like a deb at first ball, blast him. I can't afford to give him offense. Damn it all, don't I have a single clean white tie to my name?"

"I brought one for you," Seton told him, gesturing to the needed article, which was now spread out neatly on the bed beside his suit and the undergarments that he'd already laid out himself. "Mrs. Richmond pressed it."

"Ah." Relieved, happy to abandon his search, Jamie took up his jewel case from where he'd laid it on the chiffonier earlier, then crossed to the foot of the bed where Seton was waiting to assist him. Dropping the jewel case onto the counterpane, he reached for the sash of his robe.

"Hand me those underdrawers," he ordered, and started to slide his dressing robe off his shoulders, but he paused as Seton made a choked sound and turned away.

"Are you all right?" Jamie asked, his robe caught at his elbows, noting the other man's flushed face with some concern.

Seton nodded, his face turned away, and coughed several more times. "Yes, my lord," he managed after a moment. "Just a . . . ahem . . . tickle in my throat."

"When we're finished, put the boys to bed, then go down to the kitchens, have Mrs. Richmond make you a tisane, and go to bed yourself," Jamie ordered, sliding his dressing robe off his shoulders and letting it fall to the ground. "The last thing anyone in this house needs is for you to catch a cold."

Seton nodded, still coughing, his head buried in the crook of his elbow. Leaving the other man to compose himself, Jamie leaned over the bed to retrieve his underdrawers, but he'd barely picked them up before he tossed them down again with a sound of aggravation. "Damn. I forgot my collar. Choose me some studs and links while I find one, will you?"

Nodding to the case on the bed, he turned away and padded naked across the room to rectify his earlier oversight. Thankfully, his supply of fresh collars was more plentiful than his supply of white ties, and Jamie was soon able to find one.

Seton had stopped coughing and was rummaging through the now-open jewel case by the time Jamie returned to the bed. Head bent, the younger man didn't even look up as Jamie paused beside him, seeming quite preoccupied choosing just the right jewelry for the occasion. Too preoccupied, Jamie realized.

Deuce take it, he thought, noting Seton's still-pink cheeks and bent head in some amusement as he pulled on his drawers and tied the drawstring. *I believe the poor lad's embarrassed.*

If so, it was understandable, Jamie supposed, reaching for his undershirt. Sickly as a child, educated at home, Seton had obviously been accustomed to a level of privacy that no boy who'd attended public school could ever have enjoyed. The dormitories of Harrow were anything but private.

He pulled his undershirt over his head and buttoned it himself, then donned his socks and pulled on his trousers. Dressed, more or less, Jamie decided he'd been patient long enough. "Seton, I'm running late," he reminded. "Let's get on with it, if you please."

"Of course." The younger man straightened away from the case, a shirt stud of black enamel and silver clasped in his fingers. He turned, looking so pained that Jamie almost grinned. Taking pity, Jamie suppressed any sign of humor. "My dear chap," he said gently, "studs won't do me much good without a shirt."

Flushing again, the lad set the stud back in the case. "Sorry," he mumbled, his face red again as he reached for Jamie's dress shirt. "I've never . . . umm . . . dressed . . . anyone. Not a man anyway."

"Indeed?" This time the urge to tease was irresistible. "But you've dressed a few women, is that it?"

"That isn't what I meant." The poor chap's face was quickly turning from rosy pink to crimson red. "I meant I've only dressed the boys. And m . . . myself, of c . . . course. I've never valeted a man before."

Aware that time was getting on, Jamie left off the teasing, pulled his shirt from Seton's outstretched fingers and put it on, but once he had tucked the tails and buttoned his trousers, he left the other man to fasten his collar, place his studs, fasten his braces, and tie his tie, for those were tasks accomplished more quickly if done by a valet. At least, that was usually the case, but when it came to doing up a tie, Seton once again proved he was no valet.

"Still crooked," he said, pulling the ends of Jamie's tie to try again. "Sorry, my lord, but this is . . . ahem . . . harder to do on someone else than it is on oneself."

"Is it?" Jamie said, curbing his impatience, reminding himself that his lack of a true valet was his own damn fault. "For my part, I find tying my own ties more exasperating than nearly anything on earth."

"That makes two of us," Seton muttered as he started over. "I don't have the knack of it either. You should have asked Colin to do this."

"Colin knows how to tie a bow tie?"

"He does, and he's far better at it than I am."

Startled, Jamie tilted his chin down enough so that he could look into Seton's face. He opened his mouth to ask how his son had learned that particular skill, but something in the countenance of the lad before him made Jamie pause.

Seton's eyes were narrowed in concentration, his lower lip caught between his teeth, and his cheeks flushed, making him seem even more youthful than usual, but despite that, it seemed exactly the same face he remembered from two weeks ago—the same intense hazel eyes and straight brows, the same square jaw and pointed chin, the same mop of hair that looked, as always, in need of a trim and some pomade. And yet, with the other man's face so near to his own, Jamie couldn't help feeling that something about what he was seeing was different. Or wrong. Or . . . something.

He felt as if he was looking at one of those modern paintings where the artist had deliberately skewed the perspective, making it impossible to discern at close quarters what one was really looking at. He had the sudden desire to retreat a step or two, assume a proper distance as one did in galleries to gain a better view, but he couldn't, for Seton still had hold of his tie.

Unable to move, he slid his gaze down a notch to the hands at his throat. They were at the edge of his vision, but even on the periphery, they seemed absurdly small. He noted the slender wrists, the faint, delicate trace of the veins, the soft, pale skin.

Seton pulled the loops of the bow taut, knuckles brushing the underside of his jaw, and at the skin-to-skin contact, Jamie felt an unexpected sensation, a rush of heat that caught him low in the groin, a sensation that no valet, no man, had ever evoked in him.

Startled, appalled by his own body, he jerked, sucking in a sharp breath as an insane realization flashed into his mind, and as Seton's hands fell away, he knew with sudden, awful clarity just what was wrong and what he was really looking at.

"Good God." He jumped back, staring at the face before him as if he'd never seen it before, the truth hitting him like a splash of freezing water, even as the heat of arousal flamed in his body. "You're a woman!"

"Well, I can't help that!" Seton countered crossly. "It's not like I had a choice."

It was such a nonsensical reply that Jamie laughed in disbelief. He shut his eyes, rubbing his hands over his face, trying to get his bearings. Maybe this was a dream, he thought desperately, one of those bizarre dreams akin to the vicar's wife wearing scarlet silk for Sunday service and no one noticing, or bears in ballerina tutus pirouetting through the drawing room while a party was in progress.

But even as his mind tried to persuade him he was dreaming, he very much feared that he wasn't, for in Seton's absurd reply and defensive voice, there had been no denial.

Seton a woman? Dressing as a man à la George Sand? It was too ludicrous for words. He'd have known. He'd have seen. For God's sake, he thought, had it really been so long since he'd had a woman that he couldn't even recognize them anymore?

He opened his eyes and lowered his gaze to scan the slim frame in men's clothes that stood before him. He could see no sign of feminine curves, but given that ghastly double-breasted jacket, it was hard to tell. And the figure before him was tall, nearly as tall as he, a rare height for a woman, for he was over six feet.

He lifted his gaze a notch, but that did little to help him, for Seton's high collar would conceal the lack of an Adam's apple quite well. Perhaps, Jamie thought, still searching desperately for explanations, his failure to see the woman beneath the clothes was somewhat understandable.

But then, he looked again at Seton's face—the fine, pale complexion, the delicately molded nose, the lack of a beard—and his attempts to justify his woeful lack of observation crumbled. The femininity of the face before him seemed painfully obvious now, as obvious as the proverbial elephant in the drawing room.

His body had perceived the difference before his brain. With a single touch, his body had recognized that there was a woman in those masculine clothes and had responded accordingly. Jamie could take little solace in that, however, for arousal was still coursing through him, making him hot, embarrassed, and randy as hell.

He had to get clear. He took another step backward, shaking his head, staring into those extraordinary, multicolored eyes, eyes that now seemed so utterly feminine, and he felt like a complete idiot.

"A woman." He laughed again, this time at himself. "My God."

"My lord," Seton began, "I'm sorry. I—"

"Get out," Jamie ordered. "Get out of my room."

Seton hesitated a moment, then gave a nod, turned away, and started out of the room. At the door, however, the tutor paused and looked at him over one shoulder. "You can sack me, but—"

"Rest assured, I just did."

"It won't change anything. Hire another tutor, hire a nanny, ship your sons to school—do whatever you like, but nothing will change until you give them the affection and attention they need and deserve. You're their father. Don't be content to watch them play from your window."

Her words were like paraffin on flames, coalescing rage, frustration, arousal, and pain into a white-hot fire, but when he spoke, his voice was controlled, calm, and stone-cold. "You will stay away from my sons, pack your things, and leave first thing in the morning. Now, get out."

Seton departed, and as the door swung shut behind her, his friend Rex's words of a month ago rang loudly in his ears.

You need a woman, my friend, and badly.

At the time, he'd dismissed that notion, but now, he was forced to appreciate how brutally true his friend's wicked remark had been.

Seton's masculine clothes and short hair aside, Jamie knew that if he couldn't recognize a woman the moment she walked through his door, he'd gone too long without one in his bed. Perhaps, he thought grimly, he should invade a brothel and rectify that situation.

A pity he couldn't do it now, for he was still fully aroused, a painful reminder of what he'd been missing the past three years. Unfortunately, however, he didn't have time for brothels and courtesans, not tonight anyway. He moved to undo his trousers, thinking to relieve the unbearable tension the way he always had in the past, but the clock on his mantel began to chime the eight o'clock hour, and he knew that the short walk from here to Grosvenor Square in the cool night air was the only means of relief he had time for.

Swearing like a sailor, he buttoned his trousers back up, grabbed his evening jacket, and followed Seton out the door.

Chapter 10

Of all the things Amanda might have expected to feel should she be discovered, relief had never been among them. But as she went down the servants' staircase, amid the keen disappointment of losing a job she loved, melancholy at the idea of leaving the twins of whom she'd grown terribly fond, and fear of the grim future that awaited her, there was an undeniable hint of relief.

She felt no surprise at having been found out; indeed, she'd known all along that eventually that would happen. But as she had explained to Mrs. Finch, she'd hoped it would take longer than this, long enough for her second plan to come to fruition.

But the future in America that she'd envisioned, where no one knew what she'd done, where she was no longer an object of scandal and shame, wasn't going to happen, at least not for a long, long time. Amanda went down to the kitchens, and as she tried to accept that her foreseeable future was to be a parlor maid in her former landlady's lodging house, her momentary relief evaporated, replaced by a sense of hopelessness.

There was nothing wrong with being a maid, she reminded herself sternly. It was a respectable post in a respectable household, and given her circumstances, she was fortunate to have even been given such an offer. But in taking it, she knew she would be turning her back on the only thing in the world she had ever wanted to do. Other than weekly lessons with Mrs. Finch and Mr. Mackenzie, she would not be able to teach again for a long time. Perhaps never.

Amanda paused at the bottom of the staircase. At least she wouldn't have to live on the street, she thought, her hand gripping the round knob of the newel post as she strove to look on the bright side. She ought to be grateful.

Without warning, a tear slid down her cheek, efforts at optimism and gratitude went to the wall, and she sank down onto the stairs with a sob, overwhelmed by despair.

"Mr. Seton? Is that you?"

At the sound of Mrs. Richmond's voice echoing along the corridor, Amanda jerked upright, brushing away tears with her fingertips. She opened her mouth to answer, but she couldn't seem to make her mouth form words.

Mrs. Richmond came out of the kitchen, wiping her hands on her apron as she emerged into the corridor, and Amanda ducked her head, blinking hard.

"Mr. Seton?" The little cook's voice held lively surprise at the sight of her. "Whatever are you doing sitting on those hard stairs?"

She hastily invented an excuse. "Shoelace," she said, bending over one of her oxfords and making a great show of retying the lace, but Mrs. Richmond didn't seem convinced.

"What's wrong, lad?" she asked gently.

Amanda took a deep breath and forced herself to look up. "I'll be leaving tomorrow. I've been sacked."

"You never have! I don't believe it."

"Nonetheless, it's true."

"He didn't sack you because you didn't prove a good enough valet, surely?"

"I'll go first thing in the morning. My termination was effective immediately, so you shall have to put me in a servant's room tonight."

"Of course, but—"

"When Samuel returns tonight, he'll need to move his things into the nursery and sleep there until a new tutor can be found."

"But what's happened, lad? Won't you tell me?"

"I . . . he . . . ahem . . ." She paused and gave a cough. "It's complicated. But his lordship was quite justified in his action." As she spoke, Amanda didn't bother altering the pitch of her voice to the low, masculine-sounding one she'd been so careful to maintain during the past month. "I deserved to be fired, I assure you."

Mrs. Richmond noticed the change in her voice at once, but her next words proved she didn't yet appreciate the truth behind it. "You sound quite strange, Mr. Seton," she asked, frowning. "Are you ill, is that it? But his lordship would never sack someone for illness—"

"I'm not ill." Not physically anyway, she added to herself, and she felt a sudden wild desire to laugh, because her mental stability was clearly in doubt. Didn't one have to be a bit mental to think different clothes and a new job were all that was needed to erase past mistakes? That replacing a skirt with a pair of trousers could transform one into a different person with a different life?

"Then what is this about?" the little cook demanded, frowning, her round, current-bun face scrunched up with bewilderment and concern. "Tell me this instant, Mr. Seton," she ordered gruffly. "What the bloody hell is going on?"

"It's difficult to explain." Amanda looked down at her masculine clothes, thought of her chopped-off hair, and reminded herself that the farce was over. Time for Adam to go and Amanda to return.

She stood up. "It might be easier to explain things if you could find me a maid's dress," she suggested. "And perhaps a corset?"

"A maid's dress and a *corset*?" Mrs. Richmond stared, her frustration fading back into confusion. "What for? Why on earth does a man require a maid's kit?"

"Well, that's just it, you see." Amanda bit her lip, giving the other woman a look of apology. "I'm not a man."

DURING THE WALK to Grosvenor Square, Jamie was able to bring his wayward body back under his stern regulation, but his mind still reeled with the shock of his discovery.

Seton a woman?

He stalked rapidly through the foggy autumn night, appalled by his discovery and astounded by his blindness. Why hadn't he seen the truth straightaway? Granted, one didn't expect a woman to come strolling in bold as brass to apply for a man's job, especially one who'd gone so far as to chop off her hair, don a man's suit of clothes, and claim in a convincingly deep voice to actually *be* a man—or boy, in this case.

One took things at face value far too often, he realized. That was how confidence swindlers plied their trade, convincing poor sods they could talk to dead relations or make a profit of thousands of pounds in a month off a hundred-guinea investment. And he hadn't been the only one fooled here. All the other members of his household had been equally taken in. But these were cold comforts in the aftermath of his discovery, and he could only deem himself a first-class chump.

He had no time for further contemplations on the matter, for the walk to Weston's house in Grosvenor Square was a short one, and because of his tardiness, his steps had been hurried. Nonetheless, he was a quarter hour late, and his tardiness set the meal back half an hour. This earned him no small degree of resentment from his host and colleagues, ruined the fish course, and threatened to put the discussions that would come over the port on very shaky ground.

The meal was a long one, however, and by the time all seven courses and several fine wines had been consumed, the mood had lightened, the other gentlemen had forgiven his faux pas, and Jamie had managed to put the Seton debacle out of his mind. Over some of Weston's fine vintage port, questions regarding the education bill and various other pieces of legislation important to Jamie were put forth, and the discussions regarding them were far less contentious than he had anticipated.

Still, there were strong differences of opinion among the men present, and it took several hours of discussion to hammer things out. By the time he returned to Upper Brook Street, it was nearly midnight.

He had his own key, so there was no need to ring for Samuel to let him in, but he found the footman was still awake when he went upstairs.

"My lord," Samuel greeted, setting aside the book he was reading and rising to his feet as Jamie entered the nursery.

"Samuel," he answered, glancing at the darkened doorway that led into the bedrooms beyond the nursery. "Boys get to sleep all right?"

The footman nodded. "It took a while to settle them after they heard that Seton—Miss Seton," he corrected at once, "is leaving."

"It had to be, Samuel."

"I suppose," the footman acknowledged, looking doubtful. "It seems a right shame, though, my lord, if you don't mind my saying."

"So, the boys were excited by the news of Seton's departure? I'm sure they've been crowing ever since they heard, knowing another tutor's gone the way of Mr. Partridge."

"But they weren't," Samuel denied, much to Jamie's surprise. "In fact, they seemed quite put out about the whole thing."

"They didn't appreciate being tricked either, I daresay."

"Well, they were amazed they didn't tumble to her game sooner, but they also admired her for pulling one over on us all." He paused and shook his head. "I still can't quite believe it though. Seton a woman? It seems obvious now that I think about it, but it makes me feel a right fool that I didn't see it for myself."

Jamie set his jaw, feeling grim. "You're not alone."

"Yes, sir, but you've at least got an excuse. You've hardly seen her. And the boys . . . well . . . you wouldn't expect them to guess, would you? But Mrs. Richmond and I have seen her every day. We should have known." He paused again, giving a sigh. "Now you'll have to start the search for a tutor all over again."

"He wouldn't have to," said a voice from the doorway into the bedrooms, "if he'd let Seton stay."

Both men turned to find a pajama-clad Colin in the doorway, his twin right behind him. "Really, Papa," he went on, frowning at Jamie. "We finally find someone we like, and you have to go and ruin it."

As surprised as he was to hear that his sons liked Seton, he refused to be drawn into an argument about her departure. "Aren't you two supposed to be asleep?"

"How can we sleep when you two are talking out here? You woke us up."

"So, Seton's a girl," Owen said, pushing his brother into the room and following him through the doorway. "So what? Why does she have to leave just because of that?"

"That's not why she's leaving, and you know it. She's leaving because she lied."

"It was just a joke, and a jolly good one, too," Colin said with obvious admiration.

"Better than any we've pulled," Owen added, sounded envious. "Bit nauseating though, that we got tricked by a girl." Turning to his brother, he added, "We'll have to up our game."

Colin nodded agreement, but before Jamie could take issue with that ghastly prospect, the boy turned to him and said, "Samuel says a girl can't be a tutor. Is that true?"

"Female tutors are called governesses," Jamie explained. "And they only teach girls."

"But what's it matter?" Colin said impatiently. "*We* don't care."

This was certainly a night for surprises. "It doesn't bother you that Seton's a woman?"

"Why should it?" Colin countered with a shrug. "We've had plenty of nannies, you know."

"Yes, and you've driven every one of them off."

"Seton's different. He—she," the boy amended at once, "knows some smashing things, and she doesn't giggle. And Oscar likes her."

"I'm so glad she meets with the cat's approval," Jamie said.

Colin missed the sarcasm. "She promised to show us how to walk on water. That'll never happen now," he added mournfully.

Jamie blinked. "Walk on water?"

"She said there was a way to make water so you could walk on it, and she promised to show us how."

Jamie had no time to consider how a biblical miracle might be achieved by the use of science, for Colin went on, "We finally find someone decent to watch us," he said, frowning at his parent, "and you sack her. Really, Papa, you're impossible!"

"I can't believe I'm hearing this," Jamie muttered. "After she made you polish all the silver and scrub the big pots, you want Seton to stay? Why this one and not any of the others?"

"She was a true sport about being tied up, and she didn't blink an eye over the slop water. She did squeal a bit when she found the slugs," he added, "but she's still heaps better than any other nanny we've ever had."

"And she's nice, too," Owen added, "even if she does make us scrub things. She's not mean."

Jamie tensed, momentarily diverted. "You've had mean nannies?"

"The Hornsby," Colin said promptly. "She was awful, always rapping our knuckles with a ruler."

A ruler, Jamie thought, trying to console himself for past mistakes in judgment, wasn't so bad, was it? Unless . . .

He drew a deep breath. "Is that all she did? Rap your knuckles with a ruler?"

"She'd pinch, too. Hard. Left a bruise on my arm once."

Jamie felt like a rotter. "I'm sorry. But why didn't you tell me about any of this? I've told you to tell me when nannies are cruel like that. I'd have sacked her at once."

"Maybe so," Owen answered, "but we don't tattle, Papa. It's not playing the game. And if the nanny is mean, we can take care of it ourselves." He grinned suddenly. "It's easy to get rid of the ones we don't like."

There was no arguing with his sons' success in this regard, but Jamie knew that wasn't the point. "You should have told me—"

"Forget about the Hornsby, Papa," Colin cut in impatiently. "She's gone. What about Seton?"

"She's leaving in the morning."

"Why? Because she played a smashing trick? How silly."

"It wasn't just a trick," Jamie said. "She lied."

"But, Papa," Colin persisted, "why does that mean she has to leave? We lie . . . not very often," he amended at his father's raised eyebrows. "But you don't kick us into the street."

"It's a bit different."

"Can't you just dock her wages, or take away her day out, or something? You do realize," he added when Jamie shook his head, "that she hasn't anywhere to go? She's got no family. She's all alone in the world."

Jamie refused to be mollified by a hard-luck story. "And how do you know that? She told you, I suppose? Well, how did you find out, then?" he asked when they shook their heads. "Samuel?"

He turned to the footman, who raised both hands, palms toward him in a gesture of denial.

"It wasn't Samuel," Colin said. "We overheard Mrs. Richmond talking to her about it."

"Overheard?" Jamie frowned. "You mean you eavesdropped on a private conversation."

"We didn't!" Colin denied at once. "We were having our high tea in the kitchen, and they went into the butler's pantry, which is right next door. They shut the door, but the transoms were open, so we heard everything without even moving from our seats. And we think it's ripping heartless of you to kick her out when she's got nowhere to go."

"And without her pay, too," Owen added. "We never thought you could be such a tyrant, Papa."

"I am not a tyrant," Jamie denied, irritated by the accusation and by the idea that his sons seemed to adore someone who'd made a right fool of him. "She—"

"Mrs. Richmond asked her if she had any family, and Seton said no one she could go to. And then Mrs. Richmond asked her if you'd paid her wages to date and given a character, and she said no, but that she didn't ask for them and that you didn't offer. She didn't blame you, she said."

"That was good of her."

Like his brother, Owen was impervious to sarcasm. "Mrs. Richmond got very cross then, and said you were being callous."

"Callous? Me? Of all the cheek!"

"She said if you didn't give Seton a reference, no one else would hire her. Is that true?"

Jamie stirred. "Possibly," he admitted, feeling a nudge of guilt, "but—"

"If that happens, she'll be dest—dest—what's the word?"

"Destitute," Samuel supplied.

Jamie refused to be moved by this mention of the inevitable future that awaited the Miss Setons of the world. "What she does and where she goes from here is not our concern."

"It's not *ours*, Papa," Colin said as if correcting him. "It's yours. When Uncle Geoffrey died, and you became Grandpapa's heir to the title, you told us all about what that meant. You would become the marquess one day, you said, and it would be up to you to take care of our people. Isn't Seton one of our people?"

"Not anymore. Seton," he said with emphasis, "is not our people. Seton is a liar. I cannot have a liar teaching my children. And someday, Colin, when you are the marquess and you have children of your own, you will understand."

"But we like her, Papa. She makes lessons fun."

"And she doesn't fuss over stupid things," Owen put in. "We want her to stay. We want her to be our tutor."

He ignored this chorus of protest and praise. "She can't. A woman cannot be a tutor. It's quite improper."

"Things that are improper aren't always wrong," Colin said adamantly.

He tensed. "Who told you that?"

"Mama."

That was so much like something Pat would have said that Jamie had to pause and take a breath before he could reply. "When was this?" he managed after a moment.

"It was when we stole the pancakes," Owen said as if that explained everything.

"Pancakes?" Unenlightened, Jamie looked at Samuel, but the footman seemed equally at sea. "What pancakes?"

"They were left over after Shrove Tuesday—four years ago, now, was it, Colin?"

His brother shook his head. "Three and a half," he corrected. "Shrove Tuesday's in the spring, before Lent."

Pat had been pregnant that spring, Jamie reflected and shut his eyes. By the end of summer—

"Right," Owen went on, interrupting the bleak direction of Jamie's thoughts and forcing him to open his eyes. "Anyway, we took some of the leftover pancakes out of the larder to give Mr. Leach."

Jamie was still lost. "Who?"

"Mr. Leach. He sleeps on the bench by the Arch. Until the constables wake him up and make him leave, of course. But he always comes back."

"You made friends with an indigent man?" Jamie rubbed a hand over his forehead, muttering an oath. "We really need to have a talk about the two of you conversing with strangers in the park."

"It was only once, and Mama was with us. She was very nice to him, even though he called her Sally and said he wasn't coming home with her ever again, which didn't make any sense—"

"Homeless men often say things that don't make sense. They're a bit mad. Which is why you should stay away from them," Jamie added, hoping to impress upon them the risks inherent in befriending indigent strangers.

He might as well have been talking to the air.

"That's why we decided to take him the pancakes," Colin said, taking up the tale again. "He was hungry, and he asked if we had any food. Mama gave him the tin of bonbons in her pocket, but that didn't seem like very much to eat. And we always have ever so many pancakes left the day after Shrove Tuesday, so we thought we'd take some for Mr. Leach."

It was late, he was tired, it was hours past the twins' bedtime, and he really didn't want to hear about pancakes or the boys' praises of Miss Seton, so he tried to cut the story short. "Is there a point to all this?"

"We're trying to tell you, Papa, if you'd let us finish."

Jamie gave up thoughts of anyone in this family getting to bed anytime soon. "Right," he said, forcing himself to be patient. "Sorry. Go on."

"When we got caught, Nanny Olivet was fit to be tied—"

"And she tattled to Mama," Owen took up the tale. "She told Mama taking food out of the larder was most improper, and she asked what our punishment ought to be. We were sunk, we thought."

"But Mama," Colin said, "hushed Nanny up and said that kindness shouldn't be punished. And that sometimes, it's important to do what's right, even if it's not proper. Wanting to help someone, she said, was a right and proper thing."

"She said one should always try to help those in need," Owen added, and his eyes opened innocently wide. "Isn't Seton in need, Papa?"

Jamie looked from Owen to Colin and back again, appreciating anew their talent for finding anyone's weak spots, even his.

A sound from the doorway interrupted before he could recover enough to reply, and he turned to find Mrs. Richmond standing in the doorway.

"I've given her a bed in one of the maid's rooms, poor thing," the cook said, shaking her head. "Worn out, she is."

"Lying all the time makes one tired, I imagine," Jamie said. "Was there something you wanted, Mrs. Richmond?"

"I heard you come in earlier, and I thought I'd see if there was anything you need, my lord."

"There isn't."

Mrs. Richmond didn't seem inclined to leave in the wake of that bit of news. Instead, she reached into her pocket and pulled out several pound notes. "She asked me to return the money to you. She never bought the clothes, she said. Whatever that means. Her circumstances, from what I gather, were quite dire before she came to us."

Guilt nudged him again, a little stronger this time, and he glared resentfully at the cook as he took the money from her fingers.

"Oh, I'm sure," he said in irritation. "No doubt she was eager to tell you her sad, sad story, explain her unfortunate circumstances, and justify her actions."

"No, my lord. Quite the contrary. She didn't once try to justify what she'd done. In fact, getting any information out of her at all was like prying open an oyster."

Jamie gave a laugh that sounded terribly cynical to his own ears. "And yet, it seems all of you learned her hard-luck story just the same."

Mrs. Richmond stared back at him, unperturbed. "Sometimes, a woman knows things about another woman without the need for much explanation. Call it intuition."

He shoved the money into his pocket. "That's hardly reason to overlook what she did."

"My lord," Samuel put in, "it's obvious Seton was in desperate need of a job, since she was willing to go to such lengths. While you, my lord," he added, as Jamie opened his mouth to reply, "were in desperate need, too, of someone to watch and teach the boys. If she leaves, you're both in desperate need again, but if she stays, everyone may ultimately benefit. No harm was done, really. Can't you give her another chance?"

Jamie was shaking his head before the footman had even finished. "Even if I forgave the lying, which I'm not at all sure I'm prepared to do, the boys need a tutor, and a woman can't be a tutor. It isn't done, as I've already explained."

Mrs. Richmond made a choked sound that sounded suspiciously like a laugh.

"Do you have something to say, Mrs. Richmond?" Jamie asked, folding his arms, glaring at her.

She coughed. "Well, begging your pardon, my lord, but I've been second cook to Mrs. Mason a long time, well before you married Lady Patricia, and from what I remember, you were never one to care much about the proprieties." She smiled a little. "That's one of the reasons, I do believe, why Lady Patricia was so taken with you. Her father, as you know, was always very strict. Her brother, too."

Jamie stirred, uncomfortable with stories of what had caused Pat to fall in love with him and impatient with reminders of the scapegrace he'd been before he met her. "I'm a father now, Mrs. Richmond, and a Member of Parliament. I can't allow things in my own household that would raise eyebrows. A woman tutor is unthinkable. And what of our friends? Surely they'll notice if Mr. Seton transforms into someone of the opposite sex."

"We haven't seen any of our friends," Owen put in before either of the servants could reply. "They're all in the country still. Some will come back when Parliament opens, but no one we know has been introduced to her. Have they?"

He turned to the servants, who both shook their heads.

"There, you see, Papa?" Colin added. "If anyone does happen to notice how much she looks like our previous tutor—a shopkeeper, or a tradesman, or someone like that—well, Adam was her brother—filling in for her, so to speak."

Pushing aside any contemplations about Colin's talent for inventing such believable stories, Jamie tried another tack. "Even if I forgave her and went along with this, Torquil would never approve. This is his house, mind, and he's a stickler for the proprieties. A female tutor is out of the question."

"Why can't she be a nanny, then?" Samuel put in. "The boys' nannies have always given them lessons of a sort, so it wouldn't be anything out of the common way for Seton to do so. Why can't we just call her the nanny?"

"Would she have to wear a black dress and a hideous hat?" Owen wanted to know, then gave a shudder. "I hope not. I'd hate her to start looking like Nanny Hornsby."

Jamie thought of the yellowed, toad-like complexion of the boys' previous nanny, compared it to the finely textured skin of Miss Seton, and he feared that no matter how hideous the hat, Miss Seton was far too pretty to ever look like Nanny Hornsby.

"As a nanny," Samuel went on, interrupting Jamie's rather dangerous train of thought, "she could still teach the boys just as she has been."

"That's an idea," Mrs. Richmond said eagerly. "No one has to know she ever posed as a man, or that she was ever hired as a tutor. She's just the latest nanny."

"She has nowhere to go, Papa," Owen said when Jamie did not reply.

"No family," Colin added in woeful accents. "No friends but us. If you kick her out, she'll be like poor Mr. Leach, living in the park and sponging bonbons from strangers."

Her fate would probably be worse. What would Pat think of that?

For the first time, Jamie felt himself wavering. "You realize you'll have to collude in this lie—all of you—and so will I?"

No one replied. They all remained silent, their hopeful faces making Jamie feel like a pompous ass, and yet he persevered. "Which means I am teaching my sons the horrible lesson that lying is rewarded."

"Don't be daft, Papa," Colin cut in before either of the servants could answer. "We already know lying is wrong. We know she oughtn't to have done it. She knows it, too. What's important is that we need someone to watch us, she needs a job, and she's someone we actually *like*, which means we won't misbehave anymore."

Jamie was not the least bit fooled by that, but the fact remained that Seton was the first person to be in charge of his sons whom they found acceptable. And their behavior, according to the servants, had vastly improved under her tutelage. She was, as he'd already acknowledged, a very good teacher.

Mrs. Richmond gave a little cough. "The Commons reconvenes the day after tomorrow, doesn't it, my lord?"

With that, Jamie knew he'd lost the battle.

"All right, all right," he muttered, raking a hand through his hair. "I can't fight all of you. She can stay and be a nanny. But," he added, cutting off the celebratory sounds of the boys and the relieved murmurs of the servants, "I have certain conditions for her employment, which I will discuss with her, and with Mrs. Richmond, first thing tomorrow. As for you two," he added, nodding to his sons, "you had better live up to your promise and behave yourselves. If you don't, if she or you disappoint me, out she goes, and Harrow will be dealing with you. Is that understood?"

"Yes, Papa," they murmured together, looking so earnest that it would have been impossible for anyone who didn't know them to question their sincerity. Jamie, however, knew better.

Still, they'd probably be good for a while. And as he left the nursery, he could only deem a little domestic peace, however temporary, an agreeable change from the usual chaos.

Chapter 11

*I*t was still dark when Jamie woke, but dawn was breaking by the time he'd finished dressing, and a faint glimmer of morning light illuminated his way as he left his own room and crossed to the west wing. This side of the house was dead quiet, indicating that the boys, and perhaps Samuel as well, were still asleep in the nursery.

He was glad, for it wasn't to his sons' rooms that he was going. He passed that corridor, opened the baize door to the servants' staircase, and took a seat on the landing to wait.

He didn't have to wait long. Within a quarter of an hour, he heard footsteps above him on the stairs, and he turned his head, watching the stairwell beside him that led to the attic rooms above. The tap of footsteps grew louder, and a moment later, he saw a pair of black-shod feet and slim, black-stockinged ankles come into view below the too-short hem of a black skirt.

Jamie felt a hint of surprise. He'd been expecting to see Seton in that dreadful brown suit of hers, and as she descended a few more steps and the rest of her body came into view, the sight of her in a dress threw him utterly off balance. It was a maid's uniform, probably borrowed from the housekeeper's stores—severe and plain with nothing feminine about it but the skirt itself, a skirt inadequate to cover her exceptionally long legs. And yet, as plain and unadorned as it was, the dress succeeded in making obvious what had heretofore been hidden from Jamie's eyes—the curves of a woman's body.

She was carrying a large suitcase, an awkward thing to do on such a narrow staircase, and when she reached the landing, she bumped the newel post. She stopped and shifted the case to her opposite hand to better navigate the sharp U-turn of the stairs, but as she turned on the landing, she spied him on the landing below. She stopped again, the suitcase slid from her fingers to the floorboards with a thud, and she gave an astonished, "Oh!"

She was not the only one astonished.

His gaze slid down, pausing at the gentle swell of her breasts against the bodice of her dress, and he realized she must have been binding them with linen all this time, for though her breasts were not large, they could not have been so successfully hidden without that sort of assistance.

She stirred and he lifted his gaze from her chest, feeling rather a lout. "Sorry," he said at once, "but you can't really blame me for staring, can you? You in a dress is a bit disconcerting, Seton."

"I suppose it is," she admitted and looked down, smoothing the folds of black linsey-woolsey she wore. "Mrs. Richmond loaned it to me. It belongs to the house. I'll have it laundered and returned when I come back for my books."

"Of course," he murmured politely. "No hurry, I'm sure."

Despite this attempt at ordinary civility, he couldn't resist another look at what to him seemed extraordinary. Sliding his gaze back down, he noted the decided curves of a waist and hips, though whether these were obvious due to the dress or to the corset that was probably beneath it, Jamie couldn't be sure. Either way, he now understood just why he'd never seen her without that awful, double-breasted jacket. Dress or no, corset or no, trousers would have hugged her shape, molded to those curving hips and long legs in a way a skirt could never do.

With that thought, heat flickered inside him, a hint of what he'd felt last night when her knuckles had brushed beneath his jaw. The first stirrings of arousal.

It was a feeling he'd always been glad to suppress on the infrequent occasions during the last three years when it had cropped up, and he'd never found it a particularly difficult thing to do. Without Pat, arousal was unwelcome, wrenching, and always carried with it the vague sense of betrayal. And yet, as he felt it starting inside him now, he wondered what it would be like to give in to it, to loosen the tight leash of his control, to hold a woman in his arms again and allow lust to overtake him, to be just for a few fleeting minutes the wild chap he'd been in his youth—

"Do you always skulk about on the back stairs in your leisure time?"

Her question, both amused and bemused, was enough to pull Jamie out of these prurient contemplations. From long practice, he shoved down the desires of his baser nature and returned his attention to the reason he was standing here. "I've been waiting for you."

"Why? To say good-bye and good luck?" She laughed a little, tugging self-consciously at one of the short, curly locks of her hair, her cheeks going pink. "Or just to stare at the real me?"

He stiffened, fearing she had realized what he was feeling just now, and it was mortifying to think he was standing here as randy as an adolescent, especially about someone he hadn't even known was a woman until last night. He shifted his weight, making the floorboards of the landing creak beneath his feet.

"Yes, well," he mumbled after a moment, "I'm discovering that nothing makes a man feel more of a fool than failing to recognize a woman when she's right under his nose. Forgive me if I'm still trying to understand and accept that such a thing happened to me."

She swallowed hard. "It was never my intention to make a fool of you, my lord," she said after a moment.

"Was any of it true, what you told me?" he demanded. "Your father, your education, tutoring your landlady and the pubkeeper—was any of it true, or was it a string of lies from start to finish?"

"Does it matter?"

"Answer my question."

"If I don't, what shall you do? Fire me?"

"You're in no position to be cheeky, Miss Seton. If that's really your name."

If she noticed the question in that remark, she gave no sign. "Is that why you've been waiting for me?" she asked. "To find out how many lies I've told you?"

"Not quite. Well, partly," he amended as one of her straight black brows curved up in a skeptical arch. He turned, pushed open the green baize door behind him, and held it wide. "I wish to speak with you. Come with me, please."

She hesitated as if wanting to refuse, but after a moment, she shrugged and started down the stairs toward him, leaving her suitcase behind. She followed him through the baize door, across the wide empty gallery, and down the corridor that led to the family rooms and guest quarters on the opposite side of the house from the nursery.

He led her into his own private study, the same room where he'd originally interviewed her, and as he circled his desk to his chair, the view of the park beyond reminded him that it had been a woman, this woman, he'd seen that afternoon a month ago flying kites with his boys.

Don't be content to watch them play from your window.

He turned abruptly and faced her across the desk, gesturing to the chair beside where she stood. "Sit down, answer my questions, and for a change, try to be truthful."

"Very well." She took the offered chair, folded her hands in her lap, and launched into speech. "My father was American, as I said. He was educated at Harvard, he taught there, he taught me as a young girl. I was not sickly—that was a lie, I'm afraid. But the rest was true. My father is the one who educated me."

"You didn't have a governess?"

"No." A faint smile curved her lips. "Papa had a poor opinion of governesses. He wanted a true education for me. He wanted me to read books, not just practice walking with them on top of my head. He wanted me to learn mathematics, the sciences, Latin. Governesses don't teach those things, or if they do, they don't usually teach them well."

"He seems to have had an abnormally high standard of education for women."

"For me anyway. I think Papa always secretly wanted a son. He never said he was disappointed that I was a girl, of course, but he never let me think for a moment that my sex was any excuse to be ignorant on any subject. I received as good an education as any preparatory school could provide—a better one, in fact. My knowledge and education, my love of learning, my desire to teach others—all the things that I am, I owe to him."

"And would your father's desire for a son allow him to condone you dressing up as a man and applying for a man's post?"

Her smile vanished, she stiffened, and for a moment, he thought she wasn't going to answer. "No," she said at last. "He would not condone it. In fact, if he could see me now, I fear he would be very disappointed in me." She bent her head, looking at her hands clasped in her lap. "For many things," she added softly.

His curiosity deepened, but before he could think to satisfy it by asking to what things she might be referring, she looked up.

"It was wrong, of course, to do what I did, but I needed a job, and you had one available. A man's job, yes, but one I was fully qualified to do. So, I posed as a man to get it."

"You seem a bold, confident bit of goods, Miss Seton. As such, did it never occur to you to apply for the job without resorting to subterfuge? To use your faith in your own abilities and your powers of persuasion to convince me that a woman could be a perfectly good tutor?"

She shook her head. "You'd never have considered hiring a woman for the post."

She was probably right, but nonetheless, he was a bit nettled by her complete certainty on the subject of what he would or would not do. "You didn't even know me. You couldn't possibly have known what I would have done."

"But I did know. I overheard you say it."

"What?" He frowned, taken aback. "When was this?"

"The newspaper office. I was there when you came in and spoke to Lord Galbraith. He told you the twins had written to Lady Truelove, and you—"

"There *was* a woman there, I remember," he interrupted, his mind conjuring a vague image of a wide-brimmed hat and a dull black coat and skirt. He couldn't recall a face, but then, he'd been preoccupied with thoughts of the boys at the time and hadn't paid any attention to the woman sitting in the *Gazette* offices. He certainly hadn't recognized her when she'd come in men's clothes to be interviewed. "That was you?"

"Yes. I heard you say that a woman couldn't prepare boys for Harrow. I'm afraid you rather flicked me on the raw with that comment."

"And you felt compelled to prove me wrong?"

"I'd prefer to say that it seems quite unfair and downright silly to me that a woman be deprived of the chance to apply for a job simply because she is female. And I don't like hearing that I can't do something just because I'm a woman. I'm stubborn that way."

"So I'm discovering," he muttered. "And the landlady and the pub-keeper?" he went on, watching her closely. "You asked them to fabricate letters of character for you?"

She met his gaze without flinching. "They didn't mind. They thought it rather a lark, if you want to know the truth."

"Yes, yes," he countered in some irritation, "I seem to be the only person in this entire situation without a sense of humor."

She pressed her lips together, demonstrating that she was suffering at least a tiny pang of conscience at having made a fool of him. "Having heard your conversation with Galbraith, I knew he intended to insert an ad for the tutoring post on your behalf, and when I saw it appear the next day, I wrote to you as Adam Seton, obtained the character letters from my friends in that name, and requested the interview. My real name is Amanda, by the way," she added carelessly, "in case you were wondering. And now, I believe you know the whole story."

"Not quite. Weren't you afraid I'd recognize you?"

"I hoped you wouldn't." She paused and licked her lips as if they were dry. "I needed a job, as I said."

"And why was your need so great that you felt forced to such lengths? Because your father had died?"

"Partly. He left almost no money."

"With the superior education he'd given you, you could not obtain a teaching position?"

"Before I came here, I was a governess." There was a long pause, and then she looked at him, her eyes wide and dark. "But I lost my post."

"Because?" he prompted when she paused.

She shifted in her chair and said nothing, but he was of no mind to respect reticence on this topic.

"Were you fired?" he asked.

Curiously, that made her smile a little. "Would you believe me if I said I'm not quite sure?"

"What sort of answer is that?"

She shrugged. "I didn't wait for my employer's official notice of dismissal, although I'm sure if you make inquiries, you will be told that my employment was definitely terminated. You will be told I was impertinent—"

"You?" He pretended surprise. "I'm shocked. Go on," he prompted when she didn't reply.

"What would be the point? You won't believe my version of events anyway."

"Probably not," he agreed. "That is one of the difficulties all proven liars must face."

She opened her mouth as if to fire off a defensive retort, but then closed it again as if remembering she had no defense. Nonetheless, when she folded her arms, every line of her body made it clear he was not going to learn the details without a bit of spade work.

"How long were you in this post?" he asked.

"A little less than two years."

He raised an eyebrow. "It took that long for your employer to find you impertinent? I knew that about you in less than a minute."

She looked away. "Yes, well," she mumbled, "this wasn't the sort of impertinence you're thinking of."

"Indeed? I am becoming more curious by the moment."

He waited, and after a moment or two, the silence seemed to make her uncomfortable, for she frowned at him. "I would really prefer not to discuss it."

"I daresay. Tell me anyway."

Color came into her pale cheeks. "I see no reason why I should."

"To keep your job here. Is that a good enough reason?"

"Keep it?" Understandably startled, she stared, her arms falling to her lap as her bravado slipped a notch. "But I already lost it. You fired me."

"My sons have asked me to reconsider." Leaning back, he steepled his fingers together, and rested his elbows on the arms of his chair. "You have the singular honor, Miss Seton, of being the only person in charge of my sons for whom they have ever expressed the slightest shred of approval."

That seemed to please her, for a smile touched her lips. "It's amazing what a bicarbonate and vinegar volcano can do."

"That, and the fact that you can apparently walk on water."

She blinked. "I beg your pardon?"

"I'm told you know how to make water so one can walk on it. My sons were upset that you were not going to be here to teach them that trick. For my part, I'm not sure how you thought you'd ever manage it."

"Simple chemistry. Water and corn flour mixed together make a non-Newtonian fluid—"

"Of course," he exclaimed, suddenly remembering his own childhood lessons on the subject. "It would pour like a liquid but act like a solid under pressure. Still—" He broke off, considering. "How can you possibly walk on it?"

She laughed. "You use a lot of corn flour and run very fast."

He almost laughed with her, but then he remembered why they were having this conversation, his momentary amusement faded, and he returned to the subject at hand. "However interesting and entertaining your lessons may be, Miss Seton, that is not the basis for my sons' favorable impression of you. Their approval stems mostly from the very thing that caused me to sack you. The trick you played impressed them. They thought how you fooled everyone into thinking you were a man was a right good joke. To my sons, a joke well played is the pinnacle of accomplishment."

"I see." She tilted her head, studying him across the desk. "Either way, I wouldn't have thought their preferences would cut any ice with you."

"Then you would be wrong." He straightened in his chair and leaned forward, folding his hands atop his desk. "I am also forced to consider Mrs. Richmond and Samuel, who might very well give notice if you leave. And given the fact that the Commons reconvenes tomorrow, leaving me almost no spare time to find a suitable replacement, I am prepared to reconsider your termination. If," he added, meeting her gaze across the desk, "you answer my questions fully and without prevarication or evasion."

"All right then, if you insist." She squared her shoulders, meeting his gaze head-on. "Unbeknownst to me, my previous employer, a widower, had an expectation that the governess in his household would perform certain duties in addition to educating his daughters, duties which involved entertaining him, if you understand what I mean."

He did, and he felt a bitter distaste. Chivalry demanded he abandon the topic, but he could not afford to do so. She'd already proven herself a liar; it was not so great a leap to imagine her having an eye on the main chance as well, and he needed to be sure that had not been the case. "And you objected to this arrangement?"

She stuck up her chin, the gold lights in her hazel eyes flashing like sparks, answering his question in no uncertain terms, but when she spoke, her voice held a hint of mockery. "Why do you ask? Now that you know I'm a woman, are you considering me for a similar arrangement?"

He stiffened. "I don't shag the help, Miss Seton," he said bluntly. "I may have been a wild, undisciplined rake in my youth, but I am not that sort of man now, and if you doubt me, there is nothing more for us to discuss. You may retrieve your suitcase and go in search of your next post."

Her battle stance relaxed, her mockery faded. "It seems I misunderstood you," she muttered.

"Yes," he agreed mildly. "You did. Though given the circumstances, I suppose I can't blame you for it."

"Then you believe me?"

He wasn't ready to go quite that far, not yet, and he shrugged. "Having been obliged on occasion to sit over the port with men who brag about such exploits, I know quite well they happen. So, how did you handle this proposition?"

"It wasn't a proposition." She wriggled a little in her chair. "Not exactly, not at first. There were signs that was the way the wind was blowing, but I refused to let myself see them, for I could not afford to lose my post. I told myself I was imagining things, that his hand brushing my arm as we talked or resting it against the small of my back as I preceded him out of a room were accidental, though my instincts said otherwise. I took pains to avoid giving him any wrong impression, and I discouraged these advances as best I could, hoping to avoid an open confrontation on the topic. But over time, my attempts to ignore the problem and evade him were not enough. One day, he cornered me in a closet and kissed me. I objected, but he did not take kindly to my objection."

As she fell silent, Jamie felt a sick twist in his guts, a twist of dread and anger. The gentlemanly thing to do would have been to let this go, but he could not. He was driven to find out just what had happened to her, for reasons he began to fear went beyond his reconsideration of her employment. "So, your impertinence was your refusal to capitulate to him?"

"No." She bit her lip, giving him a look of mock apology. "My impertinence was when I dropped him to his knees by using one of mine."

Jamie gave a shout of laughter. He couldn't help it; his relief and surprise were too great to be wholly suppressed. But at once, he gave a cough and worked to find an appropriately grave reply. "I didn't realize," he said at last, "that you were so athletic."

"Neither did I." Unexpectedly, she grinned. "Neither did he, I imagine."

"No," he agreed, glad she could smile after what had happened. "You probably gave him the shock of his life." He tilted his head, studying her thoughtfully. "Is that the reason you applied for a man's post?" he asked. "You feared what might befall you as a woman in a widower's house?"

"Partly," she admitted. "But I also knew I could do the job. And more than that—" She broke off and leaned forward, a sudden eagerness in her expression, an eagerness to explain that had not been there before. "I *wanted* this post. After hearing what you and Lord Galbraith were saying, I wanted to tutor your sons. I wanted the challenge."

He couldn't help another laugh at that. "Well, they are that, all right. But I fear you had no idea what you were letting yourself in for."

"Oh, but I did. You and Galbraith were quite open about the difficulties."

"You had no qualms? No doubts?"

"About your boys?" She shook her head. "No. It sounds conceited, I know, and I don't mean it to be, but I knew I could handle them, I knew I'd be good with them. Teaching is what I do, you see. And in tutoring your sons, I knew I'd have the chance to teach important subjects like science and mathematics. I wouldn't be a governess teaching the silly things that girls are supposed to learn, but subjects that really matter, that can help my pupils to do great things in the world." She waved her hands impatiently, as if she found her explanations inadequate to the passion of her feelings. "Oh, do you see at all what I mean?"

He studied her without replying, noting the genuine joy with which she talked of her vocation, the sparkle in her eyes and the glow in her face, and he was struck anew by his own idiocy.

How could he ever, in a thousand years, have mistaken her for a boy? At this moment, her cropped hair notwithstanding, she looked every inch a woman. Not beautiful, he supposed, but striking just the same, with her high cheekbones, ebony hair, and pale, luminous skin. There was something else about her, though, that went beyond coloring and bone structure and conventional notions of beauty, something that seemed to penetrate the void of his existence, something akin to a candle being lit in a dark, empty room.

She had a gambler's heart and a pirate smile and a zest for life. She had a reckless disregard for rules and conventions and a love of adventure. There was pain in the dark abyss of her eyes, but there were shafts of light and hope as well. Jamie feared that any light in his own eyes had been snuffed out a long time ago.

As a boy, he'd crossed lines and defied rules, not out of any passion for a vocation like the girl before him, and not really to gain attention as his own boys were wont to do. No, he'd been driven by a darker, more insidious need: to fill up a life that was empty.

And then he'd met Pat, and it was as if dawn had broken in his soul. Pat had filled all the empty, cold, lonely places within him like sunlight. Before her, he'd been an angry, defiant, and bitter youth, breaking rules, making trouble and doing anything to kick against the pricks. After her, he was a blackened, burned-out shell of a man, going through the motions of life, getting out of bed each morning not because he welcomed what the day would bring, but because the existence of his sons left him no other choice.

Now, as he looked into the vivid, passionate face of the girl before him, longing hit him with unexpected force. It had been three interminable years since he'd seen in his own mirror what he saw in Amanda's face, and he wished—God, how he wished—he could see it again. It was the joy of being alive.

"My lord?"

The sound of her voice jerked him out of his pointless reverie. Life moved only one way, and that was forward. One could never go back. Some joys, once lost, were lost forever. Some lights, once extinguished, could never glow again.

He jerked to his feet.

"Very well," he said as she also stood up. "Has anyone of my family's acquaintance met you or learned your name?"

"No one's been introduced to me, if that's what you mean. As for the rest, you'll have to ask Mrs. Richmond and Samuel if they've mentioned me to anyone by name."

He already had asked them, late last night. "What about tradesmen? Or shopkeepers?"

"Some have seen me with the boys, of course, but none of them know my name. Why do you ask?"

He didn't answer that question directly. "We shall begin again," he said instead. "You will be the boys' new nanny, but your actual duties will remain just as they have been."

She gripped the edge of his desk, suddenly, as if her knees were threatening to give way, and watching her, he knew she must truly have been facing destitution, or something close to it.

"Thank you, my lord," she said, recovering sufficiently to abandon the death grip she had on his desk. "Thank you."

"For the sake of respectability, you will be Mrs. Seton from now on," he added. "A widow. And if anyone notices that you look like the male tutor who was here before you . . ." He paused and sighed, capitulating to yet another lie. "He was your brother."

She smiled a little at that. "I shall have to give Adam a different last name, then, since I am now a respectable widow."

"A woman requires a certain degree of privacy," he went on, "and my sons are now fully aware that if they sneak out at night, or if they misbehave in any other way, you will be the one to answer for it. So, I've instructed Mrs. Richmond to move you into the nanny's room and restore Colin to his own. That will be all."

She nodded, gave a curtsy, and turned to go.

"Seton?"

She paused, hand on the doorknob of his study, and looked at him over her shoulder. "Yes?"

"Lie to me again, about anything, and I will not forgive it. Do you understand?"

There was a slight pause, an indrawn breath, and then she squared her shoulders and met his gaze. "Yes, my lord."

"And you needn't worry that your history will repeat itself. Even in a dress, you're quite safe from me."

She nodded, seeming to take him at his word, but as he watched her walk away, he was painfully aware that this woman had inspired more in him than just a longing to enjoy life. She'd also reawakened masculine desires he'd been trying to smother for three years, and as he watched her walk out the door, her slim figure moving with willowy grace, he almost regretted that he wasn't the sort to bed the governess.

An omission wasn't really a lie.

At least, that's what Amanda tried to tell herself as she returned to the back stairs to collect her suitcase. After all, he hadn't asked for her entire employment history. Of course, that was partly due to the fact that she'd managed to steer the conversation rather adroitly away from her own past. And if he had the impression that she'd lived with her father until his death, taking the post as governess only after his passing, well, it wasn't because she'd actually said so.

If she'd told him about her post at Willowbank, he'd never have agreed to give her another chance, but how many people told their employers everything? She'd wager none. Everyone had chapters in their life they'd prefer others never read, and she was no different.

Even as she reminded herself of all these things, however, she knew she was attempting to justify actions that were questionable at best. Lord Kenyon certainly wouldn't care about such fine distinctions, not when it came to the person in charge of his boys, and if he found out the real story of her past, she knew there would be no reprieve, no third chance.

Still, she'd have to cross that bridge if and when she came to it, and in the meantime, there was no point brooding on the topic. She paused on the landing where she'd left her suitcase, picked it up, and retraced her steps, heading for the nursery and, as was her usual custom, she tried to look on the bright side. She still had a job, at least for now. She'd be able to continue working with the twins. And best of all, she could be herself—a woman—again.

Yes, she still had to keep a few secrets, but the relief of not having to live a lie every single minute was like a ten-ton weight had been lifted off her shoulders, and she couldn't help being glad about that.

No more speaking in a voice two octaves lower than her own. No more sneaking rags in and out to the laundry when her monthly came, and no more being Adam.

She could be Amanda again. She could let her hair grow, and wear dresses, and stop trying to learn to tie a bow tie. And once she started wearing a corset again, her back would stop aching, thank heaven.

At that thought, Amanda grinned. Before this started, she'd never have thought she'd be glad to put herself back in a corset.

Life, she reflected, was full of surprises.

Chapter 12

During the two weeks that followed, Jamie had little time to worry about Amanda Seton or his decision to keep her on. Almost from the moment the Commons reconvened, he found himself inundated with more work than ever. He scarcely had time to interrupt the boys' lessons late in the morning for a quick farewell before he was off to Westminster, and since the votes were seldom called before midnight, the boys and their tutor were always in bed long before he arrived home.

Nor did his work come to an end with end of the week. He did attend early service each Sunday with the boys, Amanda, and the servants, but other than that, his time at home was taken up with writing letters, drafting legislation, and composing speeches.

He didn't mind the hard work. In fact, he usually welcomed it. He'd stood for his seat in the Commons not out of any noble notion that he could change the world, but simply out of a need to fill his days, and though he had come to find satisfaction in it, his primary purpose was still to occupy his mind and block out memories of happier days.

There were times, however, when no amount of work was enough to distract him. One Saturday afternoon in mid-November, one of those beautiful autumn afternoons England so seldom offered, where the sun was shining and the air was crisp and the breeze was just strong enough to blow away the malodorous haze that hung over the city, Jamie found nothing even remotely satisfying about being an MP.

He stared down at his speech, and as he read the lines he'd spent hours composing with such painstaking care, he could not escape the dismal realization that they were pure tosh. His third attempt today, and he still couldn't seem to even convey the importance of the Education Bill with coherence, much less with eloquence. No one in the Commons would ever be persuaded by this rubbish.

Exasperated, he tossed his pen down, rubbed his hands over his face, and stood up. After stretching his cramped muscles, he stepped to the window and lifted the sash, then he leaned down, propped his forearms on the sill, and stared out over the park, breathing deeply, hoping the cold, invigorating air could invigorate his powers of inspiration as well.

Across the street, a constable approached a man who was stretched out on a bench—the same bench, he remembered, where Seton had been sitting that first day when Colin's kite had nearly landed on her head. With his truncheon, the constable prodded the sleeping man—Mr. Leach, he could only assume. Awakened from his nap, the man rose and shuffled off, the constable continued on his round, and Jamie's gaze moved on.

Beyond the bench was the space of open turf where the boys liked to fly their kites, and beside it, the cricket pitch where Samuel, or more rarely, Jamie himself, took the boys to hone their skills at bowling and batting.

The boys were there today, he realized, and he straightened, squinting to get a sharper look. Amanda was with them, but she was not watching from a comfortable place on the sidelines. No, she was playing batsman, the autumn breeze whipping her black skirt sideways, stirring the enormous puffy sleeves of her white blouse and the ribbon bow on her straw boater hat as she stood in front of the cricket stumps, bat in her hands, waiting for Colin, as bowler, to pitch the ball in her direction.

Her stance was off; he could see that at once, and when Colin sent her the bowl—a decent throw with a good bounce that made Jamie proud— she missed the ball by a mile. Not that it would have mattered anyway, for even if she'd made a splendid hit, she'd also employed too much force. Carried by her own momentum, she swung too far and hit the stumps behind her, an automatic out.

"Dismal," he murmured, shaking his head. "Simply dismal, Amanda." That was how he thought of her now, by her Christian name. He couldn't think of her as Seton any longer, for to his mind, that name conveyed a man. Mrs. Seton was the name everyone in the household, including him, used when addressing her, but Jamie never thought of her that way, though he could not have said quite why. In his thoughts, she was simply Amanda.

Colin left the pitch, Owen left his place as keeper, both boys coming over to explain what she'd done wrong, and Jamie moved to close the window, thinking he'd best get back to work.

But when he saw the sad excuse for a speech that was waiting atop his desk, he decided he could spare a few more minutes. He retrieved a pair of field glasses from his desk, returned to the window, and continued to watch the cricket lesson across the street.

The boys had resumed their places, Colin bowled again, and Amanda swung the bat, but she stepped over the crease in the process, which was a shame, because she'd managed to hit the ball this time. Retaining the bat in one hand just as a batsman ought to do, she hoisted her skirt a bit off the ground with her other hand and started to run, clearly not aware she'd broken the rules a second time. Owen, acting as umpire as well as keeper, followed her, waving his arms in a crossing motion and probably shouting as well to get her attention.

She slowed, stopped, and turned around as Owen approached her, and as he began to explain what she'd done wrong, Jamie chuckled at the indignant look on her face. She might not know much about cricket, but she certainly had a competitive streak.

Rolling her eyes in exasperation, she stalked back to where she'd started and lifted the bat to give it another go. Through his field glasses, he had a good view of her face, her eyes narrowed beneath the brim of her boater, her square jaw set, her black brows furrowed in concentration.

None of that helped her, and she missed again, making it plain that she needed clearer instruction on how to bat than his two sons were providing.

He could help her, of course, for he'd been quite a good batsman in his day. He'd taught both his sons to bat, and bowl as well. And the boys would be delighted if he'd abandon work and join them. But sadly, his speech wasn't finished, meaning he didn't have time for cricket in the park.

He lowered the field glasses, but as he shut the window, Amanda's words from that night in his room echoed back to him, and he stopped.

You're their father. Don't be content to watch them play from your window.

Jamie looked at the work piled on his desk, work that seemed to arrive in a never-ebbing tide. Work was all he did, for when a man needed to fill his life with distractions, work was one of the best.

Still, there were other distractions.

He looked out the window again, and when he saw Amanda swing the bat, whack the ball straight up into the air, and send the boys into peals of laughter, he decided it was high time he took an afternoon off.

CRICKET, AMANDA THOUGHT glumly, was just not her game. A few practice swings, all of them muffed, and she'd been heartlessly booted from consideration and dispatched to the sidelines.

Prevented from joining the group of boys now forming into teams, Amanda set aside her cricket bat and settled herself on the blanket she'd unfolded earlier, resigned to watching the match from a distance along with the various other nannies and tutors who'd brought their charges to the park. She slipped on her jacket and wrapped a knitted scarf around her throat as protection against the chilly autumn air, then opened the picnic basket Mrs. Richmond had prepared. But she'd barely retrieved a sandwich and a bottle of lemonade before a voice spoke beside her.

"Given up already, have you?"

Amanda looked up, twisting her head to find Lord Kenyon coming toward her across the grass. "I might say the same about you," she said in surprise. "Weren't you supposed to be working on a speech, or something?"

He paused at the edge of the blanket with a heavy sigh. "Don't remind me."

She eyed him with sympathy as he doffed his hat, sank down on the blanket beside her, and folded his long legs beneath him. "Not going well?"

Unexpectedly, he flashed her a grin. "About as well as your batting."

She made a face. "No wonder your speech isn't finished, if you've been up there watching my awful attempts at cricket. Is that why you came down? To tease?"

"No." He paused, his grin fading to a serious expression. "I'm here because I decided it's time I took your advice."

"My advice?"

"Yes." He nodded toward the cricket field. "To play with my sons instead of watching them from the window."

Happiness rose within her, sweet and painful, pressing against her chest until she could hardly breathe. She told herself this dizzying burst of happiness stemmed from how much his presence would please the boys, but as she slid a sideways glance over his profile, she knew what she felt wasn't only on behalf of Colin and Owen. "I'm glad."

He turned his head to look at her again. "So am I, Amanda."

At the sound of her name, the happiness inside intensified, and she looked away, forcing herself to speak. "The boys will be over the moon," she managed, nodding toward the cricket field. "They'll be quite willing to have *you* join their team, I'm sure."

"They'll have to wait a little bit." He gestured to the picnic basket near their feet. "I can't play cricket without sustenance. Unless there's not enough?"

"Oh, there's still plenty of sandwiches," she assured him, happy to talk about something innocuous like food while her breathing resumed a normal rhythm. "There's cold ham as well, if you'd prefer that, and a few apples. There might be some sweet biscuits, too, unless the boys ate them all."

"Sounds a bit of all right." He leaned forward to rummage through the basket near their feet, then retrieved a sandwich and a bottle of lemonade. "So why aren't you still playing?" he asked, nodding toward the cricket field as he unwrapped his sandwich from its covering of brown paper. "It doesn't seem like you to give up on anything after only one go."

"I didn't give up!" she said with indignation. "A boy named Archie arrived, so I had to give up my place on the team."

"Why? Because you're a girl? Now that surprises me."

"I can't think why," she countered, wrinkling up her nose. "Boys exclude girls from their games all the time."

"Well, yes, but . . ." He paused to take a swig of lemonade, giving her a rueful look. "We both know you're not the sort to let a pesky detail like gender stop you."

She gave him a reproving nudge with her foot. "And a good thing, too! Or you'd have gone through at least half a dozen tutors by now."

"Not that many, surely."

"You think I'm exaggerating? The boys told me that the first one you hired, a Mr. Partridge, only lasted three days. You make the appropriate calculations." She laughed as he grimaced.

"And," she added, "the fact that I'm female wasn't the reason I was booted off. At least, that's not the reason the boys gave me. Archie, they said, can wag the tail." She gave a sniff of injured dignity, still stinging from her dismissal. "Whatever that means."

Jamie laughed. "It means he's a very good batsman."

"Unlike me," she admitted, her indignation fading into discouragement.

"You just need practice. And a bit of proper instruction."

"I'll take instruction, if you're offering it," she said at once. "What was I doing wrong?"

"Your grip was off, for one thing. And your stance, too. Which reminds me," he added, gesturing to her skirt. "You should always wear pads when you bat. To protect your legs."

"Yes, so the boys told me, but that's rather difficult in a skirt. Of course," she added, laughing, "I could always put my trousers back on."

He didn't laugh with her. Instead, he looked down. "Ladies wear them underneath their skirts," he murmured, his gaze gliding over her legs, a slow perusal that made Amanda feel suddenly hot and flustered. But when he looked up again, his impassive face told her nothing. "The pads, I mean."

He looked away, and Amanda felt a tiny jolt of disappointment, a feeling that caused her to become immediately irritated with herself. For heaven's sake, she didn't want him staring at her legs and thinking things. Did she?

Mr. Bartlett's mind had clearly turned in that direction, and look how disastrously that had turned out. But even as she reminded herself of past history, she was also more acutely aware than ever before that Jamie was nothing like Mr. Bartlett. Her previous employer's gaze roaming over her had been an invasion of her privacy and had never impelled her to any feeling beyond a desire to slap his flushed round face.

Jamie's look was inspiring an entirely different feeling, but she knew that wasn't the point. Jamie was her employer, and however lusciously feminine she felt when he looked at her legs, nothing good could result from it.

With that reminder, Amanda returned to the topic of cricket, a far safer one than the topic of what she ought to wear under her skirts. "You said my grip was wrong. How so?"

"I'll show you." He popped the last bite of his sandwich into his mouth, set aside his lemonade, and turned toward her, reaching for the bat that lay on the blanket between them. But before he could show her how to hold it properly, he suddenly gave a chuckle. "I'll be damned," he murmured. "This is my old bat from schooldays."

"Is it? The boys dug it out for me to use. They told me their bats wouldn't do, that I needed a longer one. I hope you don't mind?"

"No, not at all," he assured her. "And the boys are quite right. You're too tall for a child's bat."

Amanda frowned, puzzled. "But you said this was your bat from schooldays. Or did you mean university?"

"No, it's definitely from Harrow days. But I was quite tall, even then." He turned it over and laughed again. "By God, this brings back memories. Where did they find it?"

"The attics, I think." She leaned closer, a bit dubious. "Are you sure it's yours?"

"Absolutely. Why do you ask?"

"It has a girl's name on it." She pointed to the handle of the bat and the name carved into the wood with delicate precision. "Sarah."

"Ah, yes." He smiled a little, staring down at the bat. "Sarah Dunn. She was the daughter of a neighboring farmer."

"Your first love?"

"Yes, although I'm not sure love had much to do with it, honestly," he answered, looking up. "After all, we were only fifteen. It was an adolescent infatuation—violent and passionate, to be sure, but we were far too young for it to be anything more."

She thought of the first time she'd seen Kenneth Halsbury, leaning indolently against the boot of a carriage in the drive at Willowbank, smoking a cigarette while he waited for his father, who'd been meeting with Mrs. Calloway, the headmistress. It had been a warm, still evening just before the start of summer term, and she'd been walking up the drive. He'd turned at the sound of her heels on the gravel, and the sight of his face had sent her entire life spinning into chaos. Her passion for teaching had given way to passion of a different sort, and three months later, she'd found herself ruined and left on her own to face her broken heart, destroyed career, and shattered dreams.

Looking back, she didn't know quite why one look at Kenneth on that fateful day should have had such a powerful effect on her. Perhaps because she'd been twenty-six but knew nothing of men, or perhaps because Papa had just died and she was still mired in grief, or perhaps because at Willowbank she'd been surrounded by females twenty-four hours a day. Whatever the reason, the first moment she'd set eyes on him, her heart had leaped in her chest with a joy so acute, it had felt more like pain. A bit like when Jamie had looked at her legs.

"Infatuation," she said with feeling, "can feel like love. No matter what your age."

"Only until one finds the real thing."

"Perhaps," she allowed, though she was somewhat skeptical that the real thing even existed. "Did you break this girl's heart?"

"No. Not that I haven't broken my share, I'm sorry to say," he added at once. "I was quite wild in my youth, and if a girl got too close to me, I was usually off like a shot, her heart be damned. But Sarah was different. Still, it didn't matter what either of us felt."

"What happened?"

"I was home for the summer holidays, and we were meeting in secret. My father caught us behind the hedgerows one day, and the fat was in the fire, as they say." He paused and looked down at the cricket bat, rubbing the letters carved there with his thumb. "He called Sarah a name I won't repeat and went for me with his walking stick. Got me a good whack to the head, too. Gave me quite a scar." He shifted the bat to one hand and pulled a lock of hair back from his forehead with the other, revealing a jagged dent at his left temple just below the hairline. "See? Right there. Gave me a concussion, too."

"Oh God, Jamie," she whispered, too sickened by the story to bother with proper forms of address.

"It was a blessing," he assured her. "I'm quite glad it happened."

"Glad?" she echoed, incredulous. "How can you be?"

His eyes suddenly glittered, like green glass in the sun. "Because that was the day I hit him back. My father never laid a hand on me again."

Amanda felt sick. "What about your brother? Couldn't he have protected you at all?"

He shook his head. "Geoff's health was always poor, especially when we were boys. Weak chest. Good thing, too."

"Good thing?"

"Yes. When he was only five, the doctors recommended sending him to the spas in France to get stronger, and my father didn't want a sickly heir, so he agreed. Geoff and his tutor were gone most of the time when we were growing up, which kept him safe from the old man's notions of discipline. Later, when I was old enough and strong enough to defy the old man, I made it clear that if he ever laid a hand on Geoff, I wouldn't just cosh him with his walking stick, I'd kill him with it."

"You shouldn't have had to." Amanda felt a flash of impotent rage. "Someone should have been there for you—an uncle, a cousin—someone should have protected you! Both of you."

At those words, his expression gentled. "Don't look so stricken, love," he said softly. "That day the old man found me with Sarah, everything turned out all right. And even if it hadn't," he added with a wicked smile, "that kiss was worth it."

Amanda stared at him, her anger giving way in the wake of that smile to an entirely different emotion. Her heart began to pound hard in her chest, her lips began to tingle, and when he lowered his gaze to her mouth, she felt desperately compelled to say something, anything, to divert his attention. "My first love was a poet," she blurted out. "At least, he wasn't really a poet, but he wanted to be."

"Was he any good?"

"I thought so at the time." She paused a moment. "Probably not," she amended, making both of them laugh.

Jamie reached for his bottle of lemonade and took a swallow. "Did he write poems about you? He must have done, if he was in love with you."

Had Kenneth ever been in love with her? She was inclined to doubt it. He'd said he loved her, but Kenneth had said a lot of things in the heat of passion, and it hardly mattered now anyway. Whatever his true feelings had been, Kenneth's notions of love had never included matrimony.

"He composed one or two poems about me," she admitted. "He once wrote—" She broke off, strangely embarrassed and well aware that if she wanted to keep her ruined reputation a secret, she probably shouldn't say anything about the man who had ruined it. "Never mind."

"No, tell me. What did he write about you? I'm keen to know."

"I can't think why," she said, and laughed a little, feeling awkward and cursing her impulsive tongue. But Jamie was watching her, waiting for a reply, and she reluctantly went on, "Very well. He once wrote that my eyes were like sunlight in a forest's dark embrace."

She forced another laugh, a dismissive one. "It sounds quite torrid, doesn't it?"

"Torrid, perhaps, but . . ." He paused, looking at her. "It's an apt description."

"Is it?" That took her back. She considered a moment, still doubtful even after all this time. She shook her head, looking away. "I never could see it. I still can't."

"I can."

The intensity in his voice startled her, and when she looked at him, her breath caught, for there was a hint of something she'd never before seen in those clear, cool eyes. Tenderness.

Suddenly, everything around them—the brightly colored autumn leaves on the trees, the grass of mottled green and gold, the topaz-blue sky—seemed to grow dim and fade away. The sounds of traffic along Park Lane and the voices of the people all around receded into silence. The only thing she saw was him, and the only thing she heard was the rush of excitement pulsing through her veins, and the only thing she felt was longing.

His gaze slid to her mouth, his eyes darkening to a duskier green, and wildly, she wondered if he was going to kiss her. She imagined it, his mouth on hers and his arms strong and tight around her, and the longing within her deepened and spread, bringing with it something she hadn't allowed herself to face, or even admit existed: her own deep and profound loneliness.

She wanted Jamie's kiss. For the first time in over two years, she wanted a man's mouth on hers and his arms around her and his hands on her, and for all the same reasons: to banish the emotional isolation of her existence, and to ease, if only for a few glorious, stolen moments, the pain of being alone.

Did he want that, too? she wondered, staring into eyes that were the foggy, misty green of frost on an English meadow. He must, she thought, looking at the lines that suffering and grief had carved into the edges of his face. Surely he must.

He leaned another fraction closer. So did she, aching with hungers of both body and soul.

"Papa? You're here!"

He jerked back, and the spell was broken. She ought to have been relieved, but when he turned away, relief was not what she felt. Instead, disappointment pierced her chest, and as he stood up and walked away, she berated herself for a fool.

A kiss, however wonderful it might feel, couldn't change her life. It couldn't erase the colossal error in judgment that had led her here; it could only tempt her to make that error a second time.

Romance had no place in her life now. She'd had that once, it was over, and now, she had no romantic illusions left. She had only her work and her pupils. She looked past Jamie, and when she saw Colin and Owen racing toward him across the grass, she knew their happiness would have to be her consolation.

SOMETIMES, TAKING A holiday could clear one's head and make work easier, but if Jamie thought his afternoon off would do that for him, he was destined for disappointment. And if he'd hoped that resuming the composition of his speech would be a distraction from what had almost happened in the park with Amanda that afternoon, he was sadly mistaken.

Even after hours in his study, the wastepaper basket beside him overflowing with a fresh lot of crumpled, pathetic efforts, his speech was no further along, Amanda was still vivid in his mind, and the arousal he'd felt, though banked at the moment, was still there, burning deep and low and waiting for any excuse to ignite.

He'd nearly kissed her. His hand tightened around his pen, the nib spreading ink across the page of his speech, but he barely noticed. In a park, surrounded by people, he'd almost kissed a woman he barely knew. When he hadn't kissed a woman, or even wanted to, in over three years. A woman who was not Pat. A woman who, less than three weeks ago, he'd thought was a man, for God's sake.

There was only one explanation for the entire baffling episode. Jamie tossed down his pen with a sound of exasperation, plunked his elbows on the desk, and rubbed his hands over his tired eyes. He was going mad.

Perhaps it was the strain of work. Or perhaps his body was rebelling at last against three years of self-imposed celibacy. But whatever the cause, his sanity was definitely slipping.

The admission didn't help, for even as he made it, the arousal he'd felt that afternoon stirred within him again, and he just couldn't summon the will to fight it, not this time.

When he closed his eyes, her face came first to his mind, her parted lips, her black lashes half closed over those extraordinary eyes, the delicate pink flush in her cheeks. There'd been desire there, in her face, and as he recalled it, his own body responded. His breathing quickened, his muscles tightened, and the arousal he'd banked only hours ago flared up within him, but instead of putting out that fire, he chose to fan the flames.

Easing back in his chair, he conjured pictures from imagination and guesswork—pictures of small, perfect breasts and long, slim legs. He imagined caressing her, sliding his hands along her waist and hips, cupping her buttocks, drawing her closer. He imagined kissing her, the satiny feel of her lips, the lush, sweet taste of her mouth.

Something, a vague whisper of uneasiness, intruded on these erotic imaginings. He frowned, working to push the feeling away, his body rebelling against any interruption to a hard-won, well-deserved, long-suppressed sexual fantasy.

He would not let me out until I kissed him.

Damn it.

Jamie opened his eyes and straightened in his chair, hating himself—not, sadly, for his illicit and inappropriate imaginings of Amanda, but for the pangs of conscience that had just ruined them.

Cursing, he reached for the glass of whisky on the desk beside him, downed it all in one swallow, and set the glass back down. Then, with the determination and self-restraint borne of long practice, he pushed erotic thoughts of his employee out of his mind, picked up his pen, and tried to resume his work.

He read the opening paragraph of his speech, trying to judge it objectively, but after the torrid thoughts that had been running through his mind, any words about why it was vital to increase the budget for the education of Britain's poorer classes seemed terribly dull.

He inked his pen, crossed out the opening, and valiantly tried again. "The British have always taken great pride in the education of the children in our upper classes," he murmured as he wrote. "Surely the accident of birth should not deprive those less fortunate—"

He stopped, his concentration broken again, but not because of any erotic imaginings. No, he thought he'd heard a noise directly overhead. He looked up, frowning at the ceiling, but though he waited several moments, the sound was not repeated, and he concluded it must have been a mouse he'd heard, or perhaps Oscar, the boys' cat. He bent his head and went on with his task.

"Nor should we be prevented from doing right by all our people," he resumed, writing as he spoke. "Surely the great wealth and prosperity of our nation can only be enhanced by a well-educated populace—"

The noise came again, louder this time, and he realized it was no mouse or cat he was hearing. It was the unmistakable tread of footsteps.

He looked up again, his gaze following the sound across the floorboards of the attic above as they passed directly over his head.

Maids' quarters were in the attics, but with the family at Ravenwood, no maids were in residence. Amanda was in the nanny's room beside the nursery, and Mrs. Richmond and Samuel's rooms were below stairs, so there should be no one up in the attics, especially not in the room directly above, a room used only for storage.

The footsteps stopped, but then Jamie heard a sliding sound and a soft thud, and he put down his pen, knowing it had to be the boys. They'd gotten out of bed, sneaked out of their rooms, and for a reason he had no doubt involved mischief of some sort, were rooting around in the attics.

He picked up the lamp on his desk and went up to investigate.

At the top of the attic stairs, he found the corridor to his left completely closed off, as it should be, but the door leading to the one on the right was open, and he could see lamplight spilling down the corridor from the room at the very end of the passage, the room directly over his study.

Wondering what on earth his two scapegraces were up to, he started down the corridor, but when he reached the doorway, he found that it was not Colin and Owen rooting about amid broken-down furnishings, old trunks, and storage crates.

"Amanda?"

She turned around with a gasp, pressing a hand to her pin tuck shirt-front. "Heavens, you startled me."

"My apologies. I heard noises up here, and I thought I'd better investigate."

"I was trying to be quiet. I didn't wake you, did I?"

"No. I was working."

"Still?" She eyed him with sympathy. "I thought surely you'd have finished by now."

"No such luck," he muttered and decided to change the subject. "What are you doing up here?"

"I was looking for the croquet set. Samuel had mentioned there was one in one of the trunks up here. If it's fine out tomorrow afternoon, I thought the boys and I might have croquet. Or clock golf. Or badminton."

He grinned. "Given up on cricket, have you?"

"Well, the boys did boot me off the team," she reminded him. "My pride demands we have at least one game at the ready that I can play without feeling like a fool."

"Don't be so hard on yourself. You only began learning the game today, and believe me, cricket's not as easy as it looks. With a bit more practice, you'll do all right."

She made a face. "Forgive me if I'm doubtful," she said, and returned her attention to the trunk she'd been searching through upon his arrival.

He stared at the shapely hips that were being presented to his gaze with such erotic innocence, and when she wriggled, trying to push the trunk aside, all his suppressed fantasies came roaring back, as lusty as before and every bit as immune to the admonitions of his conscience.

"Really, my lord, where are your manners?"

"What?" Jamie blinked, trying to regain his wits as her amused question about his manners penetrated his aroused, very unmannered senses. "I beg your pardon?"

Without straightening, she twisted around to look at him. "A chivalrous man would come and help me move some of these trunks."

"Right. Of course." Relieved at the idea of a task to divert his attention from her luscious hips, Jamie set the lamp he was holding on a nearby packing crate and came to where she stood. "Best move out of the way," he told her.

"Careful," she warned, stepping back. "That one's full of books and quite heavy."

He didn't even bother trying to lift it; he merely shoved it aside with his foot, then moved several crates out of the way as well so that she could reach the trunks that were against the far wall. But when she moved to his side and opened one of the trunks, he decided he'd flirted with the line of propriety long enough.

"I shall leave you to it then," he murmured with a bow, and turned to go, but before he'd taken three steps, she gave a kind of groaning laugh that made him pause.

"What is it?" he asked, turning around.

"I cannot seem to get away from this game." She turned toward him, a cricket bat in her hands, and when he saw her laughing face, he couldn't resist flirting with the line just a little bit longer.

She gripped the bat and gave it swing, then looked at him. "Well?" she asked. "Was that any better? What?" she added as he laughed. "Why are you laughing? What am I doing wrong?"

"Where should I start?"

"You offered to help me this afternoon," she reminded. "And laughing," she added, frowning at him, "is not helpful."

"Sorry," he apologized at once. "But you're swinging that bat as if it's rounders you're playing."

"Is that such a bad thing?" she countered at once. "I can hit a ball in rounders."

"Cricket's a bit different. But," he added as her shoulders slumped in discouragement, "if you can hit a ball in rounders, you can probably hit a ball in cricket, too. You just have to learn how it's done. Didn't the twins give you any pointers this afternoon?"

She shook her head. "They just said if I wanted to join the team, I'd have to prove myself. Then, they handed me the bat and said I had to hit the ball and run for the opposite wicket."

He gave her a dubious look. "They didn't persuade you to wager anything on the outcome of this audition, did they?"

"They tried. I didn't fall for it. I've learned a thing or two since Cowboys and Indians."

He chuckled and came to take the bat from her. "I'll show you how to bat properly. Then you can turn the tables and trick them for a change."

Glancing around to be sure nothing was in his way, he squared off and swung the bat, moving slowly so she could observe precisely what he did. "See?" he said, and did it again. "You swing down toward the ground, then up, not straight across. And you keep the lower half of your body facing sideways, your upper body facing the bowler. Now, let's get you in the proper position."

He bent down, rummaged in the trunk she'd pulled the bat from, and pulled out three cricket stumps. "Come with me."

He walked to the center of the room where there was some open space, then he set up the wicket and straightened. "Notice how I've placed the stumps?"

"Stumps?" She moved to stand beside him. "You mean these three sticks? I thought those were called the wicket."

"They are, but the packed dirt you run across is also called a wicket, so to avoid confusion, most of us just call these the stumps. See how I've stood them upright in a row?" When she nodded, he removed the center stump and tossed it aside, then stepped back a few feet and took a batting stance. "To practice your batting, you'll face the stumps, like this."

"Face them? But aren't they supposed to be behind you when you bat?"

"Yes, but we're indoors, so we can't use a cricket ball to practice with. Having the stumps in front of you with the middle one missing is how you practice your swing when you don't have a ball. You'll want to swing the bat between the two remaining stumps without touching them. Like this."

He swung again, demonstrating the point. "Notice how I'm keeping the flat side of the bat facing forward?" When she nodded, he stepped back and tapped the floor where he'd been standing with the end of the bat. "Come, stand here."

When she had positioned herself in the exact place he'd been a moment before, the wicket to her left, he moved to stand a few feet in front of her. "See how the seam of one floorboard is straight through the center of the wicket?" he asked, gesturing to the floor with the bat in his hand. "That seam," he went on as she nodded, "can act as your sight line and help you position your body in the proper stance. Where are your toes?"

She lifted the hem of her skirt several inches to peer down at her feet, and when he caught sight of her ankles, he sucked in a sharp breath. Even in opaque black stockings, her ankles were not helping him maintain his equilibrium.

"Put the tips of your toes on the sight line," he muttered, averting his gaze as he held out the bat to her, and when she took it, he moved back to a safe distance, reminding himself to pay attention to her stance, not imagine the shape of her legs.

"Bend your knees a bit and lift your right elbow higher. Good," he added when she complied. "Now, keeping in your mind what you saw me do, try to do the same."

She did, but when she swung the bat, she hit one of the stumps and knocked it over.

"That's because of your grip," he said. "The way you're holding the bat is preventing you from keeping the flat side forward. I'll show you."

He stepped forward, putting his hands over hers on the bat, thinking to maneuver her fingers into a better position, but the moment he touched her, he realized he'd made a serious mistake.

He stilled, staring down at his hands, feeling her smaller ones beneath, warm and soft, her skin silky against his palms. He should step back now, while he still could, but it had been so long, so damned long, since he'd even touched a woman, and he just couldn't make his body obey his mind's command.

She stirred, but she didn't pull her hands away. Nonetheless, he opened his, lifting them a fraction so that he was no longer touching her, giving her the clear choice to withdraw, hoping like hell she wouldn't take it.

She didn't move.

He closed his eyes. Slowly, ever so slowly, he leaned closer, and when he caught the fresh, pristine scent of talcum powder, he appreciated the reason at once.

She must have bathed.

The thought was so erotic, it made him dizzy. He stilled again, his hands suspended just above hers, his eyes closed, his heart pounding so hard, it hurt his chest. He could not move, he could only stand here, taking in the scent of her skin and the sound of her soft, quick breathing, and the warmth of her body so close to his own. He wanted to stand here forever.

"Jamie?"

He heard his name and the question in it. He opened his eyes, but he could not reply. He could only stare at her, helpless, as lust flooded through him in thick, hot waves.

She'd said he had a poker face, but as he watched her eyes widen and rosy color wash into her cheeks, he knew any talent he had for hiding his feelings had chosen now to desert him. Her lips parted, drawing his gaze like a magnet, and when the tip of her tongue touched her bottom lip, he knew he had to draw back, before he did something that he would regret and she would despise him for.

"I should go." He started to step back, but then, for no reason, he stopped. "Or you should," he added, hating that he was so desperate to hang on to this moment that he would put the burden of proper conduct on her, when the burden was his. He compromised. "One of us should go."

"Yes," she agreed, but she didn't move.

"I don't . . ." He paused, and then he laughed, a short, caustic sound. "I don't want to."

Her eyes, wide and pretty, looked into his. "Neither do I," she whispered.

And then, just like that, she was in his arms. The cricket bat clattered to the floor, and he kicked it out of the way. Then he pulled her close, tilted his head, and captured her mouth with his.

So long since he'd kissed a woman, he almost felt as if he'd never done it in his life before. Her lips were like warm velvet, and the feel of them against his own mouth sent exquisite shimmers of pleasure throughout his body.

His hand pressed into the small of her back, urging her closer, and when she came, he slid his arm fully around her waist as his other hand lifted to cup her face. The skin of her cheek was soft against his palm, the wisps of her hair tickled his fingertips, and after his self-imposed exile in the desert of celibacy, her kiss was like water and food to his body and a sweet balm of solace to his soul. But it was not enough. Not nearly enough.

He slid his hand to the back of her neck, raking it through the short, silky crop of her curls, then tightening to tilt her head back. He deepened the kiss, parting her lips with his, and her low moan into his mouth harkened to his need, urging him on. He responded gladly, his tongue entering her mouth, tasting deeply of her as he slid his hands down to shape the contours he'd already imagined—the gentle swell of her breasts, the slimness of her waist, the more generous curves of her hips. How, he wondered, had he ever managed to deny himself the pleasures of a woman for so damn long? Self-denial like that seemed ridiculous now, absurd.

He tightened his embrace again, wrapping one arm around her waist and the other around her back, wanting her even closer, needing even more.

She must have felt the same, for her arms came up around his neck, bringing the delicate scent of powder and the womanly heat beneath it to his nostrils, and he gave an agonized groan as his masculine instincts perceived her arousal.

His palms glided over her buttocks, and he made a sound of appreciation against her mouth as he cupped their fullness in his palms. And when he lifted her, pressing her hips to his hard arousal, the pleasure of it nearly drove him to his knees.

He wanted that. He longed to take her down to the floor with him, to pull up her skirts, to pleasure her with his hands and his mouth, and to feel those long, long legs of hers wrap around him as he came inside her.

But that, he knew, could not be. She was in his employ, and as he'd told her—promised her—he wasn't the sort to bed the help. In these circumstances, the wild, reckless chap he'd been at twenty might have done it, but he wasn't that man anymore.

Because of Pat.

The thought of his late wife gave him the will to stop, if not the desire. He eased Amanda to the ground, and as her hips slid down along his shaft, the pleasure was so unbearably exquisite, he groaned against her mouth, and when he tore his lips from hers and stepped back, it felt as if he was ripping himself in half.

For a long moment, neither of them moved. In the dim light and dusky shadows of the attic, they stared at each other, their rapid, mingled breathing the only sound.

She lifted her hand to her lips, still puffy from his kisses, and he knew that he could not stand here a moment longer or he would come apart.

"Forgive me," he muttered as he picked up his lamp and turned away.

He walked toward the door. He didn't dare look back, for he had anarchy inside him, and if he paused, if he turned, if he took even one more look at Amanda's long legs, gorgeous eyes, and kiss-stung lips, the promise he'd made to her just two weeks ago would be broken beyond amendment, any integrity he thought he had would be proved a joke, and any notion that he was a responsible and honorable man would be lost.

His body in full rebellion against what he'd just done, he departed the attic and returned to his study. Closing the door behind him, he walked to the nearest window and flung up the sash, his only thought to cool the fire raging in his blood.

He stood there, one shoulder propped against the window frame, breathing deep and trying not to wish he was still the wild, skirt-chasing rake he used to be. He stood there a long time.

Chapter 13

Amanda watched the door swing shut behind Jamie, but she scarcely heard the squeak of the hinges or the click of the latch or the tap of his footsteps as he descended the stairs.

Her blood was a roar in her ears, her heart was thudding in her chest, and she couldn't seem to catch her breath. And if all that wasn't enough to confound a woman, her knees didn't seem to work properly.

Amanda sank down onto a trunk with a thud as her wobbly legs gave way beneath her. "Oh dear," she murmured, and gave a wild little laugh, wondering if she were having some sort of glorious, erotic dream.

She pressed a hand to her mouth and grimaced, for her lips felt tender and swollen, as if rasped by sandpaper. No dream, she realized, and with that, her exhilaration faded. She lowered her hand into her lap, trying to get her bearings.

It was just a kiss, she reminded herself, nothing new to a ruined, scandal-ridden woman like her. Kenneth, after all, had kissed her many times. He'd also seduced her and bedded her. Thanks to him, nothing about physical love ought to be any sort of surprise to her now, and yet, Jamie's mouth on hers was like nothing she'd ever experienced before.

Unlike Kenneth's kiss, Jamie's had not been sweet and tender and a slow path to a virgin's seduction. And it had certainly not been like Mr. Bartlett's kiss, forced on her in a closet and impelling her to use force to escape.

No, Jamie's kiss had been exhilarating and wild and scorching hot, and had left her with the strange, bizarre feeling that she'd never really been kissed in her life before.

Still, despite how it had felt, she knew one thing for certain. It had been a mistake. Jamie was her employer, and letting him kiss her had been inappropriate, foolish, and possibly disastrous.

Not that allowing him to kiss her was what had happened, precisely. In fact, when she thought back, she wasn't quite sure who had kissed whom. One moment, he'd been teaching her how to hold a cricket bat, and the next, his lips had been on hers, and her arms had twined eagerly around his neck, and everything in the world had gone spinning out of control.

Regardless of who had made the first move tonight, the fact remained that stopping it had never entered her head. Quite the contrary, for Jamie had been the one to call a halt, Jamie the one who had pulled back and walked away.

In fact, if stopping had been left up to her, Amanda suspected she and Jamie would still be standing here, their lips locked together, their arms wrapped around each other in a passionate embrace.

Chagrined by her own idiocy, Amanda groaned and buried her hot face in her hands. Hadn't she learned her lesson by now? Hadn't Kenneth taught her that carnal desires meant ruin for an unmarried woman? Hadn't Mr. Bartlett reminded her that it was up to women to firmly and clearly enforce the boundaries because men could not be trusted to do so?

Either way, the question remained: what was she supposed to do now?

Amanda lifted her head at that question and forced herself to stop this stream of self-recrimination. Regrets were a waste of time. What mattered was what her next action should be.

Her first thought was to run away, so that she wouldn't have to face him tomorrow. But she didn't have the luxury of such cowardice, for she had nowhere to go, and little money to get there. And besides, she thought in aggravation, why should she have to run away? Why should she have to surrender a job she loved because of one mistake?

And there were the boys to consider. They were doing so well now. If she left, what would happen to them? They'd revert to their previous naughty ways, and that would be such a shame, given the progress they'd made. They were good boys, both of them, and they didn't deserve to be abandoned by her because she and their father had made a stupid mistake.

No, leaving was not the answer. Perhaps she and Jamie could just pretend that kiss had never happened. Perhaps they could ignore it and carry on.

The moment Amanda considered that course, she knew she couldn't take it. Ignoring the problem between herself and her employer was what she'd done in her previous post, and though this situation and her feelings about it were quite different this time around, nothing would be resolved by sticking her head in the sand. Jamie wasn't Mr. Bartlett, not by a long way. But he was a man, and what had happened tonight might lead him to believe her virtue was open to question.

She had to face him, confront the situation head-on, and make it clear that though both of them were equally to blame for what had happened tonight, she wanted no repetition of it. Then perhaps they could both forget about it.

Amanda rose and left the attic, relieved that she had a plan to deal with the situation. But her relief proved short-lived, for as she lay in bed later that night trying to fall asleep, her lips still tingled from Jamie's kiss, her body still burned everywhere he had touched her, and she knew that for her, at least, forgetting about that extraordinary kiss was going to be easier said than done.

IT TOOK THREE days for Jamie to regain his equilibrium.

Kissing Amanda had shattered the numbed state of body and mind that had kept him from going mad these past three years. It had reawakened raw physical needs within him that he'd almost forgotten, and three days of cold baths, relentless work, and sleeping at his club were required before Jamie was able to put his priorities back in order.

He owed her an apology for what had happened. Even now, he wasn't quite sure if he had made the first move that night in the attic or if she had, but he also knew distinctions like that didn't matter. He possessed position and wealth, and the power that came with them. She had none of those things. As tempting as it might be to fashion excuses for himself, he knew his conduct had no excuse.

He also had a duty to his sons, a duty he'd spent far too long neglecting in the past, a duty Amanda had been the one to finally force him to face. She was an excellent tutor and the first person he'd found capable of watching over his sons with any degree of success, and he had no intention of losing her.

By Tuesday morning, he'd managed to force any erotic notions about her out of his mind, and he felt sufficiently master of himself to make his apologies. The timing was ideal, for Tuesday was her day out, and Samuel had already taken the boys for an outing, giving Jamie the perfect opportunity to speak with her alone before she departed to enjoy her day of freedom.

He found her at her desk in the nursery, the boys' pet cat, Oscar, asleep in her lap. She was writing a letter and seemed so preoccupied with her task that she didn't notice his arrival.

Sunshine coming through the window fell over where she sat, making her short black curls gleam almost blue in the bright morning light, but that wasn't what made him pause in the doorway. In the sunlight, the silhouette of her shape was faintly visible through her white blouse, and the shadowy curve of her breast nearly sent his hard-won composure sliding off into oblivion.

Suddenly, Oscar woke, lifting his head to give Jamie a warning hiss. Interrupted in her letter writing, Amanda looked at the animal, then turned her head toward the doorway, and when she spied Jamie standing there, she looked away again at once, rosy color washing into her cheeks and reminding him forcibly of the reason he was here.

He watched her shove the letter she was writing into her blotter, and fearing the worst, he cursed himself for waiting three days. "Good morning," he greeted.

At once, she moved to stand up, causing Oscar to jump off her lap with an indignant wail and stalk off in a huff.

"My lord," she greeted, not quite looking at him. "The boys aren't here this morning, I'm afraid. They've gone with Samuel to the London Zoo. They wanted to see the Aquatic Vivarium."

"Yes, I know. Samuel told me where they were spending the day when he valeted me this morning."

That garnered her full attention. "You slept here last night? So, you've decided to stop—" She broke off, but her unfinished question hung in the air so clearly he could almost hear it.

You've decided to stop avoiding me?

He gave a cough. "I've elevated Samuel formally to the position of valet, by the way. I wrote to Torquil about it last week, and he agreed to the change, and he promised to send another footman from Ravenwood. So now, there will be three servants to watch the boys on your day out, or to help you with them when they become overwhelming."

"Yes, Mrs. Richmond told me this morning. Is that . . ." She paused, shifted her weight a bit nervously, then went on, "Is that why you've come up? To tell me this news?"

"No. But I did want to speak to you alone, and when I learned you hadn't yet departed for your day out, this seemed a good opportunity." He gestured to the space between them. "May I?"

The color in her cheeks deepened, and he hastened on before she could refuse. "I wouldn't intrude upon your free time if it wasn't important. I do hope you can give me a moment?"

"Of course." She gestured to the wooden chair by her desk. "Please, do sit down, my lord."

He crossed the room, pulled the straight-backed wooden chair around so that he could face her directly across the desk, and once she had resumed her seat, he sat down as well.

The sun coming through the window had, thankfully, moved behind a cloud. If it hadn't, he feared his task would have been even harder than it was already proving to be. "I hope I'm not intruding. You looked quite preoccupied when I came in."

"No, no. I was just writing you a letter."

"Me?" His half-formed apprehensions realized, dismay rocked him, and he tried to brace himself for the worst. "Is it a letter of resignation?"

Her eyes widened a bit, in surprise or alarm, he couldn't tell, but when she spoke, her voice was quiet and composed. "Should it be?"

Realizing what she meant, he hastened into speech. "No, God, no. I only ask because I wouldn't blame you if you did resign. God knows, most women would, after—"

He stopped, cursing himself. Damn it all, what was he doing? Trying to push her out the door? He knew what he needed to say, and it was best to get on with it before he said anything else that would only make things worse. But as he opened his mouth to express regret for his conduct and offer the requisite apologies, he couldn't make the words come out.

The reason, he appreciated in chagrin, was that he felt not a scrap of regret for that kiss. Even now, desire to repeat the experience was rising within him, and he feared only the flimsiest excuse was needed for him to act on it. Hell, if there weren't a desk between them right now, he feared he'd be more inclined to repeat his mistake than apologize for it.

Thankfully, the cat decided to stop sulking and jumped up into Amanda's lap again, providing Jamie with a much-needed neutral topic. "Oscar seems quite fond of you."

"Thankfully, yes. If he wasn't, I think the boys' opinion of me would be much lower."

"They do adore that cat. Sadly, no one else does."

That surprised her. "But why?" she asked, stroking the gray tabby's head. "He's very sweet."

"To you, perhaps," he countered wryly. "And he loves the boys. I, however, am beneath his contempt."

"Perhaps because you just don't show him enough affection." She grinned, lifting the cat to face him, and Oscar immediately began spitting at Jamie. "Want to hold him?"

"Not a chance."

They both laughed, and Oscar, clearly not liking this show of comradery between the two humans, wriggled free of Amanda's grasp, gave Jamie one last hiss, and jumped off the desk.

"You see?" Jamie said, watching as Oscar departed the nursery in a huff, his tail swishing indignantly behind him. "He hates me. Other than the boys, he hates everyone else in the house, too, including the servants. He always has."

"If that's so, why did you let the boys keep him?"

He gave her a wry look. "Deny those boys the half-starved, pathetically hissing baby cat they rescued from a tree? I'd have liked to see you try."

"I see your point." She settled back in her chair and gestured to the blotter on her desk. "But to answer your question, I was writing you a report of the boys' progress to date. Given how busy you've been, I wasn't sure when we'd have time to talk in person. Is that . . ." She paused and gave a little cough. "Is that why you came up? To talk about the boys?"

He seized on that excuse, even though he knew he was only postponing the inevitable. "I do need to keep abreast of how they are progressing," he said.

"Of course," she agreed at once. "You'll be pleased to know they seem to be settling down a bit."

"No practical jokes recently?"

"Well, there was the rash on Colin's hands," she began.

"Rash?" He stiffened in his chair. "What rash?"

"Don't be alarmed, my lord. It was nothing. I applied some cream, made him wear gloves the past few days, and he's healed quite nicely."

"But what caused it, do you know?"

"Oh yes. I recognized the rash at once. He had plucked bunches of rue leaves out of the kitchen garden with his bare hands, and since it was a bright, sunny afternoon, of course he got the reaction. In sunlight, rue oil has a detrimental effect upon the skin."

"Rue allergy?" Jamie frowned, still puzzled. "But how could that possibly be a practical joke?"

"Because he did it on purpose. You may remember, I'm making them polish all the duke's silver, one hour every day, as punishment for the slugs in my bed? Well," she added when he nodded, "the day of the rue incident, they'd been polishing silver as usual. That afternoon when the rash appeared, he tried to claim it was the silver polish that was causing it and declared that I couldn't possibly be so cruel as to make him continue."

Jamie grinned. "My son is so clever."

"Not as clever as he thinks he is," she countered dryly. "His little ploy didn't fool me for a second. I know rue allergy when I see it."

"Still, you must admit, it was rather ingenious," he said, still grinning. "With a rash on his hands, he surely got a reprieve from the silver."

"A very temporary one, I assure you. I will have him back to his task in a day or two. Those boys shall not be allowed to stop until they've polished every last piece."

He wiped the grin off his face. "You're a hard taskmaster, Amanda," he said, striving to sound appropriately solemn.

"Perhaps, but I doubt I'll have slugs in my bed ever again. And the rue provided the perfect opportunity to explain the scientific principles behind phototoxicity."

"You do like to use real-world examples in your teaching, don't you?"

"As much as possible. It's more effective than merely studying academic texts, and so much more interesting. By the way, there's something I want to ask you. Because your work takes up so much of your time, I feel the boys ought to understand what you do and the importance of it, so we are commencing lessons on the workings of Parliament. I was hoping you might be able to take some time and give us a lecture on the subject?"

"I'd be happy to, but I think I might have a better idea than a mere lecture. Since you're so fond of teaching by example, why don't you bring the boys to Westminster one day? I can give them—and you—a tour, explain what I do—"

He broke off at the sight of her smile, a smile filled with such pleasure that it drove his own suggestion—and any other coherent thought—straight out of his head.

"Oh, what a wonderful idea," she exclaimed. "That will be so much better than a schoolroom lecture. Thank you, my lord. Given how busy you are with Parliament in session, it's very kind."

He stirred in his seat, embarrassed, well aware that kindness wasn't at all what he felt right now. Shifting a little, he went on in a rush, "Well, you did say I ought to spend more time with them, and I've been letting you down in that regard. And it would be good for them to see for themselves how our government functions. They'll be able to envision so much better what they're learning about if they've seen the rooms and chambers for themselves."

"Oh, I'm so glad we spoke about this," she cried excitedly. "The boys will love it."

He wanted to ask if she would love it, too, but he refrained. "I have to be in the Chamber before the end of Question Time," he said instead, "so if you come about two o'clock, that gives us plenty of time for a tour beforehand, and tea as well."

"Can we watch the debates?"

"Of course. The view from the Ladies' Gallery isn't much, I'm afraid, but nonetheless, you can see and hear everything that goes on."

"What day should we come? Perhaps," she added before he could reply, her smile taking on a teasing curve, "we ought to visit on the day you give that speech of yours?"

He groaned. "Must you?"

"The boys would love to hear it."

"I doubt that, since it's utter rubbish."

Her teasing smile immediately vanished, and she eyed him with sympathy. "It can't be that bad."

"Honestly, I can't say." He sighed. "But I do know that every time I practice it, it seems boring as hell—so boring, in fact, it even makes me want to fall asleep. I doubt it will persuade anyone to vote to send the bill to committee, much less agree to bring it back for a second reading."

"Do you want some help? I am a teacher, after all. I could read over what you've got, give my opinion, perhaps assist you with editing it?"

His gaze slid down, his body began to burn, and he hauled his gaze back up. "I don't think that would be wise, Amanda."

She looked down, fidgeting with her blotter. "No," she murmured. "Perhaps not."

"I don't wish you to misunderstand me," he said hastily. "I appreciate the offer, I do, but . . ." He paused, staring at her, knowing he may have given offense but unable to quite make the humiliating admission that he didn't trust himself where she was concerned and that he needed more time and distance before he dared to chance it. "It wouldn't be wise," he said again.

"Of course," she agreed at once, nodding fervently, not quite looking at him.

It was time, he realized, to stop stalling. "We've come, I think, to the perfect place for me to say what I came here to say." He paused, then went on, "Amanda, I owe you an apology. I behaved abominably the other night. No, please," he added as she started to speak. "What happened should not have happened, and that is my fault. It's just that it's been so long since I've wanted—"

He broke off, appreciating that he'd nearly ruined his apology by attempting to justify what was unjustifiable. Worse, he'd almost confessed aloud the barely containable desire he felt for her. How mortifying.

Taking a deep breath, he tried again. "I broke my word that you were safe from my attentions, and I have no explanation to give or excuse to offer. I'm sure it's little consolation to you, but please know that I berate myself bitterly for my actions, being aware of how your previous employer had subjected you to the very same attention—"

"Oh, but it wasn't," she protested, cutting off his stream of self-recrimination midsentence, and even as she spoke, color flamed in her cheeks again. "It wasn't . . . it didn't . . . that is, it didn't feel . . . I mean . . ."

Her voice trailed off, and her tongue darted out to lick her lips as if they were dry, riveting his attention and sending his imagination onto even more dangerous ground. "It wasn't the same at all, Jamie," she whispered.

"It wasn't?" That was such a gratifying piece of news that he couldn't help grinning. "Truly?"

At once, her severe dark brows drew together in a frown of reproof, and he hastily wiped the grin off his face. "But nonetheless," she went on, "it was a mistake."

He ought to wholeheartedly agree, but then he glanced down, and as he envisioned the curves he'd had a shadowy glimpse of earlier and remembered how she'd felt in his arms the other night, that kiss began to seem less like a mistake and more like the most ripping thing he'd ever done.

"One we should never have made."

At the sound of her voice, he jerked his gaze back up. "Quite so, yes," he agreed, his voice firm, hearty, and so patently insincere, it almost made him wince. "You may be assured that it won't happen again," he added, praying he was a strong enough man to make that assurance the truth.

She nodded, but she did not reply. His goal had been accomplished, they seemed in complete accord, and it would be a good idea if he departed now, before he was tempted to act on any of the erotic thoughts and impulses that were still plaguing him. Lingering here, he appreciated, was akin to lighting matches in a room full of gunpowder, and yet he didn't move.

Instead, he looked into her eyes, with all their deep, murky colors, and suddenly, he felt as if he was hanging on the edge of an abyss. He tried to think of his boys, and Pat, and the honorable, responsible man he had spent over a decade trying to become. But as he looked into Amanda's eyes, he didn't want to be that man. He didn't want to think of Pat. He didn't want to mourn and grieve. He didn't want to be good and responsible and keep his promises and set an honorable example for his sons. He wanted . . . oh God, what he wanted . . .

The yearning that came over him was so strong, it felt like a hand reaching into his chest and pulling his heart out. A yearning for what, he couldn't have said, but it was an ache far deeper than unslaked lust.

He drew in his breath, caught the powdery scent of talc, and forced himself to pull back from the brink. It felt like tearing himself in half.

"I really must be on my way, or I'll be late," he said, and stood up. "Again, please accept my apologies for my conduct. As to Westminster," he added as she rose to her feet, "if you think the boys would really want to hear me speak, then come on Tuesday, one week from now. Tuesday's your day out, I know, but that's the first day of debate on the Education Bill, and it's scheduled first on the docket, so that's when I have the best chance to give my speech. I can't guarantee that I will catch the Speaker's eye, of course, especially since I'm not a minister, just an ordinary backbench MP, but Peel likes me, so there's a good chance he'll call on me when I stand. If so, I expect it will be well before the dinner bell— somewhere between five and seven would be my guess."

She nodded. "Should we come in by the visitor's entrance?"

"Yes, by the Clock Tower. Go across Westminster Hall, and I'll meet you on St. Stephen's Porch at two o'clock." He bowed. "Enjoy your day out."

With that, he departed the nursery and went down to where his carriage waited at the curb outside, breathing deeply of the cool air to get the soft, womanly scent of her out of his nostrils. He started to step into the vehicle, but suddenly changed his mind.

"I'll walk for a bit," he told his driver, "then pick up a hansom. Take the carriage back around to the mews if you would. And don't worry about fetching me tonight. I'll be quite late, so I'll take a hansom back from Westminster as well."

"It's quite cold today, my lord. Are you sure?"

"I'm sure. I've a bit of a headache," he lied as his driver gave him a dubious glance. "The cold air will do me good."

He turned away. "I just hope it cools my damned imagination," he muttered under his breath as he started down the sidewalk.

Chapter 14

The twins were so excited about their outing to Westminster that during the week that followed Jamie's offer to give them a tour, both boys were absolute angels. They did their lessons, perpetrated no practical jokes on her or the other servants, and polished the remaining silver without a single complaint.

Their new footman, William, arrived from Ravenwood as planned, and he was so impressed by the improvement in the boys' behavior, he declared that Amanda must have the patience of a saint.

Amanda, however, knew she was anything but saintly.

Jamie's kiss came back into her mind at least a dozen times a day, and whenever she thought of it, her spirits soared with an unreasoning joy. Sometimes at night, the taste of his mouth and the hot burn of his caress invaded her dreams and she would awaken with her body aching with desire, but she knew there was no future in longings of that sort.

Most young women, she supposed, would assume a kiss as searing and intimate as the one she and Jamie had shared would mean that a marriage proposal was in the offing, but Amanda was too worldly for such expectations. Passion, as she well knew, wasn't love, and it wasn't necessarily a prelude to marriage.

And though Jamie clearly desired her, she could not delude herself into believing that his kiss had been inspired by a deeper feeling. For him, there had been only one great love, and though the woman who had inspired it was dead, he'd made it quite clear there would never be another.

For her own part, she wasn't sure she wanted marriage anyway, from any man. She'd dreamed that dream already—marriage, children, a future shared with her one true love—but Kenneth had killed that dream, and she'd come to accept her spinster's life. She was married to her vocation, her pupils were her children, and she vastly preferred taking care of herself by a profession she loved than relying on a man to do it for her.

But though she didn't dream of marriage anymore, in the wake of Jamie's kiss, there were times, late at night in the darkness of her room, when she dreamed of him, of his mouth on hers and his arms around her, and when she woke, her body aching with desire, the loneliness of her celibate life seemed almost unbearable. His kiss had reminded her of the pleasures of physical love and the surcease of loneliness that could accompany it, and it was all Amanda could do not to sneak over to the other side of the house, slip into his room, and fling herself at him with shameless abandon. She already had the reputation of a strumpet, after all, and when she woke from these fevered, erotic dreams, she was tempted almost beyond restraint to live up to that reputation.

The main reason she didn't do it was the boys. She loved those boys, loved them with a depth of feeling that was so fierce, it sometimes shocked her. In the nearly two months she'd been here, Colin and Owen had stolen her heart, and she couldn't bear the idea of risking her job and losing them. She'd have to leave them someday, of course, in a few years when they went off to school, but she wasn't about to precipitate that heartbreak by igniting an affair with their father that could only offer her an even lonelier future than the one she already had.

He stopped sleeping at his club, but by unspoken agreement, they took great pains to avoid being alone together. Each morning, she sent the boys down to have breakfast with him, and afterward, when he brought them back to the nursery, he was so politely stiff and formal that no one observing him would dream anything untoward had ever occurred. Amanda tried her best to mirror his demeanor, but she found it almost unbearably difficult. A woman just couldn't be stiff and formal when notions of kissing a man kept invading her imagination every time she looked at him. She couldn't speak in brisk, no-nonsense accents when her lips were tingling. She couldn't pretend his presence was of no consequence when her skin flushed with heat and her pulses raced every time he was in the room.

As a result, by the time the day came for their outing to Westminster, Amanda was every bit as excited as the boys, so excited, in fact, that they arrived early, passing the Clock Tower and crossing New Palace Yard with seven minutes to spare.

Despite their precipitate arrival, Jamie was already waiting for them, and when they turned the corner at the end of Westminster Hall and she saw him on the steps leading to St. Stephen's Corridor, her heart leaped in her chest with such pleasure that it hurt.

The boys saw him, too, and it was only because she was holding each of them by the hand that they couldn't break into a run as their father came down the steps to greet them.

"No running," she ordered, but though she'd intended her order to be the firm one of a proper nanny, Jamie's approach and her own pounding heart made her voice nothing but a breathless rush of air, and she had to grip the boys' hands hard and haul them back to ensure they minded her. "We talked about this before we came today, remember?" she added, forcing a firm note into her voice by sheer willpower. "No running inside Westminster."

Jamie descended the last step, and as he halted in front of them, removed his tall, black opera hat, and gave her a bow, Amanda felt as jumpy as a cat on hot bricks.

"We're here," she said, and almost groaned aloud at the inanity of that remark.

It wasn't lost on him, either, much to her chagrin, for his mouth twitched at one corner as he settled his hat back on his head. "Yes," he agreed, his voice suspiciously grave. "So I see."

"Can we see the Commons first, Papa?" Colin asked. "And can we see where we'll sit? And what about the Royal Gallery? Can we see that?"

"Slow down, slow down," Jamie said, laughing. "No, you can't see the Royal Gallery, I'm afraid. The Queen isn't here, and even if she were, I'm not important enough to warrant an invitation into her presence, sadly. But as for the rest, yes, we'll go to the Commons first."

He turned to Owen, and his smile changed to a quizzical expression. "You're very quiet, Owen?" he remarked. "Is something wrong?"

"No, Papa. It's just that I didn't expect to see you wearing a hat."

"You've seen me in a hat before. Every day, in fact."

"I know, but don't you have to wear a wig in Parliament?"

"No, only the Speaker and the clerks are required to wear wigs, thank heaven. Most of us do retain our hats, though we don't always wear them. A hat's important, because if any member needs to raise a point of order during a division, he must have his hat on before doing so."

"Why?" Colin wanted to know.

"Oh, it's tradition. But any time a Member stands up, he must remove his hat—to speak, for example, or to leave the Chamber. That's tradition, too."

"But you used to wear a wig, didn't you?" Owen asked. "When you were a barrister?"

"I did. Which is why I gave up the bar and became an MP. A hat's much more comfortable than a wig."

"You're having us on, Papa," Colin accused, clearly skeptical. "That seems a silly reason to run for election."

"You only say that because you've never had to wear a wig," Jamie countered. "I have, and they itch like mad, especially in summer when it's hot. Now, then," he added, gesturing to the immense arched doors behind him. "We'll go through St. Stephen's Hall and head for the Commons, then see the gallery, the Lords, and all the rest."

He turned, holding out his hands, and when Amanda relinquished her hold, he took each of his sons by the hand and led them up the stone steps, through a pair of wood and glass doors overhung by an arched Gothic window, and into St. Stephen's Corridor. Amanda fell in step behind them, content to recede into the background as Jamie took his sons through the Members' Lobby, let them peek through the windows beside the door to the House of Commons, where things were already well underway, and took them up to the gallery where they would sit later to watch debates.

"Why do we have to sit in the Ladies' Gallery?" Owen wanted to know as they descended the stairs again. "We're not ladies."

"Mrs. Seton is, though," Jamie reminded. "And you're not old enough to sit alone in the men's galleries, so you have to sit with her."

"But all that brass grillwork is in the way." Owen sounded quite aggrieved. "We won't be able to see very well."

"That's rather the point," Amanda muttered, but though the boys didn't hear that tart remark, Jamie did, and he gave her a rueful look.

"I daresay you're right," he told her as they left the Commons and started across the Central Hall to the House of Lords, weaving their way amid the crowd. "The grillwork is ridiculous."

"It's more than ridiculous. It's unfair. It's wrong. And what's the purpose? To make it so hard to see what they're doing down below that we won't come at all."

"You can stand at the windows by the door to the Chamber if you prefer," he said, though he supposed that wasn't much of a consolation. "Ladies are allowed to do so, and the view is better."

"Yes, but there's nowhere to sit. And we don't know if or when you'll be called, so we could be standing for hours. A fact which rather proves my point."

"Believe me, you're not telling me anything I haven't already heard," he assured her. "Every female in my family hates the Ladies' Gallery."

Owen spoke before Amanda could suggest he do something about that problem. "Why are the benches green in the Commons, Papa?" he asked over his shoulder as they started down the Peers' Corridor to the House of Lords.

"Because that's the Queen's favorite color," Jamie answered at once.

"Really?" Owen asked.

Colin gave a snort. "Papa's joking," he told his younger brother. "The seats were green long before Victoria."

"But *why* are they green?"

"No one knows, really," Jamie confessed. "It's another tradition."

"But the ones in the Lords are red, aren't they, Papa?"

"Really, Owen," Colin cut in impatiently. "Who cares what color the seats are? What I want to know is when you'll show us the cellar where Guy Fawkes hid with the gunpowder."

"I say, that's a ripping idea," Owen endorsed, seat colors apparently forgotten. "Let's go down there."

"I'm afraid we can't," Jamie told them. "That cellar was destroyed in the fire of 1834."

Both boys groaned in disappointment at that piece of news, but they weren't deterred from asking more questions.

"Do you have an office, Papa?" Colin asked. "Can we see that?"

"No office, I'm afraid. MPs are only allowed a locker and a coat peg."

"Can we see the Robing Room?"

"And what about the Prince's Chamber?"

The boys continued firing questions at their parent as they crossed to the House of Lords, and as Amanda listened, she was overcome by feelings both poignant and bittersweet. She was glad, so very glad, that he was spending more time with them, and it was gratifying to know her influence had brought about that happy circumstance. But watching them like this also brought a sense of melancholy, because she knew that for her, it was only temporary. In two years or so, Colin and Owen would be off to Harrow, and she would have to say good-bye to them and to their father.

That was the nature of her occupation, a perpetual cycle of hullo and good-bye. To come into children's lives, influence them in all the positive ways she could, then to part from them as they journeyed without her into their future was a cycle she was well accustomed to by now, but as she watched Jamie with his sons, as she listened to them talk and laugh together, she felt both the pleasure and the pain of her teacher's life more keenly than she ever had before.

Jamie took them up to the galleries overlooking the House of Lords so the boys could see the red seats for themselves, then they went back down to explore the libraries and stroll along the terrace beside the Thames. At last, they circled back to retrace their steps along St. Stephen's Corridor.

"That pretty well does it," Jamie said as they halted where they had begun, at St. Stephen's Porch. "You've seen everything visitors are allowed to see, and since it's now a quarter to three, might I suggest refreshments? The tearooms for visitors inside Westminster are always stuffy and crowded, but there's quite a nice tearoom around the corner." He gestured toward Westminster Hall and the exit beyond. "Shall we?"

Owen and Amanda happily endorsed this plan. Colin, however, wasn't nearly as enthusiastic. "But Papa, our tour can't be over yet," he protested, pulling his hand from Jamie's, a move that compelled his father, his brother, and Amanda to stop as well. "You haven't shown us Auntie Irene's cupboard."

Jamie, it was clear, knew at once what the boy meant, for he threw back his head and laughed. "I don't believe Auntie Irene had a particular cupboard in mind," he told his son.

Colin seemed satisfied by that answer, but Amanda was baffled. "What is Auntie Irene's cupboard?" she asked as they stopped by the cloakroom and she handed over the claim ticket to retrieve their wraps and coats. "I've never heard of such a thing."

"Because it doesn't exist—not yet anyway. The boys' aunt Irene, the Duchess of Torquil, has often declared that when the Government conducts the next census, she intends to come to the House of Commons, duck into one of the broom cupboards here, and spend the night."

For the life of her, Amanda could see no reason a duchess, or anyone else, for that matter, would want to do such an uncomfortable, seemingly pointless thing. "For what purpose?"

"I'm not sure I should tell you." He gave her a rueful look. "Knowing you, Amanda, you'd be likely to join her."

The clerk interrupted before Amanda could reply, handing over an armful of garments, and it was only after she and Jamie had helped the boys into their mackintoshes, gloves, and mufflers, Amanda had buttoned up her cloak, and they had emerged into the cold autumn air that she could return to the subject they'd been discussing.

"I can't imagine any reason to spend the night in a cupboard at Westminster," she told Jamie as they started across New Palace Yard side by side, each of them holding one of the boys by the hand. "What would be the point?"

"My sister-in-law is a staunch suffragist. Her main ambition in life is to gain women the right to vote. If she could manage to spend the night inside Westminster while they are conducting the government census, she could legitimately declare the House of Commons as her valid address, her contention being that she could then claim the same political rights as men, including the right to vote."

It was Amanda's turn to laugh. "I see. But would that work?"

"Well, it is a loophole in the law, rather, but if you want my opinion as a member of the bar, it wouldn't have a prayer of succeeding."

"You're probably right," Amanda said, making a face. "You men are very stubborn about hanging on to your power."

He grinned at her. "Understandably."

"I'll be in the Commons someday," Owen said before Amanda could rebuke Jamie for his teasing remark. "And I'll give women the vote, if they don't have it already."

"Hear, hear," Amanda said as Jamie groaned.

"Don't you start," he admonished her. "I'm already in the suds with many of my colleagues because of Irene's suffragist work. My electorate, too, for I barely won my seat. The margin was less than a hundred votes." He leaned around Amanda to look at his younger son, who was walking on her other side. "So, you'd agree to give women the vote, would you, Owen? Why?"

"Mama wanted the vote," he said simply. "I'd do it for her."

At once, she glanced at Jamie, but though his profile gave nothing away, it hurt somehow to look at him.

They had one mother. One. And she died. Any stepmother would be nothing but a second-rate substitute, and they don't need that.

As his words from that first day in the newspaper office echoed through her mind, they were a stark reminder of reality. Jamie would never love another woman as he had loved his wife. She'd known that all along, so why should it matter now? Why should it hurt now?

Because she was falling in love with him.

Oh no, she thought, looking away, trying desperately to deny it. *No, no, no.* She was not going to make the same mistake twice. She was not going to let herself fall in love with a man who was incapable of loving her in return.

But even as she made that vow, she had the sick feeling it was already too late.

BECAUSE JAMIE HAD to be in the Chamber before Question Time ended, tea was a hurried affair. He then escorted Amanda and the boys to the Ladies' Gallery and raced down the stairs to take his place in the Chamber.

Asquith was being grilled about inefficiencies in the British railways as Jamie took his seat, giving him time to review his speech. He already knew the blasted thing by heart, but he wasn't the least bit confident about it, and when he pulled the speech out of his jacket pocket to peruse it, his dismal opinion was only reinforced, for his words seemed duller and more tedious than ever, and he wondered if he ought to have taken Amanda up on her offer to help him with it.

But even as he wondered, he knew that would have been unwise. In the wake of that kiss, being anywhere near her was a risky thing. He'd broken his promise that she was safe in his company once already, and he had no intention of doing so again, as deliciously tempting as it might be.

Asquith stopped rambling on about the government's efforts to improve railway efficiency, veering Jamie off the precarious path his thoughts had started down. He sat up straighter on his seat, readying himself as Asquith sat back down. When Speaker Peel announced that debate for the Education Bill would now commence, he stood up, but Peel's gaze moved right past him, and when the Speaker called on his colleague, Colonel Forrester, Jamie sat back down.

He glanced again at his notes, but as Forrester began talking about demographics, budgetary needs too long ignored, and how little had been spent on educating the lower classes in the past—words very similar, in fact, to the ones he himself had composed—Jamie knew why his speech dissatisfied him. It was pedantic, it was dull, it had no heart. What was the point of it?

Hell, he thought as Forrester sat down and he stood up and Peel called on a member of the opposition, *what was the point of anything he was doing here?*

He sat back down and turned his head, looking up at the Ladies' Gallery. He spied Amanda at once, for the teal blue of her walking dress was plainly visible through the brass grillwork. She was in the front row, he noticed, the boys flanking her. He squinted, and when he did, he could make out her face—a fractured view, to be sure, but that didn't matter, because her piquant features and deep, murky eyes were always vivid in his mind.

There were mysteries in those eyes of hers, mysteries a man would need an entire lifetime to uncover.

A lifetime, he thought, the word piercing him right through the chest like an arrow. *His lifetime.*

Suddenly, Jamie felt as if the entire world was slipping sideways, turning over, and cracking apart, reshaping itself into something else, something new and unforeseen.

The life he'd had with Pat was gone and would not come back. He'd scorned that brutal truth, he'd raged against it, he'd wept over it, and finally, at last, he'd come to accept it. Resigned, he had trudged on, moving toward the future for the sake of his children, but it was a future that to his heart and mind had seemed bleak and dim, colorless and without joy.

But suddenly, he could see a different future. For the first time in three years, he could see color and light. He could see hope. He could see love.

As if from a great distance, he heard the Liberal MP on the opposite side of the chamber fall silent, and tearing his gaze from the gallery, Jamie looked at the Speaker's Chair and stood up.

Strangely, he knew Peel was going to call on him even before the other man did so, and with a nod of acknowledgment, he turned away just long enough to drop his notes on the seat behind him. Notes weren't necessary, because he knew exactly what he was going to talk about and it wasn't the words he'd written down. He was going to talk about the future.

Chapter 15

Jamie, Amanda decided, was touched in the head. He'd told her his speech was rubbish, but it wasn't. Not at all.

When he spoke of the Members' duty to the children of Britain, even her half-American heart soared with pride. When he spoke of the Members' obligation to their posterity, her eyes stung. And when he voiced his prayer for a safe, secure future, she prayed for it as well.

It was an inspired speech, eloquent and moving, and she knew she wasn't the only one who thought so. When she glanced over the room, she noticed that no one was talking. There were no heads bent together for whispered comments, no jeering or laughter from the opposition. The room was pin-drop silent. Heads nodded in quiet agreement on his side of the chamber and in tacit acknowledgment on the other side. When he sat down, not one Member of the opposition stood up to counter his remarks. When the Speaker moved for a vote, the bill was moved forward to committee by a substantial margin.

"Papa is really good at this, isn't he, Mrs. Seton?" Colin whispered as the Speaker moved on to the next piece of legislation.

"Indeed, he is." She stood up and gestured to the door behind them. "We'd best leave him to it and go home. It's nearly dinnertime."

"Can we come see Papa speak again?" Owen asked as they went down the stairs.

"If your father is willing, of course we can."

They paused by the cloakroom once again to retrieve their coats.

"Shall we take a taxi home?" she asked as she buttoned Colin into his mackintosh. "Or the train?"

"The train?" they echoed in unison.

Amanda straightened, glancing from Colin to Owen and back again. "What?" she asked, laughing at their surprised faces. "Haven't you ever ridden in a train before?"

They both shook their heads, their blue eyes wide as saucers, but it was Colin who replied. "Not in London," he said, and she laughed again.

"Well, then," she said as she wrapped Owen in his mackintosh, "we have to take the train now, don't we?"

Amanda donned her own cloak, then took one boy by each hand, led them across Westminster Hall, and out through the exit. But before she could turn them in the direction of Charing Cross, the closest station, she heard a voice calling to her.

"Amanda? Amanda, is that you?"

She slowed her steps, turning her head as a slim, dark-haired man hurried toward her across New Palace Yard, and at the sight of his face, she came to an abrupt stop, a move that compelled the boys to halt as well.

"Kenneth?" She let go of the boys and turned around, staring in astonished dismay as the man who'd called her name halted in front of her.

Six million people living in London, she thought wildly, and she had to encounter the very one who'd ruined her, shamed her, and broken her heart. What a rum thing life was.

When he tipped his hat and bowed, she felt a strange sense of unreality, as if she was watching one of those newfangled moving picture shows. He seemed flat and unidimensional, not the least bit real. When he straightened, the smile beneath his small, perfectly groomed mustache was so agreeable and charming, she wondered if he'd simply forgotten his ruination of her, or if he simply assumed she'd forgiven it. Or perhaps he thought there was nothing to forgive.

"How smashing it is to see you, Amanda. You look more beautiful than ever." His voice held all the warmth of those days together in Kent, halcyon days she'd thought at the time, and yet, what she felt now was so different from what she'd felt then that even Amanda was startled.

How handsome he is, she thought. *And how little it moves me.*

"What are you doing at Westminster?" she asked. "You've never been political."

"I am now. It's a ghastly business, but I've taken my seat in the Lords. My father died last spring. Surely you heard?"

She hadn't, but then, it wasn't as if she'd been keeping track. Kenneth Halsbury's life had ceased to be of any interest to her ages ago. Suppressing the rather petty desire to point that out, she took a deep breath and said the expected, conventional thing instead. "I'm so sorry."

He glanced at the boys, then back at her, still smiling. "I see you have champions to the left and right of you."

Her own smile was equally pleasant. "But none in front of me."

A flush came into his cheeks, her only indication her shot had gone home.

"How do you know Mrs. Seton?" demanded Colin, his voice fierce and protective and displaying that even at the age of ten, he was far more perceptive at discerning the true character of people than she had been at twenty-six. What a humbling thought.

"*Mrs.* Seton?" he echoed, his brows rising with a soupcon of mockery as he gave her the title of a married woman.

She opened her mouth to make excuses and depart, but he turned to Colin before she had the chance. "Mrs. Seton and I are old friends." He looked at her again. "Aren't we, Amanda?"

"Friends?" She gave a wild little laugh of disbelief. "Hardly."

"Well, acquaintances, then, if you prefer. Speaking of acquaintances, aren't you going to introduce me?"

She didn't want to, but he'd put her in the awkward position of being uncivil if she refused. To avoid an introduction now, she'd have to cut him and turn her back, and given that he knew her for who she really was, she reminded herself that it was wiser not to antagonize him, especially since it would serve no purpose, and she reluctantly performed introductions. "Boys, this is Lord Halsbury—sorry," she corrected at once, striving to remember his late father's title. "Lord Notting. My lord, may I present Baron Knaresborough, and Mr. Owen St. Clair."

"Knaresborough? St. Clair? Ah, yes, of course." Kenneth laughed. "Earl Kenyon's famous boys." He bowed. "How do you do?"

"Do you know our father?" Owen asked.

"Of course. We met at Cambridge. He was quite wild in those days, as I recall, always getting into scrapes." He returned his attention to Amanda, but though his smile was pleasant, something in it made her stiffen. "He's turned his life around nicely, it seems. So clever of him to marry a duke's sister, wasn't it? It salvaged his respectability, got him back in his father's good graces, opened all sorts of doors for him."

"I'm sure," Amanda said politely, glancing past him, hoping he'd take the hint. "Well," she began, preparing to make the excuse to depart, "we really must—"

"And now, he's one of the party's most promising members, with the potential of a brilliant political career ahead of him."

He was watching her as he spoke, still pleasant and smiling, and yet, beneath the complimentary words, she sensed a definite malice. But why should Kenneth feel any malice toward Jamie? Or toward her, for that matter? Two years had passed, after all. And he hadn't wanted her anyway when all was said and done. He'd made that fact painfully clear, to her and everyone else.

"It would be a shame," he went on slowly, his smile widening, "if he blotted his copybook in some way. Wouldn't that be a shame, *Mrs. Seton*?"

She sucked in a sharp breath. The malice in his eyes was obvious now, but she still couldn't pinpoint the cause. He might be thinking there was something more between her and Jamie than employer and nanny, but so what? Why should he care? Granted, after he'd laughed at the idea of marrying her, she'd refused his suggestion of a more sordid arrangement, but that wasn't cause enough for him to make trouble for a fellow peer. Even Kenneth wouldn't do something like that, surely.

But as Amanda tried to reassure herself with that thought, she nonetheless felt a pang of fear because the look in Kenneth's eyes defied reassurance.

She swallowed hard and forced herself to reply. "It's a shame when scandal hurts anyone," she said, her gaze steady, her voice icily polite. "Now, if you'll excuse us, Lord Notting, it grows late, and we need to be on our way."

"Of course. But," he added before she could move to depart, "we really must catch up, my dear. I shall call on you tomorrow," he added as she opened her mouth to refuse. "We can talk about old times. Perhaps we could even . . ." He paused, his faint, knowing smile becoming a definite smirk. "Discuss the possibility of new times? The post I once offered you might still be open, if you're interested?"

"She isn't!" Colin said before she could reply. "She's got a post already, as our nanny."

"Nanny?" Kenneth echoed and looked at her, making no effort to hide his amusement. "You could be so much more, Amanda."

She gave a laugh of scorn and disbelief. "I refused your *offer* once before. Why would I accept it now?"

"Well, now that the old man's gone, I can afford to be much more generous than I was able to be then. And you may soon be in need of employment. It's amazing how quickly gossip can spread, my dear."

She inhaled sharply, appreciating the threat. "How kind you are to be so concerned for my well-being," she said with biting sarcasm. "But I must once again decline."

"The Commons is an elected body, you know," he went on, his silky voice making Amanda's stomach twist with dread. "It's not like the Lords. In the Commons, one breath of scandal can ruin an MP's entire career."

Oh God, Amanda thought, feeling sick. *Oh God.*

"It could destroy everything he wants to achieve," Kenneth went on as she strove for calm. "It could hurt his good name, his family—"

"What scandal?" Colin cut in. "Our father's not involved in any scandal!"

Amanda squeezed the boy's hand tightly. "Lord Notting is speaking in general terms, Colin," she explained, keeping her gaze locked with Kenneth's. "He's not referring to any scandal specifically involving your father."

Kenneth leaned closer to her. "Not yet anyway," he murmured, his voice just loud enough for only her to hear, then he straightened away from her and went on, "Having turned his life around so admirably, I'm sure Lord Kenyon wouldn't want to see all his good work undone now."

"I'm sure," she managed. "But as I said, we must be going."

"Of course." He bowed. "Forgive me for detaining you, and please do keep my offer in mind."

Before she could reply that she'd rather swallow corrosive acid, he tipped his hat again and walked on.

She turned to stare after him, powerful emotions surging with her. Anger that he would threaten her, especially in front of the boys. Regret that she'd wasted herself on a man like him. Bafflement that she'd ever fancied herself in love with him. Repulsion at the thought of what he wanted from her, and bewilderment as to why he still seemed to want it.

Despite all the chaotic emotions swirling around inside her, one thing was clear. She could not allow Jamie and the boys to be tainted by her mistakes.

Her heart lurched, twisting with pain at the knowledge of what she must do. Her soul rebelled, frantic to find another way. Her mind, however, knew with brutal clarity that there was no other way. She had to leave.

"I don't like that man."

Colin's voice broke into her tumultuous thoughts, reminding her she was standing here as if she'd been turned to a pillar of salt. "Your instincts are sound, Colin," she assured the boy. "Lord Notting's a rotter."

"He said he was your friend."

"He isn't, and he never will be." She glanced back over her shoulder, but thankfully, he had turned at the corner and vanished. "I'd rather be friends with Lucifer."

THE HOUSE ADJOURNED just past midnight, but because of his success in persuading the Members to send the bill forward, others in the party insisted on standing him a drink, and it was closer to one o'clock by the time he entered the house on Upper Brook Street.

The house was dark and quiet, indicating that everyone, including his new valet, had gone to bed, but after Jamie had lit a lamp and mounted the stairs, he realized that he'd been mistaken, at least in regard to one member of his household.

"Amanda?" he asked, stopping in surprise as she rose from one of the chairs that furnished the wide, shallow gallery at the top of the stairs and came toward him out of the shadows. "What are you doing sitting here in the dark? In fact, what are you doing up at all? Do you know how late it is?"

"I was waiting for you."

"At this hour?" He felt a jolt of alarm. "Why? Has something happened? Is one of the boys ill?"

"No, no," she answered at once. "I just . . . I wanted . . . I needed to see you." She paused in front of him and lifted her face, her eyes dark as ebony in the circle of lamplight around them. "That was a fine speech you gave today. I can't believe you thought it was rubbish."

She'd waited up for him until one in the morning to tell him she liked his speech? "It wasn't the one I'd intended to give," he muttered, not quite sure what else to say. "At the last minute, I tossed out the one I'd written and gave my speech extempore."

"You mean you just pulled those beautiful words out of thin air?"

"Well . . ." He paused, considering how to explain. "Let's just say it was a speech from the heart."

"That makes you a rare commodity in politics. I think you'll go far in your career. I'm not . . ." She paused again and took a deep breath. "I'm not the only one who thinks so."

"That's nice to hear, but I can't believe you've been waiting up for me all this time so that we could discuss my political future."

"I said I wanted to see you." Something in her voice quickened his pulses, and when she edged closer to him, pulled the lamp from his hand, and set it on the table by the stairs, his heart began to race, and when she spoke again, hope sparked to life within him. "I never said I wanted to talk."

He hardly dared to believe what he was hearing, but then she rose on her toes and pressed her mouth to his, and the arousal he'd been suppressing for weeks flared up like kindling set alight. But aware of what had happened to her in her previous post, he strove to contain what he felt, for he didn't want to take anything for granted.

"If this is how you intend to react every time I give a successful speech in the House," he murmured, his lips brushing lightly against hers as he spoke, "I can see I shall have to up my oratory game."

She laughed softly, her breath warm against his mouth, and when she slid her arms around his neck, pressed her body close to his, and kissed him again, the pleasure of it was so great, it nearly knocked him off his feet. Despite that, he wasn't quite ready to capitulate. "What are you say-ing, Amanda?"

"Can't you guess? After all," she added, pressing kisses to his chin, his jaw, and the edges of his mouth, "I'm not flinging myself at you in this shameless way because I want to have a conversation."

Inside, he began to shake, for the effort of holding back was becoming intolerable. "I hope I'm not dreaming," he muttered instead. "Because I want you so badly, I can hardly breathe."

"Then why are we still standing here?"

"I just need to be sure you know what you're asking for."

"Why?" she asked, smiling against his mouth. "Are you afraid a knee will come between us at an inopportune moment?"

Despite the agonizing uncertainty his body was in, that made him laugh. "In these particular circumstances, I'm willing to take the chance. But—"

He broke off, deciding he had to be blunt. He grasped her wrists and pulled her arms down. "We're talking about your virtue, Amanda. I think you know enough about the world to know what that means."

She tilted her head, studying his face for a moment, then she said, "I can see I shall have to disillusion you about me a little. Remember that day in the park when I told you I'd been in love once?"

"Yes."

"It wasn't a chaste love, Jamie."

The news took him back. "You're not a virgin? Is that what you mean?"

She nodded. "It was a mistake," she went on. "One I bitterly regret, but it wasn't until it was too late that I realized he wasn't worthy of me. I hope . . ." She paused, looking at him in uncertainty. "I hope you don't think less of me now."

"God, no." He grasped her hands in his, entwining their fingers. "I told you how wild I was in my salad days. I chased anything in a skirt. I've no right to judge."

She gave a little laugh. "That doesn't stop most people," she whispered. "Women are expected to be chaste until their wedding day. But I thought I was in love with him, you see. And at the time, I was so, so lonely."

He knew all about loneliness, especially now because it was gone. He let go of her hands and cupped her face. "You're not still in love with this man, are you?"

"God, no."

"Then that's all I need to know about him."

She smiled, a wide, radiant smile that took his breath away and sent his control slipping another notch.

"Shall we, then?" she asked. "Or do I have to shamelessly fling myself at you again?"

He didn't need any more persuading. He wrapped one arm behind her back and bent to slide the other beneath her knees. "It'll have to be my room," he murmured, lifting her into his arms. "Yours is too close to the boys. They might hear us."

She nodded, and he turned, nodding to the lamp she'd taken from him earlier. "Grab the lamp," he instructed, and when she did, he started down the darkened corridor and through the open doorway into his bedroom. There, he kicked the door shut and set her on her feet, then reached behind him to turn the key in the lock.

Her hair gleamed raven black in the soft lamplight, and he lifted his hands to rake his fingers through it, smiling a little.

"What are you smiling about?" she asked.

"I'm thinking about that first day when you came swaggering into my study—"

"Oh, I did not swagger!"

"Oh yes, you did." He twisted the strands in his fingers and tilted her head back. "Like you were the best person for the post and you knew it."

He kissed her before she could reply, and as her lips parted beneath his, it was a kiss so lush, so deep and ardent, that it sent all his senses reeling. But he wanted to look at her, see her face, as he undressed her, so he pulled back, his hands sliding down to the ribbon tie at her throat.

Looking into those amazing eyes of hers, he tugged the bow apart, and the ribbon fell to the floor. He began unbuttoning her blouse and guiding her backward toward the bed, but the last button came undone before he got there. Unable to wait any longer to see her body, he paused beside the dressing table, pulled the edges of her blouse apart, and slid the garment off her shoulders, tugging it free of her skirt and letting it fall to the floor. Her skin gleamed like alabaster in the lamplight, and he leaned in, pressing his lips to the bare skin at her collarbone, relishing the way she shivered in response.

Her soft, powdery scent was pristine, almost maidenly, and yet, it only seemed to deepen his own desire, harkening to his wild side. He breathed in fully, savoring the fragrance as he trailed kisses along her shoulder and continued to undress her.

Striving to keep his desire in check, he removed her clothes with slow, painstaking care, for he wanted to heighten her anticipation as much as possible, and by the time he had her down to her chemise and drawers, he knew he was succeeding.

Her skin was flushed a delicate pink, and her breathing had quickened. As he traced tiny circles over the skin of her shoulders and breastbone, he could feel the delicate tremors running through her, and when he lowered his gaze, he could see her hardened nipples jutting out against the thin muslin of her chemise, and the fire in his loins grew hotter and stronger, and he decided not to finish undressing her yet, for the sight of her naked might unravel any control he had left. Instead, he spread his arms wide. "It's your turn, I think."

She stared up at him, her eyes wide, her breath coming as fast as his. "You want me to undress you?"

"Turnabout's fair play, darling. Unless," he added as she hesitated, "you don't want to?"

Unexpectedly, she chuckled. "The question is if *you* want me to. Last time I valeted you, if you recall, it was rather a disaster."

"On the contrary." Despite his rather vulnerable state at present, he couldn't help a grin. "In hindsight, I have to say that finding out you were a woman ranks as one of the most smashing discoveries I've ever made."

That pleased her, he could tell, for she was smiling as she began to undo the buttons of his waistcoat. Once they were unfastened, she slipped it from his shoulders along with his jacket and let both garments fall to the floor behind him. As he unfastened his collar and cuff links, she set to work on his studs. She must have been nervous, though, for her fingers fumbled on the second one, and both slipped through her fingers to the floor. "Oh dear," she murmured, laughing a little as one stud bounced along the carpet and the other rolled beneath the dressing table. "I'm not a very good valet, I'm afraid."

"I'll do it," he offered, dropping his cuff links on the table by the lamp. He tugged his shirt out of his trousers and pulled it off, but when he reached for his undershirt, she stopped him.

"No, I want to do it."

"All right. Just—" He broke off as she pulled his undershirt off, waiting until it had joined his shirt on the floor before going on, "Just don't take too long. I don't know how much longer I can hold out, to be honest."

"Indeed?" She slanted a mischievous look at him as she lifted her hands to the waistband of his trousers. "What, no willpower?"

"Not much," he admitted freely. "Not with you in my vicinity."

"I'll keep that in mind." She began undoing the buttons of his trousers, and as she worked, her hands brushed teasingly against his groin. He inhaled sharply, tilted his head back, and endured the exquisite torture, but it seemed to take forever, and he realized just what she was doing.

"Oh, you cheeky girl," he murmured, giving an agonized laugh. "This is the game you want to play, is it?"

Before she could answer, he grasped her wrists, and she gave a shriek of laughter as he lifted her arms overhead and turned their bodies toward the wall. "When you sow the wind, my sweet," he said, pressing her to the wall, holding her wrists overhead with one hand as he bent his head, "you reap the whirlwind."

Her laughter ended in a gasp of shock as he bent his head and opened his mouth over one of her hardened nipples, dampening the fabric of her chemise as he flicked his tongue against it.

She moaned as he used his tongue and the texture of the fabric to toy with her and arouse her. She arched into him with a moan that begged for more, and he was glad to comply. Keeping hold of her wrists overhead, he suckled one breast as he slid his free hand underneath the hem of her chemise. And when he cupped her other breast in his hand, shaping it against his palm, he gave a groan of appreciation at the small, plump perfection of it.

He toyed with her, shaping one breast and suckling the other until she was trembling all over and her breath was coming in soft, quick gasps.

Amanda had never dreamed such delicious torture existed. She pulled, straining against Jamie's hold, wanting to wrap her arms around him fully, freely, but he would not let her. Instead, he held her wrists above her head and suckled her harder, tearing deep moans of pleasure from her throat. Desperate, she did the only thing she could: she rocked her hips.

He groaned, and so did she. The feel of him against her, hard and fully aroused, was exquisite, but it was also agony, for each time she surged her hips forward, he pulled back.

"Jamie," she cried, bucking her hips, demanding more.

He laughed, the wretch, but he did not relent. Instead, keeping firm hold of her wrists, he suckled harder as his free hand lowered to the apex of her thighs, eased between them, and cupped her mound.

Sharp sensation shot through her, and she cried out, her knees caving beneath her. He released her wrists at once, wrapping his arm around her to keep her from falling. He turned her sideways, and she thought vaguely that he might be intending to pick her up and carry her to the bed as he had carried her up the stairs, but then he stopped, and she realized she'd been mistaken.

He moved to stand behind her, and when she felt his hard erection brush against her buttock, she felt a stab of disappointment. Was he intending to take her right here, from behind, over a dressing table?

She stirred, uneasy, wanting to turn around. "Jamie?"

"It's all right, I promise," he murmured, his hand moving up along her ribs in a slow caress, his head lowering to kiss her bare shoulder. "Open your eyes."

She complied, and when she saw her own reflection and his in the mirror, she caught her breath, realizing his true intent. When he cupped her breasts, the view of his hands on her was every bit as exciting as his touch.

The dim lamplight shot gold through his brown hair and seemed to enhance the hard muscles of his chest and shoulders, sculpting them with shadow and light. The view of his naked chest surprised her, for though she wasn't an innocent woman, she'd never seen a man unclothed. Kenneth, she recalled dimly, had always made love to her in the dark.

Jamie had no such reticence. "You're lovely," he murmured, seeming to relish the sight of them this way as much as she did. "So, so lovely."

Lost in a sensuous haze, Amanda watched as he caressed and toyed with her, and when he pinched her nipples lightly in his fingers, sharp sensation shot through her, so overwhelming that she cried out, her knees gave way again, and she understood why he had turned her toward the dressing table. She sagged forward, resting her forearms against the wood surface, a move that pressed her buttocks flush to his hips, and even through the fabric of her drawers and his trousers, the feel of his erection, full and turgid against her bum, was so exquisite that she moaned, and she was glad for the dressing table. If it hadn't been there to support her, she feared she'd have melted into a puddle on the floor.

She moved her hips up and down, savoring the feel of him against her, and instead of being disappointed by the idea of Jamie taking her in this position, she began to crave it.

But he didn't satisfy that craving. Instead, when she jerked her hips again, he groaned and pulled back, his hands sliding away.

"Jamie," she wailed in frustration, her fingers curling into fists on the dressing table, desire clawing at her.

His palms, scorching hot, glided over her hips and up to her waist, and then his hands eased between her tummy and the dressing table, undoing the ribbon of her drawers. "Yes," she gasped, wriggling her hips to urge him on, welcoming eagerly what had seemed so disappointing only moments ago. "Yes, yes."

But again, she was denied. Instead of pushing down her drawers and moving to unbutton his trousers, he knelt behind her, his hands sliding away.

What on earth? She turned her head, but she couldn't see him. He was no longer touching her. "Jamie?"

"Lift your foot," he said. "I need to take your shoes off."

She didn't want to wait for that. "Damn my shoes," she muttered, panting.

For some reason, he laughed. "Patience, sweetheart."

Patience? She had no patience. She had only need, the driving, desperate need for completion.

Thankfully, he was quick, removing her shoes, stockings, and drawers in only a few seconds, and when he stood up again, she spread her legs, bracing herself against the dresser, sure he would take her now.

He didn't. Instead, he eased his hand beneath her bum and between her thighs, and when the tip of his finger touched the seam of her sex, the pleasure was so great, she cried out, her hips jerking.

He shifted his position at once, flattening his free hand on the dressing table to brace his weight and leaning his hip against her buttock to anchor her in place.

His other hand between her thighs, he began to caress her, his fingertip sliding slowly back and forth along the seam of her sex. Desperate, hungry with need, she tried to jerk her hips, but her range of motion was limited by his superior weight, and she could only stand there, pinned, helpless, moaning with need as his knowing fingers teased and tormented her.

It was an exquisite agony, this sensation of pleasure held just out of reach. She moved her hips back and forth the scant fraction he would allow, but he didn't increase the pace, and soon, the tension within her became unbearable. A sob of frustration tore from her throat.

He leaned down, his bare chest scorching hot against her back, his warm breath against her ear making her shiver. "Is there something you want?" he murmured. "Tell me."

Tell him what she wanted? Impossible. She couldn't talk. She could hardly breathe. She pumped her hips again, insistent, hoping that was enough to urge him on, but instead of deepening the caress, he did the opposite, pulling back a fraction, his fingertip circling the nub of her pleasure, lightly, softly, barely touching her. "Tell me."

"More," she ground out, her hips jerking again, her hot cheek pressed against smooth mahogany. "More, Jamie, more."

He complied, his fingers spreading the moisture of her arousal across her clitoris and just inside her opening as he began to caress her, and mercifully, he eased back, giving her freedom at last to enjoy it fully. Her arousal rose with each tender lash of his fingers, her hips working, her need rising higher and higher, until at last, she climaxed in a shattering rush of pleasure and collapsed, panting, against the dressing table.

Smiling a little, Jamie leaned down to press a kiss to the corner of her mouth, feeling her lips curve in a little smile against his. Then he drew back, relishing how she looked at this moment, beautiful and ravished even in profile, her skin flushed from her orgasm. He wished he could linger here, pleasure her more, but his years of self-imposed celibacy had taken their toll, and his body simply couldn't endure waiting any longer. "I want you," he said, pressing kisses along her cheek to her ear. "I want to be inside you."

"Yes," she gasped, nodding in willing accord. "Oh yes, Jamie, yes."

He'd had vague thoughts of moving them to the bed, but when she spread her legs apart, positioning herself for him to take her, he simply couldn't resist. He straightened, his hand sliding from between her legs so that he could unbutton his trousers. He shoved them down to his knees along with his linen, releasing his aching cock, then positioned himself directly behind her, his hands holding her hips.

"I want to see your face, Amanda. Open your eyes, my love."

She did, lifting her head, and when her gaze locked with his in the mirror, he began to enter her. He wanted to go slowly, but she was so wet, so hot and inviting, that as the head of his penis pushed between her warm, silken folds, he just couldn't hold back, and he thrust into her hard and deep.

She came almost at once. He felt it, her muscles clenching around him again and again, as her head tilted back, her eyes closed, and her body shuddered with pleasure. The sensations of her climax were just too much for his starved body to withstand. With a force he could no longer contain, he began to move in her, the dressing table thumping against the wall as he held her hips in his hands and thrust into her again and again and again, losing himself in the warmth and scent of her body.

Despite the maelstrom, he kept his eyes open, for the sight of her flushed face in the mirror as he took her from behind was one of the most beautiful and erotic things he'd ever seen in his life. He could feel his climax coming, but he held it back as best he could, waiting for her, and when at last she came again, sobbing his name, he came as well, an orgasm so intense, it nearly blinded him in a white-hot flash of sensation.

He closed his eyes then, savoring the shudders of pleasure that rocked his body and hers. Sated at last, he collapsed against her in complete release, and they both sank against the dressing table, his forearms resting on either side of hers, his chest against her back, his labored breaths mingling with hers in the glorious aftermath. He kissed her cheek, her hair, the side of her neck, murmuring her name.

She didn't answer, and he looked at her in the mirror, his body still locked with hers. "Amanda, are you all right?"

"Oh God," she whispered, her eyes opening to meet his, wide with wonder. "I never knew it could be like this, Jamie."

At those words, he felt a wave of satisfaction that was better than any orgasm he'd ever had. Joy filled his chest, squeezed his heart, flooded through his veins, and he savored the feeling.

In his wildest dreams he never thought he'd fall in love again. But as he gathered Amanda against him, as he wrapped his arms around her waist and looked at her beautiful face in the mirror, his love for her overwhelmed him and awed him, and for the first time in three long, lonely years, he felt as if life was worth living.

Chapter 16

*T*he bang was like an explosion, a sharp, loud report that woke Jamie out of a deep, sound, blissfully contented sleep.

"What the hell?" he mumbled, lifting his head from his pillow as his bedroom door bounced back from the wall against which it had slammed, and two very loud, carrot-headed hurricanes came rushing toward him.

"Wake up, Papa," Colin shouted, hurling himself onto the bed, landing on top of him before Jamie could roll sideways and planting his elbows right on Jamie's stomach.

He grunted at the impact. "I am awake, Colin," he muttered. "Thanks to you."

"You've got to come downstairs, Papa." Owen joined his brother on the bed, landing on Jamie's legs, barely missing his groin. "It's an absolute disaster, and you've got to stop it."

Thanks to having his body pummeled in this rough-and-tumble manner, Jamie was awake enough to remember the events of the night before. With a pang of alarm, he turned his head, but the place beside him was, thankfully, empty. To have his sons find Amanda in his bed would have been awkward, to say the least.

"What are you two on about, bursting in on me at this hour?" he asked. "What time is it anyway?"

"Half past eight, but who cares what time it is? You've got to get up now." Colin pounded a fist against his chest. "She's going. You've got to stop her."

"Going?" He stiffened. "What do you mean?"

"Just what we said." Owen poked him several times in the ribs. "It's a tragedy, and you've got to stop it."

"For God's sake, Owen," he muttered, rubbing his bleary eyes and try-ing to think, "stop prodding me as if I'm a recalcitrant sheep, and tell me what's going on."

Colin, clearly exasperated that his parent wasn't already flying out of bed, grabbed him by the hair and pulled, hard enough that Jamie uttered an anguished, "Ouch!"

Colin paid no heed. "She's leaving us," he said with another tug on Jamie's hair. "Quitting. Going off forever. Her clothes are packed and everything!"

Fully awake now and genuinely alarmed, Jamie pushed his sons aside and sat up in bed. "You're joking," he said, hearing the doubt in his own voice as he spoke. "You must be."

"It's no joke, my lord."

Jamie looked up to find Samuel in the doorway.

"Her trunk is in the foyer," the footman went on, "and she's waiting for William to fetch her a taxi." Samuel pulled an envelope out of his jacket pocket and held it up. "She's asked me to give you her letter of resignation."

Jamie was out of bed even before his valet had finished speaking. "Don't let her leave," he ordered Samuel, snatching the letter and tossing it on the dressing table, then bending to retrieve his trousers from the floor where he'd dropped them last night. "Keep her there until I come down."

"Very good, my lord."

Not bothering with his linen, Jamie slid into his trousers and began doing up the buttons as his valet departed. "Why is she going?" he asked the boys, opening the armoire to retrieve his dressing robe. "Did you two do something to drive her away?"

It was a logical question, but even as he asked it, Jamie wondered if perhaps he, not his sons, had been the one to blame. He'd broken his word to her. Granted, last night had been a mutual decision. At least he'd thought so. What if she was leaving out of regret? Or shame?

"We didn't do anything, Papa!" Colin replied indignantly, cutting into his speculations. "We haven't played any jokes on her in ages."

"We haven't, Papa," Owen added. "It's no fun to play jokes on Mrs. Seton because she doesn't get upset or angry or anything. She just acts all cheerful and happy, no matter what prank we pull. But she still makes us do chores afterward," he added woefully.

"We asked her if she was leaving because of us," Colin added, "and she said she wasn't."

"It didn't have anything to do with us, she said," Owen added, and frowned at his father. "Maybe she's leaving because of you, Papa."

"Me?" Jamie's gaze slid guiltily away as he slid into his dressing robe. "Did she say that?"

"No, but why else would she be going?"

Jamie hadn't the least idea, but he damn well intended to find out. He took up the letter and shoved it into his pocket, then started out of the room, tying the sash as he went along the corridor and down the stairs, his sons on his heels.

When he turned at the landing, he saw Samuel standing like a stalwart sentry by the front door below. Mrs. Richmond was there, too, and facing her, seated on the chair beside the calling-card tray, was Amanda.

She was dressed to go out, a cloak around her shoulders and a straw boater on her head, a trunk beside her and a leather suitcase at her feet. Dismayed, he paused on the landing as she looked up.

"My lord," she said.

The sound of her voice stirred him to action, and as he came down the remaining stairs, the boys still on his heels, she rose and turned to face him.

"I heard you were leaving," he said, feeling as if the words were being torn out of him. "But I'd hoped it was just an unfounded rumor."

"No," she said, tilting back her head to meet his gaze, and the pain in her eyes felt like an arrow through his chest. "It's not a rumor."

He swallowed hard. "Might I ask why? Is it . . ." He hesitated, glancing at the boys and the servants. "I can think of only one reason why you'd be leaving, and if . . . if it's about that, then—"

"It's not," she cut in. "I know what you're thinking, and it's not that at all."

"Then what is it?"

She hesitated, and it was her turn to glance at the others present. "I wrote you a resignation letter giving my reasons," she murmured, shifting her weight from one foot to the other. "Didn't you read it? Perhaps you should," she added when he shook his head. "It would make things easier."

He was in no frame of mind to make things easier. "Easier for me?" he asked. "Or you?"

She flinched, but she didn't look away. "For everyone."

He set his jaw, feeling grim. "Letter or no, I always prefer to hear things like this face-to-face. I think," he added, meeting her pain-filled gaze with a level one of his own, "I deserve at least that much. Don't you?"

They stared at each other for several seconds, then she capitulated with a nod. "Very well," she said, "if that's what you prefer, but I don't think we should discuss it in front of the boys."

He frowned, more bewildered than ever. "Then it is about what I thought," he said. "If not," he added when she shook her head, "then I think the boys deserve to know why you're going as much as I do." He leaned down, and took each boy by the hand, then looked at her again. "More, in fact."

Her pale face went even whiter. "I can't, Jamie," she choked. "I can't explain in front of them. Believe me, you'll understand why when you hear my reasons."

"I know the reason," Colin said abruptly. "It's that man, isn't it? The one who offered you a post yesterday. You're taking it, aren't you? You said you weren't, but you are. That's why you're leaving us."

"Man?" Jamie frowned, glancing from his son to Amanda and back again. "What man?"

"It doesn't matter," Amanda said before Colin could answer. "He is not the reason I'm going, and I am certainly not taking any post working for him." She turned to the boy. "I swear it to you on my life, Colin. I'd rather jump off a cliff than accept that man's offer."

"What man?" Jamie repeated.

"He was at Westminster yesterday," Colin said. "He—"

"Samuel," Amanda cut in, her voice sharper than Jamie had ever heard it before, slicing through Colin's words like a razor, "would you take the boys upstairs, please?"

"No!" cried Colin. Jerking his hand out of Jamie's, he stepped forward and wrapped his arms around Amanda. "You can't leave us. You can't!"

Owen tried to follow his brother's move, but Jamie tightened his grip on his younger son's hand.

"Colin," Amanda began, but then, her face twisted, her calm fractured, and she gave a sob, pressing a gloved hand to her mouth.

Jamie could stand no more. "Samuel, do as Mrs. Seton asks and take the boys to the nursery—"

A torrent of anguished protest from his sons interrupted him, but Jamie overrode them. "Now, Samuel," he said, his voice harsh to his own ears, "if you please."

He relinquished his hold on his younger son, and when Samuel took Owen by the hand, the boy went without further protest. Colin, however, was another matter, and Jamie had to pull him away from Amanda by force. It felt like tearing himself in half, and it seemed like hours before the footman could get them up the stairs and out of earshot.

That wrenching task accomplished, he turned to Mrs. Richmond. "Have the boys had breakfast?" he asked the cook.

"No, my lord. Not yet. What with one thing and another—"

"Then would you be so kind as to go down and begin preparing it?"

"Yes, my lord." She gave a curtsy and departed, casting a bewildered glance at Amanda before vanishing behind the green baize door at the other end of the foyer.

Once the door had swung shut behind her, Jamie returned his attention to Amanda. "Now, for God's sake, tell me what this is about. Who is this man the boys are talking about?"

"It doesn't matter. He's an . . . old acquaintance. He offered me a post, but I refused it. As I said, he's not the reason I'm leaving here."

"Then what is the reason?" He leaned closer, lowering his voice. "Is it because of last night? If you're worried about losing your post because of what happened between us—"

"That's not it!" she cried. "That's not why."

"Then what the hell is it?"

She took a deep breath as if bracing herself. "I've been lying to you, Jamie. Lying to you all along."

He tensed, suddenly wary. "Lying about what?"

"Who I really am. My father was American, yes. He did graduate from Harvard—summa cum laude, in fact—and he did go on to teach there as well. He was a brilliant mathematician, and well regarded by all his peers. But if you had written to Harvard to make inquiries about Professor Seton, you would have found that no man by that name ever attended that university or taught there."

"But that makes no sense—"

"Yes, it does, because his name was not Seton. My father," she rushed on before he had the chance to ask why she'd lied about her name, "saw no reason his daughter should not receive the same excellent education he had been given, the same education he would have provided a son. His dream was for me to attend Radcliffe, and go on to teach there, but when my mother became ill and we returned to England, that became impossible, and I attended Girton instead."

"Girton?" He was startled. "You went to Girton?"

"Yes." She smiled a little. "That day in the newspaper office when you said no woman could prepare a boy for Cambridge, it was like throwing down the gauntlet to me, because I'm a woman, and I did attend Cambridge, and I knew I could prepare your sons for a Cambridge education as well as any male tutor. I wanted, so badly, to show you how wrong you were in what you said."

"But why didn't you tell me all this when I discovered you were posing as a man? I realize you couldn't have known, but I would have been delighted to have the boys taught by a Girton graduate. Why keep that a secret or lie about your name?"

She gazed at him helplessly. "Because my real name is Leighton. I am Amanda Leighton. Now do you see?"

He didn't. She was looking at him as if that explained everything, but though the name seemed quite familiar, Jamie could not place it. "Who?"

For some reason, she gave a laugh, but he had the awful feeling she wasn't laughing because he'd said something amusing. "You obviously don't read the scandal sheets."

"Not usually. Any politician who reads the scandal sheets is a glutton for punishment. What does the piffle printed in the gutter press have to do with you?" But even as he asked the question, her confession of a false name and her mention of scandal began to sink in, and an awful fear knotted his stomach. "Are you saying . . ." He paused, telling himself not to jump to conclusions, and it was his turn to take a deep breath. "What are you saying, Amanda?"

"My father was a brilliant man, but he was also a driven and determined one, and after my mother's death, my entire life became about my education. It was his obsession. Parties, dances, meeting young men . . . I had no time for such things. I only had time for my studies. I didn't really mind, but then, I never knew there was anything else. I wanted the same things my father wanted for me, to be well educated, to be brilliant, to be published, to teach and lecture. But a life like that, a life composed wholly of academic considerations, takes its toll."

The suspense was killing him, but though he wanted to ask what toll it had taken on her, the question was stuck in his throat. Perhaps because he was afraid to hear the answer. "Go on," he said instead.

"Growing up," she went on, "I had a very small circle of acquaintance, and most of them were professors my father's age. Later, at Girton, I was surrounded by women every bit as earnest and insular as myself. I knew enough facts to fill the Encyclopedia Britannica, but I knew nothing of life. I knew nothing of men."

Jamie stiffened, beginning to see where this was going, and he felt suddenly afraid. He didn't want to know any more about it. He wanted to tell her to stop, that none of what she was saying mattered at all, not to him.

"Go on," he said instead.

"When I graduated from Girton, I decided I didn't want to teach there. I wanted to teach children, not adults. Looking back, I think I chose that course because I knew an academic career meant I'd never have children of my own. Schoolmistresses can't be married. My father didn't like it, for he'd have preferred I teach at the university level, but I got my way in the end, and I accepted a post at Willowbank Academy."

"Willowbank?" The mention of that famous school was another spark to his memory, but a vague one. "Go on."

"I'd been there several years—still surrounded by women and girls all the time. I thought I was happy and content at Willowbank, but underneath, I know now that I was desperately lonely. And then, in my sixth year there, my father died, and I think something inside me . . . just snapped."

She was looking at him, but not seeing him. She was staring through him, looking into the past, and he knew why he found her eyes so hauntingly lovely. The loneliness in their depths harkened to his own lost and lonely soul.

He took a step toward her. "Amanda," he began, but when she took a step back, he stopped.

"Something happens to a girl when she's too sheltered from the world for too long," she said in a musing voice, as if she was talking about someone else, and curiously, her detachment made what she was saying all the more moving. "It's not natural, you know—that sort of suppression. Raised under such rigorous discipline, with the burden of such heavy parental expectations, any girl is bound to snap one day, to break out, to rebel. I'd seen it several times among my pupils." She paused, then shook her head, laughing a little. "I was twenty-six years old. I'd never dreamed it would happen to me. Or the price I would pay for it."

Suddenly, in a flash, he knew who she was. All the pieces— Willowbank, Amanda Leighton, scandal sheets—came together like the pieces of a puzzle falling into place, forming a clear and devastating picture. "Amanda Leighton? Good God."

Something of the shock he felt must have been in his voice, for she sensed it, and her gaze shifted, coming into the present, seeing him again. "Yes, Jamie," she said simply. "I am Amanda Leighton. I am the notorious and wanton schoolteacher who was caught fornicating with an earl's son on school grounds. Yes, I was naked as a jaybird. Yes, it was the middle of the afternoon. Yes, the headmistress herself, along with several of her colleagues and pupils, came across me with my lover while they were on a nature walk." She gave a laugh, a harsh sound that made him wince. "They got far more nature than they bargained for."

Jamie didn't know what to say, or even what to think. His head was reeling, but unfortunately, his memory was now crystal clear. Two years ago, Amanda Leighton had been the most talked about scandal in England, her name a headline in the gutter press for weeks, her past investigated, her career dissected, her colleagues and former pupils interviewed, and all of it served to the public for their greedy and avid consumption.

Her lover, Viscount Halsbury, the son of the Earl of Notting, had refused to marry her, adding fuel to the scandal fire by declaring that Miss Leighton had seduced him. He had been painted by the journalists as the innocent victim of a scheming harlot.

But Jamie, who'd known Halsbury slightly at Cambridge, and who now knew Amanda, and who had done more than his fair share of carousing in his own youth, suspected he had a better understanding than the gutter press or the reading public of what had really happened two years ago and who had seduced whom. He knew all about seduction, for once upon a time, he'd been pretty damn good at it.

"That day, in the park, when you mentioned the man you once loved, the one who wrote poetry, it was him, wasn't it? It was Viscount Halsbury."

"Yes. My love, needless to say, was not reciprocated. At least—" She broke off, giving a brittle laugh. "At least not quite in the way I'd hoped. I fell in love in a month, lost my virtue in two, and was abandoned in three." Her face twisted, and she looked down at the floor. "Not exactly a starved spinster's romantic dream," she mumbled.

He studied her bent head, his chest aching. He knew about pain; he understood it well, for it had been his companion for most of his life. But what Amanda had gone through was something beyond pain, and he could not begin to imagine the agony and humiliation she had endured. He'd been behind a hedgerow with a naked girl a time or two, but had they been caught, he'd never have had to suffer the humiliation Amanda had endured, and the knowledge of that shamed him—as a former rake, as a man, and as a human being.

For years, he had regretted the heedless ways of his youth, fully aware he'd been very lucky not to have ruined any of the girls he'd been with. Unlike Halsbury, he'd have done the honorable thing required of a gentleman, but he was grateful fate had never forced him to that course. He'd also been lucky not to have sired a child because of his thoughtless, pleasure-loving ways. And it suddenly occurred to him that his luck regarding the latter may have at last run out because of last night.

"Marry me," he said.

Her head came up, and she stared at him in shock. "What?" she whispered.

His gaze slid to her belly, then back up. "Marry me," he said again. "Let me do right by you as Halsbury would not."

The shock in her face softened, then vanished, replaced by a tender, sad smile. "Oh, Jamie," she said with a sigh, "you don't want to marry me. You don't want to marry anyone. No one can ever replace Pat in your heart, and that's been clear from the beginning. And anyway, I couldn't bear to be a second-rate substitute for her."

He grimaced at having his own words from that day in the newspaper office quoted back to him at such a moment as this. "I said that before I knew you. You're not a second-rate anything, Amanda. Not to me."

"No? You say that—you may even mean it—but what about the rest of the world? To them, I'm something far worse than a second-rate substitute. I'm a first-rate slut."

He winced at the brutal language, but it didn't deter him. "Who cares what the world thinks?"

"You do, Jamie."

"I don't. I've never given a damn what people think of me."

"Not in your wilder days, no. But now?" Her smile widened a fraction, turning sweet, and she looked so poignantly beautiful, it took his breath away. "You're in politics, Jamie. You have to care what people think. And I am ruined beyond amendment. Do you think any of your constituents would vote for you again if you married me? Do you think your own political party, or any of the others, would support you with a notorious woman like me as your wife? You have a brilliant career ahead of you. Marrying me would ruin it. I can't let that happen to you."

"Hang my career."

"And the boys?" she asked softly. "Would you taint their future with a stepmother who is notorious?"

He sucked in his breath, feeling the impact of that question like a blow to the chest. It was a pain so great, he couldn't think, and he said the first thing that came into his head.

"Be my mistress, then." The words were barely out of his mouth before he saw the hurt in her eyes, but he was too desperate to care, too driven to keep her here with him. "I'll provide you a house, an income. No one will judge me for having a mistress, and the boys won't suffer because of it. Even my constituents wouldn't care."

"But I would," she said, and with that soft, simple declaration, she defeated him utterly. "I would care, Jamie."

The door opened, and William came in, somewhat out of breath. "I got your taxi, Mrs. Seton. I had to go all the way up to New Oxford Street, but I got it. It's at the curb."

"Thank you, William. Take my trunk and portmanteau, will you?"

He did, opening the door, then hefting the truck onto his back. He grasped the end strap to hold it steady, took up her suitcase with his free hand, and carried both pieces of luggage out to the waiting hansom cab, kicking the door shut behind him.

Amanda turned to Jamie, and her lips parted for what he knew was good-bye, but he couldn't let her go, not yet, not this way. "Stay. Keep your post here. I won't—"

He stopped, unable to make the same promise he'd broken twice already. What had happened last night would happen again if she stayed. He knew it, because even now, as she was leaving him, he wanted her.

She seemed to know it, too, for she lifted her hand to cup his cheek, and in her face was a tenderness that nearly annihilated him.

"The months I've been here have been the happiest of my life," she whispered, "but I can't stay. We both know what would happen if I did. And even if last night hadn't happened, or we both made every effort to ensure it never happened a second time, your family and your acquaintances will eventually find out about me, discover who and what I am, and that will only hurt you and the boys."

She rose up on her toes and kissed him, and with the touch of her lips, Jamie felt as if he'd just had his last chance at heaven snatched away and smashed to bits.

And then, she was opening the door and walking away, and he couldn't bear it. "Amanda, wait."

She stopped, but only long enough to pull the hood of her cloak over her head to protect her hat against the rain. She walked on, going down the steps to the waiting taxi without a backward glance.

He started to follow her, but then he stopped, remembering that he wasn't even dressed. He could hardly go chasing a taxi up one of London's most elegant and prestigious streets wearing nothing but a pair of trousers and a dressing robe. And what good would it do anyway? She'd been right in everything she'd said. Going after her would only prolong the pain for both of them.

The taxi jerked into motion, and he shut the door, but he couldn't walk away. Instead, he ran into Torquil's study, flung up the sash of the nearest window, and stuck his head out. Heedless of the rain pouring down, he watched in silent agony as the cab rolled away along Upper Brook Street, taking her out of his life.

Only after the cab had turned onto Park Lane and disappeared did he pull back from the window. He closed the sash, turned around, and leaned his back against the glass, then slowly, he lowered his face into his hands.

The clattering of footsteps coming down the stairs roused him before he could give in to anything as maudlin as self-pity. He straightened, raked his fingers through his now-wet hair, and returned to the foyer.

"I hope it's all right I brought the boys down," Samuel said as they paused at the bottom of the stairs. "We saw her go from the nursery window."

"You didn't stop her," Colin said, and when Jamie looked at his son and saw the tears on his face and the condemnation in his eyes, he almost came apart.

"No," he said as gently as he could. "I didn't."

"Why didn't you stop her?" the boy burst out furiously, his hands balling into fists. "You should have stopped her."

He whirled around without waiting for an answer and ran back up the stairs, his brother on his heels.

"She's gone for good, then?" Samuel asked, and when Jamie nodded, he gave a deep sigh. "What do we do now, my lord?"

Jamie looked up the stairs, watching as his sons turned on the landing and vanished. "We carry on," he said dully. "We get through the days, one at a time."

Even as he spoke, he felt his heart crumbling to dust in his chest, leaving the black emptiness he knew so well. "What else is there?"

Chapter 17

*L*ike most London newspapers, the premises of Deverill Publishing, Ltd. were located in Fleet Street. Surrounded by the opulent, granite-faced, marble-tiled offices of literary giants such as the *London Times* and the *Daily Telegraph*, the new headquarters of Deverill Publishing were much more modest, consisting of a plain limestone facade, two floors, four printing presses, and twenty-four employees.

On the ground floor, several young ladies in severe white blouses and neckties sat behind desks, pecking away at typewriting machines, and clerks with ink-stained cuffs and pince-nez perched on their noses scribbled in accounting journals. A harried-looking youth with a laden tray moved among them depositing cups of lukewarm tea and hot cross buns, for those people employed by an evening paper had no time to break for a proper tea, not at half past four o'clock.

Behind them, a doorway led to the production room, where the printing presses hummed, churning out copies of the evening edition of the *London Daily Standard* at an efficient clip and strong young men with ink-stained hands bundled the papers with twine and stacked them by the back for the delivery boys, who would begin taking them to the various newspaper sellers around the city in less than an hour.

A haughty receptionist, dressed in a well-cut tailor-made suit of dark gray and a white blouse with a lace jabot, sat at the front of this controlled chaos, her blond hair rolled into a tidy bun at the back of her neck.

As receptionist, Miss Pitman's primary duty was to greet anyone coming through the tall glass doors, determine the intent of each new arrival, and where he or she ought to be sent. Customers wishing to place an advertisement were taken at once through a baize door to their right and into a nice, quiet room where polite young secretaries took down their words and accepted their money. Anyone with a story to tell was guided to the journalists' press room upstairs. Any tradesmen with the temerity to enter through the front doors were summarily directed back outside to the tradesman's entrance on the left.

The latest arrivals at the offices of Deverill Publishing, however, did not fit into any of these categories. Miss Pitman, who had only been employed by the newspaper company for six weeks, stared in some surprise at the pair of boys with identical freckled faces, bright red hair, and short pants who stood in front of her.

"May I help you?" she asked, sounding doubtful, thinking perhaps they were part of a contingent of schoolchildren on an outing who'd gotten separated from their group. They were not wearing uniforms, but still—

"We want to see Lady Truelove," one of them said, his voice surprisingly decisive for one so young. "Would you take us to her, please?"

Miss Pitman relaxed a fraction, surer of her ground now. Lady Truelove was rather a legend in London nowadays, having been the city's most popular advice columnist for over two years. Many people of all sorts called wishing to see her, and Miss Pitman was already quite accustomed to dealing with that sort of thing.

"I'm sorry, but Lady Truelove is not in at present." Her elegant hands moved to reach for pencil and paper. "May I take a message for her?"

The two boys looked at each other. This news was clearly unexpected.

"No," the second boy said after a moment, his voice a bit less assertive than that of his twin. "Could we see Lady Galbraith?"

"Lady Galbraith is also out, I'm afraid." She looked past the children, wondering what to do with them. What did one do with lost schoolchildren? Call the police? Her bourgeois mind was appalled by the prospect. Surely not the police.

"Lord Galbraith then," the second boy suggested, interrupting Miss Pitman's speculations.

"Lord Galbraith does not see anyone without an appointment."

"He'll see us," the first boy said with a confidence that ruffled Miss Pitman's sense of self-importance a little bit. "We're his nephews."

"Oh." That put the situation in an entirely new light, and she stood up, glad to have found a course of action appropriate to the situation. "I will take you to Lord and Lady Galbraith's secretary, Miss Huish."

She led them to an electric lift and escorted them upstairs to the first floor, where she deposited them in the capable hands of Miss Evelyn Huish and hurried away with profound relief.

Miss Huish, the boys discovered, was much friendlier and less haughty than her predecessor. Prettier, too, with hair of a darker red than theirs and nice brown eyes. "So, you two are Lady Galbraith's nephews?" She grinned. "Pleasure to meet you."

She looked past them, and her grin faded, replaced by a little frown. "Isn't anyone with you?"

The boys looked at each other, unsure what to say that wouldn't get them into trouble. Fearing it might be too late for considerations of that sort, they looked at Miss Huish and shook their heads, deciding quite wisely to refrain from explanations. The more one explained, after all, the more trouble one usually got into.

Miss Huish rose. "Well, then," she said briskly, "it's clear you must see your uncle at once. Wait here. I'll be right back."

She turned and walked to one of the two doors behind her, tapped on it, then opened it, and went inside. Her voice floated to the boys through the open doorway.

"My lord, your nephews are here and would like to see you."

"The twins are here?" Uncle Rex sounded understandably surprised. "Is their father with them? Or their tutor?"

"Neither. They are alone."

"Alone? Good lord." He groaned. "They came all the way across London by themselves?"

The two boys grinned at each other, rather proud of their accomplishment. Good thing Mrs. Seton had shown them how to use the trains during the journey home from Westminster.

"Send them in."

"Yes, my lord."

Miss Huish reemerged, pushing the door wide invitingly. "You may go in, gentlemen."

The boys ran past her and into Uncle Rex's private office, where he rose from behind his desk and gave a nod to Miss Huish, who departed and closed the door behind her.

"Good afternoon, boys," he greeted them. "What on earth are you doing here? And where is your tutor?"

"Nanny," Owen corrected at once. "Mrs. Seton's our nanny. Or she was." He gave a mournful sigh. "She's left us."

"Left you?" Rex eyed them with worrisome severity. "What do you mean? Left you where?"

"She quit two days ago."

"You drove another nanny away? What did you do?"

"Nothing!" Colin cried. "We didn't do anything. At least," he amended as his uncle's brows rose, "we don't think we did. She said we didn't. She said it wasn't us."

"But we must have done something," Owen put in. "Why else would she leave?"

"Maybe it was because of that man, after all, and she was lying to us about it."

"Man?" Rex inquired, but occupied with their own speculations, the boys paid no heed.

"I don't think she lied," Owen said slowly. "Not about that. It was plain as a pikestaff she didn't like him. Why would she go to work for him when she has a smashing post with us?"

"Then I think it was Papa. Otherwise, why would she insist on telling him her reasons for going without letting us be there? Or," Colin added at once, "why didn't she just leave a note and slink away before dawn, like most of them do when they go?"

"That's easy," his brother said. "She likes us, and she didn't want to leave us without saying good-bye. But—"

"Where is your father?" Uncle Rex asked, his voice cutting into these speculations.

Both boys looked at him in surprise.

"At Westminster, of course," Colin said. "Where else would he be?"

"No one is watching you?"

"Samuel. He's Papa's valet now."

"And yet, he is not here, apparently."

The boys looked at each other, then at their uncle. "We snuck out," Owen said reluctantly. "When he wasn't looking."

"We left him a note," Colin added as Uncle Rex gave a groan. "We told him not to worry and that we'd be back soon."

"The note was my idea," Owen said proudly, but much to both boys' chagrin, Uncle Rex did not seem impressed by this display of consideration and responsibility on their part.

"If Samuel is supposed to be watching you," he said, frowning like thunder, "then how did you manage to sneak out? And why did you come all the way across town by yourselves to see me?"

"We didn't come here to see you, Uncle Rex," Colin told him.

"Your Auntie Clara, then? Well, who?" he added as they shook their heads.

The boys looked at each other, then back at him, and with the uncanny talent of twins for being in complete accord, they said simultaneously, "We came to see Lady Truelove."

JAMIE WAS IN the Chamber, trying his best to pay attention to Mr. Fortescue, the member from Welsham, for he was in desperate need of distraction. Unfortunately, his colleague had no talent for oratory, and as his speech droned on and on in one long, ceaseless stream of pontification, Jamie occasionally came out of his daze to wonder with weary forbearance how anyone in Welsham had stayed awake long enough to hear the man's views, much less be inspired enough by those views to elect him to public service.

Still, even if Mr. Fortescue were the greatest public speaker since Pericles, Jamie suspected it wouldn't have made a difference to his own state of mind. Ever since Amanda had walked out his door two days ago, he felt as if he'd been moving through fog. He could see nothing, no present and no future. Everything around him seemed drab, gray, and curiously devoid of substance.

Despite the dampening of his other senses, Jamie did not feel numb.

Quite the contrary. He ached with pain. In a strange way, he relished the feeling, for pain meant he was alive, and if he was alive, he could surely find a solution to this conundrum. Couldn't he?

I am the notorious and wanton schoolteacher caught fornicating with an earl's son . . .

Some men, he supposed, would be repelled by such a confession. But then, some men were blatantly hypocritical about that sort of thing.

I am ruined beyond amendment. Do you think any of your constituents would vote for you again if you married me?

He'd meant what he'd told her—he didn't care about that. But he also knew what he cared about wasn't the only consideration.

And the boys? Would you taint their future with a stepmother who is notorious?

He knew he would suffer a thousand years in hell rather than cause them a moment's pain. He leaned back in his seat, despair washing over him. And because of that, there was no solution. How could there be?

Suddenly, all around him, gentlemen were standing up, and he came out of his reverie with a start, appreciating the dinner break had come.

Colonel Forrester, seated beside him, rose to his feet and clapped him on the back. "The MP's dining room?" he suggested as Jamie also stood up. "Or perhaps we should duck out altogether and go have a decent meal for a change? The Criterion, perhaps? All this talk of statute revision is so trivial—we can surely give the debates on it a miss. They're mind-numbingly dull."

Jamie, relieved he wasn't the only one who thought so, gave a nod. He wasn't the least bit hungry, but even so, the Criterion had a better chance of distracting him from thoughts of Amanda than debates over statute revisions ever could.

But the moment the two men left the Chamber and entered the Members' Lobby, Jamie's dinner plans were interrupted by a tap on his shoulder, and he turned to find a clerk beside him, holding a letter. "Lord Kenyon? This came for you an hour ago. From Lord Galbraith."

"Galbraith?" Jamie echoed in surprise, taking the letter.

"Yes, my lord. The clerk who delivered it said to tell you it's about your sons."

Alarmed, shaken out of his dazed state, his own troubles forgotten, Jamie tore open the envelope, broke Galbraith's seal, and unfolded the letter, then scanned the contents and muttered an oath of both exasperation and relief. "Oh, for God's sake."

"Nothing wrong, I hope?" Forrester asked him as he refolded the letter.

"Just the usual," he muttered wryly. "You know my sons."

Forrester chuckled. "The scamps are in trouble again, eh?"

"They arrived at Galbraith's offices in Fleet Street unescorted. He's dealt with the situation, however, and he's taking them to dinner, then bringing them here."

Forrester chuckled. "Given their nanny the slip, have they? No harm done, I trust? Well, well," he went on as Jamie shook his head, "if that note came an hour ago, they may be here already."

"Probably," he agreed and shoved the letter into his breast pocket. "I shall have to forgo dinner with you, my friend."

"Of course." Colonel Forrester gestured to the corridor nearby. "I'll walk out with you. If they are here, perhaps I can share your taxi home? The Criterion is on your way to Upper Brook Street."

"Certainly."

But when the two men entered the Central Lobby, Jamie appreciated that finding his sons and procuring a taxi to take them anywhere wasn't going to be easy, for the Lobby was crowded with men making their way to various exits. Some were MPs, evidently as bored by statute revisions as Jamie and his companion, others were peers streaming through from the Lords, which had just adjourned for the evening. But as Jamie scanned the room, he did not see either his sons or Galbraith amid the crowd.

"Do you see them?" he asked his companion.

The Colonel shook his head. "It might be best to wait over here by the reception desk, and let them find us."

The two men adopted this plan, but they had waited only a few minutes before Rex and the boys emerged from the throng.

The twins knew they were in trouble, for the moment they saw him, they hung their heads in their best woeful fashion, shuffling forward on either side of Rex as if headed for a firing squad.

"Well, gentlemen," Jamie said, straightening away from the wall beside the reception desk as they stopped in front of him, "you must really enjoy polishing silver. At the rate you're going, I fear you'll be doing it every morning for the rest of your lives."

They didn't reply, a wise move on their part. "I'm sure you've worried Samuel half to death," Jamie went on. "You vanished on his watch, you know."

"We left him a note," Colin mumbled.

"About that," Rex put in, "Samuel knows the boys are with me. I telephoned the house at Upper Brook Street before I left the newspaper office."

He looked at his brother-in-law. "Back from France, I see. Thank you for bringing the boys to me. You didn't ask your taxi to wait, by chance?"

The other man shook his head. "We let it go. We didn't know how long you'd be. If you need to stay, I can take the boys home."

"No, I'll take them. You're welcome to share the taxi with us."

"If we can manage to find one. The queue was miles long when we came in."

"The Lords just let out. It should be easy enough to secure a taxi if we wait a bit."

Rex nodded, and Jamie returned his attention to the boys. "In the meantime," he said severely, "you two can tell me what you thought you were doing, coming across town by yourselves. If you wanted a tour of the new offices, I'm sure your uncle Rex would have been happy to take you, had you just asked nicely."

"That wasn't why we went there," Colin said. "We wanted to see Lady Truelove."

Jamie groaned. "Not that business again."

"She didn't answer our letter, so this time, we thought we'd go in person to ask her advice."

"I wish you two would stop trying to find me a wife," he said with a sigh, wishing he could have told them he'd already found her himself. But Amanda had not allowed him that. Perhaps she was wiser than he.

"We don't care about that, Papa," Owen said.

Jamie blinked. "You don't? Then why did you go to see Rex—I mean," he corrected when his brother-in-law gave a pointed cough, "why did you go to see Lady Truelove?"

"As to that, Jamie," Rex put in hastily, "you'll be relieved to hear that finding you a wife was not their intent."

"It wasn't?"

"No. In a stunning reversal of feeling, the boys have decided they actually want—brace yourself for the happy news—a nanny instead."

"Not any nanny, Uncle Rex," Colin said. "We want the nanny we had."

"I stand corrected," Rex said, and grinned at Jamie. "Seems to me there's a simple solution to all of this. Why not just marry the nanny? That way, the boys get a new mother, and you get a nanny who can't ever quit. And you get a wife thrown into the bargain. Perfect all 'round, I say."

"Don't," Jamie said, his voice fierce enough to cause the teasing gleam in his friend's eyes to vanish at once. "You don't know the first thing about it, so don't interfere."

"I seem to have touched a nerve. Sorry, Jamie. I was only teasing."

Jamie sighed, rubbing his fingers over his forehead. "Never mind," he said, lifting his head. "It's just—"

He stopped, for coming toward him, moving with the unsteady gait of a blatantly drunken man, was Lord Notting, flanked by two companions.

As he watched the other man approach, a picture of Amanda's pain-filled eyes flashed through Jamie's mind, and suddenly the fog that had been enveloping him for two days dissipated, and a cold, blinding, snow-white rage took its place. It was a feeling akin to what he'd felt seventeen years ago when his father had called Sarah Dunn a whore and had hit him for the last time, but it was stronger and deeper, because he wasn't a skinny youth of fifteen anymore. Jamie also knew that at this moment, the Earl of Notting was in a very dangerous place.

Walk away, he told himself. *Walk away, now.*

He didn't move.

"Ah, Lord Kenyon," the other man greeted him, and perversely, Jamie was pleased that it was now too late for walking away. "Lord Galbraith. And Baron Knaresborough and Mr. St. Clair as well? My, my, a real family party."

"Notting," he said shortly and gave a curt nod to the other man's companions.

"We have a mutual friend, I understand," Notting said, smiling.

"Do we?" Jamie countered, his voice as icy as his anger, and he was never more grateful for his "poker face," as Amanda called it, than he was right now. "I wasn't aware I had any friends with such bad taste."

The other man's smile faltered, but only a fraction. Then he laughed as if Jamie had been joking. "Indeed, we do. Amanda Leighton."

In his peripheral vision, he saw Rex stiffen, clearly recognizing the name. But then, who wouldn't?

"I could hardly believe it when I saw her the other day," Notting went on, clearly enjoying himself by teasing Jamie, unaware of just how precarious a hold Jamie had on his control at this moment. "She was here at Westminster with your sons, and she conveyed the great honor of introducing them to me."

He managed to make the honor sound like theirs rather than his, and involuntarily, Jamie's lip curled a little with contempt. He didn't bother to check it.

"Amanda Leighton, a nanny?" Notting shook his head. "My, my, who'd ever have thought that?"

"That's not her name," Colin said. "You've got it wrong. It's not Leighton. It's Seton. Mrs. Seton."

Notting didn't argue the point. Instead, he gave the boy a pitying glance. "Is that what she told you?"

Colin started to speak again, but Jamie put a hand on his shoulder to silence him, and in the awkward breach that followed, Colonel Forrester, standing nearby, gave a cough. "Well, well," he began, but Notting cut him off.

"It was quite a shock, of course, seeing her after all this time. Even more shocking to find she was your . . . ahem . . . nanny."

"Go home, Notting," Jamie said, smiling softly. "You're drunk, and I'm tired."

It was a warning, and it was ignored.

"But then," Notting went on, "perhaps it's not so shocking, really. If she's calling herself by another name, perhaps you didn't know who you were really hiring. Or perhaps," he added, laughing, "you did. Amanda's still a beautiful woman. Her first freshness is gone, of course, but—"

Jamie stiffened, his control slipping, and as if sensing it, Rex laid a hand on his arm. "We really need to be going, old chap."

Jamie shrugged, feeling Rex's hand slide away. "Who told you she was my nanny?" he asked Notting.

"Why, Amanda did, of course."

"That's not true," Colin cried. "I told you that, you codfish." Twisting his head to look up at his father, he went on, "He's the man I was talking about, Papa. The one who offered her a job."

"Guilty as charged," Notting admitted. "I did offer Amanda a job. But not," he added, laughing, "as a nanny."

"That's enough," Jamie cut in before Colin decided to ask what job Notting had been offering. The cur might actually tell him, and Jamie didn't know if he could keep hold of his control if that happened. He wasn't, he found, the least bit surprised by the idea that Lord Notting was the man from the other day. In fact, he realized, that notion had been a vague, half-formed theory in his own mind from the moment Amanda had explained what had occurred. There was one thing, however, that needed to be made clear here and now.

He moved closer to Notting, as he gently but firmly pushed Colin behind him, out of harm's way. Just in case.

Rex, thankfully, had known him a long time. He took his cue and moved in front of Owen.

Adopting a confidential manner, Jamie leaned in until he could speak directly into Notting's ear. "Understand this, you pathetic excuse for a man," he murmured. "If you approach her, if you speak to her, if you ever come anywhere near her again, I will thrash you within an inch of your life. Touch her, and I will kill you."

"Touch her?" Notting murmured in reply, sounding amused. "I've already had that pleasure." He laughed, taking a step back. "I did offer her another go the other day, I admit, but I didn't realize you were now in possession. Enjoy her, Kenyon," he added, grinning as he clapped Jamie on the shoulder. "God knows, I did."

The words were barely out of his mouth before Jamie's fist came flying, slamming into Notting's face with bone-jarring force. Witnesses, no doubt, would see it as a rash act borne of temper, but for Jamie, it had been a deliberate one, with both intent and purpose, and as the pain of the impact shivered up his arm, he happily accepted all the other consequences he knew would follow in its wake.

Notting's head swung sideways at the blow, he staggered and fell, but he wasn't out cold, unfortunately, for with the help of one of his companions, he managed to get to his feet. His lip was bleeding, Jamie noted with satisfaction, and in a day or two, he'd probably have one hell of a black eye.

Notting touched his fingers to his lip, stared at the blood on his fingertips, then scowled at Jamie. "You'll regret this."

"Regret it?" Jamie grinned. "I *relished* it. Go, Notting, or I'll happily relish it again."

A gleam of fear came into the other man's eyes, and Jamie widened his grin, hoping for any excuse to continue the fight, but in the other man's moment of hesitation, others quickly intervened, depriving him of the chance. Colonel Forrester stepped between them, and Rex wrapped his arms around Jamie's shoulders, holding him back. Notting, the coward, retreated, turning away, making for the exit as quickly as he could without breaking into a run.

"God, man, what have you done?" Colonel Forrester muttered, turning around to look at Jamie in horror as Rex eased his hold and stepped back.

Colin's astonished voice intruded before Jamie could reply. "Papa, you hit him. You bloodied his lip and everything."

"Yes," he agreed, flexing his hand, savoring the pain. *And damned satisfying it was, too.*

"Jamie, I hope you know what this means." Colonel Forrester put a hand on his arm. "You struck a fellow peer, a Member of the House of Lords, in an unprovoked attack."

Jamie wouldn't have described it as unprovoked, but he didn't quibble. Instead, he tugged at his cuffs, glaring at Notting's back as the swine ducked out the door of St. Stephens and vanished, his companions following in his wake. "I dispensed justice."

"Justice?" Colonel Forrester spluttered. "By brawling inside the Houses of Parliament? Good God, man, you've just thrown your entire political career onto the rubbish heap and ruined your future."

"Yes," he said, flexing his hand again. "Believe me, I know exactly what I've done."

Oblivious to his friend's stunned expression, indifferent to the stares and murmurs of the men all around him, Jamie turned to his sons, who were staring at him in understandable shock.

"Why, Papa?" Owen asked. "Why did you do it?"

"It was because of what he said, wasn't it?" Colin asked before Jamie could reply. "About Mrs. Seton."

"Yes." It hurt Jamie to look into their faces because he knew that he'd just made an irrevocable choice that, if it succeeded, would affect them throughout their lives. At school and at university, and even beyond it, their peers would tease them, fling obscene words at them that now, in their youthful innocence, they didn't know. When that happened, they might feel compelled to respond by doing what he had just done. But though he hated that they would have to face that sort of pain and violence because of his choice, he also knew the courage and fortitude that came with facing those things. He knew that some things in life were worth pain, worth sacrifice, worth fighting for. He wanted his sons to know that, too.

"But, Papa," Owen said, "you've always told us it's wrong to hit people."

He knelt down in front of them. "It's usually wrong, but not always. There are exceptions. This was one of them. But you must remember that it *is* an exception. It is not the rule. Do you understand?"

"Yes, Papa," they said in unison.

"Good." He retrieved his hat from where it had fallen to the floor nearby and started to stand up.

"But, Papa," Colin said, tugging on his sleeve to stop him, "how do you know when it's an exception and when it's not?"

"You'll know, son," he said, and put on his hat. "Trust me, you'll know."

"Is it true what Colonel Forrester said?" Owen asked. "That you just ruined your future?"

"Probably. But . . ." Jamie paused, putting a hand on each boy's shoulder. "A woman's honor is more important than a man's future. Remember that, my sons. Always remember that."

Chapter 18

Amanda tried to tell herself being a parlor maid wasn't so bad. In sheer physical terms, dusting bookshelves, making beds, helping with laundry, and serving tea was easier than watching over two energetic, mischievous boys all day, but Amanda, who'd always welcomed hard work that challenged her brain, knew before the end of her third day as a parlor maid that for her, domestic service was going to be unutterable boredom.

She was determined to do her best, however, for she was truly grateful to Mrs. Finch for the post and well aware that her situation could be much, much worse.

Leaving Jamie and the boys had been the hardest decision of her life, but it had also been inevitable. For the past two months, she'd enjoyed the illusion that she was sheltered from the slings and arrows of ruin and disgrace, but like a shimmering city on the edge of a desert horizon, it had been a mirage.

Jamie and the boys had driven away her unbearable loneliness. They had made her feel as if she had a family, a rock to cling to, a safe haven.

The night she had spent with Jamie had been the most glorious experience of her life. His touch and his caress had been a balm to her wounded soul. His arms around her had made her feel cherished and protected. And for those few extraordinary hours in his arms, she had been untainted, without shame and without regrets.

That night had been a dream, a blissful, beautiful dream. But as with all dreams, one eventually had to wake up, and in the early morning hours afterward, when she'd opened her eyes to the sight of him still sleeping beside her, she'd known the dream had come to an end.

She loved him, but he wasn't in love with her. He was still in love with his wife, and she could never give him the happy perfection of his first marriage. And even if that was not the case, even if he were to fall in love with her somehow, Amanda knew love could never be enough.

Even Jamie's strong arms could not hold back the condemnation of the world. His position, his money, his influence, even his affection and tenderness, could not make pure what another man had sullied.

But then, she'd never expected that. She'd known from the start that her place in Jamie's world was temporary. Posing as a man, she'd hoped to keep her past away long enough to earn the money to make a fresh start in America. That was as far as she'd allowed her expectations to go.

When Jamie had uncovered the truth that she was a woman, she'd let herself believe nothing had changed, that her plan was still viable. But with each passing day, she'd fallen a little bit more in love with him and with his two beautiful, splendid boys. Without realizing it, she'd begun to harbor the ridiculous hope that somehow, she could stay with them forever, that some way, her past could remain undiscovered, but her encounter with Kenneth outside Westminster had brought reality back to her with painful clarity. There was no way to erase her past or prevent it from hurting and shaming Jamie and his sons.

When she decided to leave, she hadn't expected him to offer her marriage, and though she'd seen his offer for the fantasy it was, in that moment, she'd wanted desperately to accept it, to selfishly choose her own safety and security over what was right. But she could not saddle him and his family with the burden of choices she had made, or ruin his career, or give his sons a stepmother who was notorious.

Walking out of the house in Upper Brook Street had been the right thing to do, but it had felt like tearing herself in half, and though she'd managed to keep the pain at bay long enough to get herself to Holborn, the minute she'd arrived at the lodging house, she'd fallen utterly apart.

Mrs. Finch had taken one look at her face and one glance at her luggage and opened her arms. Amanda had run into them, sobbing as if she were a little girl instead of a mature woman of the world. Half a dozen handkerchiefs and three cups of strong India tea later, her luggage was up in the maids' attic, and she was in a black dress, white apron, and cap, learning all about what it meant to be a parlor maid.

Ever since her arrival, Betsy and Ellen had been chaffing her about her too-short maid's dress and teasing her good-humoredly about how much less attractive she was as a woman than she'd been as a man. They had laughed at her first attempts to properly make beds, and Betsy, as head housemaid, had been forced to teach her step-by-step how to remove spilled candle wax with a hot iron and blotting paper and how to clean carpets with a dustpan and brush as if she was the rawest of raw tweenies. But the addition of Amanda to the household staff meant less work for them, and though they were often confounded by her woeful ignorance of even the simplest household tasks, they had cheerfully helped her learn the ropes of domestic service.

She was expected to make the beds of all the lodgers and tidy their rooms. Afterward, her duties seemed to consist mostly of battling dust— shaking it out of draperies, punching it out of pillows, flicking it off of bric-a-brac, and sweeping it up with brushes and dustpans. By the end of her third afternoon dealing with the problem, Amanda decided there had to be a more efficient tool for dusting bookshelves than a bunch of feathers on the end of a stick, and she was contemplating just how her knowledge of engineering could help her design such a device, when the front doorbell rang.

Aside from dust removal, opening the door to callers was also part of her job, so as the chiming of the bell echoed through the lodging house. Amanda stuck the feather duster behind a potted fern, left the parlor, and started across the foyer, but then she caught sight of herself in the mirror and stopped, giving a groan of dismay at her dust-covered face, apron, and cap.

She had no time to tidy her appearance, however, for the bell rang again, and she could only hope whoever had come to call wasn't anyone important.

That hope was dashed the second she opened the door, for to Amanda's eyes, the three people standing on the stoop were the most important ones in the world.

"Jamie?" she whispered, staring in disbelief. "Colin? Owen? What are you doing here?"

"We're here to get you back," Colin began, but he was immediately silenced by a kick in the leg from his brother.

"Papa said we could only come along if we're quiet and let him do the talking," Owen said. "We promised."

Bewildered, Amanda looked up from the boys to their father, who doffed his hat and bowed. "Jamie, I can't come back," she murmured. "We talked about this."

He smiled a little. "As I recall, you're the one who did most of the talking."

She shook her head, taking a step backward. "Either way," she choked, "we agreed that I had to leave."

"I wouldn't say we agreed, precisely. It would be more accurate to say your decision to leave caught me off guard, your news about your past rather shattered me, and then you were gone before I could think of any way to counter your arguments."

"Counter them?" She sighed. "Jamie, there's no way to do that. You know the circumstances."

"Yes, well . . ." He paused and gave a cough. "The circumstances have changed a bit since we last spoke. I changed them."

"What?" She felt a jolt of hope, then shoved it down ruthlessly. "That's not possible. You can't change things like that."

His smile widened a fraction. "Can't I?"

She glanced at the boys, then leaned closer to their father, curiosity tugging at her like a mischievous imp. "Jamie, what did you do?" she whispered.

"It's a bit complicated." He gestured to the foyer behind her with his hat. "May we come in?"

She hesitated, dying to hear, knowing it wouldn't matter. Letting him stay would only prolong her pain, it wouldn't make any difference, and yet . . . and yet . . .

Before she could decide, footsteps sounded on the stairs. "Amanda?" Mrs. Finch called. "Was that the bell? If it's one of those horrid rag-and-bone men, send him off—oh!"

She stopped halfway down the last flight of stairs, staring at Jamie and the boys through the open doorway. "Your lordship."

"Good day, Mrs. Finch." He bowed. "May I introduce my sons to you? Baron Knaresborough and Mr. Owen St. Clair, this is Mrs. Finch."

"How do you do?" she murmured, descending the remaining stairs as the boys bowed to her. "Would you care to come in, gentlemen?"

"No," Amanda said sharply, then flushed, remembering that wasn't her choice to make. Mrs. Finch was looking at her expectantly, and she capitulated, making a sound of aggravation as she opened the door wide for Jamie and the boys to enter the house.

They followed Mrs. Finch into the parlor, Amanda trailing behind them.

"Would you care for tea?" the landlady asked.

"We'd adore tea," Jamie said at once. "Thank you."

"I'll fetch it," Amanda said, glad of the perfect excuse to compose herself. She moved to depart, but Mrs. Finch stopped her.

"No, no, my dear. I can't let you see to the tea when your friends have made a special visit. Take a moment with them. I shall go down and see to the tea myself."

Amanda made a sound of protest, but Mrs. Finch ignored it. When she passed Amanda to depart for the kitchens, she also ignored Amanda's pleading stare. And when Amanda called over her shoulder, rather crossly, "There's a bellpull, you know," Mrs. Finch ignored that, too.

Left with no choice and no escape, Amanda forced her attention back to Jamie and the boys, and the sight of them was so sweet, so wrenching and awful, that she knew she had to get this over with as quickly as possible or she'd come apart right in front of them. Tea could go hang.

"Whatever has happened," she said, "I can't see how it matters. I left because of . . ." She hesitated, glancing at Colin and Owen. "I left for very good reasons, Jamie, as we both know," she reminded. "Reasons nothing can change."

"You mean us," Colin said, making a sound of derision as if at the idiocy of adults.

"Colin!" Owen admonished, anguished. "Shut up. I don't want to go wait in the taxi."

"But we're the reason she left," Colin said, turning to his brother, his jaw showing that stubborn line Amanda knew so well. "We ought to at least be allowed to tell her we know all about it and we don't care."

"What do you mean, you know all about it?" Amanda asked, dismayed. "You don't know. You can't. And you certainly couldn't understand. You're too young."

"I explained the circumstances to them," Jamie said before either of his sons could reply. "I told them what happened to you."

"Oh no," she groaned, appalled and mortified, her face growing hot. "What did you say? Why did you tell them anything about it?"

"He had to tell us, because of that man, Notting," Colin said. "And what happened at Westminster the other night. We saw it happen, so he didn't have a choice."

Her mortification and dismay deepened tenfold at the mention of Kenneth, and she couldn't make heads or tails of what Colin was saying about Westminster. She shook her head, staring at Jamie in bewilderment. "Westminster? The other night? I don't understand. What happened?"

Jamie turned to his sons. "Boys, go sit down," he said, gesturing to a nearby settee of crimson velvet. "And keep quiet, as you promised. I will handle this."

With uncharacteristic docility, they complied, and Jamie returned his attention to her. "I had to explain certain things to them because of this." He reached into the breast pocket of his jacket, pulled out a folded sheet of newspaper, and handed it to her. "This was in one of the morning papers yesterday."

She opened it and stared at the headline in dumbfounded dismay. "Oh my God."

She read the story—Kenneth's insulting remarks about her, the presence of the boys, the gathering crowd, Jamie's hard right hook to Kenneth's jaw, the certainty of every witness that Lord Kenyon's unprovoked assault on another peer had ruined his political future forever—she read every lurid detail, and by the time she'd finished, her face was afire. "Oh,

Jamie," she groaned, looking up at last, miserable and heartsick that he'd ruined his future because of her. "What have you done?"

"As I told my friends, I dispensed a little justice to a cad." He smiled, leaned closer to her, and added in a whisper, "It was one of the most satisfying things I've ever done."

The tenderness of his smile was almost her undoing, but she forced herself to rally, trying to harden her resolve even as she felt it start to crumble. "Fighting is never satisfying," she said loudly enough for the boys to hear, realizing as she spoke that she sounded like the most rigid schoolmistresses at Willowbank. "And I don't see how this changes the fundamental issue anyway."

She held the newspaper cutting out to him, stuffing it into his outside breast pocket when he wouldn't take it, crumpling his handkerchief. "If I come back, this would just be the first of many such incidents. You know that as well as I do. What are you going to do, Jamie? Get in a fight every time someone insults me?"

"I hope it won't come to that."

"It will. Are you going to take on the entire world for the sake of my honor?"

"If I have to, yes."

Fear gripped her, fear and hope, joy and despair, and inside, she began to shake. "And the boys? You would make them fight for my honor, too?"

"He wouldn't have to make us!" Colin said stoutly and jumped to his feet. "We're gentlemen," he added as Owen followed suit and stood up. "We know what's right."

Amanda pressed her hands over her flushed cheeks, watching them as they came to stand on either side of their father, certain they couldn't understand what they would be taking on. "It's not that simple," she said miserably.

"Yes, it is," Jamie told her with a quiet finality that made her desperate.

Taking a deep breath, she tried again. "You don't know what it would be like."

"Yes, we do," Owen told her. "We saw it for ourselves, the other night. And afterward, Papa talked to us about it, told us that he wanted you to stay with us forever and be our stepmother, but that we had to decide if we wanted that, too, now that we knew what we'd be taking on."

"And, of course, we said yes," Colin added.

"But then," Owen resumed, "Papa explained why Notting had said the things he'd said. Papa explained that you had been be—be—be—oh, blast it, Colin, what's the word?"

"Besearched. I think."

"Besmirched," Amanda corrected gently, not knowing whether to laugh or cry.

"That's it," Owen said gratefully. "Anyway, Papa told us other people might say things about you to him and to us, and that what he'd done to Notting might happen again, and that even though he'd try not to fight, he might have to sometimes."

"He also said if we wanted you to stay with us forever," Colin added, "we might get into fights, too."

"But that's what I don't want!" Amanda cried. "I don't want your names dragged through the mud. I don't want you to fight, or have to defend me, or be teased and shamed."

"But that's our choice," Owen said with his usual stoic calm. "Isn't it?"

She opened her mouth, but her throat was clogging up, and she couldn't reply.

"So," Colin added in the wake of her silence, "the three of us talked it over, and we decided we didn't care about being teased or called names or anything like that. Sticks and stones, you know. And if they call you names, well, they'll have all three of us to deal with, won't they?"

"More than three," Jamie said, reaching into his pocket again to pull out another slip of paper. "I sent a telegram to Torquil, explaining the situation. I felt I must, for what happened at Westminster will appear in the Hampshire papers in a day or two. This was his reply."

He cleared his throat. "'Scandal nothing new to our lot. Will do all we can to help of course. Tell Miss Leighton welcome to the family. Torquil.'"

"Family?" Amanda echoed, feeling all her defenses crumbling around her. She bit her lip, glancing from Jamie to the boys and back again, loving them so much, wanting so badly to protect them from what would be their fate with her, fearing that she no longer had the strength to save them from it.

"Let us do this," Jamie said tenderly. "We are your champions. Let us fight for you. Let us love you, and protect you, and defend you."

"You would do that?" she whispered, staring at him. "You would fight the world? For me?"

"Yes," he said simply.

"You might have to do it every day," she choked.

"For a while, yes."

"For the rest of your life."

"I doubt that. The furor will die down after a bit."

"A bit?" She snorted. "After a decade, maybe."

He shrugged as if the length of time involved didn't matter.

"Why?" she whispered, miserable and scared and happy all at once. "Why would you do this?"

He looked down, staring at the hat in his hand for a long moment, then he stepped back, placed his hat on a chair, and resumed his place in front of her.

"Do you remember that day in the park when the boys played cricket?"

"Of course."

"Remember what I told you? That when the real thing comes along, you know it?"

Amanda tried to speak, but the only reply she could manage was a choked sound, halfway between a snort and a sob. She pressed her hand to her mouth and nodded.

"Well, there you are." He reached out, gently pulled her hand down from her face, taking it into his own. "I love you, Amanda. I love you, and I know it. I first began to fear you would steal my heart that morning when we talked in my study."

She stared. "The morning after you fired me?"

"Yes."

"But . . . but . . . that's not possible! Twelve hours earlier, you thought I was a man!"

He smiled. "I told you I fall in love fast."

She shook her head, not believing him. How could she?

"You were talking about teaching children," he said, "and why you love it, and the happiness it gives you, and I envied you that feeling. That purpose and that passion. That zest for life."

He paused, hesitating, then went on, "Before I met Pat, I'd never had that. I think I was born cynical, and growing up, I stayed that way. I was wild and reckless, and I did all manner of mad things, and the reason, though I didn't realize it at the time, was that I was seeking that inner joy of life. I think I'd been chasing it always, but never finding it. It was with Pat that I started to understand what true happiness was, but when she died, I felt as if all the joy had vanished from the world and would never return." He paused, lifting his free hand to cup her cheek. "Then you came."

Amanda was astonished and overwhelmed, humbled and proud. She didn't know what to say in reply to something so beautiful.

"And when I looked into your face that morning in my study," he went on, "I was seeing you in a whole new light, obviously, but I was also seeing that spark, that joy that was inside of you, and as you talked, I felt it come alive inside of me. For the first time in three years, I wanted to live again. To love again. That was when I first started to fall in love with you."

As he spoke, she knew just what he meant, for that joy he talked about was squeezing her chest at this very moment, pressing against her heart, making it impossible for her to speak, or even breathe.

"And then," he went on, "the other day at Westminster when I was about to give my speech, I looked up and saw you in the gallery. I couldn't really see your face, but I knew you were there, and I knew with absolute certainty that you were part of my future, that you were the woman I wanted to share my life, and my sons' lives. You were what inspired my speech that day. I love you, Amanda, and I don't care about your past. I don't care what other people think, or what they say. And I certainly don't care about having a political career, because no career would mean a damn thing without you. And, hell, I don't need a career now anyway, really, because I'm the son and heir of a marquess. The point I'm trying to make is that if you don't come back, the spark of joy you brought to me will die again, and I will be what I was before you came—a hollowed-out shell of a man."

Suddenly, he blurred before her eyes, and she felt a tear slide down her cheek. He caught it with his thumb, caressing her cheek. "So, will you, Amanda?" he asked. "Will you save me from that terrible fate and marry me and spend your life with me?"

Before she could answer, another voice entered the conversation. "You have to kneel down, Papa," Colin said, tugging at his coat. "Mrs. Richmond says it doesn't count unless you kneel down."

Amanda laughed through her tears as Jamie sank down to one knee in front of her, still holding her hand. He opened his mouth to continue, but he was once again interrupted.

"The ring, Papa," Owen whispered, nudging him in the shoulder. "Show her the ring."

"You bought a ring?" she choked.

"Of course." Jamie let go of her hand, patted his pockets, and pulled out a small box of white velvet. When he opened it, the pear-shaped sapphire set in platinum and surrounded by diamonds took her breath away.

"I chose this one," he said as he pulled it out and handed the box to Colin, "because I think it looks a bit like the kite. Remember the kite?" he asked, taking up her hand.

"Of course, I do! It was this shape, and this exact shade of blue."

"Yes. I chose it because it will remind you every day of your primary responsibility as my wife and the mother of my children."

"Kite flying?" she asked, laughing through her tears. "That's my primary responsibility?"

"No, my darling. It is taking me to task whenever you catch me watching my children play from a window instead of joining them. Can you do that? Will you?"

"Yes," she cried, capitulating utterly. "Oh, Jamie, I love you so."

The ring slid onto her finger, and then his arms were around her, his lips were on hers, and she knew in a haze of bliss that she would never have to face the world alone again.

After a moment, a cough interrupted them, and they pulled apart as

Owen said rather disapprovingly, "I thought people weren't supposed to kiss until they're married. You're not married yet, you two."

Jamie pressed his forehead to Amanda's. "Isn't it about time we sent them to school?"

"No," three voices told him at once.

"They're not ready for school yet," Amanda added, twining her arms around his neck, laughing as the twins cheered. "But at least they've finished polishing all the silver."

"Yes, well . . ." Jamie's voice trailed off and he sighed. "About that . . ."

She groaned. "What have they done now?"

"Kiss her quick, Papa," Colin said before his father could answer. "Then maybe she'll forget all about it, and you won't have to tell her anything."

"Now that," his father murmured, "is excellent advice. Who needs Lady Truelove, when we have these two to guide us? I think, Amanda, I shall have to employ Colin's strategy whenever you and I have an argument."

"If I kiss you first, there won't be an argument," she said, and pressed her lips to his before he could say another word.